QUOTES FROM READERS' LETTERS REGARDING THE
Mark of the Lion trilogy

"I cannot begin to tell you as a 'handicapped' person what Hadassah's story meant to me. . . ."

—C. C., Portland, OR

"Hadassah's story shook me. I looked at my life and felt a yearning for her quiet, trusting faith and self-sacrificing love for others."

—J. H., Internet

"My husband, who rarely reads, couldn't put these books down."

—T. G., Columbia Falls, MT

"I am a Captain for United Airlines and enjoy reading God's word while traveling around the world. Francine Rivers' books help me to keep focused on God and not on the worldly things."

—J. K., Laguna Niguel, CA

"I found little Hadassah's faith a breath of fresh air and fire to ignite my own faith."

—D. E., Internet

"Hadassah has been an inspiring fictional role model for me."

—M. S., Buena Park, CA

AN ECHO IN THE DARKNESS

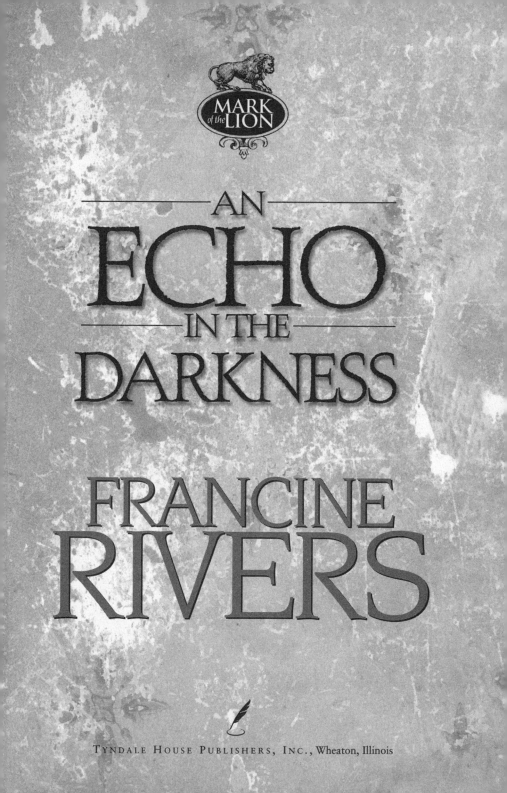

MARK
of the LION

AN
ECHO
IN THE
DARKNESS

FRANCINE
RIVERS

TYNDALE HOUSE PUBLISHERS, INC., Wheaton, Illinois

Visit Tyndale's exciting Web site at www.tyndale.com

Check out the latest about Francine Rivers at www.francinerivers.com

Discussion Guide section written by Peggy Lynch.

Designed by Zandrah Maguigad

This novel is a work of fiction. Names, characters, places, and incidents are either the product of the author's imagination or are used fictitiously. Any resemblance to actual events, locales, organizations, or persons living or dead is entirely coincidental and beyond the intent of either the author or publisher.

Library of Congress Cataloging-in-Publication Data

Rivers, Francine, date
  An echo in the darkness / Francine Rivers.
    p. cm. — (Mark of the lion)
  ISBN 0-8423-1307-9
    1. Church history—Primitive and early church, ca. 30-600—Fiction.
2. Women slaves—Rome—Fiction. I. Title. II. Series: Rivers, Francine, date
Mark of the lion.
PS3568.I83165E24 1994
813'.54—dc20   94-5909

Printed in the United States of America

08 07 06 05 04 03 02
22 21 20 19 18 17 16

This book is dedicated to
PEGGY LYNCH and LYNN MOFFETT,
beloved friends and prayer warriors.

CONTENTS

FOREWORD

In 1992, Tyndale House made a conscious decision to begin publishing excellent fiction that would help us fulfill our corporate purpose—to "minister to the spiritual needs of people, primarily through literature consistent with biblical principles." Before that time, Tyndale House had been known for many years as a publisher of Bibles and of nonfiction books by well-known authors like Tim LaHaye and James Dobson. We had dabbled in fiction before "Christian fiction" became popular, but it was not a major part of our publishing plan.

We began to recognize, however, that we could carry out our purpose very effectively through fiction, since fiction speaks to the heart rather than to the head.

Fiction is entertaining. Well-written fiction is gripping. As readers, we'll stay up until 2:00 A.M. to finish a good novel. But Tyndale has a greater goal than simply entertaining our readers. We want to help our readers grow!

We recognize that authors have something of a bully pulpit for communicating their worldview and values to their readers. But with that opportunity comes a danger. Just what worldview and values is an author communicating? At best, most contemporary novelists present a squishy worldview. At worst, they sow negative values and unhealthy attitudes in the hearts of their readers. We wanted to set a whole new standard for fiction.

So we began looking for novelists who had a heart message that would help our readers grow. And we met Francine Rivers.

Francine had been extremely successful as a writer of romance novels for the general market early in her career. But when she became a Christian, she wanted to use her talents to communicate faith values to her readers. One of her early projects was the Mark of the Lion trilogy.

When I read the manuscript for the first book in the series, *A Voice in the Wind*, I was blown away by the power of the story. I was transported back to the first century—to Jerusalem, Germania, Rome, and Ephesus. I lived with Hadassah as she struggled to live out her faith in the midst of a pagan Roman household. I felt the terror of the gladiator as he faced his foes in the arena. Above all, through their experiences I learned lessons in courage.

We are proud to present this new edition of the Mark of the Lion. I trust it will speak to your heart, as it has to mine and to hundreds of thousands of other readers.

MARK D. TAYLOR
President, Tyndale House Publishers

PREFACE

When I became a born-again Christian in 1986, I wanted to share my faith with others. However, I didn't want to offend anyone and risk "losing" old friends and family members who didn't share my belief in Jesus as Lord and Savior. I found myself hesitating and keeping silent. Ashamed of my cowardice and frustrated by it, I went on a quest, seeking the faith of a martyr. *A Voice in the Wind* was the result.

While writing Hadassah's story, I learned that courage is not something we can manufacture by our own efforts. But when we surrender wholeheartedly to God, He gives us the courage to face whatever comes. He gives us the words to speak when we are called to stand and voice our faith.

I still consider myself a struggling Christian, fraught with faults and failures, but Jesus has given me the tool of writing to use in seeking answers from Him. Each of my characters plays out a different point of view as I search for God's perspective, and every day I find something in Scripture that speaks to me. God is patient with me, and through the study of His Word, I am learning what He wants to teach me. When I hear from a reader who is touched by one of my stories, it is God alone who is to be praised. All good things come from the Father above, and He can use anything to reach and teach His children—even a work of fiction.

My main desire when I started writing Christian fiction was to find answers to personal questions, and to share those answers in story form with others. Now, I want so much more. I yearn for the Lord to use my stories in making people thirst for His Word, the Bible. I hope that reading Hadassah's story will make you hunger for the real Word, Jesus Christ, the Bread of Life. I pray that you will finish my book and pick up the Bible with a new excitement and anticipation of a real encounter with the Lord Himself. May you search Scripture for the sheer joy of being in God's presence.

Beloved, surrender wholeheartedly to Jesus Christ, who loves you. As you drink from the deep well of Scripture, the Lord will refresh and cleanse you, mold you and re-create you through His Living Word. For the Bible is the very breath of God, giving life eternal to those who seek Him.

Francine Rivers, 2002

ACKNOWLEDGMENTS

I want to acknowledge and thank two very special editors, both of whom have burned the midnight oil over my work, past and present: my husband, Rick Rivers, who has had a hand in my writing from the beginning, and Tyndale House editor Karen Ball. Rick cuts to the point. Karen polishes. Both have braved the wilderness of untitled chapters, tread through the marshes of run-on sentences, and slashed their way through thickets of unique punctuation and original spellings.

May the Lord bless you both.

PROLOGUE

Alexander Democedes Amandinus stood at the Door of Death waiting for the chance to learn more about life. Never having enjoyed the games, he had come reluctantly. Yet now he was transfixed by what he was witnessing, amazed into his very marrow. He stared at the fallen girl and felt an inexplicable triumph.

The mad intensity of the mob had always filled him with an unrest. His father had said some found release in watching violence done to others, and Alexander had thought of this when he had seen, on occasion, an almost sick relief in faces among the crowd. In Rome. In Corinth. Here, in Ephesus. Perhaps those who beheld the horrors were thankful to the gods that it was not they who faced the lions or a trained gladiator or some other more grotesque and obscene manner of death.

It was as though thousands came to find a catharsis in the bloodletting, that this embracing of planned mayhem protected each of them from the growing chaos of an increasingly corrupt and arbitrary world. No one seemed to notice that the stench of blood was no less strong than the stench of lust and fear permeating the very air they breathed.

Amandinus' hands gripped the iron bars as he looked out upon the sand where the young woman now lay. She had come out from among the other victims—those who walked to their deaths—calm and strangely joyful. He could not look away from her, for he had seen in her something extraordinary, something that defied description. She had sung and, for the briefest moment, her sweet voice had drifted on the air.

The mob had overwhelmed that sweet sound, rising en masse as she had continued forward, walking across the sand serenely, straight toward Alexander. His heart had pounded harder with each step she took. She had been rather plain in appearance, and yet there had been a radiance about her, an aura of light surrounding her. Or had it just been his imagination? When the lioness had hit her, Alexander had felt the blow himself.

Now, two lions fought over her body. He winced as one beast

sank its fangs deeply into her thigh and began to drag her away. The other lioness sprang, and the two rolled and clawed at one another.

A little girl in a ragged, soiled tunic ran screaming past the iron-gridded gate. Alexander gritted his teeth, trying to harden himself against the sound of those terrified cries. In trying to protect the girl, the child's mother was taken down by a jewel-collared lioness. Alexander's hands whitened on the iron-grated door as another lioness raced after the child. *Run, girl. Run!*

The sight of so much suffering and death assaulted and nauseated him. He pressed his forehead against the bars, his heart pounding.

He had heard all the arguments in favor of the games. The people sent to the arena were criminals, deserving of death. Those now before him belonged to a religion that encouraged the overthrow of Rome. Yet he couldn't help but wonder if a society that murdered helpless children did not deserve to be undone.

The screams of the child sent a chill through Alexander's body. He was almost grateful when the lioness' jaws closed upon that small throat, extinguishing the sound. He let out his breath, hardly aware he had been holding it, and heard the guard behind him laugh harshly.

"Hardly a mouthful in that little one."

A muscle jerked in Alexander's jaw. He wanted to shut his eyes to the carnage before him, but the guard was watching now. He could feel the cold glitter of those hard dark eyes shining through the visor of the polished helmet. Watching *him*. He would not humiliate himself by showing weakness. If he was to become a good physician, he had to overcome his sensibilities and aversions. Hadn't his teacher, Phlegon, warned him often enough?

"You have to harden yourself against those tender feelings if you are to succeed," he'd said more than once, his tone ringing with disdain. "After all, seeing death is part of a physician's lot in life."

Alexander knew the older man was right. And he knew that, without these games, he would have no opportunity to further his studies of the human anatomy. He had gone as far as he could by studying drawings and writings. Only by performing vivisection could he learn more. Phlegon had been well aware of his aversion to the practice, but the old physician had been adamant, closing him in a trap of reason.

"You say you want to be a physician?" he had challenged.

"Then tell me, good student, would you have a physician perform surgeries without firsthand knowledge of human anatomy? Charts and drawing are not the same as working on a human being. Be thankful the games give you such opportunity!"

Thankful. Alexander watched as, one by one, the victims went down until the horrific sounds of terror and pain were deadened by the relative quietude of feeding lions. Thankful? He shook his head. No, that was one thing he would never feel regarding the games.

Suddenly another sound more dangerous than the lions began to hum. Alexander recognized it quickly—the ripple of boredom, the growing swell of discontent among the spectators. The contest was over. Let the beasts gorge themselves in the dark interiors of their cages rather than tax the crowd with tedious feasting. A dark restlessness swept through the stands like a fire in a cheap tenement.

The warning was quickly heeded by the editor of the games.

The beasts heard the gates swing open and dug in their claws and teeth more fiercely as armed handlers came out to drive them back into their cages. Alexander prayed to Mars, that the men would work quickly, and to Asklepios that there might be the flicker of life in at least one of the victims. If not, he would have to remain here until another opportunity presented itself.

Alexander was not interested in the drama of separating feeding animals from their kills. His gaze swept across the sand, searching for a survivor, any survivor, holding little hope that there was one. His eyes fell upon the young woman again.

No lion was near her. He found that curious, since she was far from the men driving the animals toward the gates. He saw a flicker of movement. Leaning forward, he squinted his eyes against the glare. Her fingers moved!

"Over there," he said quickly to the guard. "Near the center."

"She was the first one attacked. She's dead."

"I want to take a look at her."

"As you wish." The guard stepped forward, put two fingers to his lips, and gave two quick, sharp whistles. The guard made a signal to the plumed visage of Charon, who danced among the dead. Alexander watched the costumed actor leap and turn toward the fallen girl. Charon leaned down slightly, his feathered, beaked head turned as though listening intently for some sound or sign of life, all the while waving his mallet around in the air theatrically, prepared to bring it down if there was. Seemingly satisfied that the girl was dead, he grabbed her arm and dragged her roughly toward the Door of Death.

At the same moment, a lioness turned on the animal handler who was driving her toward a tunnel. The crowd came to its feet, shouting in excitement. The man barely managed to escape the animal's attack. He used his whip expertly to drive the enraged lioness back away from the child she had been eating and toward the tunnel to the cages.

The guard took advantage of the distraction and swung the gate at the Door of Death wide. "Hurry up!" he hissed and Charon ran, dragging the girl into the shadows. The guard snapped his fingers and two slaves hurriedly grasped her by her arms and legs and carried her into the dimly lit corridor.

"Easy!" Alexander said angrily as they tossed her up onto a dirty, bloodstained table. He brushed them aside, sure that these oafs had finished her off with their rough handling.

The guard's hard hand clamped firmly on Alexander's arm. "Six *sesterces* before you cut her open," he said coldly.

"That's a little high, isn't it?"

The guard grinned. "Not too high for a student of Phlegon. Your coffer must be full of gold to afford his tutelage." He held out his hand.

"It's emptying rapidly," Alexander said dryly, opening the pouch at his waist. He didn't know how much time he had to work on the girl before she died, and he wasn't going to waste any haggling over a few coins. The guard took the bribe and withdrew, three coins in reserve for Charon.

Alexander returned his attention to the girl. Her face was a raw mass of torn flesh and sand. Her tunic was drenched in blood. There was so much blood, in fact, he was sure she was dead. Leaning down, he put his ear near her lips, amazed as he felt the soft, warm exhalation of life. He didn't have much time to work.

Motioning to his own slaves, he took a towel and wiped his hands. "Move her back there away from the noise. *Gently!*" The two slaves hastened to obey. Phlegon's slave, Troas, stood by watching as well. Alexander's mouth tightened. He admired Troas' abilities, but not his cold manner. "Give me some light," Alexander said, snapping his fingers. A torch was brought close as he bent over the girl on the slab in the dim recesses of the corridor.

This was what he had come for, his one purpose for enduring the games: to peel back the skin and muscle from the abdominal area and study the organs revealed. Stiffening his resolve, he untied the leather case and flipped it open, displaying his surgeon's tools. He selected a slender, razor-sharp knife from its slot.

His hand was perspiring. Worse, it was shaking. Sweat broke out on his forehead as well. He could feel Troas watching him critically. Alexander had to move quickly and learn all he could within the space of the few short minutes he would have until the girl died of her wounds or his procedure.

Silently, he cursed the Roman law that forbade dissection of the dead, thus forcing him to this grisly practice. But how else was he to learn what he had to know about the human body? How else could he achieve the skill he had to have to save lives?

He wiped the sweat from his brow and silently cursed his own weakness.

"She will feel nothing," Troas said quietly.

Clenching his teeth, Alexander cut the neckline of the girl's clothing and tore the bloodstained tunic to the hem, laying it open carefully and exposing her to his professional assessment. After a moment, Alexander drew back, frowning. From breasts to groin, she was marked only by superficial wounds and darkening bruises.

"Bring the torch closer," he ordered, leaning toward her head wounds and reassessing them. Deep furrows were cut from her hairline down to her chin. Another cut scored her throat, just missing the pulsing artery. His gaze moved slowly down, noting the deep puncture wounds in her right forearm. The bones were broken. Far worse, however, were the wounds in her thigh where the lioness had sunk in her fangs and tried to drag her. Alexander's eyes widened. The girl would have bled to death had not sand clogged the wounds, effectively stanching the flow of blood.

Alexander drew back. One swift, skillful slice and he could begin his study. One swift, skillful slice and he would kill her.

Perspiration dripped down his temples, his heart pounded heavily. He watched the rise and fall of her chest, the faint pulse in her throat, and felt sick.

"She will feel nothing, my lord," Troas said again. "She is not conscious."

"I can see that!" Alexander said tersely, flashing the servant a dark look. He stepped closer and positioned the knife. He had worked on a gladiator the day before and learned more about human anatomy in the space of a few minutes than in hours of lectures. Thankfully, the dying man had never opened his eyes. But then, his wounds had been far worse than these.

Alexander closed his eyes, steeling himself. He had watched Phlegon work. He could still hear the great physician speaking as he cut expertly. "You must work quickly. Like this. They are nearly dead when you get them, and shock can take them in an instant. Don't waste time worrying about whether they feel anything. You must learn all you can with what little time the gods give you. The moment the heart stops, you must withdraw or risk the anger of the deities and Roman law." The man on whom Phlegon had been working had lived only a few minutes before bleeding to death on the table to which he was tied down. Yet, his screams still rang in Alexander's ears.

He glanced at Troas, Phlegon's invaluable servant. The fact that Phlegon had sent him along spoke loudly of the master physician's hopes for Alexander's own future. Troas had assisted Phlegon many times during the past and knew more about medicine than most practicing free physicians. He was an Egyptian, dark of skin and with heavy-lidded eyes. Perhaps he held the mysteries of his race.

Alexander found himself wishing he hadn't been afforded so great an honor.

"How many times have you overseen this done, Troas?"

"A hundred times, perhaps more," the Egyptian said, his mouth tipping sardonically. "Do you wish to stand aside?"

"No."

"Then proceed. What you learn here today will save others tomorrow."

The girl moaned and moved on the table. Troas snapped his fingers, and Alexander's two servants stepped forward. "Take her by the wrists and ankles and hold her still."

She uttered a rasping cry as her broken arm was drawn up. "Yeshua," she whispered, and her eyes flickered open.

Alexander stared down into dark brown eyes filled with pain and confusion, and he couldn't move. She was not just a body to work on. She was a suffering human being.

"My lord," Troas said more firmly. "You must work quickly."

She muttered something in a strange tongue and her body relaxed. The knife dropped from Alexander's hand and clattered onto the stone floor. Troas took a step around the slab table and retrieved it, holding it out to him again. "She has fainted. You may work now without concern."

"Get me a bowl of water."

"What do you mean to do? Revive her again?"

Alexander glanced at that mocking face. "You dare question me?"

Troas saw the imperiousness in the young, intelligent face. Alexander Democedes Amandinus might only be a student, but he was *free*. No matter the Egyptian's own experience or skill, he acknowledged resentfully that he himself was still a slave and dared not challenge the younger man further. Swallowing his anger and pride, Troas stepped back. "My apologies, my lord," he said without inflection. "I only meant to remind you that she is condemned to die."

"It would seem the gods have spared her life."

"For *you,* my lord. The gods spared her that you might learn what you need to become a physician."

"I will not be the one to kill her!"

"Be rational. By command of the proconsul, she is already dead. It's not your doing. It was not by word of your mouth that she was sent to the lions."

Alexander took the knife from him and put it back among the other tools in his leather case. "I'll not risk the wrath of whatever god spared her life by taking it from her now." He nodded to her. "As you can clearly see, her wounds have damaged no vital organs."

"You would rather condemn her to die slowly of infection?"

Alexander stiffened. "I would not have her die at all." His mind was in a fever. He kept seeing her as she walked across the sand, singing, her arms spreading as though to embrace the very sky. "We must get her out of here."

"Are you mad?" Troas hissed, glancing back to see if the guard had heard him.

"I don't have what I need to treat her wounds or set her arm," Alexander muttered. He snapped his fingers, issuing hushed orders.

Forgetting himself, Troas grasped Alexander's arm. "You cannot do this!" he said in a firm, barely restrained voice. He nodded pointedly toward the guard. "You risk death for us all if you attempt to rescue a condemned prisoner."

"Then we'd better all pray to her god that he will protect us and help us. Now stop arguing with me and remove her from here immediately. Since you appear afraid of the guard, I'll handle him and follow as soon as I'm able."

The Egyptian stared at him, his dark eyes unbelieving.

"*Move!*"

Troas saw there was no arguing with him and gestured quickly to the others. He whispered commands in a low voice as Alexander rolled the leather carrier. The guard was watching them curiously. Taking up the towel, Alexander wiped the blood from his hands and walked calmly toward him.

"You can't take her out of here," the guard said darkly.

"She's dead," Alexander lied. "They're disposing of the body." He leaned against the iron-grated gate and looked out at the hot sand. "She wasn't worth six sesterces. She was too far gone."

The guard smiled coldly. "You picked her."

Alexander gave a cold laugh and pretended interest in a pair of gladiators. "How long will this match last?"

The guard assessed the opponents. "Thirty minutes, maybe more. But there will be no survivor this time."

Alexander frowned with feigned impatience and tossed the blood-stained towel aside. "In that case, I'm going to buy myself some wine."

As he walked past the table, he picked up his leather case. He strode along the torchlit corridors, curbing the desire to hurry. His heart beat more quickly with each step. As he came out into the sunlight, a gentle breeze brushed his face.

"*Hurry! Hurry!*" Startled, he glanced behind. He had heard the words clearly, as though someone whispered urgently in his ear. But no one was there.

His heart pounding, Alexander turned toward his home and began to run, urged on by a still, small voice in the wind.

THE ECHO

1

ONE YEAR LATER

Marcus Lucianus Valerian walked through a maze of streets in the Eternal City, hoping to find a sanctuary o0f peace within himself. He couldn't. Rome was depressing. He had forgotten the stench of the polluted Tiber and the oppressive, mingled humanity. Or maybe he had never before noticed, too involved in his own life and activities to care. Over the past few weeks since returning to the city of his birth, he had spent hours wandering the streets, visiting places he had always enjoyed before. Now the laughter of friends was hollow, the frenetic feasting and drinking exhausting rather than satisfying.

Downcast and needing distraction, he agreed to attend the games with Antigonus. His friend was now a powerful senator and held a place of honor on the podium. Marcus tried to still his emotions as he entered the stands and found his seat. But he could not deny he felt uncomfortable when the trumpets began blaring. His chest tightened and his stomach became a hard knot as the procession began.

He hadn't been to the games since Ephesus. He wondered if he could stomach watching them now. It was painfully clear that Antigonus was more obsessed with them than he had been when Marcus left Rome, and he was betting heavily on a gladiator from Gaul.

Several women joined them beneath the canopy. Beautiful and voluptuous, they made it apparent within moments of their arrival that they were as interested in Marcus as in the games. Something stirred in Marcus as he looked at them, but disappeared as quickly as it came. These women were shallow, tainted water to Hadassah's pure, heady wine. He found no amusement in their idle, vain conversation. Even Antigonus, who had always amused him, began to shred his nerves with his collection of ribald jokes. Marcus wondered how he had ever thought such obscene stories amusing or felt any pity for Antigonus' litany of financial woes.

"Tell another one," one of the women laughed, obviously enjoying the crude joke Antigonus had just related to them.

"Your ears will burn," Antigonus warned, eyes dancing.
"Another!" everyone agreed.

Everyone but Marcus. He sat silent, filled with disgust. *They dress up like vain peacocks and laugh like raucous crows,* he thought as he watched them all.

One of the woman moved to recline beside him. She pressed her hip against him enticingly. "The games always stir me," she said with purring softness, her eyes dark.

Repulsed, Marcus ignored her. She began to talk of one of her many lovers, watching Marcus' face for signs of interest. She only sickened him further. He looked at her, making no effort to hide his feelings, but she was oblivious. She simply continued her intended seduction with all the subtlety of a tigress pretending to be a housecat.

All the while, the bloody games went on unabated. Antigonus and the women laughed, mocked, and shouted curses down on the victims in the arena. Marcus' nerves stretched tight as he watched his companions . . . as he realized they relished the suffering and death going on before them.

Sickened by what he was seeing, he turned to drink for escape. He drained cup after cup of wine, desperate to drown out the screams of those in the arena. And yet, no amount of the numbing liquid could hold off the image that kept coming to his mind . . . the image of another place, another victim. He had hoped the wine would deaden him. Instead, it made him more acutely aware.

Around him, the masses of people grew frenzied with excitement. Antigonus caught hold of one of the women, and they became entangled. Unbidden, a vision came to Marcus . . . a vision of his sister, Julia. He remembered how he had brought her to the games her first time and laughed at the burning excitement in her dark eyes.

"I won't shame you, Marcus. I swear. I won't faint at the sight of blood." And she hadn't.

Not then.

Not later.

Unable to stand more, Marcus rose.

Shoving his way through the ecstatic crowd, he made his way up the steps. As soon as he was able, he ran—as he had in Ephesus. He wanted to get away from the noise, away from the smell of human blood. Pausing to get his breath, he leaned his shoulder against a stone wall and vomited.

Hours after the games were over, he could still hear the sound of the hungry mob screaming for more victims. The sound echoed in his mind, tormenting him.

But then, that was all he had known since Hadassah's death. Torment. And a terrible, black emptiness.

"Have you been avoiding us?" Antigonus said a few days later when he came to pay Marcus a visit. "You didn't come to Crassus' feast last night. Everyone was looking forward to seeing you."

"I had work to do." Marcus had thought to return to Rome permanently, hoping against hope that he would find the peace he so desperately longed for. He knew now his hopes had been in vain. He looked at Antigonus and shook his head. "I'm only in Rome for a few more months."

"I thought you had returned to stay," Antigonus said, clearly surprised by his statement.

"I've changed my mind," Marcus replied shortly.

"But why?"

"For reasons I'd rather not discuss."

Antigonus' eyes darkened, and his voice dripped with sarcasm when he spoke. "Well, I hope you'll find time to attend the feast I've planned in *your* honor. And why do you look so annoyed? By the gods, Marcus, you've changed since going to Ephesus. What happened to you there?"

"I've work to do, Antigonus."

"You need distraction from these dark moods of yours." He became so cajoling, Marcus knew he would soon be asking for money. "I've arranged entertainment guaranteed to drive away whatever black thoughts plague your mind."

"All right, all right! I'll come to your bloody feast," Marcus said, impatient for Antigonus' departure. Why couldn't anyone understand that he just wanted to be left alone? "But I've no time for idle conversation today."

"Graciously said," Antigonus said mockingly, then rose to leave. He swept his robes around himself and made for the door, then paused and looked back at his friend in annoyance. "I certainly hope you're in a better humor tomorrow night."

Marcus wasn't.

Antigonus had neglected to tell him that Arria would be in attendance. Within moments of arriving, Marcus saw her. He gave Antigonus an annoyed look, but the senator merely smiled smugly and leaned toward him with a sly expression. "She was your lover for almost two years, Marcus." He laughed low. "That's far longer than anyone has lasted since." At the expression on Marcus' face, he raised a questioning brow. "You look displeased. You did tell me you parted with her amicably."

Arria was still beautiful, still intent on gaining the adoration of every male in the room, still amoral and eager for any new excitement. However, Marcus saw subtle changes. The soft loveliness of youth had given way to a harder-edged worldliness. Her laughter held no exuberance or pleasure—rather, it carried a quality of brashness and crudity that grated. Several men hovered around her, and she alternately teased each, making jokes at their expense and offering whispered suggestive observations. She glanced across the room then, looking at Marcus in question. He knew she was wondering why he hadn't been caught by the smile she had cast him when he came in. But he knew that smile for what it was: bait for a hungry fish.

Unfortunately for Arria, Marcus was not hungry. Not any longer.

Antigonus leaned closer. "See how she looks at you, Marcus. You could have her back with a snap of your fingers. The man who's watching her like a pet dog is her current conquest, Metrodorus Crateuas Merula. What he lacks in wit, he more than makes up for in money. He's almost as rich as you are, but then our little Arria has money of her own these days. Her book created quite a furor."

"Book?" Marcus said and gave a sardonic laugh. "I didn't know Arria could write her name, let alone string enough words together to make a sentence."

"Obviously, you know nothing of what she's written or you wouldn't be making light of it. It's hardly a laughing matter. Our little Arria had secret talents unbeknownst to us. She's become a woman of letters, or more precisely, erotica. A do-all, tell-all collection of stories. By the gods, it's stirred up trouble in high places. One senator lost his wife over it. Not that he minded the loss of the woman, but her family connections cost him dearly. Rumor has it he may be forced into suicide. Arria has never been what you would call discreet. Now, I think she's addicted to scandal. She has scribes working night and day making copies of her little tome. The price for one copy is exorbitant."

"Which you undoubtedly paid," Marcus said dryly.

"But of course," Antigonus said with a laugh. "I wanted to see if she would mention me. She did. In chapter eleven. To my dismay, it was a rather cursory mention." He glanced at Marcus with an amused smile. "She wrote about you in detail—and at length. No wonder Sarapais was so enamored of you at the games the other day. She wanted to see if you were all Arria said you were." He grinned. "You should buy a copy for yourself and read it, Marcus. It might bring back a few sweet memories."

"For all her exquisite beauty, Arria is crass and best forgotten."

"A rather cruel assessment of a woman you once loved, isn't it?" Antigonus said, measuring him.

"I never loved Arria." Marcus turned his attention to the dancing girls undulating before him. The bells on their ankles and wrists jingled, grating on his nerves. Rather than be aroused by the boldness of their sensual dance and transparently veiled bodies, he felt discomfited. He wished their performance would end and they would depart.

Antigonus reached out to grasp one of the women and pulled her down onto his lap. Despite her struggling, he kissed her passionately. When he drew back, he laughed and said to Marcus, "Pick one for yourself."

The slave girl cried out, and the sound sent Marcus' insides instinctively recoiling. He had seen the look on the girl's face before—in Hadassah's eyes when he had let his own passions burn out of control.

"Let her go, Antigonus."

Others were watching Antigonus, laughing and calling out encouragement. Drunk and provoked, Antigonus became rougher in his determination to have his way. The girl screamed.

Marcus found himself on his feet. "Let her go!"

The room fell silent, all eyes staring at Marcus in astonishment. Laughing, Antigonus raised his head and looked at him in mild surprise. His laughter died. Alarmed, he rolled to one side, releasing the girl.

Weeping hysterically, she stumbled to her feet and scrambled away.

Antigonus regarded Marcus quizzically. "My apologies, Marcus. If you wanted her that badly, why didn't you say so earlier?"

Marcus felt Arria's eyes fixed on him like hot coals, burning with jealousy. He wondered fleetingly what punishment the slave

7

girl would receive at Arria's hands for something that had nothing to do with her. "I didn't want the girl," he said tersely. "Nor
any other in this room."

Whispers rippled. Several women glanced at Arria and smirked.

Antigonus' countenance darkened. "Then why intrude upon
my pleasure?"

"You were about to rape the girl."

Antigonus laughed dryly. "Rape? Given another moment, she
would have enjoyed it."

"I doubt that."

Antigonus' humor evaporated, his eyes flashing at the insult.
"Since when did a slave's feelings matter to you? I've seen you
take your pleasure in like ways a time or two."

"I don't need to be reminded," Marcus said grimly, downing
the remainder of the wine in his cup. "What I *do* need is a breath
of fresh air."

He went out into the gardens, but found no relief there, for
Arria followed him, Merula at her side. Gritting his teeth, Marcus
bore their presence. She talked about their love affair as though it
had ended yesterday and not four years before. Merula glared at
Marcus, who felt pity for the man. Arria had always enjoyed tormenting her lovers.

"Have you read my book, Marcus?" she said, her voice dripping honey.

"No."

"It's quite good. You'd enjoy it."

"I've lost my taste for trash," he said, his gaze flickering over
her.

Her eyes flashed. "I lied about you, Marcus," she said, her
face contorted with rage. "You were the worst lover I ever had!"

Marcus grinned back at her coldly. "That's because I'm the
only one who walked away from you with blood still in his
veins." Turning his back on her, he strolled away.

Ignoring the names she called him, he left the garden. Returning to the banquet, he looked for distraction in conversations
with old acquaintances and friends. But their laughter grated;
their amusement was always at someone else's expense. He heard
the pettiness behind the amusing remarks, the relish as new tragedies were recounted.

Leaving the group, he reclined on a couch, drank morosely,
and watched people. He noticed the games they played with

8

one another. They put on masks of civility, all the while spewing their venom. And then it hit him. Gatherings and feasts such as this had once been a large part of his life. He had *relished* them.

Now, he wondered why he was here . . . why he had ever returned to Rome at all.

Antigonus approached him, his arm thrown carelessly around a richly clad, pale-skinned girl. Her smile was sensual. She had the curves of Aphrodite, and for an instant his flesh responded to the dark intensity of her eyes. It had been a long time since he had been with a woman.

Antigonus noted Marcus' appraisal and smiled, pleased with himself. "You like her. I knew you would. She's quite luscious." Removing his arm from around the woman, he gave her a gentle nudge, though she needed none. She fell lightly against Marcus' chest and gazed up at him with parted lips. Antigonus smiled, obviously pleased with himself. "Her name is Didyma."

Marcus took hold of Didyma's shoulders and set her back from him, smiling wryly at Antigonus. The woman looked from him to her master in question, and Antigonus shrugged. "It would appear he doesn't want you, Diddy." He waved his hand carelessly in dismissal.

Marcus set his goblet down firmly. "I appreciate the gesture, Antigonus—"

"But . . . ," he said ruefully and shook his head. "You perplex me, Marcus. No interest in women. No interest in the games. What happened to you in Ephesus?"

"Nothing you would understand."

"Try me."

Marcus gave him a sardonic smile. "I would not entrust my private life to so public a man."

Antigonus' eyes narrowed. "There's a bite in your every word these days," he said softly. "How have I offended you that you take on such a condemning air?"

Marcus shook his head. "It's not you, Antigonus. It's all of it."

"All of *what?*" Antigonus said, baffled.

"Life. Damnable *life!*" The sensual pleasures Marcus had once savored were now dust in his mouth. When Hadassah had died, something within him had died with her. How could he explain the wrenching, profound changes within himself to a man like

Antigonus, a man still consumed and obsessed with fleshly passions?

How could he explain that everything had lost meaning to him when a common slave girl had died in an Ephesian arena?

"My apologies," he said flatly, rising to leave. "I'm poor company these days."

He received other invitations over the next month but declined them, choosing to immerse himself in his business enterprises instead. But no peace was to be found there, either. No matter how frenetically he worked, he was still tormented. Finally, he knew he had to be clear of the past, of Rome, of everything.

He sold the rock quarry and the remaining building contracts—both at sizable profit, though he felt no pride of satisfaction in his gain. He met with managers of the Valerian warehouses on the Tiber and reviewed the accounts. Sextus, a longtime associate of his father's, had proven himself loyal to Valerian interests over many years. Marcus offered him the position of overseer to the Valerian holdings in Rome, with a generous percentage of the gross profits.

Sextus was stunned. "You've never been so openhanded, my lord." There was subtle challenge and unspoken distrust in his words.

"You may distribute the monies as you see fit, without answering to me."

"I wasn't speaking of money," Sextus said bluntly. "I speak of *control*. Unless I misunderstand, you're handing me the reins of your business holdings in Rome."

"That's correct."

"Have you forgotten I was once your father's slave?"

"No."

Sextus assessed him through narrowed eyes. He had known Decimus well and had been long aware that Marcus had brought his father little but grief. The young man's ambition had been like a fever in his blood, burning away conscience. What game was he playing now? "Was it not your goal to control your father's holdings as well as your own?"

Marcus' mouth curved into a cold smile. "You speak frankly."

"Would you not have it so, my lord? Then by all means tell me so that I might flatter you."

Marcus' mouth tightened, but he held his temper. He forced

himself to remember this man had been a loyal friend to his father. "My father and I made our peace in Ephesus."

Sextus' silence revealed his disbelief.

Marcus looked straight into the older man's eyes and held his gaze. "The blood of my father runs in my veins, Sextus," he said coolly. "I haven't made this offer lightly, nor do I have ulterior motives that threaten you. I've given it a great deal of thought over the last few weeks. You've handled the cargoes that have been brought into these warehouses for seventeen years. You know by name the men who unload the ships and store the goods. You know which merchants can be trusted and which cannot. And you've always given a solid accounting for every transaction. Who better for me to trust?" He held out the parchment. Sextus made no move to take it.

"Accept or decline, as you see fit," Marcus said, "but know this: I've sold my other holdings in Rome. The only reason I haven't sold the ships and warehouses is because they were so much a part of my father's life. It was his sweat and blood that built this enterprise. Not mine. I offer this position to you because you are capable—but more important, you were my father's friend. If you refuse my offer, I will sell. Have no doubts about that, Sextus."

Sextus gave a harsh laugh. "Even if you were serious about selling, you couldn't. Rome is struggling to survive. Right now, no one I know of has the money to buy an enterprise of this size and magnitude."

"I'm well aware of that." Marcus' eyes were cold. "I'm not against disposing of my fleet ship by ship, and the dock holdings building by building."

Sextus saw he meant it and was stunned by such opportunistic thinking. How could this young man be the son of Decimus? "You have over five hundred people working for you! Freemen, most of them. Do you care nothing about them and the welfare of their families?"

"You know them better than I."

"If you sell now, you'll make a fraction of what all this is worth," he said, alluding to Marcus' well-known love of money. "I doubt you would carry this through."

"Try me." Marcus tossed the parchment onto the table between them.

Sextus studied him for a long moment, alarmed by the hardness in the younger man's face, the determined set of his jaw. He wasn't bluffing. *"Why?"*

"Because I'll not have this millstone around my neck holding me in Rome."

"And you would go so far? If what you said is true and you made your peace with your father, why would you tear apart what took him a lifetime to build?"

"It's not what I want to do," Marcus answered simply, "but I will tell you this, Sextus. In the end, Father saw it all as vanity, and now I agree with him." He gestured toward the parchment. "What is your answer?"

"I'll need time to consider."

"You have the time it'll take me to walk out that door."

Sextus stiffened at such arrogance. Then he relaxed. His mouth curved faintly. He let out his breath and shook his head on a soft laugh. "You are very much like your father, Marcus. Even after he gave me my freedom, he always knew how to get his own way."

"Not in everything," Marcus said cryptically.

Sextus sensed Marcus' pain. Perhaps he *had* made his peace with his father after all and now regretted the wasted years of rebellion. He took up the parchment and tapped it against his palm. Remembering the father, Sextus studied the son. "I accept," he said, "on one condition."

"Name it."

"I'll deal with you the same way I dealt with your father." He tossed the parchment onto the burning coals in the brazier and extended his hand.

Throat closing, Marcus grasped it.

The next morning, at sunrise, Marcus sailed for Ephesus.

Over the long weeks of the voyage, he spent hours standing on the bow of the ship, the salt wind in his face. There, at last, he allowed his thoughts to turn again to Hadassah. He remembered standing with her on a bow like this one, watching the soft tendrils of her dark hair blowing about her face, her expression earnest as she spoke of her unseen god: *"God speaks . . . a still, small voice in the wind."*

Just as her voice seemed to speak to him now, still and small, whispering to him in the wind . . . beckoning him.

But to what? Despair? Death?

He was torn between wanting to forget her and fear that he

would. And now it was as though, having opened his mind to her, he couldn't close it again.

Her voice had become an insistent presence, echoing throughout the darkness in which he now lived.

2

Disembarking in Ephesus, Marcus felt no sense of homecoming or relief that the voyage was over. Leaving his possessions in the hands of servants, he went directly to his mother's villa set in a hillside not far from the center of the city.

He was greeted by a surprised servant, who informed him that his mother was out but expected home within the hour. Weary and depressed, he went into the inner courtyard to sit and wait.

Sunlight streamed down from the open roof into the *atrium,* casting flickering light on the rippling water of the ornamental pool. The water sparkled and danced, and the comforting sound of the fountain echoed through the lower corridors. Yet there was no comfort for him as he sat in the shadows of a small alcove.

He leaned his head back against the wall, trying to let the musical sound wash over and ease his aching spirit. Instead, haunted by his memories, his grief grew until he felt almost suffocated by it.

It had been fourteen months since Hadassah had died, yet the anguish of it swept over him as though it had been yesterday. She had often sat on this same bench, praying to her unseen god and finding a peace that still eluded him. He could almost hear her voice—quiet, sweet, like the water, cleansing. She had prayed for his father and his mother. She had prayed for him. She had prayed for *Julia!*

He shut his eyes, wishing he could change the past. If only that was all it took to bring Hadassah back again. Wishing. If only, by some stroke of magic, the agony of the past months could be wiped away, and she would be sitting here beside him, alive and well. If only he could speak her name, as an incantation, and make her, through the power of his love, rise from the dead.

"Hadassah . . . ," he whispered hoarsely, *"Hadassah."* But instead of her rising from the mists of his imagination, there came the obscene, violent images of her death, followed by the turmoil of his soul—the horror, grief, and guilt, all of which were collapsing into a deep and relentless anger that now seemed his constant companion.

14

What good did prayer do her? he wondered bitterly, trying to obliterate the vision in his mind of her death. She had stood so calmly as the lion charged her. If she had screamed, he had not heard it above the din of cheering Ephesians . . . one of whom had been his own sister.

His mother had said before he left for Rome that time healed all wounds, but what he had felt that day as he watched Hadassah die had only grown heavier and harder to bear, not easier. Now his pain was a constant solid mass within him, weighing him down.

Sighing, Marcus stood. He couldn't allow himself to dwell on the past. Not today when he was so tired, bone-weary from the long monotonous sea voyage. Going to Rome had done nothing to obliterate the inertia he felt; it had only made life worse. Now here he was, back in Ephesus, no better off than the day he had left.

Standing in the *peristyle* of his mother's hillside villa, he was filled with an aching, unspeakable sadness. The house was filled with silence, though there were servants in the household. He sensed their presence, but they had wisdom enough to keep their distance. The front door opened and closed. He heard soft voices and then hurried steps coming toward him.

"Marcus!" his mother said, running to him and embracing him.

"Mother," he said, smiling and holding her at arm's distance to see how she had fared in his absence. "You look well." He bent to kiss both cheeks.

"Why are you back so soon?" she asked. "I thought not to see you for years."

"I finished my business. There was no reason to linger."

"Is everything as you hoped it would be?"

"I'm richer than I was a year ago if that's what you mean."

His smile lacked heart. Phoebe looked into his eyes, and her expression softened. She lifted her hand gently to his cheek, as though he were a hurt child. "Oh, Marcus," she said, full of compassion. "Your journey didn't make you forget."

He stepped back from her, wondering if every mother could look into the soul of her child as his own could. "I've given management of the warehouses to Sextus," he said briskly. "He's capable and trustworthy."

Phoebe followed his lead. "You've always had your father's instincts about people," she said quietly, watching him.

"Not in all cases," he said heavily and then veered his thoughts away from his sister. "Iulius informed me you were taken with fever for several weeks."

"Yes," she said. "I'm fine now."

Marcus assessed her more closely. "He said you still tire easily. You are thinner than last I saw you."

She laughed. "You need not worry about me. Now that you're home again, I'll have more appetite." She took his hand. "You know I always worried when your father was on one of his long journeys. I suppose, now, I will be the same with you. The sea is so unpredictable."

She sat on the bench, but he remained standing. She saw he was restless and thinner, his face lined and harder. "How was Rome?"

"Much the same. I saw Antigonus, with his retinue of syco-phants. He was whining about money, as always."

"And did you provide him with what he required?"

"No."

"Why not?"

"Because he wanted three hundred thousand sesterces, and every coin of it would go to sponsor games." He turned away. Once he would have agreed without qualm and, in fact, enjoyed witnessing them for himself. Of course, Antigonus would have shown his gratitude in government building contracts and refer-rals of rich aristocrats who wanted bigger, more elaborate villas.

A politician like Antigonus had to court the mob's favor. The best way to do that was by sponsoring the games. The mob cared nothing about what a senator stood for, as long as they were entertained and distracted from the real issues of life: an imbal-ance of trade, civil unrest, starvation, disease, slaves flooding in from the provinces and taking the jobs of freemen.

But Marcus no longer wanted part in any of it. He was ashamed he had given hundreds of thousands of sesterces to Anti-gonus in the past. All he had thought about then was the business advantage of having a friend in high places. Never once had he thought of what his actions meant in terms of human lives. In truth, he hadn't cared. Financing Antigonus had been expedient. He had wanted the contracts to build in the burned-out wealthier sections of Rome, and lining Antigonus' pouch with sesterces had been the quickest avenue to financial success. Bribery had bought him opportunity; opportunity had brought him wealth. His god: Fortuna.

Now, as though looking in a mirror, he saw himself as he had been: bored and drinking wine with friends while a man was nailed to a cross; eating delicacies served by a slave while men were pitted against one another and forced to fight to the death. And for what reason? To entertain a bored, hungry mob, a mob of which he had been a paying member. Now he was paying an even higher price: the knowledge that he had been as much a part of Hadassah's death as anyone.

He remembered laughing while a man ran in terror, trying to escape a pack of dogs when no escape was possible. He could still hear the thousands screaming and cheering wildly as the lioness tore Hadassah's flesh. What had been her crime other than having a sweet purity that had smitten the conscience and roused the jealousy of a foul harlot. A harlot who was Marcus' sister. . . .

Phoebe sat silently on the bench in the shade and studied her son's bitter face. "Julia asked when you would return."

The muscles in his jaw clenched at the mention of his sister's name.

"She wants to see you, Marcus."

He said nothing.

"She needs to see you."

"Her needs are the very least of my concern."

"And if she wants to make amends?"

"Amends? How? Can she bring Hadassah back to life? Can she undo what she's done? No, Mother. No amends are possible for what she did."

"She is still your sister," she said gently.

"You may have a daughter, Mother, but I swear to you, I have no sister."

She saw the fierceness in his gaze, the uncompromising set of his jaw. "You cannot set the past aside?" she pleaded.

"No."

"Or forgive?"

"Never! I tell you I pray every curse under heaven falls on her head."

Tears filled his mother's eyes. "Perhaps if you try to remember how Hadassah lived instead of the way she died."

The words struck his heart, and he turned slightly, angry that

17

she should so remind him. "I remember all too well," he said hoarsely.

"Perhaps we don't remember in the same light," Phoebe said softly. She raised her hand to feel the pendant concealed beneath her *palus*. On it was the emblem of her new faith: a shepherd carrying a lost lamb across his shoulders. Marcus didn't know. She hesitated, wondering if this was the time to tell him.

It was strange that in watching Hadassah, Phoebe had found the path her own life must take so clearly before her. She had become a Christian, baptized by water and the Spirit of the living God. It had not been a struggle for her, not like it had been for Decimus, who had waited to the very end to accept the Lord. Now it was Marcus, who was so like his father, who fought against the Spirit. Marcus, who wanted no master over his life and would acknowledge none.

Looking at his stance, his hand clenching and unclenching, Phoebe knew this wasn't the time to speak of Jesus and her faith. Marcus would be angry. He wouldn't understand. He would be afraid for her, afraid he would lose her the same way he had lost Hadassah. Oh, if only he could see that Hadassah was not lost at all. *He* was.

"What would Hadassah have had you do?"

Marcus shut his eyes. "Had she done things differently, she would still be alive."

"Had she been different, Marcus, you would never have loved her the way you do, with all your heart and mind and soul." Like he would love God, but he couldn't see that it was the Spirit within Hadassah that had drawn him.

Seeing his pain, she ached for him. Rising from the bench, Phoebe went to her son. "Is your monument to Hadassah going to be your unrelenting hatred for your own sister?"

"Leave it be, Mother," he said hoarsely.

"How can I?" she said in sorrow. "You are my son, and no matter what Julia's done, she remains my daughter. I love you *both*. I love Hadassah."

"Hadassah is *dead*, Mother." He glared down at her. "Did she die because of any crime she committed? No! She was murdered out of petty jealousy by a whore."

Phoebe laid her hand on his arm. "Hadassah's not dead to me. Nor to you."

"Not dead," he said bleakly. "How can you say that? Is she

here with us?" He moved away from her and sat on the bench where Hadassah had often sat in the quiet of the evenings and the stillness before dawn. He looked exhausted, his back against the wall.

She came and sat on the bench beside him and took his hand. "Do you remember what she told your father just before he died?"

"He took my hand and placed it over Hadassah's. She belonged to me." He could still see the look in her dark eyes as he had closed his hand firmly around hers, taking possession. Had his father known then she was in danger? Had he been telling him to protect her? He should have taken her from Julia then and there rather than await her convenience. Julia had been with child at the time, her lover gone. He had felt pity for her situation, never realizing the danger. Had he been wise, Hadassah would still be alive. She would be his wife.

"Marcus, Hadassah said that if you but believe and accept God's grace, you will be with the Lord in paradise. She told us that whosoever believes in Jesus will not perish but have eternal life."

He squeezed her hand. "Words to comfort a dying man who saw his life as meaningless, Mother. There's no life after death. Just dust and darkness. Everything we have is right here. Now. The only kind of eternal life anyone can expect is in the heart of another. Hadassah is alive, and she'll remain so as long as I live. She's alive in me." His eyes hardened. "And because of my love for her, I will never forget how she died and who brought it to pass."

"Will you ever understand why she died?" Phoebe said, eyes glistening with tears.

"I *know* why. She was murdered out of jealousy and spite. Her purity exposed Julia's impurity." He took his hand from hers, tense and fighting the emotions raging within him. He didn't want to take it out on his mother. It was no fault of hers that she had birthed a poisonous snake. But why did she have to speak of these things now when he felt so raw?

"Sometimes I wish I could forget," he said, lowering his head into his hands and kneading his forehead as though his head ached with memories. "She told me once that her god spoke to her in the wind, but I hear nothing except the faint echoing of *her* voice."

"Then listen."

"I can't! I can't bear it."

"Perhaps what you need to do is seek her God to receive the peace of which Hadassah spoke."

Marcus raised his head sharply and gave a harsh laugh. "Seek her god?"

"Her faith in him was the essence of who Hadassah was, Marcus. Surely you know that."

He stood and moved away from her. "Where was this almighty god of hers when she faced the lions? If he exists, he's a coward, for he abandoned her!"

"If you truly believe that, you must find out why."

"How do I do that, Mother? Do I inquire of the priests in a temple that no longer exists? Titus destroyed Jerusalem. Judea is in ruin."

"You must go to her God and ask."

He frowned, his gaze penetrating. "You're not beginning to believe in this accursed Jesus, are you? I told you what happened to him. He was nothing more than a carpenter who got on the wrong side of the Jews. They handed him over to be crucified."

"You loved Hadassah."

"I still love her."

"Then isn't she worth your questions? What would she have wanted you to do, Marcus? What one thing mattered to her more than life itself? You must seek her God and ask him why she died. Only he can give you the answers you need."

Marcus's mouth twisted sardonically. "How does one seek the face of an unseen god?"

"As Hadassah did. *Pray.*"

Grief filled him, followed closely by bitterness and anger. "By the gods, Mother, what good did prayer ever do her?"

At her surprised look and fallen expression, he knew he had hurt her deeply. He forced himself to relax, to be rational. "Mother, I know you're trying to comfort me, but there is no comfort. Don't you understand? Maybe time will change things. I don't know. But no god will do me good." He shook his head at her, his voice growing angry again. "From the time I was a child, I remember you placing your offerings before your household gods in the *lararium.* Did it save your other children from fever? Did it keep Father alive? Did you ever once hear a voice in the wind?" His anger died, leaving only a sense of terrible emptiness. "There are no gods."

"Then everything Hadassah said was a lie."

He winced. "No. She believed every word of what she said."

"She believed a lie, Marcus? She died for nothing?" She saw his hand clench at his side and knew her questions caused him pain. But better pain now than death forever.

She rose and went to him again, laying her hand gently against his cheek. "Marcus, if you truly believe Hadassah's God abandoned her, ask him why he would do such a thing to one such as she was."

"What does it matter now?"

"It matters. It matters more than you know. How else will you ever be at peace with what happened?"

His face grew pale and cold. "Peace is an illusion. There is no true peace. If I ever go looking for Hadassah's god, Mother, it wouldn't be to praise him as she did, but to curse him to his face."

Phoebe said no more, but her heart cried out in anguish. *O Lord God, forgive him. He knows not what he says.*

Marcus turned away from comfort, believing all he had left was the sweet echo of Hadassah's voice in the darkness that had closed around him.

3

"That one over there," Julia Valerian said, pointing to a small brown goat in the stall just outside the temple. "The dark brown one. Is he perfect?"

"All of my goats are perfect," the merchant said, pushing his way through the herd crowded into the pen and grasping the one she demanded. He looped a rope around its neck. "These animals are without defect," he said, lifting the struggling animal and making his way back to her as he named his price.

Julia's eyes narrowed angrily. She looked from the scrawny beast to the avaricious merchant. "I will not pay you so much for such a small goat!"

His gaze swept pointedly over her fine woolen palus and lingered on the pearls in her hair and the carbuncle necklace about her neck. "You appear able to afford it, but if it's a bargain you're looking for, may it be on your head." He set the goat down and straightened. "I will not waste my time in haggling, woman. Do you see this mark on the ear? This animal is anointed for sacrifice by one of the *haruspices*. This concession is provided by the seers for your benefit. The money you pay for this animal goes to the haruspex and the temple. Do you understand? If you want to buy a cheaper goat somewhere else and try to bring it before the gods and their ordained representatives, do so at your own peril." His dark eyes taunted.

Julia trembled at his words. She was fully aware she was being cheated, but she had no choice. The dreadful man was right. Only a fool would try to fool the gods—or the haruspicex, whom the gods had chosen to read the sacred signs hidden in the sacrificed animals' vital organs. She looked at the small goat with distaste. She had come to find out what ailed her and if that meant she had to purchase a sacrificial animal at an outrageous price, then she would do so. "My apologies," she said. "I will take him."

Julia removed her bracelet and opened the compartment built into it. She counted three sesterces into the merchant's hand while trying to ignore his smugness. He rubbed the coins between his fingers and slipped them into the pouch at his waist. "He is yours," he said, handing her the rope, "and may he bring you improved health."

"Take him," Julia ordered Eudemas tersely and stepped aside so her slave girl could drag the bleating, struggling animal from the crowded stall. The merchant watched and laughed.

As Julia entered the temple with Eudemas and the goat, she felt faint. The heavy cloying scent of incense failed to overwhelm the smell of blood and death. Her stomach turned. She took her place in the line behind others waiting. Closing her eyes, she swallowed her nausea. Cold sweat beaded her forehead. She couldn't stop thinking about the night before and her argument with Primus.

"You've become quite a bore, Julia," Primus said. "You impose your gloom on every feast you attend."

"How kind of you, *dear* husband, to think of my health and welfare." She looked to Calabah for sympathy, but saw her motion to Eudemas to bring the tray of goose livers closer. Selecting one, she smiled in a way that made the slave girl blush and then pale. Waving her away, Calabah watched the girl carry the tray to Primus. Calabah hadn't noticed until then that Julia was watching her. When she did, she merely arched a brow, her cold, dark eyes empty and indifferent. "What is it, dear?"

"Don't you care if I'm ill?"

"Of course I care," Calabah said, her quiet voice tinged with impatience. "It's you who seems not to care. Julia, my love, we have talked about this so many times before it's becoming tedious. The answer is so simple you refuse to accept it. Set your mind on being healthy. Let your will heal you. Whatever you set your mind upon you can, by your own will, bring it to pass."

"Don't you think I've tried, Calabah?"

"Not hard enough, my dear, or you would be well. You must center your thoughts on yourself each morning and meditate as I taught you to do. Empty your mind of everything but the one realization that you are your own god, your body merely the temple in which you dwell. You have power over your temple. Your will be done, Julia. The problem is you lack faith. You *must* believe, and in believing, you will bring forth whatever you want."

Julia looked away from the woman's dark eyes. Morning after morning, she had done exactly as Calabah said. Sometimes the fever came upon her in the midst of her meditations, and she trembled with weakness and nausea. Overwhelmed by a sense of hopelessness, she spoke quietly. "Some things are beyond anyone's will to control."

Calabah gazed at her disdainfully. "If you have no faith in yourself and your own inner powers, perhaps you should do as Primus suggests. Go to the temple and make a sacrifice. As for me, I have no faith in the gods. All I have achieved came by my own efforts and intellect, not through leaning on some supernatural, unseen power. However, if you truly believe you have no power of your own, Julia, what other logical course have you but to borrow what you need from elsewhere?"

After their months of intimacy, Julia was stunned by Calabah's disdain and callous indifference to her suffering. She watched Calabah eat another goose liver and then ask Eudemas to bring her the scented water to wash her hands. The girl did as she was bade, gazing at Calabah with rapt adoration and blushing when those long jeweled fingers stroked her arm before she was dismissed. Julia saw the dark speculation in Calabah's eyes as she watched the servant girl withdraw. A faint, predatory smile played on the older woman's lips.

Julia felt sick. She knew she was being betrayed before her very eyes, and she knew equally well that there was nothing she could do about it but boil in her own blood. Primus noticed also and took cruel amusement in letting her know.

"The proconsul goes frequently to the haruspices to inquire of the gods," he said into the stifling silence. "They'll know if there's been an outbreak of disease. At least you'll know if what ails you is something that has been ordained by the gods."

"And how will knowing that help me?" she said angrily. It was all too apparent that neither Calabah nor Primus really cared what happened to her.

Calabah gave a heavy sigh and rose. "I grow weary of this conversation."

"Where are you going?" Julia said in dismay.

Sighing, Calabah gave her a long-suffering look. "To the baths. I told Sapphira I would see her this evening."

Julia grew even more distressed at the mention of the young woman. Sapphira was young and beautiful and came from a well-known Roman family. Upon their first meeting, Calabah had said she found her "promising."

"I don't feel up to going anywhere, Calabah."

Calabah's brow arched again. "I didn't ask you."

Julia stared at her. "Have you no consideration of my feelings?"

"I *have* considered your feelings. I knew you'd say no and saw no reason to include you. You've never liked Sapphira, have you?"

"But you do," Julia said in accusation.

"Yes," Calabah said with a cool smile, her answer a twisting knife thrust. "I like Sapphira *very* much. You must understand, my dear. She's fresh, innocent, full of a world of possibilities."

"The way you said I was once," Julia said bitterly.

Calabah's smile grew mocking. "You knew what you embraced, Julia. *I* have not changed."

Julia's eyes shone with angry tears. "If I have changed, it is because I wanted to please you."

Calabah laughed softly. "Ah, Julia, beloved. There is but one rule in this world. Please yourself." Calabah's cold gaze moved over Julia's face and down her slender body. "You mean as much to me now as you ever did."

Julia took little comfort in those words. Calabah tilted her head slightly and assessed her with dark, unblinking eyes, daring her to respond. Julia remained silent, knowing the challenge had to go unanswered. Sometimes she felt Calabah was simply waiting for her to do or say something that would give her the excuse to desert her completely.

"You do look pale, my dear," Calabah said with damning insouciance. "Rest this evening. Perhaps you will feel better about everything tomorrow." She walked gracefully from the room, pausing briefly to lightly brush her fingertips against Eudemas' cheek and say something for the servant's ears only.

Helpless to stop her from leaving, Julia clenched her hands. She had thought she could trust Calabah with her heart. Now she was filled with fury.

All her life she had suffered at the hands of men. First, her father had structured and controlled her life, dictating her every move up until he married her off to Claudius, a Roman intellectual who owned land in Capua. Claudius had bored her to distraction with his intellectual pursuits into the religions of the Empire, and she had been thankfully saved from a life of drudgery with him by his accidental death.

She had been madly in love with her second husband, Caius, sure this was the union that would bring her all she had hoped for: pleasure, freedom, adoration. Then she found him worse by far than Claudius could ever have been. Caius opened the purses of her estate, spending thousands of her sesterces on races and on other women while venting his ill luck and dark moods on her. Julia had stood the abuse for as long as she could. Finally, with Calabah's guidance, she had made sure Caius would never hurt her again. She recalled with a shiver his slow death, a result of the poison she had slipped into his food and drink.

Then there was Atretes . . . her one great passion! She had given her heart to him, making herself totally vulnerable, asking only that he not ask her to give up her freedom. And he had deserted her because she turned from his marriage proposal and married Primus to ensure her financial independence. Atretes had refused to understand why it had been necessary to do so. The pain of their last, angry encounter stabbed through her momentarily, and she gave an angry shake of her head. Atretes had been nothing more than a slave taken in the Germanic revolt, a *gladiator*. Who was he to dictate to her? Did he think she would marry *him* and relinquish all her rights to an uneducated barbarian? Marriage by *usus* to Primus had been the more intelligent course open to her—it gave her the freedom of being a married woman but none of the risk, for Primus would have no claim on her finances or estate—but Atretes had been too uncivilized to understand.

Even Marcus, her beloved, adored brother, had betrayed her in the end, cursing her at the games because she saved him from making a fool of himself over a slave girl. The pain of his defection had been the greatest blow of all. His words, filled with disgust and anger, still rang in her ears. She could still see the cold fury on his face as he had turned from her to Calabah.

"You want her, Calabah?"

"I've always wanted her."

"You can have her."

He had refused since then to speak with her or see her.

Father, husbands, and brother had failed her. So she had given herself into Calabah's keeping, trusting her absolutely. After all, wasn't it Calabah who swore undying love for her? Wasn't it she who had pointed out and finally opened her eyes to the frailties and infidelities of men? Wasn't it Calabah who had nurtured, spoiled, and guided her?

And now Julia had found that Calabah was no more to be

trusted than the others, and her betrayal was deepest and most astonishing.

She was pulled from her thoughts when Primus poured more wine into his goblet and raised it to her. "Perhaps now you have a better understanding of how I felt when Prometheus' affections turned to another," he said wryly, reminding her of his handsome catamite, who had run away. "Don't you remember? He was enraptured with Hadassah's every word, and she finally stole his heart from me."

Julia's eyes glittered. "Calabah is free to do as she likes," she said, pretending indifference though her tone was brittle. "Just as I am." She wanted to hurt him for reminding her of Hadassah. The slave's name alone, like a curse, always roused an incomprehensible loneliness and fear in Julia. "Besides, Primus, Calabah's affections can't be compared to those of Prometheus. He didn't come to you of his own accord, did he? You had to *buy* him from one of those foul booths beneath the arena stands." Seeing her words had struck their mark, she smiled and shrugged. "I've nothing to worry about. Sapphira is little more than a temporary diversion. Calabah will tire of her soon enough."

"As she's already tired of you?"

Julia raised her head sharply and saw his eyes shine with malicious triumph. Fury rose in her, but she pressed it down, speaking quietly. "You dare a great deal, considering your own precarious position in *my* household."

"What are you talking about?"

"My father is dead. My brother has relinquished all rights over me and my possessions. I have no further *need* of you as a husband, do I? What is mine is mine with—" she smiled coldly—"or *without* you."

His eyes flickered as he understood her threat, and his demeanor changed as swiftly as a chameleon changes colors. "You ever misunderstand me, Julia. Your feelings are uppermost in my every thought. I only meant that if anyone can understand what you're going through, it is I. I *empathize,* my dear. Haven't I suffered myself? Who was it who comforted you after Atretes deserted you? I did. Who was it who warned you that your slave was stealing your brother's affections and poisoning his mind against you as she did with Prometheus?"

Julia turned her face away, not wanting to think about the past, loathing him for reminding her of it.

27

"I care about you," Primus said. "I am the only true friend you have."

Friend, she thought bitterly. The only reason Primus remained was because she paid for the villa, the clothes and jewels he wore, the lavish, rich food he loved, and the pleasures of the flesh he embraced. He had no money of his own. What little money he did make came from patrons afraid he would turn his acerbic wit on them and expose their secrets. However, that means of support had proven more and more dangerous of late, his enemies increasing. He now relied heavily on her financial support. Their mutual need of one another was what had made this marriage convenient in the beginning. He needed her money; she needed to live with him in order to retain control of her money.

Or had.

Now, no one cared any more what she did with her money. Or her life.

Primus came to her and took her hand, his own cold. "You must believe me, Julia."

She looked into his eyes and saw his fear. She knew he feigned concern merely to protect himself, but she was desperate for someone to care about her. "I do believe you, Primus," she said. She wanted someone to care.

"Then go to the haruspex and find out what causes these fevers and bouts of weakness."

And thus, Julia found herself here in this dark, torchlit sanctuary, witnessing a grim ritual. Having studied the texts and tablets, the haruspex slit the throat of the small thrashing goat. Turning her face away as its terrified bleating gurgled into silence, Julia swayed and struggled not to faint. With another expert stroke, the priest laid open the animal's belly and removed the liver. Servants removed the carcass as the priest reverently placed the bloody organ on a golden platter. He probed at it with his fat fingers, studying it, certain that the answers to whatever disease had befallen Julia would be found on its slick, black surface.

The priest gave his opinion and sent her away with little understanding of what ailed her. His veiled sentences hinted at myriad possibilities, and he made few suggestions. For all the good her visit had done, he might as well have said, "The gods refused to speak" and dismissed her. As she looked around, she saw others, more important, who were waiting—government officials concerned about possible outbreaks of disease or coming disasters. And she understood. What did the fate of one sick, frightened, and lonely young woman matter to anyone? What mattered were the gold coins she had given for the goat.

"Perhaps a votive offering would help," a novice priest said as she was led away.

To which god? she wondered in despair. How would she know which deity among the pantheon would intercede on her behalf? And to whom would that god appeal? And if she had offended one god among them all, how would she know which one to appease with an offering? And what offering would suffice?

Her head ached with the endless possibilities.

"All will be well, my lady," Eudemas said, and her comfort grated on Julia's already raw nerves. Julia was well aware Eudemas' sympathy lacked sincerity. The slave pretended to care because her survival depended on the goodwill of her mistress. Julia had Prometheus to thank for the way the slaves treated her. Before he had run away, he had told every servant that she had sent Hadassah to the arena.

Tears smarted Julia's eyes as she looked away from the girl. She should have sold all of her household slaves and bought others fresh off ships from the farthest reaches of the Empire. Foolishly, she had chosen to sell only a few, never considering that those new to the household would soon hear what happened to those before. Within a few days of their arrival, Julia felt their fear like a palpable force around her. No one ever looked her in the eye. They bowed and scraped and obeyed her every command, and she hated them.

Sometimes, against her will, she remembered what it was like to be served out of love. She remembered the sense of security she had felt in trusting another human being completely, knowing that person was devoted to her even when faced with death. At such times her loneliness was greatest, her despair the most debilitating.

Calabah said fear was a healthy thing for a slave to feel toward her mistress. "One who is wise in the ways of the world should learn to cultivate fear. Nothing else gives you more power and advantage over others. Only when you have power are you truly free."

Julia knew she held the power of life and death over others, but it no longer gave her advantage or security. Hadn't she hated her father when he controlled her life? Hadn't she hated Claudius, and then Caius, for the same reason? And even when she had fallen in love with Atretes, she had feared his hold over her.

Power was not the answer.

Over the past six months, Julia had begun to wonder whether life had any meaning at all. She had money and position. She answered to no one. Calabah had shown her every pleasure the Empire had to offer, and she had embraced them all wantonly. Yet, still, something within her cried out, and the abysmal emptiness remained, unfulfilled. She was so hungry, hungry for something she couldn't even define.

And now she was sick, and no one cared. No one loved her enough to care.

She was alone.

This wretched lingering illness only made matters worse, for it made her vulnerable. When the fevers were upon her, she was forced to rely on others: Like Calabah, whose lust for life was turning to others. Like Primus, who had never cared about her in the first place. Like Eudemas and all the others who served out of fear.

Julia walked out of the temple. She craved the warmth of sunlight. Jannes, a well-proportioned slave from Macedonia who had taken Primus' fancy, assisted her onto the sedan chair. After sending Eudemas to the market to buy a vial of sleeping potion, she gave Jannes instructions on how to reach her mother's villa. He and the three others lifted her and carried her through the crowded streets.

Weary from the ordeal in the temple, Julia closed her eyes. The sway of the chair made her dizzy, and perspiration broke out on her forehead. Her hands trembled. She clenched them in her lap, struggling to squelch the rising sickness. Glancing out once, she saw they were carrying her up Kuretes Street. She was not far from her mother's villa, and hope made her bite her lip. Surely her own mother would not refuse to see her.

Only twice in the last months had her mother come to her own villa. The first time, conversation had been strained and stilted. Primus' anecdotes about high officials and well-known personages made her mother uncomfortable. Julia had grown accustomed to his crass innuendoes and acid humor, but in her mother's presence, his words embarrassed her. She had also become acutely aware of her mother's subtle reactions to

Calabah's openly possessive and affectionate manner. Julia had begun to wonder if Calabah was behaving so deliberately and had given her a pleading look. She had been surprised at the venomous anger sparkling in those dark eyes.

On the second visit, Calabah made no effort to be discreet or polite. As Julia's mother was ushered into the *triclinium*, Calabah rose, tipped Julia's chin up, and kissed her full and passionately on the mouth. Straightening, she gave a taunting, contemptuous smile to Julia's mother and retired without excuse. Julia had never seen her mother look so pale or repulsed, and Julia found herself mortified by Calabah's behavior. The scene had caused the first rupture in Julia's infatuation with her mentor.

"You deliberately shocked her! You were rude!" she said later in their upstairs apartment.

"Why should I concern myself with the feelings of a traditionalist?"

"She's my *mother!*"

Calabah arched her brow at Julia's imperious tone. "I don't care who she is."

Julia stared into the cold blackness of Calabah's eyes, fathomless as a dark, bottomless pit. "Do you care at all about me and my feelings in the matter?"

"You ask foolish questions and make unwarranted demands. I will not suffer her presence in order to please you. You are indulged by me enough as it is."

"Indulged? Is it indulgence to show common courtesy to the only relative I have who speaks to me?"

"Who are you to question me? You were nothing but a foolish, naive child when I met you in Rome. You didn't even know your potential. I guided you and taught you. I opened your eyes to the pleasures of this world and you've been drunk with them ever since. It is *I* who deserve your loyalty, not some woman who by accident of biology gave birth to you!" Calabah glared at her with chilling intensity. "Who is this *mother?* How important is she when measured against *me?* She is a narrow-minded, backward-thinking fool who has never approved of the love we have for one another. She looks upon me as a foul, anomalous creature who has corrupted her daughter. She suffers me in order to see you. I tell you, she pollutes the air I breathe just as your little Christian slave did. I despise her and all those like her, and you should as well. They should be made to bow down before me."

31

Julia shuddered now as she remembered Calabah's face, grotesque with hatred and rage. Calabah had quickly regained her composure, but Julia was left shaken, wondering if the smooth, smiling face was but a mask to Calabah's true nature.

As the chair was lowered, Julia drew the curtain aside and looked up at the marble wall and stairway. She had not come back to this villa since her father had died. A wave of longing swept over her at the thought of him, and she blinked back tears. "I need help," she said hoarsely and held out her hand. Without expression, Jannes assisted her from the chair.

She looked up at the marble steps, feeling weary. She stood for a long moment, gathering her strength and then began the climb to her mother's villa. When she reached the top, she dabbed the perspiration from her face before she pulled the cord. "You may go back and wait with the others," she told Jannes and was relieved when he left her. She didn't want a slave present should she be humiliated and turned away by her own family.

Iulius opened the door, his homely face taking on an expression of surprise. "Lady Julia, your mother was not expecting you."

Julia lifted her chin. "Does a daughter need an appointment to see her mother?" she said and stepped past him into the cool antechamber.

"No, my lady, of course not. But your mother is not here."

Julia turned and looked at him. "Where is she?" she said, disappointment tingeing her voice with impatience.

"She's taking clothing to several widows who have come to her attention."

"Widows?"

"Yes, my lady. Their husbands worked for your father and brother. Lady Phoebe has taken it upon herself to provide for them."

"Let their children provide for them!"

"Two have children too young to work. Another's son is with the Roman army in Gaul. And the others—"

"Never mind," Julia said. "I don't care about them." The last thing she had come for was to hear the troubles of others when her own were so burdensome. "When will she return?"

"She usually returns at dusk."

Utterly dejected, Julia wanted to weep. She couldn't wait that long. Dusk was hours away yet, and Calabah would want to know why she was so long in returning from the haruspex. If she admitted she had come to see her mother, she risked Calabah's further displeasure.

She pressed her fingers against her throbbing temples.

"You look pale, my lady," Iulius said. "Would you like some refreshment?"

"Wine," she said, "and I'll have it in the peristyle."

"As you wish."

She walked along the marble corridor and went beneath one of the arches. She sat in the small alcove on the far side. Her heart beat fast, as though she had been running. She had sat here the day her father died, crying inconsolably while the others had gathered around him. She hadn't been able to bear seeing him so emaciated with illness, his sunken eyes full of pain and sorrow. She hadn't been able to face his disappointment in life. In her.

Tears of self-pity filled her eyes. In the end, it hadn't mattered anyway. During those last precious moments of his life, he had called for *Hadassah* and not his own daughter. He had given his blessing to a slave rather than his own flesh and blood.

She clenched her hand, angry again. None of them understood her. They never had. She had thought Marcus understood. He had been just as hungry for life as she, and he still would be if he hadn't been fool enough to fall in love with a homely Christian slave girl. What had he ever even seen in her?

Julia sighed. Maybe Calabah was right. Maybe no one was capable of understanding her, of comprehending the hunger that drove her, the desperation she felt, the terrible yearning and fear that were her constant companions. They were satisfied with their simple, placid lives, comforted by their dull routines, self-righteous in their conventional mores. They had crushed her beneath their expectations.

Just as Calabah and Primus are now crushing me beneath theirs.

The unbidden thought came as a shock to Julia, and she fought the wave of nausea and light-headedness that washed over her. Calabah and Primus both professed to love her. But did they? How had they shown their love lately?

"You've become quite a bore, Julia. You impose your gloom on every feast you attend."

"There is but one rule in this world. Please yourself."

Julia closed her eyes and sighed wearily. Perhaps it was her illness that roused such disloyal thoughts.

Or was it?

Sweat beaded her forehead, and she dabbed at it with the back of her hand.

She had thought she was safe with Calabah, that Calabah was her only true friend. She thought Calabah, and only Calabah, loved her for who she was. But of late Julia wondered if Calabah was capable of love at all, and wondering made her insecure and afraid. What if she had made a terrible mistake?

Since the argument over her mother, Julia had become increasingly aware of the way Calabah and Primus looked at everyone, including one another, including her. It was as though they were ever hunting for that careless word or expression that might reveal some hidden distaste for their way of life. And when something did emerge, in truth or their fertile imaginations, the attack was immediate and ferocious. Primus unleashed words so acrimonious and vitriolic that his listeners winced, thankful they were not the target he shredded. Calabah used intellectualism to overwhelm those who questioned her ethics and morality, and contempt when she failed, dismissing anyone with an opposing viewpoint as obtuse or archaic. Ever on the defensive, Primus and Calabah were armed for offense. Why was it so necessary if they were truly in the right?

Julia's mind was clouded with nameless dreads. *What if they were wrong. . . ?*

Iulius entered the peristyle, rescuing her from her grim contemplations. "Your wine, my lady."

She took the silver goblet from the tray and glanced up at him. "Has my mother had any word from Marcus?"

"He visits her several times a week, my lady. He was here yesterday."

Julia felt as though she had been struck in the stomach. "I thought he went to Rome," she said, forcing her voice to sound normal.

"Oh, he did, my lady, but he returned within a few months. It was a pleasant surprise for your mother. She didn't expect to see him for several years."

Julia pressed the goblet between cold hands and looked away. "When did he arrive?"

Iulius hesitated, fully aware of the scope of Julia Valerian's question. "Several weeks ago," he said, wondering what her response would be. She had the habit of venting her wrath on the bearer of ill tidings.

Julia said nothing. *Several weeks.* Marcus had been back for several weeks and not even bothered to let her know. His silence was a cold proclamation that nothing was forgotten. Or forgiven. Julia's hands shook as she raised the goblet to her lips and sipped.

Surprised and relieved, Iulius lingered. She looked unwell. "May I bring you anything else, Lady Julia? I purchased cherries from Pontic Cerasus and some Armenia peaches this morning." They had always been her favorite.

"No," Julia said, warmed slightly by his consideration. How long had it been since a servant had spoken to her in that gentle way?

Not since Hadassah.

The traitorous memory sent a shaft of pain through her. "I don't want anything."

He took a small bell from the tray and set it on the bench beside her. "If you need anything, ring for me," he said and withdrew.

Julia drank her wine and wished she hadn't come. The emptiness of the villa made her own loneliness all the more unbearable. Her throat constricted and she blinked back tears.

Marcus was here in Ephesus.

Before he had gone back to Rome, she had sent him message after message, and each was returned, seal unbroken. She had even gone to his villa once. One of his servants came to her. He said, "The master said he has no sister" and closed the door in her face. She had pounded and screamed that Marcus did have a sister and there had been a misunderstanding and she must speak to him. The door remained closed. All her efforts to see Marcus and talk with him had availed nothing.

She wondered if it would make any difference if Marcus knew she was ill. She could find one of his friends and send word that way. Perhaps then he would come to her. He would beg her to forgive him for sending her letters back and refusing to see her. He would tell her she was his sister again, that he would take care of her, that he still adored her. She would make him suffer briefly before forgiving him, and then he would tease her and laugh with her and tell her amusing stories like he always had back in Rome.

Tears slipped down Julia's pale cheeks.

A wonderful dream, but she knew the true situation. Marcus had made it clear enough. If he did learn of her illness, he would say it was only what she deserved. He would say she brought it on herself. He would say again, "May the gods curse you!"

And so they had.

She could only try to forget everything. She had to wipe yesterday from her mind. Today was already too much for her to bear. She could not bring herself to contemplate tomorrow.

Her hands tightened around the goblet. She sipped the wine again, hoping to strengthen herself. As she lowered the goblet, she looked into the ruby liquid. It looked like blood. Casting it from her, she stood shakily and wiped her mouth with the back of her hand.

Iulius heard the crash and entered the peristyle. "Are you all right, my lady?" He glanced at the wine splattered across the marble tiles and bent to pick up the goblet.

"I should not have come," she said, her words directed to herself rather than him. Jannes would tell Primus, and Primus would tell Calabah.

And without Calabah, Julia was terrified her life would shatter completely.

4

Marcus dismissed his servant and removed the seal from a parchment that had arrived that morning. He read through it quickly, frowning. The epistle was from Ishmael, an Egyptian with whom he had dealt frequently in the past. All the man said in his letter still held true. Sand was more in demand now than ever as the addiction for the games grew. Ishmael reminded Marcus that he had made his first million *aurei* of gold in transporting sand from Egypt to Roman arenas. There were markets for sand in Ephesus and Corinth and Caesarea as well. Respectfully and with admirable tact, Ishmael sought the reason for Marcus' long silence.

Crumpling the parchment in his hand, Marcus tossed it into the brazier. His father's voice echoed in his memory. *"Rome needs grain."* Ah, but he, Marcus Lucianus Valerian, in his youthful lust and zeal for life's pleasures—and in his arrogance that he knew better than his father—had imported what Rome *wanted* instead: Sand to soak up blood.

An image of a gentle girl lying in her own blood on sand he had sold made him rake his hands back through his short hair. He rose from his chair and went to the window overlooking the harbor.

One of his ships had come in from Sicily laden with goods. He watched the *sacrarii* shouldering sacks of grain, bundles of hides, and crates of fine woodwork. One of his overseers, a Macedonian slave named Orestes, who had been trained by his father, stood watching and checking quantities and products against the bill of lading. Orestes knew as much about the comings and goings of Valerian ships as he did, and he was as trustworthy and loyal to the memory of Decimus Valerian as Sextus in Rome. So, too, were several others who had labored under the Valerian banner, including Silus, who stood by the scales with *mensores* overseeing the weighing of the grain. His father had been a good judge of character.

The harbor was a hive of activity, ships arriving and departing, men scrambling up and down gangplanks loading and unloading cargoes. Two of his ships were scheduled to leave before the end of the week, one for Corinth and the other for Caesarea. Marcus felt the pull to board the latter. Perhaps his mother was right. He should go in search of Hadassah's god. Hadassah had said her god was loving and merciful. Marcus' hand clenched. He would like to find out why a supposedly loving god would allow a devoted worshiper to suffer such a merciless, humiliating death.

Banging the iron lattice with his fist, Marcus left the window and returned to his worktable.

He stared at the parchments strewn across it, each a record of goods brought into Ephesus on one of his ships over the past months: From Greece were articles of bronze; from Tarshish, silver, iron, tin, and lead; from Damascus, wine and wool; from Rhodes, ivory and ebony. Beautiful garments, blue fabric, embroidered work, and multicolored rugs were transported by caravan from the East and loaded onto his ships bound for Rome. Arabia yielded lambs, rams, and goats; Beth Togarmah, horses for the races and war-horses and mules for the Roman army.

Angrily, he swept his hand across the documents, scattering them onto the floor. What he needed was sound and activity, anything to drown out his own grim thoughts. Rejecting the thought of riding on a litter to the private baths he usually frequented, he headed on foot instead for one frequented by the populace. They were closer to the docks and something beyond his usual experience. Anything for distraction.

Paying the small copper *quadrans*, Marcus entered the noisy changing room, ignoring the surprised glances of laborers. He left his folded tunic on a shelf, wondering if it would be there when he returned. It was made of the best wool and was trimmed with gold and purple thread, a garment undoubtedly coveted by some of the patrons of this chaotic establishment of commoners. He took a towel and slung it over his shoulder, entering the *tepidarium*.

His brows flickered slightly as he saw the baths were communal. He was unaccustomed to bathing with women, but supposed in this crowded atmosphere it made no difference. Marcus tossed the towel aside and entered the first pool, rinsing himself in the warm water and taking his turn beneath the fountain that was part of the circulation system.

He left the first pool and entered the second. The murals were chipped, mildew growing in the cracks. The water was slightly warmer than the first, and he allowed enough time for his body to adjust before entering the third pool of the tepidarium. All manner of citizenry were enjoying the baths, and the cacophony of mingled accents and topics filled the chamber. The noise was almost deafening, but he was glad of it, thankful to have his own dark thoughts drowned out by the chaos around him.

Marcus sank down and leaned his head back against the tiles. Several young men and women were having a splashing contest. A child running on the wet tiles fell and sent up a shrill, warbling wail. Two men were having a heated debate about politics, while several women laughed and gossiped among themselves.

Tiring of the noise, Marcus entered the smaller *calidarium*. The room had benches along the walls and a raised font in the center of which were hot stones. A Nubian slave in a loincloth ladled water over them, keeping the chamber filled with steam. There were only two others in the room, an elderly man with a balding pate and a man younger than Marcus. Sweat glistened on the man's well-muscled body, and he scraped it away with a *strigil* while talking to his older companion in a low, confidential tone.

Ignoring them, Marcus stretched out on one of the benches and closed his eyes, hoping the intense heat of the place would ease his tension. He needed a night of dreamless sleep.

Unbidden, the younger man's earnest words, his hushed voice filled with abject frustration, eased into Marcus' awareness. "I went with the best of intentions, Callistus, and Vindacius *mocked* me. He used that caustic tone he takes on when he thinks he knows more than everyone else. 'Tell me, dear Stachys,' he said, 'how you can believe in a god who sits on top of a topless throne, whose center is everywhere, but who cannot be measured? How can a god fill the heavens and yet be small enough to dwell in a human heart?' And then he *laughed* at me! He asked why anyone with the least intelligence would want to worship a god who let his own son be crucified."

Marcus stiffened. By the gods! Even here, he could not escape!

"How did you answer him?" the old man said.

"I didn't. After suffering his derision, I was too angry to say anything. Why open myself to further humiliation? It was all I could do not to ram my fist down his throat. And I went to save his soul!"

"Maybe the problem was not with Vindacius."

"What do you mean?" Stachys said, clearly dismayed by his elder's reproof.

"When I first accepted Jesus as my Lord, I was overwhelmed with the desire to convert everyone I knew. I carried my new faith out into the world like a club, ready to batter everyone I knew into believing the Good News. I was wrongly motivated."

"How can you be wrongly motivated for wanting to save people?"

"What brought the Lord down from heaven, Stachys?"

"He came to save us."

"You have spoken to me often of Vindacius. And now, I ask you. Did you go to this man you've always considered your intellectual superior to overcome him with debate and reason? Did you want him to see your righteousness in Christ? Or did you go to him out of love, to win his heart to the Lord for his own sake?"

There was a long silence, and then the younger man answered bleakly, "I understand."

Callistus consoled him. "We know the Truth. It's evident to all in God's creation. But it is the kindness of the Lord that leads man to repentance. When you speak with Vindacius the next time, remember that your struggle isn't against him. It's against the spiritual forces of darkness that hold him captive. Put on the armor of God—"

The slave poured water over the hot stones again, and the hissing drowned out Callistus' next words. As the hissing softened, Marcus heard only silence. He rose, realizing the men had left the chamber. Taking up the strigil, Marcus scraped the sweat from his body angrily.

Armor of God, the older man had said. *What armor?* Marcus wondered bitterly. If Hadassah's unseen god had given her armor to wear, it hadn't saved her from a horrifying death. Nor would it save them. He wanted to warn the young man not to preach a faith that would bring him death.

What good was this god to his followers? What protection did he offer? Marcus rose from the bench, intent on going after Stachys and confronting him with the truth. This god of kindness and mercy deserted his believers when they most needed him!

Marcus left the calidarium and entered the frigidarium. The temperature drop was stunning. Standing on a tiled mural, his gaze swept across the pool, searching for the two men. They were gone. Annoyed, Marcus dove into the cold water and swam to the end of the pool. He lifted himself out with the lithe grace of an athlete. Shaking the water from his hair, he took a towel from a shelf and wrapped it around his waist as he headed for one of the massage tables.

Stretched out on the table, he tried to empty his mind of everything and let the vigorous pounding and kneading of his muscles give him ease. The masseur poured olive oil into his palm and worked it into Marcus' back and thighs, instructing him to turn over. When he was finished, Marcus stood, and a slave scraped the excess oil away with another strigil.

Passing men exercising and women gathered around board games, Marcus headed for the changing rooms. Surprisingly, his clothing was where he had left it. Marcus shrugged on his tunic and fitted the bronze sash. He left the baths as restless as when he had entered.

Booths lined the street, hawkers promulgating a variety of goods and services to patrons going in and out of the baths. Marcus wove his way through the crowd. Earlier he had craved the chaotic noise of the populace to drown out his own thoughts, but now he wanted the solitude and silence of his own villa in order to give them full reign.

A young man shouted a name and ran by to catch up with someone. As he did so, he bumped Marcus, who fell back a step and muttered a curse as he collided with someone behind. At a woman's soft cry of pain, he turned and looked down at a small figure shrouded in heavy gray veils. She stumbled back, her small hand gripping a walking stick as she tried to regain her balance.

He caught hold of her arm and steadied her. "My apologies," he said briskly. She lifted her head sharply, and he felt rather than saw her staring up at him. He could make out no face beneath the dark gray mantle that covered her from the top of her head to her feet. She lowered her head quickly as though to hide from him, and he wondered what terrible deformity her veils covered. She might even be a leper. He took his hand from her arm.

Stepping around her, he walked away through the crowd. He felt her watching him and glanced back. The veiled woman was turned toward him, still standing in the midst of the river of people. He paused, perplexed. She turned away and limped cautiously down the street, through the crowd, away from him.

Marcus was strangely pierced by the sight of that small, shrouded figure being jostled as she made her way through the

throng of people crowding the narrow street before the baths. He
watched her until she entered one of the physicians' booths,
undoubtedly seeking a cure. He turned away and headed for his
villa.

Lycus, his Corinthian slave, greeted him and took his cloak.
"Your mother has invited you to sup with her this evening, my
lord."

"Send word I won't be able to see her. I'll stop by and visit
tomorrow." He entered his private chamber and opened the iron
lattice to his private terrace. The view of the Artemision was
breathtaking. He had paid a fortune for this villa because of it,
intending to bring Hadassah here as his wife. He had imagined
spending each morning with her on this sunny terrace overlooking the indescribable beauty of Ephesus.

Lycus brought him wine.

"What do you know of Christians, Lycus?" Marcus said without looking at him. He had bought Lycus upon his return to Ephesus. The Corinthian had been sold as a manservant and was
reputed to have been educated by his previous master, a Greek
who had committed suicide when faced with financial ruin.
Marcus wondered if his servant's education had included religious
matters.

"They believe in one god, my lord."

"What do you know about their god?"

"Only what I've heard, my lord."

"Tell me what you've heard."

"The god of the Christians is the Messiah of the Jews."

"Then they are one and the same."

"It's hard to say, my lord. I am neither Jew nor Christian."

Marcus turned and looked at him. "Which religion do you
embrace as your own?"

"I believe in serving my master."

Marcus laughed wryly. "A safe reply, Lycus." He looked at
him solemnly. "I'm not testing you. Answer me as a man and not
a slave."

Lycus was silent so long, Marcus didn't think he would answer
at all. "I don't know, my lord," he said frankly. "I have worshiped many gods in my lifetime, but never this one."

"And have any of them helped you?"

"It helped me to think they might."

"What do you believe in now?"

"I've come to believe that each man must come to terms with his own life and situation and make the most of whatever it may be, slave or free."

"Then you don't believe in an afterlife such as those who worship Cybele or those who bow down to this Jesus of Nazareth?"

Lycus heard the edge in his master's voice and answered cautiously. "It would be comforting to believe it."

"That's not an answer, Lycus."

"Perhaps I don't have the answers you seek, my lord."

Marcus sighed, knowing Lycus would not be completely honest with him. It was a simple matter of survival that a slave keep his true feelings secret. Had Hadassah kept her faith secret, she would still be alive.

"No," Marcus said, "you don't have the answers I need. Perhaps no one does. I suppose, as you imply, each person has their own religion." He drank his wine. "For some, it's the death of them," he said and set it down. "You may go, Lycus."

The sun set before Marcus left the terrace. He had changed his mind about visiting his mother. It seemed imperative that he speak with her tonight.

Iulius opened the door when he arrived. "My lord, we received word you weren't coming this evening."

"I take it my mother has gone out for the evening," he said in dismay, entering the hall. Removing his woolen cape, he tossed it heedlessly on a marble bench.

Iulius took it up and put it over his arm. "She's in her lararium. Please, my lord, make yourself comfortable in the *triclinium* or peristyle and I'll tell your mother you're here." He left Marcus and went down the tiled corridor that opened into the peristyle. The lararium was nestled in the west corner, situated there for privacy and quiet. The door stood open, and Iulius saw Lady Phoebe sitting on a chair with her head bowed. She heard him and glanced his way. "I apologize for interrupting your prayers, my lady," he said sincerely.

"It's all right, Iulius. I'm simply too weary this evening to concentrate." She rose, and in the lamplight, Iulius saw new lines of fatigue in her lovely face. "What is it?"

"Your son is here."

"Oh!" Smiling, she hurried past him.

Iulius followed and watched Phoebe embraced by her son. He hoped Marcus would notice her exhaustion and speak to her

43

about spending so much of her strength in caring for the poor. She had been gone from dawn this morning until only a few hours ago. He had overstepped himself once in trying to suggest she allow him or the other servants to deliver whatever food and clothing she wanted taken to the poor. Phoebe had insisted it was her pleasure to do so.

"Athena's son wasn't well when I saw her this morning. I want to see if he's better tomorrow," she had said, speaking of a woman whose husband had sailed for a number of years on one of Decimus Valerian's ships and been swept over the side during a heavy storm. Since the master's death, Phoebe Valerian had befriended all the families who had lost husbands or fathers while laboring on Valerian ships or docks.

Iulius always accompanied her during her visits to various families in need. One young woman, newly widowed and terrified that she would find no way to provide for her children, had prostrated herself before Phoebe when she arrived at the dreary tenement. Dismayed, Phoebe had quickly drawn the young woman up and embraced her. A widow herself, Phoebe understood grief. She remained for several hours, talking with the younger woman, sharing her anguish and offering comfort.

Iulius revered his mistress, for she gave out of love rather than a sense of responsibility or fear of the mob. The widows and orphans in the rat-infested tenements near the Ephesian docks knew she loved them and so loved her in return.

Now Iulius watched as her affection for her son lit her tired face. "Your servant sent word you weren't coming this evening, Marcus. I thought you were otherwise occupied," Phoebe said.

Marcus did notice her fatigue but made no remark. He had encouraged her to rest more the last time he had visited with her, and it had done little good. Besides, he had other things on his mind this evening.

"I had some things I wanted to think over."

She didn't press him. They entered the triclinium, and Marcus took her to her couch before reclining on another. He declined the wine Iulius offered. Phoebe whispered instructions to Iulius to bring bread, fruit, and sliced meat for him and then waited patiently for Marcus to speak, knowing that her questions would be deflected. Marcus had always hated being interrogated about his life. She would learn more by listening. For now, he seemed content to pass the time with news of ships coming in and the cargoes they brought.

"One of our ships came in from Caesarea and brought in some beautiful blue cloth and embroidered goods from an Eastern caravan. I can bring you whatever you want."

"I've little need for embroidered goods, Marcus, but I would like some of the blue cloth—and wool if you have it." With it, she could make dresses for her widows.

"Some came this morning from Damascus. The finest quality."

She watched him pick at the meal as he talked about imports and exports, his routine, people he had seen. And all the while she listened, she knew he had not spoken what was really on his mind.

Then he said, surprising her, "Did Hadassah ever discuss her family with you?"

Surely he knew more than she. He had been deeply in love with the slave girl. "You never talked with her about her family?"

"It never seemed important. I assumed they died in Jerusalem. Did she ever tell you anything about them?"

Phoebe thought back for a long moment. "If I remember correctly, her father was a potter. She never told me his name, but she said people came from other districts to watch him work and talk with him. She had a brother and a younger sister as well. Her sister's name was Leah. I remember because I thought it such a pretty name. Hadassah said she died when they were taken into the ruins of the Jewish temple and held captive in the Women's Court."

"Did her father and mother die in captivity also?"

"No. Hadassah said her father went out into the city to teach about Jesus. He never returned. Her mother died later of starvation, and then her brother was killed by a Roman soldier when the city fell."

Marcus remembered how thin Hadassah had been the first time he saw her. Her head had been shaved, and her hair was just beginning to grow back. He had thought her ugly. Perhaps he had even said so.

"The daughter of a potter in Jerusalem," he said, wondering if that knowledge would help him in any way.

"Her family was from Galilee, not Jerusalem."

"If they were from Galilee, what were they doing in Jerusalem?"

"I'm not sure, Marcus. I seem to remember Hadassah saying something about her family returning to Jerusalem once a year during the Jewish Passover. They came to celebrate Communion with other believers of the Way."

"What's Communion?"

"It's a meal of wine and bread partaken by those who embrace the Christ as their Lord. It's eaten in memory of him." It was so much more than that, but Marcus wouldn't understand. She saw the question growing in his eyes and the darkening of his countenance. Did he suspect?

"You seem to know a great deal about Christian practices, Mother."

She didn't want to alarm him and so took the easier way. "Hadassah was in our household for four years. She became very dear to me."

"I can understand how Father might have grasped for immortality with his last breath, but—"

"Your father sought peace, Marcus, not immortality."

Marcus stood, agitated. He sensed the change in his mother and was afraid of what it meant. He didn't want to ask. He had already lost Hadassah because of her uncompromising faith in her unseen god. What if his mother now worshiped the same god? His stomach knotted at the mere thought.

"Why are you asking all these questions, Marcus?"

"Because I'm thinking of taking up your suggestion and going in search of Hadassah's god."

Phoebe drew a soft gasp, her heart lighting with joy. "You will pray?"

"No, I'm going to Judea."

"Judea!" she said, stunned by his answer. "Why must you go so far away?"

"Where better to find a Jewish god than in a Jewish homeland?"

She tried to recover from the shock of his announcement, grasping at the small flame of hope in what his words implied. "Then you believe Hadassah's god does exist."

"I don't know if I believe in anything," he said flatly, crushing her. "But maybe I'll understand her better and feel closer to her in Judea. Maybe I'll find out why she embraced this religion of hers with such tenacity." He leaned against a marble column and stared out into the peristyle where he had spoken with Hadassah so often in the past. "Before I left Rome the first time and came here with you and Father, my friends and I used to sit for hours drinking wine and talking."

He turned to face her again. "Two subjects were guaranteed to rouse passionate debate: politics and religion. Most of my friends worshiped gods that gave free reign to their pleasures. Isis. Artemis. Bacchus. Others worshiped out of fear or need."

He began to pace as he spoke, as though walking helped him mull through various ideas while he sought some fleeting conclusion that eluded him. "It stands to reason, doesn't it? Soldiers bow down to Mars. Pregnant women appeal to Hera for safe delivery. Physicians and their patients lift their hands to Asklepios to bring healing. Shepherds turn to a god of mountains and lonely places, like Pan."

"So what are you saying, Marcus? That man creates gods according to his needs and desires? That Hadassah's god never existed except out of her need for a redeemer from her slavery?"

Her quietly spoken questions made him defensive. "I'm saying that the land man dwells on molds the way he lives. Is it so inconceivable then that man would mold a god to fulfill his needs?"

Phoebe listened to his theories with breaking heart. Both of her children were lost, both tormented, and there seemed nothing she could do except let them find their own way. Decimus' efforts to control Julia's impetuous high spirits had met with disaster, and it had been Hadassah who had brought Marcus closer to the family hearth. Now, sitting here in the triclinium with an appearance of calm, listening to her son, she wanted to cry out and scream and tear her hair. She felt she was standing on a safe shore while her son was drowning before her eyes in a dark, swirling sea.

What do I say, Lord? Her throat closed tightly, and she could utter nothing.

What would become of her son if he continued on his present course? If Hadassah, with all her wisdom and love, had been unable to reach him, how could she? *O God!* she cried out in her heart, *my son is as stubborn as his father, as passionate and impetuous as his younger sister. What do I do? O Jesus, how do I save him?*

Marcus saw his mother's distress and went to her. He sat on her couch and took one of her hands between his. "It wasn't my desire to cause you more grief, Mother."

"I know that, Marcus." She had watched him go back to

Rome, thinking she wouldn't see him for several years, and he had returned more deeply distressed than when he had left. Now he was saying he had to leave again and this time to go to a war-torn country that hated Rome. "But Judea, Marcus. *Judea* . . ."

"Hadassah's homeland. I want to know why she died. I have to find out the truth, and if there is a god, I'll find him there. I've no answers, Mother, and I can't seem to find the ones I need here in Ephesus. I feel as though I'm standing on sinking sand. The sound of the mob still rings in my ears."

She had seen the pain in his eyes before he lowered his head, and she wanted desperately to comfort him, to hold him in her arms and rock him as she had when he was a small child. But he was a man now, and something beyond even that held her back and told her she had said enough.

His hands tightened on hers. "I can't explain what I feel, Mother. I want you to understand, and yet I don't even understand it for myself." He looked into her eyes again. "I hunger for the peace of hillsides I've never walked over and the smell of an inland sea I've never seen." His eyes filled with tears. "Because *she* was there."

Phoebe thought she understood what her son was saying to her. She knew how Hadassah would have grieved to know Marcus had placed her on an idol's pedestal. Hadassah had been the moon reflecting the sun's light in everything she said and did; she was not the light herself and never claimed to be. And yet, that was what she had become to Marcus. His life had risen in his love for her. Would it set there as well?

She wanted to say something, to spring forth with some wisdom that would turn him from the path he was on, but nothing came. What choice did she have except to let him go and trust the Lord to guide him? The apostle John had told the gathering that Jesus promised, *If you seek, you shall find.*

Jesus said.

Jesus.

Phoebe laid her hand tenderly against Marcus' cheek, fighting back her own tears and drawing Christ's words of hope around her as a protective shield against the darkness that held her son prisoner.

"Marcus, if you believe you'll find your answers only in Judea, then to Judea you must go." They embraced. She held him for a long moment and then released him, praying with silent fervor,

O Jesus, blessed Savior, I give my son to you. Please watch over him and protect him from the evil one. O Lord God, Father of all creation, overcome my fear for my son and teach me to rest and trust in you.

Clinging to that, she kissed Marcus' cheek in blessing and whispered, "Do whatsoever you must." Only she knew the words were not spoken to her son, but to the unseen God she trusted with all her heart.

5

Alexander Democedes Amandinus lounged back on the bench in the calidarium while his two friends continued their debate over the practice of medicine. He had not seen either of them since leaving Phlegon's tutelage, where all three had been studying beneath the master physician. Vitruvius Plautus Musa had always had difficulty keeping up with the written work Phlegon required, while Celsus Phaedrus Timalchio took every word the master physician said as the final authority. After a year of study with Phlegon, Vitruvius had decided he was an empiric and sought a master physician who shared his views. Cletas apparently sufficed. Alexander had reserved his comments about him, deciding that whatever he would say would fall on deaf ears anyway.

And now, Vitruvius sat across from him, his back against the wall, his strong legs stretched out in front of him, declaring that true physicians received their healing abilities directly from the gods, a view undoubtedly touted by Cletas. Alexander smiled to himself, wondering if young Celsus had grasped yet that Vitruvius was boasting out of a sense of inferiority. Phlegon had frequently congratulated Celsus on his quick grasp of medical concepts, especially those he himself favored.

"So, now you think you're a gift from the gods," Celsus said from where he stood near the steaming font. He was pale, perspiration dripping from his body, and in no mood for Vitruvius' boasting. "Pray to the gods all you want, but I hold with what Phlegon teaches. He's proven that illness comes from an imbalance of the humors and elements, all of which are rooted in fire, air, earth, and water."

"Proven! Just because Phlegon says health comes from balancing body fluids, you swallow it as fact," Vitruvius said. "Have you no mind of your own?"

"Indeed, I've a mind of my own. Mind enough to not swallow your hogwash," he said, moving closer to the hot steam rising from the stones.

"If that old man was right about how to treat a patient, you would be able to overcome these recurring fevers you've suffered since studying in Rome. You've been 'balancing humors' since we met. If his theories worked, you'd be the healthiest man in the Empire!"

"The fever is less than yesterday," Celsus said stiffly.

"Ah, so the bloodletting and emetics helped." Vitruvius uttered a derisive snort. "If that were really so, you wouldn't be standing there shivering in this heat!"

Celsus glared at him in growing frustration. "If you're so sure of your divinely inspired abilities, give me a demonstration! By Cletas' logic, all a physician would need to do is utter the right words and give a sleight of hand to produce a cure! So whisper your incantations, Vitruvius, and let's see if you can cure someone who's *really* sick. Let's see this *gift* of yours in action!"

"Magical incantations are only the beginning," Vitruvius said haughtily. "Animal and vegetable remedies—"

Celsus held up his hand. "If you're about to suggest I swallow a brew like that last one you concocted out of lion's manure and the blood of a dying gladiator, save your breath. It almost killed me!"

Vitruvius sat forward. "Perhaps what you lack is a proper respect for the gods!"

"If I had kissed your feet, would it have made a difference?"

Seeing that what had begun as an interesting exchange of ideas had deteriorated into an argument, Alexander interceded. "What ails you, Celsus, is a common affliction of many who live in Rome. I think it has something to do with the mephitic floods that occur there."

Vitruvius rolled his eyes and leaned back again. "Another of your theories, Alexander? Have you shared it with Phlegon? Or is he still not speaking to you because of your defiance over that slave girl you smuggled out of the arena?"

Alexander ignored him as he continued speaking to Celsus. "I studied in Rome before coming to Ephesus, and I wrote extensive notes on my observations. The fevers come and go, sometimes with weeks or months between attacks. Sometimes they grow worse. . . ."

Celsus nodded. "My symptoms exactly."

Vitruvius looked at Celsus. "Alexander will now tell you again disease is spread by tiny invisible seeds, and that if medical cases were recorded in a logical, methodical manner, one could find a commonality." He waved his hand airily. "By experimentation, a trial and error method, if you will, a workable cure could be found for almost any disease."

Alexander grinned at him. "Neatly summarized, Vitruvius. One would think I have swayed you to a new way of thinking."

"You can be persuasive at times," Vitruvius conceded, "but it would take better logic than yours to convince me. Your theories make no sense whatsoever, Alex, especially in the light that *all* disease is hidden from man and in the hands of the gods. Therefore, it stands to reason that it is to the gods one must appeal."

Alexander arched his brow. "If what you say is true, why bother training physicians at all?"

"Because physicians must be knowledgeable in what pleases the gods."

Alexander smiled. "You have your professions confused, my friend. You shouldn't be training to be a physician at all. With your zeal for religion, you should be in the robes of a novice priest. A haruspex, perhaps. You could learn how to properly disembowel helpless goats and read signs from their entrails."

"You would mock the gods?"

Alexander's mouth tipped ruefully. "I worship Apollo and Asklepios just as you do, as well as a host of other healing deities like Hygieia and Pankeis. And *with* all that, I still find it impossible to believe any man can manipulate a god into doing what he wants simply by uttering an incantation and burning a little incense."

"I agree," Celsus said, wrapping a towel around his shoulders and huddling beneath it. "But what's the answer?"

"A deeper study of human anatomy."

Vitruvius grimaced. "By 'deeper study' Alexander means the practice Phlegon espouses with such gruesome relish. Vivisection."

"I abhor vivisection," Alexander said.

"Then why did you ever study with Phlegon?"

"Because he's a brilliant surgeon. He can remove a man's leg in under five minutes. Have you ever watched him work?"

"More times than I care to remember," Vitruvius said with a shudder. "The screams of his patients still ring in my ears."

"Who's your master physician now?" Celsus asked Alexander.

"No one."

"No one?"

"I've set up my own practice."

"Here in the baths?" Celsus said in surprise. It was common

enough for physicians to begin their practices at the baths, but not one of Alexander's talent and ability. He had been groomed for grander halls than these.

"In a booth just outside."

"You have too much promise to be practicing medicine in a booth," Vitruvius said. "Talk to Cletas. I'll recommend you."

Alexander strove for tact. "Cletas doesn't practice surgery, and he espouses theories I find . . . disquieting," he said, feeling his answer was unsatisfactory, but unwilling to state straight out that he thought Cletas a fraud. The man called himself a master physician, but was more a magician adorned in impressive robes and gifted with an orator's voice. Granted, he was successful, but his success lay in the fact that he always chose patients who were very rich and not seriously ill. Vitruvius, with his good looks, aristocratic accent, and lack of ethics, would probably do very well practicing the same brand of medicine.

"However unpleasant it may be," Celsus said, "vivisection is necessary if you're going to be a physician."

"I don't see how torturing and killing citizens advances medicine," Vitruvius said disdainfully.

"Phlegon has never suggested we use just any man on the walk," Celsus retorted angrily. "I've only performed vivisection on criminals from the arena."

"Do they scream less loudly than the average person?"

Celsus stiffened. "How else does a physician develop his skills in surgery unless he practices on someone? Or do you think someone with a gangrenous leg should be treated with incantation and a foul-tasting potion of bat wings and lizard tongues?"

Celsus' sarcasm hit its mark. Vitruvius' face went red. "I don't use bat wings."

"Ha. Then maybe you ought to brew some up and see if they work better than your last potion . . . which didn't work at all!"

Watching Vitruvius' face darken even more, Alexander's mouth tipped in a wry smile. "Perhaps we should go into the frigidarium so the two of you can cool off."

"Good idea," Vitruvius said and stalked from the small chamber.

Celsus swore. He sat down on the bench closest to the steaming font. He was pale and shaking, sweat pouring from his face. "I used to admire him. Now I see he's a pompous fool."

"What you admired were his family connections." Alexander

took up another towel and brought it to Celsus. He understood Celsus' sense of inadequacy. He had felt it himself upon entering the school of medicine in Rome. He was the only student whose father had once been a slave, a fact that had less impact in Rome, where he had still had unlimited funds, than it did now in Ephesus, where most of his inheritance had been used up. People tended to overlook one's lineage much more easily when one had a storehouse of wealth. Which Alexander no longer had.

He pulled his thoughts back to Celsus. "Perhaps this wet heat isn't good for you," he said, handing the towel to him.

Celsus took it and dabbed his face with it. "Did you learn how to treat this fever while you studied in Rome?"

"The master there prescribed rest, massage, and dietary controls, but without complete success. The fevers continued to recur." He hesitated. "It seemed to me in reviewing the case histories I've kept that the fevers were always worse when the patient was tired and in poor physical condition. I've had a few patients come to my booth, and I've advised all three of them to build their strength between the attacks. As soon as you're able, go on a barleyman diet and exercise regimen."

"You mean train like a gladiator?" Celsus said with a mirthless laugh.

"Not exactly," Alexander said, not taking offense. "Clearly the purges and emetics Phlegon prescribed have only served to sap your strength."

"They were meant to purify my body."

"So, now you've been purified. You need to build up your strength."

"I don't know who to believe anymore, Alexander. Vitruvius has his points. Maybe I don't revere the gods enough and they're punishing me. Phlegon says it's a matter of balance. And now you're telling me something else." Celsus sighed and put his head in his hands. "All I do know is when I feel like this, all I want to do is die and have done with it."

Alexander put his hand on Celsus' shoulder. "Come on back to my booth with me and rest a while before you head back."

They left the calidarium. Alexander dove into the frigidarium and cooled down while Celsus bypassed it and went to dry off and dress in the changing room. When Alexander left the pool, he signaled to Vitruvius that he was leaving. Vitruvius gave a slight wave and stretched out on one of the tables for a massage.

Celsus was silent as they walked the short distance from the public baths to the booth where Alexander daily practiced medicine. A heavy wooden screen had been set across the front. Hanging from the screen was a small sign saying the physician would not return until late in the afternoon. Two soldiers walked by and nodded to Alexander as he pushed aside one section of the screen, letting Celsus enter ahead of him before closing it after them.

A small oil lamp was lit and sitting on a worktable in the corner at the back. "Well," Alexander said, watching Celsus take in his surroundings. "What do you think of it?"

Sitting on a stool, Celsus pulled his cape around him more snugly as he looked around the dimly lit interior. Compared to the facilities Phlegon had, it was rude and small, almost primitive. The floor was packed dirt rather than marble. Yet, despite the crudeness of the hide awning and mortared walls, it was surprisingly well equipped for a young physician only just setting up practice.

A narrow examining bench and privacy screen were set against the west wall, and every square inch of space looked to be efficiently used. A small counter sat against the back wall. On it were pestle and mortar, fine balances, scales and weights, and marble palettes for rolling pills. Shelves above the counter displayed bottles, small amphoras, glass phials, squat jars, and dropper juglets, each meticulously labeled and categorized as astringent, caustic, cleanser, erodent, and emollient. Neatly arranged in shelves on the opposite wall were various tools of their trade: scoops, spoons, spatulas, blades, forceps, hooks, probes, scalpels, speculums, and cautery.

Picking up a scalpel, Celsus studied it.

"From the Alpine province of Noricum," Alexander said proudly.

"Phlegon claims they make the best steeled surgical instruments," Celsus remarked, putting the tool back carefully.

"And cost a veritable fortune," Alexander said grimly, adding fuel to the red coals in the brazier.

"How long have you had this booth?" Celsus said, setting a stool closer to the warmth.

"Two months," Alexander said. "Before that, I spent most of my time tending my one and only patient."

"I heard the rumors," Celsus admitted. "A slave girl, wasn't it?"

"Yes. A Christian who'd been tossed to the lions."

"Did you heal her?"

Alexander hesitated. "Not exactly, but she is healed."

Celsus frowned. "What do you mean?"

"I mean I didn't have the skills to prevent infection. The wounds in her right leg festered. An amputation was necessary, but when I prepared her, I saw the wounds were clear. She said Jesus healed her."

Celsus shook his head, glancing around again. "A pity you forfeited your position with Phlegon in order to save someone who doesn't even appreciate your sacrifice."

"I didn't mean to imply the girl was not grateful," Alexander said.

"Yet she doesn't credit you with her life."

"Well, not exactly." He grinned. "She said I was but a tool in the hand of God."

"I've heard Christians are thought to be insane."

"She's not insane. Just a little strange."

"Whatever she is, she cost you a promising career. If you apologized to Phlegon, I'm sure he'd take you back. He said once you were the most brilliant student he had ever had."

"I see no need to apologize, and I disagreed with Phlegon in several areas. Why should I go back?"

"You spent three years studying at the Hippocratic Corpus in Alexandria. Then you studied in Rome under Cato. When you learned all he could teach you, you came here to Ephesus, seeking Phlegon's teaching because of his reputation throughout the Empire. But now, here you are in a booth outside the public baths."

Alexander laughed. "Don't sound so distressed. I chose to be here."

"But why? You could have a prestigious practice anywhere, even in Rome itself if you wanted. Physician to the greatest men in the Empire. Instead, you defy Phlegon, set off on your own, and end up here, like this. I don't understand it."

"I've treated more patients in the last six months than I saw in a year under Phlegon, and I don't have Troas breathing down my neck," Alexander said, referring to the master physician's Egyptian slave, a gifted surgeon and healer in his own right.

"But what sort of patients come to you?"

Alexander arched his brow. "People with conditions other

56

than gout and mentagra or wasting illnesses caused by rich living," he said, nodding toward a pile of scrolls neatly tucked into a shelf in the corner. "Where better to learn medicine than by treating the masses?"

"But can they pay?"

Alexander looked at him with a wry expression. "Yes, they pay. Granted, I don't demand the same fees Phlegon does, but I didn't come down here to get rich, Celsus. My purpose in being here is to learn all I can and apply that knowledge for the benefit of others."

"And you couldn't have done that with Phlegon?"

"Under his conditions, no. He's too set in his thinking."

Someone began to open the partition and then drew back.

"Someone is trying to get in," Celsus said, alarmed.

Alexander rose quickly and pushed aside the heavy screen. "I should have left it open for you," he said to whomever was outside, and glanced at Celsus as a veiled figure limped through the opening. "This is the woman of whom we were speaking earlier," he said.

Celsus did not rise as a crippled woman in heavy veils entered the small cubicle. Alexander pulled the partition closed behind her. "Did you get the *mandragora?*" he asked her, taking the small basket she balanced over one arm and uncovering the contents.

"Yes, my lord," came the soft reply. "But far less than you wanted. Tetricus had just received some *opobalsamum,* and I used the money you gave me to purchase it instead."

Celsus frowned, listening intently. There was a slight impediment to her speech, but it did not disguise the heavy Judean accent.

"You did well," Alexander said, pleased. He took the squat jar with the precious balsam and set the basket on the work counter. He held the small jar carefully near the flickering flame to see the deep color. Opobalsamum was made from secretions from numerous balsam trees, the most famous being the Mecca balsam or "balm of Gilead." The drug had dozens of uses, from cleaning wounds as an erodent and a suppurative for drawing pus from a festering wound, to acting as an emollient.

"Are you making *mithridatium?*" Celsus said, alluding to an ancient antidote that was reputed to counteract poisons introduced into the body through bites, food, or drink. It had been named for its inventor, a brilliant and learned king of Pontus, Mithridates VI, who had drunk poison daily after first taking remedies to render it harmless. When ordered to take his own life, poison had proven ineffective, and he had died by the sword instead.

"Mithridatium might be in demand if I was physician to the proconsul or some other high official," Alexander said, amused. "Since I'm treating laborers and slaves, I prefer to use the opobalsamum for something far more useful. It's one of the ingredients in several poultices I make and also useful as an anodyne salve for relieving neuralgia. It's also proven effective as an eye ointment." He glanced at the slave girl. "Is it resin?"

"No, my lord," the slave told him softly. "It was boiled down from leaves, seeds, and branches."

"Does that make a difference?" Celsus said.

Alexander took down a bronze box and removed the sliding lid. "Only in price, not effectiveness," he said, placing the squat jar carefully into one of the internal compartments before sliding the lid closed again. He set the box back in its space on the shelf, which was loaded with other drugs and medicinal ingredients.

Turning, Alexander noticed Celsus had forgotten the discomforts of his chills and fever in his curiosity over the veiled girl. Many people stared at her the same way, wondering what she hid beneath the veil. He glanced at the girl. She was slightly stooped, her small hand gripping the walking stick. Her knuckles were white with the effort. Alexander took the stool by his worktable and placed it near the brazier opposite Celsus. "Sit and rest, Hadassah. I'll buy some bread and wine and return shortly."

Celsus was alarmed to be left alone with the girl—the veils made him uncomfortable. She sank down onto the stool, and he heard her soft sigh of relief. She set the walking stick to one side and rubbed her right leg. Her hand was small and delicate, with clean oval nails. It was lovely, very feminine, and young. He was surprised.

"Why do you wear that veil?" he said abruptly.

"My scars make others uncomfortable, my lord."

"I'm a physician. Let me see them."

She hesitated and then slowly lifted the veils, revealing her face. Celsus grimaced. Nodding once, he gestured for her to cover herself. Alexander had been cruel to rescue this girl. She would have been better off dead. What sort of a normal life could she have looking as she did and crippled the way she was? And what use was she as a servant, so ponderous and clumsy?

He started to shiver again and drew his cape around himself, trying to overcome the chills. He swore under his breath, wishing he had hired a litter and returned to his own apartment.

The slave girl rose with some effort. Celsus watched her limp to the back of the booth and bend down to take a bedroll from beneath the worktable. Loosening the thick woven blanket, she brought it back to him and placed it around his shoulders. "Would you be more comfortable lying down, my lord?"

"Probably not." He watched her limp to the small counter. She poured water into a small pot and set it on the brazier to heat. Then she took several containers down from the medicine shelf. She meticulously measured out ingredients from several and replaced the containers on the shelf again before grinding what she had taken with the pestle and mortar. The water had begun to boil. Sprinkling in the contents, she stirred with a slender stick. "Inhale this, my lord."

Her voice and manner were very soothing, and he was surprised by her knowledge. "Should you be making free with your master's things?" he said as he leaned forward.

"He will not object," came her soft rasping reply.

As he filled his lungs with a surprisingly pleasant aroma, he sensed she was smiling. "Do you take advantage of his kind nature?"

"No, my lord. The master has used this treatment on other patients with fevers. He would want you to be comfortable."

"Oh," he said, feeling faintly ashamed that he had criticized her when she had sought to serve her master—and him as well. He breathed in the aromatic vapor, his muscles relaxing. The weight of the blanket added to his comfort. The heat of the calidarium had drained him, and now the warmth from the brazier and the sweet vapor rising from the small pot made him drowsy. He started to drift asleep and then jerked awake as he swayed on the stool.

The girl rose and took another bedroll from beneath the worktable and laid it out on the packed-dirt floor. Celsus felt her arm ease around his shoulder and heard her whisper, "Come and rest, my lord. You'll feel much better." She was stronger than she looked and helped him up, but when he leaned more heavily against her, he heard the small catch of breath.

Her leg must pain her, he thought, then he sank down on the pallet she had prepared for him. As she rearranged the blanket over him, he smiled. "Nobody's done that for me since I was a child." She brushed her fingertips lightly over his forehead, and he felt a peculiar sense of well-being.

Rising stiffly, Hadassah limped to the stool and eased down. Sighing, she kneaded the aching muscles of her right leg. Closing her eyes, she wished she could knead away the ache in her heart as well.

Tears came unexpectedly, and she struggled against them, knowing Alexander would return soon and know she'd been crying. Then he would want to know if her leg pained her again. If she said yes, he would insist upon massaging it. If she said no, he would probe with questions she had no heart to answer.

She had seen Marcus!

He had bumped right into her on the street outside. She had been jostled so often in the crowds heading for the baths that she thought nothing of it. Then he had spoken. Stunned at the sound of his voice, she had glanced up and saw it *was* him, and not just her memory playing tricks on her again.

He was still devastatingly handsome, though he looked somehow older and harder. The mouth she had remembered as enticingly sensuous had been set in a grim line. Her heart had beaten so fast . . . just as it raced now with her remembering. When he had caught her arm to steady her, she had almost fainted.

Amazing how more than a year could be wiped away in an instant. She had looked into Marcus' eyes, and every moment she had spent with him had come back to her in a wave of longing. She had almost reached up to touch his face, but he had drawn back slightly, the same wariness on his face that she saw so often when people looked at her. A woman covered in veils was a disconcerting sight. Tilting his head, he had stared down at her with a bemused frown. Even knowing he couldn't do so, she had been instinctively afraid he might see her scarred face and lowered her head quickly. In that moment, he had turned away.

She had stood there in the middle of the milling crowd, tears filling her eyes as she watched him walk away. He was walking out of her life as he had before.

Now, sitting in the security of Alexander's booth, Hadassah wondered if Marcus Lucianus Valerian even remembered her.

"Lord, why did you allow this to happen to me?" she whispered into the stillness of the dimly lit booth. She stared through her tears and veils at the burning coals in the brazier, all the love she had felt for Marcus welling up again and filling her with an aching sadness for what might have been. "I feel yoked to him, Lord," she went on softly, beating her breast softly with her fist. "Yoked . . ."

She lowered her head.

She knew it hadn't been Marcus' habit to enter the public baths. He had always bathed at exclusive establishments reserved for those who could pay high membership fees.

So why had he come?

She sighed. What did it matter? God had removed her from his life and placed her here, in this tiny booth, with a young physician hungry to save the world from everything. Everything, that is, but spiritual darkness. He was like Julia's first husband, Claudius, insatiable for knowledge while remaining blind to wisdom.

Her heart ached. *Why didn't you let me die, Lord? Why?* She wept silently, crying out to God for an answer. No answer came. She had thought she knew God's purpose for her: to die for him. And yet she was alive, bearing her secret scars beneath the dark veils. All the serenity and acceptance she had found over the past year was shattered. And why? Because she had seen Marcus again. A chance encounter that had lasted less than a minute.

The screen moved, and Alexander entered the room. Hadassah glanced up at him, relieved by his presence. His face had become dear to her over the months of her convalescence. She had been too ill then, and in too much pain, to realize the sacrifice he had made in smuggling her out of the arena. Not until later did she learn that he had forfeited his position with a renowned master physician and gained the scorn of many of his friends for throwing so much away over a mere slave.

Hadassah knew without a doubt that God had had his hand on Alexander that day in the shadows of the Door of Death. He had been God's instrument. As she watched him now, she admitted that her feelings for him were sometimes very confusing. She was grateful, but there was more to it than that. She liked him and admired him. His desire to heal was heartfelt, not a matter of expedience or profit. He cared, even to the point of grief, when he lost a patient. She remembered the first time she had seen him weep—it had been over a young boy who died of a fever—and she had felt love for Alexander wash over her. She knew she did not love this man the way she still loved Marcus . . . yet she could not deny that they were deeply connected.

He looked at her, and their eyes met. A tired smile crossed his face. "Heat some more water, Hadassah," he said.

"Yes, my lord."

She did so, then watched as he added various ingredients to it and then hunkered down and awakened Celsus. "Come, sit up my friend," he said, and Hadassah was moved by the note of compassion in Alexander's voice. He held the brew to Celsus' lips. At the first sip, Celsus grimaced and drew back from it suspiciously. Alexander laughed. "No bats' wings or lizard tongues in it," he said, and Hadassah was left wondering what he meant as Celsus took the cup and swallowed the contents.

Alexander rose. "I've hired a litter to take you home."

"You have my gratitude," Celsus said, rising, the blankets falling in a heap around his sandaled feet. As he stepped away, Hadassah took the blankets up and folded them, putting them away beneath the worktable. Celsus readjusted his crumpled cape. "I needed to rest awhile," he said. He glanced at Hadassah and then back at Alexander. "Maybe I'll drop by again and read some of your cases."

Alexander put a comforting hand on his shoulder. "Make it in the morning then. I hardly have space to take a breath the rest of the day." He pushed the partition aside, setting the sections together so that the front of the booth was wide open, indicating he was ready to see patients.

Several were already waiting outside.

Celsus went out and climbed into the litter. "Hold," he said as the two slaves lifted him. "What was in that drink you gave me?" he called to Alexander, who was positioning a small table at the front of the booth where Hadassah was setting up an inkpot and scrolls.

Alexander laughed. "A little of this and that. Let me know if it works."

Celsus gave the carriers directions and leaned back into the folds of his cape. He looked back as they bore him away and saw that patients were already pressing forward—and he frowned, for rather than cluster around Alexander, the physician, they drew close to the quiet woman in veils.

Hadassah, unaware she was the subject of scrutiny, dropped half a dozen grains of dried lampblack into the inkhorn and added water. She mixed it carefully and took up her iron stylus. "Name, please," she said to the man who took the stool beside the writing table where she worked. She dipped the stylus into the ink and poised the tip over the waxed tablet on which she wrote the most rudimentary of information: name and complaint. The information would later be transferred onto parchment scrolls and the waxed tablet rubbed smooth for use the next day. Several scrolls were already stored in the back of the booth and included long lists of patients whom Alexander had treated, along with their physical complaints and symptoms and prescribed treatments and results.

"Boethus," the man told her flatly. "How long will it be before I can see the physician? I haven't much time."

She wrote his name down. "He'll be with you as soon as he can," she said gently. Everyone had urgent needs, and it was difficult to tell how long Alexander would take with each patient. Some had conditions that fascinated him, and he spent more time questioning and examining them. She glanced at the man through her veils. He was deeply tanned and thin, his hands gnarled and stained from hard work. His short hair was salted with gray, and the lines about his eyes and mouth were deeply cut. "What's your occupation?"

"I was a *stuppator,*" he said glumly.

Hadassah wrote his occupation beside his name. A caulker of ships. Tedious, backbreaking work. "Your complaint?" He sat silent, staring off at nothing. "Boethus," she said, placing the stylus between her two hands. "Why did you come to see the physician?"

He looked back at her, his fingers spreading on his thighs and digging in as though he were trying to keep himself together. "Can't sleep. Can't eat. And I've had a constant headache for the last few days."

Hadassah poised the stylus again and wrote meticulously. She felt him watching each stroke she made, as though fascinated. "I worked up until a few weeks ago," he said, "but there's been no work for me lately. Fewer ships are coming in, and the overseers hire the younger men to do the work."

Hadassah lifted her head. "Have you a family, Boethus?"

"A wife, four children." The lines in his face deepened, and his face grew even paler. He frowned as she laid down the quill. "I'll find a way to pay for the physician's services. I swear."

"You needn't worry about that, Boethus."

"Easy for you to say, but if I get sick to death, what'll happen to them?"

Hadassah understood his fear. She had seen countless families living in the streets, begging for a piece of bread, while just a few feet from them was a lavish temple and palaces built into the hillsides. "Tell me about your family."

He began by telling the names and ages of his son and three daughters. He spoke of his hardworking wife. The deep love he had for her was apparent in his words. Hadassah's gentle manner and quiet questions of concern encouraged him, until he was hunching forward, pouring out his deepest fears about what would become of his children and his wife if he couldn't find work soon. The landlord was wanting his rent for the small tenement where the family lived, and Boethus had no money to give him. He didn't know what he was going to do. And now, to add to all his other burdens, he was sick and getting sicker with each day.

"The gods are against me," he said in despair.

The privacy curtain was drawn aside, and a woman left the booth. She paid Hadassah the copper fee. Hadassah rose and placed her hand on Boethus' shoulder, asking him to remain where he was.

The man watched her speak with a young woman standing off by herself. He noted the woman's painted eyes and anklets with small bells that jingled softly with the slightest moment—all advertisement of her profession: prostitution.

Boethus continued watching with interest as the physician's veiled assistant took the prostitute's hand between hers and spoke again. The young woman nodded slowly, and the assistant went in to talk with the physician.

Drawing the curtain slightly, Hadassah tried to summarize what she had learned about Alexander's next patient. "Her name is Severina, and she's seventeen years of age." Careless of personal information, Alexander asked specifics. "She's had a bloody discharge for several weeks."

Alexander nodded, rinsing one of his instruments and drying it. "Send her in."

Hadassah saw that he was weary and distracted. Perhaps he was still mulling over what he had discovered about the previous patient's condition. He often worried about his patients, staying away from his bed for long hours in the evening, going over his records and making meticulous notes. He never counted his successes, which were many, but viewed each person he saw as a new challenge with illnesses to be overcome by his knowledge.

"She was a temple prostitute, my lord. She said they performed a purification ceremony on her, and when it didn't work, they put her out."

He set the instrument on the shelf. "Another patient who can't pay."

The dry remark surprised her. Alexander seldom mentioned money. He set no fees for his patients, accepting only what they could afford to give him in exchange for his help. Sometimes payment was no more than a copper coin. Hadassah knew the money mattered less to him than what he learned and what he was able to accomplish for others with that knowledge. Had he not spent his entire inheritance on traveling and learning all he could for his chosen profession?

No, it was not the money that was bothering him.

He glanced at her, and she saw frustration in his eyes. "I'm running out of supplies, Hadassah. And the rent for this booth is due tomorrow morning."

"Alexander," she said, putting her hand on his arm. "Didn't the Lord provide the rent last month?"

Her use of his name warmed him, and he smiled down at her ruefully. "Indeed, but does this god of yours always have to wait until the last moment?"

"Perhaps he's trying to teach you to trust him."

"Unfortunately, we've no time for an esoteric discussion," he said and nodded toward the curtain. "We've a line of patients outside waiting to be seen. Now, what were you saying about the next one? She's a prostitute?" Venereal disease was rampant among them.

"She *was*, my lord. She's been expelled from the temple and is living on the streets. She has problems other than physical—"

He lifted his hand, silencing her, and his mouth tipped in a wry smile. "Those problems we can't worry about. Send her in and I'll try to treat what I can. Let her gods do the rest."

"Her other problems affect her physical condition."

"If we get her well, those other problems will fade."

"But—"

"Go," he said somewhat impatiently. "We can discuss your theories later, at a less chaotic time."

Hadassah did as he commanded, then sat down at the table again, struggling with frustration. Did Alexander see these people only as physical beings in need of a quick cure? People's needs were complex. They couldn't be solved with a drug or massage or some other prescribed treatment. Alexander only took note of the physical manifestations of their diverse illnesses, and not the deeper, hidden cause. As each day had passed since she had started helping Alexander, Hadassah had become more and more convinced that many of the patients they saw could be cured by the indwelling of the Holy Spirit.

Yet . . . how was she to convince Alexander of that when he himself turned to his healing gods only as a last resort and viewed God Almighty with an awed wariness?

She saw that Boethus looked at her expectantly. She felt that look into her innermost being, and her eyes prickled with tears. She lowered her head, praying silently in desperation. *Lord, what do I say to this man? He and his family need bread, not words.*

Yet, words were what came.

She let out her breath. Tilting her head slightly, she studied Boethus' weary face. "My father once sat on a hillside in Judea listening to his Master. Many people came to hear what the Master had to say, and they came long distances and stayed all through the day. They were hungry. Some of the Master's followers were worried. They told the Master he should send the people home. He told them to feed the people themselves, but they said they had nothing to give them."

She smiled beneath her veil, a smile that lit her eyes. "One small boy had bread and a fish. He came forward and gave it to the Master, and with it the Master fed them all."

"Who was this master?"

"His name is Jesus," she said. She took Boethus' hand between hers. "He said something else, too, Boethus. He said that man doesn't live by bread alone." Leaning toward him, she told him the Good News. They talked quietly all the while the prostitute was with Alexander.

The woman came out and handed Hadassah a copper. "Keep the two *quadrantes* change for yourself," she said. Surprised, Hadassah thanked her.

Boethus watched the woman hurry away.

"Sometimes," Hadassah said, smiling again, "the Lord answers prayer in swift, unexpected ways." He glanced at her as she rose and left him again to speak briefly with a young man who had a severe cough. She went behind the curtain again.

"What do we have next?" Alexander said as he washed his hands in a basin of cold water.

"His name is Ariovistus and he's twenty-three years of age. He's a fuller and has a cough that won't go away. It's deep in his chest and has a thick sound." She took a money box from a small concealed shelf beneath Alexander's worktable. "Severina gave us a copper. She wanted me to keep the two quadrantes change."

"She was probably grateful to have someone speak to her," he said and gave her a nod. Giving thanks to God, she took the two small quadrantes from the box and replaced it beneath the worktable.

Boethus was still sitting on the stool beside the small table outside. He glanced up as she came from behind the curtain. "My headache's gone," he said, bemused. "I don't think I need to see the physician after all. I just wanted to wait and thank you for talking with me." He stood.

Taking his hand, Hadassah turned it palm up and placed the two small coins in it. "From the Lord," she said, closing his fingers around them. "Bread for your family."

Needing a moment's respite, Alexander came out of the booth. He needed a breath of fresh air. He was tired and hungry, and it was getting late. He glanced over the patients still waiting to see him and wished he was more than human, that he could command time to stop. As it was, he could not see everyone who needed him. People such as these, who had little money and even less hope, came to a physician as a last resort. To send them away without the care they desperately needed sat ill with him. But what else could he do? There were only so many hours in a day . . . and only one of him.

He saw Hadassah had set her stool before a woman who held a crying child in her lap. The mother's face was pale and intent as she spoke, her gaze flickering to him nervously. Alexander knew that patients often were afraid of him, certain that whatever cure he might dispense would involve considerable pain. Unfortunately, that too often was true. You couldn't suture wounds or set limbs without pain. He struggled with the sense of frustration that welled within him. Had he the money, he would give doses of mandragora before he did his work. As it was, he had no choice but to save the drug for use during surgery.

He sighed, then smiled at the woman, trying to ease her trepidation, but she blinked and looked quickly away. With a shake of his head, he turned his attention to the scroll on the small worktable. He ran his fingertip down the names written carefully onto the parchment and found the person he'd just finished with. He announced the next patient.

"Boethus," he said and looked over the people standing and sitting around the front of the booth. Four men and three women were waiting, not counting the woman with the crying child. He had already seen ten patients and knew there wouldn't be time to see more than two or three more before he needed to close and rest himself.

Hadassah leaned heavily on her walking stick and rose.

"Boethus!" Alexander said again, impatient.

"I'm sorry, my lord. Boethus left. Agrippina is next, but she's agreed to let Epicharis go before her. Epicharis' daughter, Helena, has a boil on her foot and it's causing her terrible pain."

He looked at the mother and gestured. "Bring her in," he said abruptly and went behind the curtain.

As the mother rose to follow, her child screamed, struggling in her arms. The mother tried to reassure her, but her own fear was evident: her eyes were wide and shining with it, and her mouth trembled. Hadassah stepped toward her and then hesitated, knowing Alexander wouldn't want her to interfere with what had to be done. Epicharis carried her child behind the curtain.

Hadassah wanted to cover her ears as sounds of terror splintered the air. She heard Alexander's voice, and it was none too patient. "By the gods, woman! You must hold her down or I can't work." Then the mother spoke, and Hadassah knew she was crying as she struggled to do as she was told. The screams grew worse.

Clenching her hands, Hadassah remembered the pain she had felt when she had revived after being mauled by the lion. Alexander had worked on her as gently as possible, but the pain had still been excruciating.

Suddenly Alexander yanked the curtain aside and ordered Hadassah into the booth. "See if you can do something with them," he said, his face strained and pale. "One would think I was performing vivisection," he muttered under his breath.

She moved around him to get near the shrieking child. Tears poured down the mother's white face, and she clutched her daughter, every bit as terrified of Alexander as the child. "Why don't you get something to eat, my lord?" Hadassah suggested mildly and turned him toward the curtain.

As soon as he was gone, the child's sonorous screams eased to gulping sobs. Hadassah set two stools near the hot brazier. She indicated the woman could sit on the one while she lowered herself painfully to the other. It had been a long day, and her leg ached so badly each movement sent pain shooting up to her hip and down to her knee. Yet, she was certain her pain was far less than the poor child was suffering. Something had to be done. But what?

Alexander was too eager with his knife.

She remembered suddenly how her mother had treated a boil on a neighbor's hand. Perhaps the same method would work here, now.

Please, Lord, let this work for your glory.

First, the child had to be calm and cooperative. Hadassah rose again, asking the woman questions about her family, while she poured fresh water into a basin and set it on the hard ground in front of Epicharis' feet. The child looked down at it suspiciously and then hid her face in her mother's breasts. Hadassah kept speaking softly, encouraging the mother to answer. As Epicharis talked, she relaxed. And as she relaxed, the child relaxed with her, turning to sit on one knee and stare at Hadassah adding salt crystals to the steaming water in the pot on the brazier.

"Why don't you take the bandage off her foot?" Hadassah said. "She'll be more comfortable. I'll put a little hot water in the basin, and she can soak the foot. It'll ease her pain."

The child moaned when the mother did as Hadassah said. "Put your foot in the water, Helena. That's it, my love. I know it hurts. I know. That's why we've come to the physician. So he can make your foot better."

"Would you like me to tell you a story?" Hadassah asked, and at the child's shy nod, she told of a young couple traveling to a distant town to register for taxes. The lady was expecting a baby, and when it came time for the child to be born, there was no place for them in the inn. In desperation, the mother and father found shelter in a cave where cows and donkeys and other animals were kept—and there the little baby was born.

"When the baby was born, Joseph and Mary wrapped him in swaddling cloths and placed him in a manger."

"Was he cold?" little Helena asked. "I get cold sometimes."

The mother stroked the fair hair back from the child's face and kissed her cheek.

"The cloths and hay kept him warm," Hadassah said. She poured some water from the basin, then added more hot water and set the pot back on the brazier. "It was spring, and so the shepherds had taken the sheep out on the hillsides. That night, up in the dark sky, they saw a beautiful new star. A star that shone more brightly than all others. And then a wondrous thing happened." She told them about the angels sent by God to tell the shepherds about the baby and, when Helena asked, explained what angels were. "The shepherds came to see the baby and bow down to him as their Messiah, which means 'the anointed one of God.' "

"What happened then?" Helena said, eager for more.

"Well, the new family stayed in Bethlehem for quite a while. Joseph was a good carpenter, and so he was able to work and support his family. Some months later, some men came from another country to see the child who had been born under the new star. They recognized that this child was very special, that he was more than just a man."

"Was he a god?" Helena said, eyes wide.

"He *was* God come down to live among us, and the men from the far country brought him gifts: gold because he was a King, frankincense because he was the High Priest for all men, and myrrh because he would die for the sins of the world."

"The baby was going to die?" the child said in disappointment.

"Shhh, Helena. Listen to the story . . . ," the mother said, caught up in it herself.

Hadassah added more hot water to the basin. "There was a wicked king who knew the child would grow up and be a King, and so he looked for him in order to kill him." She set the pot back on the brazier. "The men from the far countries knew of this king's plans and warned Joseph and Mary. They didn't know what to do and waited for the Lord to tell them. An angel appeared to Joseph and told him to take the mother and child to Egypt where he would be safe."

As she told the story, she continued pouring some of the cooled water from the basin and adding more and more hot water, until steam came up from the pan in which the child had her foot. The gradual increase in temperature caused no increase in pain and was little noticed.

"The evil king died and El Roi, 'God who sees,' sent word to them by another angel—"

Little Helena gave a startled gasp and a soft groan. The water in the basin reddened as the boil burst and emptied.

Hadassah stroked the child's calf. "Good girl. Keep your foot in the water. Let the boil drain," she said and thanked God for his mercy. "Doesn't that feel better?" Leaning heavily on her walking stick, she rose and made a poultice of herbs such as the ones Alexander prepared for patients with festering wounds. When she finished, she glanced back at them. "Your mother is going to put you on the table, and I'll bandage your foot," she told Helena, and Ephicharis rose and did as she instructed.

Hadassah gently rinsed Helena's foot and then dried it, making sure all the vicious blood-tinged, yellow-white fluid had drained. She placed the poultice gently and wrapped the foot tightly with clean linen. She washed her hands and dried them. Tapping Helena on her nose, she said playfully, "No running around for a day or two."

Sitting up, Helena giggled. Her eyes flickered and a serious expression spread across her small elfin face. "What happened to the little boy?"

Hadassah folded the extra linen. "He grew up and proclaimed his kingdom, and the government rested on his shoulders; and his name was called Wonderful Counselor, Mighty God, Eternal Father, Prince of Peace." She put the linen back on the shelf.

"There now, Helena. The little boy escaped all harm," Ephicharis said.

"No," Hadassah said, shaking her head. "The child grew and became strong. He increased in wisdom and stature and in favor with God and men. But men betrayed him. They told lies about him and turned him over to be crucified."

Helena's face fell and Ephicharis looked dismayed, clearly wishing Hadassah had left this part of the story untold.

Hadassah tipped Helena's chin. "You see, even his followers didn't understand who Jesus really was. They thought he was just a man, Helena. His enemies thought if they killed him, his power would end. His body was placed in a borrowed tomb and sealed, and they had Roman guards watch over it. But three days later, Jesus arose from the grave."

Helena's face lit with a smile. "He *did?*"

"Oh yes, he did. And he's still alive today."

"Tell me more!"

Ephicharis laughed. "We have to leave, Helena. Others are waiting." Smiling, she handed Hadassah two quadrantes and then lifted her daughter Helena. "Thank you for tending her foot—and for the story."

"It wasn't just a story, Ephicharis. It's true. My father witnessed it."

Ephicharis stared at her in amazement. She held Helena closer and hesitated, as though she wanted to stay and talk more. But she had been right. There were others in need waiting outside. Hadassah put her hand on the woman's arm. "Come back any morning, and I'll tell you all the things Jesus did."

"Oh, please, Mama," Helena said. Ephicharis nodded. She drew back the curtain and started when she saw Alexander sitting on a stool right outside. She gasped an embarrassed apology and stepped past him. Helena turned her head away and clung more tightly to her mother. Bowing slightly, Ephicharis quickly left the booth. Alexander watched her hurry away. He had seen the fear in her eyes—and in the child's eyes—when she looked at him. Yet, they both trusted Hadassah completely.

"Where are the others?" Hadassah said.

"I told them to come back tomorrow."

"Are you angry with me?"

"No. I'm the one who told you to see what you could do with them. I just didn't expect . . ." He gave a rueful laugh and shook his head. He rose and looked down at her. "I'll have to keep a closer eye on you or you'll steal my other patients out from under my nose." He gave her veil a light, good-natured tug.

Entering the booth, he closed the curtain and took the money box from its hiding place. "By the way, why did Boethus leave? Did you heal him while he was waiting?"

Hadassah decided to answer his teasing question seriously. "I think his physical complaints were caused by fear."

Alexander glanced at her, interested. "Fear? How so?"

"Worry, my lord. He has no work and a family to feed and shelter. He said his stomach troubles began a few weeks ago. That's when he said he last worked at the docks. And his headache started a few days ago, about the same time his landlord said if he had no money for rent, the family would be put out on the street."

"A sizeable problem, and not uncommon. Did you solve it?"

"No, my lord."

"So he was still suffering from his ailments when he left?" He sighed. "He probably got tired of waiting." He took some coins from the box and slammed the lid. "Not that I blame him," he added, shoving it back into its cubbyhole. "If only I could work faster, I'd be able to treat more patients. . . ."

"He said his headache was gone."

Alexander glanced back at her in surprise. Straightening, he frowned, uneasy. It wasn't the first time he had felt this way in her presence. He had been almost too afraid to touch her after her festered wounds had cleared without any logical explanation. Surely her god had intervened, and a god with such power should not be taken lightly. "Did you invoke the name of your Jesus?"

"Invoke?" she said and straightened slightly. "If you're asking did I utter an incantation, the answer is *no.*"

"Then how did you entreat your god to do your will?"

"I didn't! It's the Lord's will that prevails in all."

"You did *something.* What was it?"

"I *listened* to Boethus."

"And that was all?"

"I prayed and then told Boethus about Jesus. Then God worked upon Severina's heart, and she gave me the two quadrantes for him."

Alexander shook his head, completely baffled by her explanation. "That makes no logical sense whatsoever, Hadassah. In the first place, Severina gave you the money because you were kind to her. In the second, she didn't know anything whatsoever about Boethus' problems."

"*God* knew."

Alexander stood perplexed. "You talk too freely about your god and his power, Hadassah. I would think after all you suffered, you, of all people, would know the world is like the wicked king in your story. You don't know any of the people who come to this booth and yet you tell them about Jesus without compunction."

She realized he had been sitting close enough to the curtain to hear every word she said to Ephicharis and Helena. "Whatever it may appear, the world belongs to the Lord, Alexander. What have I to fear?"

"Death."

She shook her head. "Jesus has given me eternal life in him. Let them take my life here, but God holds me in the palm of his hand and no one can take me from him." She spread her hands. "Don't you see, Alexander? Boethus didn't need caution on my part. Nor did Severina, or Epicharis and Helena. They all need to know God loves them just as he loves me. And you."

Alexander rolled the coins in his hand. Sometimes he was afraid of her convictions. She had already proven how deep her faith ran, deep enough to give up her life. He wondered if it would someday take her from him. . . .

He quickly pushed that thought away, not stopping to analyze the sharp stab of dread that shot through him. Losing her was not something he was willing to contemplate. . . .

He was even more afraid of the power he sensed in her. Was it hers alone or was it a gift from her god that could be revoked at any time? Whatever the answer, sometimes she would say things that raised gooseflesh on him.

"I need to think," he muttered and stepped past her.

Moving along with the current of people heading away from the baths, Alexander debated what he knew about medicine with what Hadassah had said about anxiety causing illness. The more he thought about it, the more curious he became to see if what Hadassah suggested might be proven through proper record keeping. He purchased bread and wine and headed back, eager to talk with her.

Alexander took the partitions and closed off the booth for the night. He took his bedroll from beneath the worktable and sat on it. Tearing off a portion of bread, he handed it to Hadassah as she sat on her bedroll opposite him. Taking down the goatskin, he poured wine for each of them.

"I want to hear more about your theories," he said as they ate. "First, the boil. How did you know what to do?"

"My mother treated a boil for a neighbor. I tried her method. By the grace of God, it worked."

"*By the grace of God.*" He decided to remember those words. Perhaps they were more important than she realized. Perhaps in them was some of her power.

"I've seen you heal several people who've come to the booth."

"I've never healed anyone."

"Indeed you have. Boethus for one. You healed him. The man came with all manner of symptoms and went away cured. I obviously had nothing to do with it. I never even spoke with the man."

Hadassah was disturbed. "All I offered Boethus was hope."

"Hope," Alexander said and tore off a small piece of bread and dipped it in his wine. "I don't see that it'd make much difference, but go ahead. Explain." He popped the bread into his mouth.

Lord, Lord, Hadassah prayed, *he is so like Claudius, and Claudius never had the ears to hear.* Holding the wooden cup between her hands, she prayed Alexander would not only listen, but comprehend.

"God created mankind to live in a love relationship with him and to reflect his character. People weren't created to live independent from God."

"Go on," he said, waving his hand, impatient to hear.

She told of Adam and Eve in the Garden and how God had given them free will, and how they had sinned by believing Satan over God. She told him how they had been cast out of the Garden. She told about Moses and the Law and how every day, all day long, offerings were burned to cover sin. Yet, all those sacrifices could never wash it completely away. Only God had been able to accomplish that by sending his only begotten Son to die as the final atoning sacrifice for all mankind. Through Jesus, the walls were torn down and man could once again be with God by the indwelling of the Holy Spirit.

"'For God . . . gave His only begotten Son, that whoever believes in Him should not perish but have everlasting life,'" she quoted. "Yet, for all this, most people still live in a state of separation."

"And it's this state of separation that causes disease?" Alexander said, intrigued.

She shook her head. "You see things only in the physical, Alexander. Disease can come when man refuses to live within God's plan. Severina, for example. The Lord warned against the practice of prostitution. He warned against promiscuity. He warned against many things, and those who practice them bear the consequences of their sin. Perhaps many diseases are just that, consequences of disobedience."

"And so if Severina were to obey the laws of your god, she would be well again. Is that it?"

Hadassah closed her eyes behind her veil. *Lord, why did you let me live when I always fail in everything you give me? Why can't I find the words to make him understand?*

"Hadassah?"

Her eyes burned with tears of frustration. She spoke very slowly, as to a small child. "The Law was given that man might recognize his sinfulness and turn away from wickedness to the Lord. You see mankind as physical and seek solutions in that realm, but man is also a spiritual being, designed in the image of God. How will you ever learn who and what you are without learning who God is?" Her voice broke softly, and she saw his frown.

She bit her lip before going on. "Our relationship with God affects our body, yes. But it affects our emotions and our mind, as well. It affects our very spirit." Her hands tightened on the wooden cup as she lowered her head. "I believe true healing can only happen when a person is restored to God himself."

Alexander remained silent, thoughtful. He tore off another piece of bread and dipped it in his wine, giving himself extra time to think over what she had just said. His heart began to beat rapidly as it always did when an idea came to him. He ate his bread quickly and then drained his cup, setting it aside. Standing up, he dusted the bread crumbs from his hands and cleared a space on his worktable. Mixing soot with water, he prepared ink with which to write. Selecting a clear scroll, he sat and opened it, setting weights to hold it flat.

"Tell me a few of these laws," he commanded, writing down "By the grace of god" as his first notation.

Did he hear nothing, Lord? Nothing at all? "Salvation is not in the Law."

"I'm not talking about salvation. I'm talking about treating patients."

"God! Why did you leave me here? Why didn't you take me home?" It was a cry of pure anguish and frustration, and the hair on the back of Alexander's neck stood on end. She was crying, clutching her head in her hands, and it was his fault. What would her god do to him now?

He left his stool and knelt before her. "Don't call down the wrath of your god on me before you've heard what I have to say." He took her hands and touched his forehead to them.

She snatched her hands away and pushed him back. "Get off your knees to me! Am I God that you should bow down to me?"

Astonished, he drew back. "Your god has set you apart. He hears you," he said, rising and sitting on his stool again. "As you said to me once, I didn't save your life. Nor can I explain how it happened. Your wounds were putrefying, Hadassah. By all the laws of nature and science that I know, you *should* be dead. Yet, here you are."

"Scarred and crippled . . ."

"Otherwise healthy. Why would your god save you and not others?"

"I don't know," she said bleakly. She shook her head. "I don't know why he saved my life at all." She had thought she knew God's purpose for her: To die in the arena. But it seemed God had another mission.

"Perhaps he saved you so that you might instruct me in his ways."

She raised her head and looked at him through her veils. "And how do I do that when you have no ears to hear a word I say?"

"I hear."

"Then hear this. What does the body matter if the soul is dead?"

"And how do you restore a soul if the body is moldering in disease? How does one repent without understanding what sin he has committed?" His mind was reeling with thoughts more complex than he could fathom at once.

Hadassah frowned, remembering her father telling of Josiah, king of Judah, whose servant had found the book of the Law and read it to him. Upon hearing it, Josiah tore his clothing, recognizing his own sin and the sin of his people against God. Repentance had come through knowledge. But she had no written copy of the Torah. She had no copies of the Memoirs of the Apostles. All she had was her memory.

"From now on you will no longer assist me, Hadassah," Alexander said, setting his quill aside. "We'll work together."

She was alarmed. "I have no training as a physician."

"Not in the way I have, perhaps, but you have more training than you realize. I'm versed in the physical nature of man, and your god has given you insights into the spiritual realm. It's logical that we must work together in order to treat patients whose complaints are more complicated than a cut that needs immediate tending."

Hadassah was speechless.

"Do you agree?"

She sensed something deeper at work than she or Alexander understood. Was this offer of God or the evil one? "I don't know," she stammered. "I need to pray. . . ."

"Good," Alexander said, pleased. "That's exactly what I want you to do. Inquire of your god and then tell me—"

"No!" she said hastily as his words set off alarm within her. "You speak as though I were a medium like those in the booths near the Artemision."

"Then I'll make an offering to your god."

"The only offering God will accept is *you.*"

Alexander sat back slightly and didn't say anything for a long moment. He smiled wryly. "I'm afraid I'm not that self-sacrificing, Hadassah. I don't like lions."

She laughed softly. "I'm not particularly fond of them myself."

He laughed with her and then grew serious again. "Yet, you were willing to lay down your life for what you believe."

"I didn't begin my walk with God in an arena."

His mouth tipped. "Where did you start?"

Tears came as warmth filled her. She liked this man. His desire to know and understand stemmed from his deep desire to help people. Perhaps it *was* God's purpose that she instruct him in what she knew about the Lord. Perhaps there were answers in the laws that Moses had been given by God for the Israelites. Jesus had said he had come to fulfill the Law, not abolish it.

She held out her hand. Alexander took it, his own large and strong, closing firmly around hers. She eased from her bedroll, wincing as she knelt on the earthen floor. Taking his other hand, she drew him down so that they were both on their knees, hands clasped together, facing one another.

"We start here."

Imitating her, Alexander bowed his head, concentrating on her every word.

He would write them down later.

6

Eudemas entered the triclinium and handed Julia a small scroll bearing a wax seal. Julia's face paled noticeably as she took it and waved her away. Primus, sitting opposite her, smiled sardonically as she tucked it quickly into the folds of her Chinese silk tunic.

"Hiding something, Julia?"

"I'm not hiding anything."

"Then why aren't you going to read your letter now?"

"Because I don't feel like it," she said tersely, not looking at him. She drew the crimson silk shawl around her and fingered the gold and adamas bracelet on her wrist. Primus noted how she grew more agitated at his perusal. His mouth curved as he continued to study her. She remained tense and silent, pretending not to notice. The vivid colors she chose to wear only intensified her pallor and brought out the deepening circles of sleeplessness beneath her eyes. Julia, who once glowed with lust and life, was now positively sallow with ill health. Trembling, she poured herself more wine and then stared into her gold goblet with dull eyes.

After a moment she glared at him. "Why are you staring at me?"

"Was I?" Primus' smile grew taunting. "I was noticing how lovely you look this evening."

She turned her head away, well aware his flattery was empty and vicious. "How kind of you to notice," she said bitterly.

He took a delicacy from the tray. "Poor Julia. You're still trying to plead your case to Marcus, aren't you?"

She lifted her chin haughtily, her dark eyes flashing. "I needn't plead my case to anyone. I don't have to apologize for what I did."

"Then why do you persist?" He ate the morsel.

"I don't!"

"Ha. You've been begging and pleading for Marcus' forgiveness ever since he left you at the arena. He returns every message you send." He waved airily. "Just like that one, seal unbroken."

She glared at him. "And how would you know what messages I send and to whom?"

Laughing softly, he selected a stuffed cow's teat from the tray of rich delicacies. "I've always found it immensely entertaining to observe those around me." He shifted his bulk to make himself more comfortable. "You, in particular, my sweet."

"Did Eudemas tell you I wrote to him?"

"She didn't have to. I could read the signs. You were drunk last night and maudlin. When you're maudlin, you retire to your chamber early and write to your brother. It's all too predictable, Julia. Predictable to the point of boring. You know very well he'll never forgive you, yet you persist. I find his unrelenting hatred refreshing, but frankly, my dear, your relentless pursuit of his forgiveness has become pathetic."

She didn't speak for a moment, attempting to bring her heightened emotions under control. "He doesn't hate me. He only thinks he does."

"Oh, he hates you, Julia. He hates you absolutely. Never doubt that for a minute."

His words lacerated her, and her eyes burned with the tears she held back. "I despise you," she said with the dark wealth of her emotions.

He recognized her poor attempt at retaliation and mocked her openly. "Ah, I know, my dear, but then I'm all you have left, aren't I? Calabah has left you and sailed away to Rome with pretty little Sapphira. Your friends avoid you because of your illness. You've received only one invitation in the last week, and I regret to inform you that Cretaneus was decidedly relieved when you sent your regrets. So, my dear, who but me do you have to keep you company?" He clicked his tongue. "Poor Julia. Everyone leaves you. Such a pity . . ."

"I can always count on your understanding, can't I, Primus? By the way, did any of your hirelings ever find trace of your beloved Prometheus?" She tilted her head to one side, laying a fingertip against her chin, parodying a thoughtful muse. "Now why do you suppose it's become more and more difficult for you to find lovers?" She spread her hands, her face opening with pretended realization. "Could it be your growing corpulence?"

Primus' face darkened. "Your troubles and mine could've been avoided had you listened to Calabah and had that little Jewess of yours killed *earlier.*"

She grasped her wine goblet and hurled it at him, just missing his head. Breathing heavily with her frustration, she called him a foul name and rose from her couch, glaring across at him. "My troubles would've been avoided had I never made an alliance with *you!*"

He brushed the drops of wine from his face, his eyes glittering. "Blame me if you must, but everyone knows *you* made the choice." He laughed darkly. "And now you must live with it. Or die . . ."

"You're a despicable worm!"

"And you're a stupid sow!"

"I should've listened to Marcus," she said, struggling against tears. "He knew what you were."

Primus smiled smugly, seeing he had almost succeeded in reducing her to hysteria. "He did, didn't he? But then, so did you, Julia. You walked in with your eyes wide open, thinking everything would be exactly as you wanted it. And for a while, it was, wasn't it, my sweet? Exactly as *you* wanted. Money, position, Atretes, Calabah . . . and me."

She wanted to destroy him, to wipe that self-satisfied smirk from his face forever. But he was all she had left, and she knew it. Her eyes narrowed. "Perhaps I've changed my mind about what I want."

"Oh, dear. Another empty threat. I'm trembling."

"Someday you may find my threats not so empty."

Primus knew how sick she was—so sick he doubted she would survive. His eyes narrowed coldly as he embraced his secret wrath and felt warmed by it. "By the time you change your mind, you'll have gone through all your money and it'll make no difference, will it?" he said with deceiving calm. "Have you ever wondered why I remain with you? Do you think it's because I *love* you?" He saw the tiny flicker of fear in her eyes and was satisfied. He knew Julia's greatest fear was being alone, and alone she would be when the time was right. He would have his vengeance for every insult, every slight he had suffered from her. He would have his vengeance for Prometheus' defection.

But for now, he pretended remorse at causing her to feel vulnerable. He raised his hand. "I'm sorry I said that," he said with feigned regret, content he had accomplished part of his purpose. "Why do we argue so much, beloved? It comes to nothing. You must grow up, Julia. Accept what you are. You've drunk from the same well I have, and you've done it so long you can't go back. I'm the only friend you have left."

81

"If you'll excuse me," she said with acid sweetness and turned away.

"As you please, my dear. I suppose I'll save my news for another time," he said smoothly, laughing silently. "Something I overheard at Fulvius' feast last night. About Marcus."

She turned to face him, her eyes narrowing. "What is it this time?"

"Never mind," he said with a wave of his hand. Let her sweat. Let her stomach twist and turn. Let her *hope*. "It can wait until another time when you're more amenable."

"What foul gossip did you hear this time, Primus?"

"Gossip? Concerning your brother? He's become rather dull from all accounts. No women. No *men*." He laughed in derision, aware he had her full attention. "Poor Marcus. He doesn't know how to enjoy life anymore, does he? He works, goes to the baths, goes home. Day after day after day. His greatest passion is hating you, and he does that so very well, doesn't he? Such resolve. Such dedication."

Julia's face was stony, giving no hint to the anguish his words caused. She knew all too well Primus enjoyed his petty cruelties. The only way to defend herself was to pretend she felt nothing at all, but her stomach tightened with the effort, and her heart pounded.

She hated him so much a metallic taste filled her mouth. It would give her the greatest pleasure to plunge a knife into his fat belly and hear him scream. She would kill him if it didn't mean her own death in the process. But then, maybe it would be worth it. After all, what did she have to live for now anyway? Why had she ever been born in the first place?

Her mouth twisted bitterly. "You heard nothing, did you? Nothing of any import. You hate Marcus because he's twice the man you are or ever could be. He's admired. He's *respected*. And what of you? You're nothing but an insect that thrives on lies and slander about those better than you."

His eyes glittered. "Have I not kept all *your* secrets, Julia, beloved?" he said softly. "How your first husband died because of you, how you murdered your second. And what of your children? Do they yet cry out upon the rocks? How many others did you have torn from your womb before you cast away Atretes' seed?" He saw her face go even paler and smiled. "I have kept your secrets locked away, haven't I?" He put his fingers to his lips and puckered, blowing her a kiss.

She was shaking. How had he known these things? No one knew she had poisoned her second husband . . . no one, of course, but Calabah. Calabah, her trusted lover and friend, must have told him.

Primus shifted his bulk on the cushions, moving closer to the laden food tray. "I did hear something of great import that has given me cause to think. The question is, should I share this new-found information with you, oh most ungrateful of women."

She controlled her fury. He was baiting her again, but she dared not leave, afraid he might really know something. She wanted to order him out of her villa, but knew in doing so she would open herself to his cunningly malicious tongue. He would expose her deeds to everyone. Worse, he would expose the foulness of the disease that feasted on her secret flesh.

"Very well, Primus." *Spew your venom, you miserable snake. Someday, someone will cut the head from the body.* "I'm listening. What have you to tell me about my brother?"

"Marcus is leaving Ephesus. That should cheer you, my dear." His mouth curved as what little color she had left drained from her face. "Think of the advantages. You'll no longer have to find plausible excuses when others ask you why your highly esteemed, much sought-after brother refuses invitations to any gathering where you might be present."

She tilted her chin, pretending his words had no effect on her. "So he's returning to Rome. So what?"

"Rumor has it he's sailing on one of his own ships. But not to Rome."

Clenching her hands, she watched Primus select another cow's teat and devour it with disgusting relish. He sucked the grease from his fingers and reached for another while she waited.

Primus felt her impatience radiating across the room. He relished it almost as much as the feast he was eating. He possessed her full attention, and that's what he wanted. He could almost hear the heavy beat of her heart tolling in dread. He fingered the rich foods, caressing them, selecting another tidbit.

Sickened at having to watch him eat, Julia strove for control of her roiling emotions. "Sailing *where*, Primus?" she said with measured calm. "Rhodes? Corinth?"

He filled his mouth with another teat and dabbed his greasy fingers on a fold of his toga. "To Judea," he said around the food.

"Judea!"

He swallowed and licked his full lips. "Yes, to Judea, homeland of his little Jewess. And it would seem he plans on staying for a long, long time."

"How would you know how long he's planning to stay?"

"Deduction. I learned Marcus sold his interests in Rome, except for your family's villa, which he has given over to your mother's disposal. Do you know what she did? She sent word to have the property rented and the proceeds used as an *alimenta* for the poor of the district. Can you imagine all that money going to feed the ragged unwashed? What a waste! It would've been put to better purpose replenishing our dwindling coffers."

"*My* coffers."

"As you wish. *Your* coffers," he said with a shrug and dipped a strip of ostrich tongue in spiced honey sauce. Little did his Julia realize, he thought smugly, that most of her money had already been filtered into his own hands and secreted away for the future. And it was all done without her being aware. Her illness had helped him in the process; she was so obsessed with her various ailments that she paid little attention to her financial situation. She trusted her agents to protect her.

Amazing the power a bribe can give one, he thought, smiling to himself. *And a little knowledge that could prove embarrassing should it come to light.*

But her agent had sent word to him this morning that she was demanding a full accounting be done. Primus had known he had better give Julia something else to occupy her mind besides the condition of her estate.

To that end, he went on, weaving his web. "Giving away all that money," he said again and shook his head. "It's unimaginable. Unless . . . Do you suppose your mother was corrupted by that little Jewess of yours and has become a *Christian?*"

Julia winced inwardly at the suggestion. Her mother, a Christian? If that were so, she knew another door was closed against her.

Primus saw her expression alter subtly and knew he was cutting into her little by little, deeper and deeper. He wanted to lay her wide open and let carrion birds feast upon her flesh. "As for your brother's interests here in Ephesus, the ships and warehouses, he has put them under the management of trusted servants of your father. He has put everything he owns into the hands of two stewards, Orestes and Silas."

He chewed the expensive delicacy and, with a grimace, spit it onto a platter. He poured himself Falernian wine, the finest from Capua, and swished some around in his mouth to wash away the taste. He swallowed and continued. "It all suggests your brother has no plans to return any time soon, if ever. I suppose he's making a pilgrimage to the memory of his beloved, departed Hadassah." Lifting the gold goblet in a toast, he taunted Julia with a smile. "May his departure bring you a respite from your guilt, my dear," he said, savoring her torment. He relished the pain he saw in her eyes. His news had hurt her deeply. She could no longer hide it.

Julia left the triclinium. When she reached her bedchamber, she sank down on the divan and took the small scroll from the folds of her shimmering tunic. Trembling all over, she fingered the seal. It was firmly in place. Her eyes blurred with tears. Marcus probably hadn't even touched the epistle.

Judea! Why would he go so far and to such a terrible place unless Primus was right and it had something to do with that wretched slave girl?

She drew in a ragged breath. Why couldn't he forget Hadassah? Why couldn't he forget what had happened? She bit her lip, wanting to cry out in anguish. But to whom? No one cared what happened to her.

Had she known what would happen, she wouldn't have done what she did. Why couldn't Marcus forgive her? She was his sister, his own flesh and blood. Didn't he know how much she had always loved him, how much she loved him still? She had only wanted things to be the way they were when they were children, when it had seemed as though they were together against the world. Had he forgotten how close they were, how they could talk to one another about everything? She had never trusted anyone the way she had trusted him.

Except for Hadassah, a small voice whispered inside her.

The unwelcome thought lanced her with pain. She shut her eyes, willing herself to obliterate the memories that swept over her . . . memories of what it had been like to be loved, really loved. "No. *No.* I won't think of her. I won't!"

Silence closed around her, bringing darkness with it.

She clutched the small scroll in her hand. "Oh, Marcus," she whispered brokenly. "You promised me once you would love me no matter what I did." The lonely silence of her bedchamber became a crushing weight. "You promised, Marcus." Filled with hopelessness, she crumpled the final plea to her brother and threw it into her brazier. The parchment caught flame and was quickly reduced to ashes.

Julia sat watching her last hope for her brother's forgiveness disintegrating.

"You promised. . . ." Covering her face, she rocked back and forth, weeping.

THE CLAY

7

"It is a great honor for us to have you aboard, my lord," Satyros said, studying the younger man as he gestured for him to take the honored place on the couch. A simple but deliciously prepared meal was placed on the small table between them.

"The honor is mine, Satyros," Marcus said, nodding for the captain's servant to pour his wine. "You're considered a legend upon the seas. Few survive a shipwreck." He tore off a piece of bread and replaced the loaf on the silver tray.

Satyros nodded solemnly. "You speak of the shipwreck on Malta. I was not a captain then, but a mere sailor on that ship. And it was not only I who survived. There were 276 people aboard that ship. None was lost."

Someone knocked at the captain's door. The servant answered and spoke briefly with one of the sailors. He relayed the message concerning the winds to Satyros, who gave instructions to be passed on to the helmsmen. The *Minerva* was making good headway.

Satyros returned his attention to Marcus and apologized for the interruption. They discussed the cargo; the hold was filled with marble and timber from the Greek isles, materials destined for use in expanding Caesarea. A profusion of other crates was also packed below, some purchased by Marcus in speculation, others fulfilling orders dispatched by various merchants in Judea. Loaded into every available space were hides from Britain, silver and gold from Spain, pottery from Gaul, furs from Germany, fine wines from Sicily, and drugs from Greece. Most of the goods would be unloaded in Caesarea.

"We will only remain in Caesarea long enough to unload the cargo and then take on passengers destined for Alexandria," Satyros said.

Marcus nodded. In Alexandria, the *corbita* would dock and his representatives would meet the ship. The *Minerva* would take on valuable items for the Roman market: tortoise shell and ivory from Ethiopia; oil and spices from eastern Africa; pearls, dyes, and citron from the West. Within a few months, the *Minerva* would sail back to Rome, her starting point for the trade route Decimus Andronicus Valerian had established over twenty years ago.

Satyros gave a rueful laugh. "Eliab Mosad will take his time haggling over the merchandise. It always takes a few weeks to get things sorted out in Egypt before we can set sail for Rome again."

"He will want you to take on slaves," Marcus said. "Don't. Nor sand. No matter the price. I've already been in contact with him and informed him I won't deal in those commodities any more."

"We'll need ballast, my lord."

"Egyptian grain will do for ballast."

"As you wish," Satyros said. He had heard the rumors about Marcus Valerian's change in thinking—rumors that were now confirmed. He studied the younger man surreptitiously. What had happened to change Marcus Valerian's well-known axiom of giving Rome what it wanted? Marcus had amassed a fortune by trading in sand and slaves. Now he wanted no part in either cargo. Perhaps he felt enough to have his father's scruples . . . but why now and not before? What had changed?

"I'll be leaving the ship in Caesarea," Marcus said.

Again, Satyros covered his surprise with an effort. He had expected Marcus to remain aboard until Alexandria or perhaps Rome. The elder Valerian had sometimes traveled the full trade route to meet with his representatives and gain firsthand information on how his operations were being conducted.

"You'll find Caesarea an interesting departure from Ephesus, my lord. Though it lacks the elements of grandeur, it has its arenas and beautiful women." Marcus was reputed to enjoy both to the fullest.

"I intend to remain in Caesarea only long enough to outfit myself for travel."

Satyros gray brows rose a fraction. "There is little in Judea to commend it to a Roman. What is it you want to see?"

"Jerusalem."

Satyros gave a soft exclamation. "Why on earth would you of all people choose the most depressing place in all the known world to visit?" Too late, he realized the rude intrusiveness of his thoughtless question. "From all reports I've heard, Jerusalem is nothing but a pile of rubble, my lord," he added hastily. "Antonia and Mariamne towers might still be standing for defensive purposes, but I doubt it. Titus' orders were to not leave one stone standing upon another."

"I am well aware of that, Satyros," Marcus said coolly.

Satyros frowned, realizing belatedly that Marcus would, of course, know all this for himself. As owner of the Valerian ships and trade routes, he would have to keep well informed as to the circumstances in all regions of the Empire. His level of success bespoke his astuteness in this regard. Yet Satyros could not curb his own curiosity at such a surprising announcement.

"Why are you interested in such a desolate place?"

Marcus decided to answer frankly. "It's not the place that interests me as much as the god that resided there." Over the rim of his goblet, he watched the man's face, waiting for the inevitable question to come forth. Why would a Roman be interested in the Jewish God? He was unsure what he would answer to that. He was not fully aware of all the reasons himself.

However, Satyros surprised him. "Perhaps therein lies the reason for the disaster that befell the city."

"What reason do you mean?"

"Their God cannot be contained in a building."

Satyros' words so closely reflected those Hadassah had once said that Marcus' interest sharpened. "What do you know of the Jewish god?"

"Only what I learned from a prisoner long ago, on the very ship you referred to earlier. But it would hardly interest you."

"It interests me greatly."

Satyros considered this for a moment. "The man was a Jew. An insurrectionist by all reports. Everywhere he went he caused a riot. When I met him, he was under the custody of an Augustan centurion named Julius and on his way to Rome to face Caesar for his crimes. I heard later he was beheaded. His name was Paul, and he was from Tarsus. Perhaps you've heard of him."

Marcus had, but only from those who reviled him and mocked his claims of an all-powerful, loving god.

"What did this Paul tell you?"

"He said God had sent his only begotten Son to live among men and be crucified for our sins so that we might be restored and live in the heavens with the Father-God. Through this Christ, as he called him, Paul said all men can be saved and have eternal life. Nobody listened to him until the Euraquilo hit us."

Marcus was aware of the feared winds that had sunk many ships.

"Paul had warned us beforehand that we'd suffer great loss and damage, not only to the ship and cargo but in human life," Satyros said.

"You said earlier that no one was killed."

"That's true, but I'm convinced it's because Paul prayed for us. I think his God gave him what he asked for—our lives." He poured himself some wine. "We were caught in the violent winds and being driven along. We managed to take shelter at Cauda long enough to hoist the ship and undergird it with ropes. Not that it did us any good. When we got underway again, the storm hit harder. We jettisoned the cargo. By the third day, we threw the ship's tackle overboard. We couldn't see any stars, so we had no way of navigating. We didn't know where we were. We were sailing blind. There was not a sailor or passenger aboard who was not terrified for his life. Except Paul."

Satyros leaned forward and tore off a piece of bread.

"It was during the worst of the storm that he stood among us and said only the ship would be lost. He had to shout to be heard above the storm, but he was absolutely calm. He said an angel of his God had been sent to assure him of what he was telling us. He told us not to be afraid. He said we would run aground on an island but that no one would be killed."

Smiling slightly, he shook his head, bemused. "It seemed his God wanted him to live in order to speak to Caesar, and in the process of saving him, his God decided to save the rest of us as well."

"It could've been coincidence."

"Perhaps, but I'm convinced it wasn't."

"Why?"

"You would have to have been there to understand, my lord. Never before then or since have I seen such a storm. Destruction and death were certain, yet Paul was absolutely calm. He had no fear of death. He told us to have no fear. He took bread, gave thanks to God, and ate. Can you imagine such a thing? He *ate* in the midst of that chaos." He shook his head, still amazed as he remembered. "I've never seen anything like his faith before, and few times since."

Satyros dipped the bread in his wine.

Marcus remembered Hadassah walking calmly across the sand of the arena, unaffected by the screaming mob or the roar of lions.

Satyros took up a slice of brined meat. "When you see faith like that, you have to believe there's something to it."

"Perhaps it was only his own delusions."

"Oh, it was more than that. Paul *knew.* God had revealed events to him. Paul said the ship would be destroyed. It was." He ate the soaked beef.

"Go on," Marcus said, his own appetite gone in his eagerness to hear more.

"The ship began to break up, and the soldiers were set to kill the prisoners rather than let them escape," Satyros went on. "Their own lives would've been forfeit if they did. Julius stopped them. As it happened, those who could swim jumped overboard, and the rest of us floated in on planks and whatever else was available on the ship. The island was Malta. Not one person perished. Not one, my lord. That is truly amazing."

"Perhaps," Marcus said. "But why credit this Jewish Christ with saving everyone? Why not give thanks to Neptune or some other exalted member of the pantheon?"

"Because we were all crying out to our gods for help. Brahma! Vishnu! Varuna! None of them answered. And then even more amazing things happened on Malta to confirm for me and everyone else that Paul was a servant of an all-powerful God."

He saw Marcus' acute interest and sought to explain.

"The natives received us kindly. They built a fire for us, but as soon as we settled before it, a viper came out and sank its fangs into Paul's hand. He shook the snake off into the fire. Everyone knew it was poisonous and that he would shortly die of the bite. The people were convinced he was a murderer and the snake had been sent as punishment from the gods."

"Obviously, he didn't die. I was in Rome when he was brought there under guard."

"No. He didn't die. He didn't even get sick. His hand didn't swell. Nothing. The natives waited all night. By morning, they were convinced he was a god and worshiped him as such. Paul told them he was not a god, but merely a servant of one he called Jesus, the Christ. He preached to them what he had told us."

Satyros took several dried figs from the tray. "Our host, Publius, was leader of the island. He entertained us for three days, and then his father became very ill. Paul cured the old man just by laying his hands on him. One minute Publius' father was ready for death, the next he was up and in perfect health. Word spread, and the sick came from all over the island."

"Did he cure them?"

"All of them that I saw. The people honored all of us for Paul's presence. They made arrangements for us to continue our journey and even supplied us with what was needed. Paul sailed on an Alexandrian ship that had Castor and Pollux for its figurehead. I put out on another ship. I never saw him again."

The question that had plagued Marcus for months now burned through his mind like a fever. He took up his goblet and frowned. "If this god was so powerful, why didn't he save Paul from execution?"

Satyros shook his head. "I don't know. I wondered that myself when I heard of his fate. But this I know: however hidden it may be, there was a purpose."

Marcus stared grimly into his wine. "It seems to me this Christ destroys everyone who believes in him." He drained his goblet and set it down. "I'd like to know why."

"I have no answer to that, my lord. But I will tell you this. After meeting Paul, I know that the world is not all it seems to be. The gods we Romans worship cannot compare to the God he served."

"It is Rome that rules the world, Satyros," Marcus said sardonically. "Not this Jesus of whom Paul spoke. You've only to look to what happened in Judea to know that."

"I wonder. Paul said Jesus overcame death and set the way for anyone who believes in him."

"I haven't seen a single Christian overcome death," Marcus said in a hard voice. "They all face death praising Jesus Christ. And they all die just like any other man or woman."

Satyros studied Marcus intently, sensing that some deep torment was driving him across the seas to a rebellious land. "If it's this God you seek, I would tread very carefully."

"Why?"

"He can destroy you."

Marcus' mouth tipped bitterly. "He already has," he said cryptically and rose. He thanked Satyros for his hospitality and left.

The days passed slowly, though the winds held well and the conditions of the sea were advantageous.

Marcus walked the deck by the hour, struggling with the depth of his emotions. Finally, he returned to his quarters, a small private chamber that was simply furnished. He stretched out on the narrow couch built into the wall and stared at the polished wood ceiling.

He slept fitfully. Hadassah came to him in his dreams every night. She cried out to him, and he struggled against the hands holding him back. Julia was there, too, and Primus. Calabah gloated as lions roared. He saw one racing toward Hadassah and fought desperately against his bonds—and then the beast leaped and took her down.

Night after night he awakened abruptly, shaking, his body streaming with sweat, his heart pounding. He sat up and held his head. Digging his fingers into his scalp, he swore and struggled against the grief that overwhelmed him.

Closing his eyes, he remembered Hadassah kneeling in the moonlight, her hands raised to her god. He remembered cupping her face in his hands and looking into her beautiful brown eyes, eyes so full of love and tranquility. Every part of him yearned for her, yearned with a hunger so deep that he groaned.

"What kind of a god are you to kill her?" he rasped, his eyes burning with tears. "Why did you let it happen?" The anger burned in him and he clenched his fists. "I want to know who you are," he whispered through gritted teeth. "I want to know. . . ."

He rose earlier than anyone else and dressed to go above deck. He needed the stinging cold sea air, but even standing at the bow, he felt Hadassah's presence beside him. She haunted him, but he was thankful. His memories of her were all he had left.

Passengers awakened and moved about as the sun rose. He crossed to the leeward side to be alone. Most of the passengers were Arabs and Syrians who had completed their business in Ephesus and were returning home. He could speak only rudiments of their language and did not want company. The corbita could hold up to 300 passengers, but only 157 were on this ship because Marcus had ordered that most of the space be used for cargo. He was thankful there were not more people aboard.

The winds were good and the ship held a steady course. Restless, Marcus walked the deck each day until he was exhausted. He supped with the captain and returned to his quarters.

A few days yet from Caesarea, he grew calmer. He rested his forearms on a stack of crates and stared ahead at the blue-green sea as it flashed with reflected sunlight. He knew he would soon begin his quest across the land of Judea.

The sailors called to one another as they worked the lines. The square sails stretched taut above him. The ship moved smoothly through the water. The *Minerva* had made good time thus far, but Marcus remained impatient, eager to be at his destination.

A dolphin leaped below him.

He hardly noted it at first, then it appeared again. It dove and then came up, keeping easy pace with the ship. It came straight up once and made a strange chattering noise before splashing back into the sea again. One of the crew manning the sails spotted it and cried out that the gods were with them. Passengers hastened to the leeward side and crowded him in order to watch. An Arab wearing a red burnoose with a black band pushed his way forward to get a better look.

The dolphin rose again and again, just below Marcus. Arcing gracefully, it repeatedly leaped and then slipped elegantly beneath the surface of the sea. The playful animal was joined by three others, and they leaped in unison, delighting the passengers, who began to call out greetings to them in several languages.

"It is a good omen!" someone said in excitement.

"Oh, servant of Neptune!" another cried out reverently. "We thank you for blessing our ship!"

"An offering! An offering! Give them an offering!"

Several passengers tossed coins into the sea. One struck the first dolphin and startled it. It veered off and disappeared, the others following. The excitement died with the creatures' departure, and the passengers milled around and moved away from Marcus, finding places and ways to pass the time. Several groups gathered to gamble with small dice, while others dozed in the sun.

Satyros gave the helm to his first mate and came down to stand beside Marcus. "A good sign for your journey, my lord."

"Would a Jewish Messiah send word by way of a pagan symbol?" Marcus said dryly, his arms still resting on the side as he stared out at the flashes of sunlight on the blue-green water.

"According to Paul, all things were created by this god you seek. Doesn't it stand to reason, he can send word to you by any means he chooses?"

"And so an almighty god is sending a fish."

Satyros gazed at him steadily. "The dolphin is a symbol we all recognize, my lord, even those who have no faith in any religion. Perhaps God sent the dolphin to give you hope."

"I don't need hope. I need answers." His face hardened. Defiant and angry, he stretched his hand out over the water. "Hear me, messenger of the Almighty! I accept no emissary!"

Satyros felt the fear Marcus should have. "Do you challenge God without thought to the consequences?"

Marcus gripped the side. "I *want* the consequences. At least then I'd know if this god truly exists, that he isn't an illusion someone thought up to foist on gullible mankind."

Satyros drew back from him. "He exists."

"Why do you think that? Because you lived through a storm and shipwreck? Because a snake bit a man and he didn't die of it? The Paul you speak of did die, Satyros. On his knees, his head on a block. Tell me, what use is a god who won't protect his own?"

"I don't have the answers you seek."

"No one does. No man, at least. Only God, if he speaks." He raised his head and called out loudly. "I want to know!"

"You mock him. What if he hears?"

"Let him hear," he said and then repeated it, *"Do you hear?"* He called the words out over the sea like a challenge, unaware and uncaring of the curious glances he drew. "I want him to hear, Satyros. I defy him to hear."

Satyros wished now he had kept his distance from Marcus Valerian. "You risk your life."

Marcus gave a brittle laugh. "My life, such as it is, means nothing to me. If God chooses to take it, let him. It is empty and meaningless anyway." He leaned on the side again, body rigid, jaw hard. "But let him face me when he does so."

8

Alexander entered the courtyard of the Asklepion. Two men with
an empty litter hurried past him to the gate and disappeared
beyond the walls. Frowning, he leaned forward, assessing the dismal scene before him.

His father had brought him to the Asklepion in Athens when
he was a boy, hoping their offerings and a daylong vigil would
save Alexander's younger brother and older sister from fever. It
had been dark when he and his father had come, as it was now,
with only the flickering torches to cast eerie shadows over the glistening marble of the grand court. The scene he had faced then
upon entering the gates had gripped his stomach with an unspeakable anguish. . . .

And now, as he looked at the tragic sight before him, he was
filled again with that same anguish—and with an overwhelming
sense of helplessness.

More than twenty men and women lay upon the temple steps,
ill, suffering, dying. Discarded humanity. Most had been abandoned in the dead of night by uncaring owners, left without even
a blanket to cover them. Alexander fought his emotions as he let
his eyes scan the forms scattered about him, then he turned to
Hadassah.

Her stunned expression stopped him cold, and his heart sank.
He had been afraid of her reaction to what she would see and
had tried the night before to prepare her.

"My father was a slave," he had told her, watching her face in
the flickering light of the small oil lamp on the table between
them. He could see the surprise in her eyes at what he had said,
for Alexander had seldom spoken of himself or his past. He only
did so now to help her understand what he planned to do.

"He was fortunate enough to have belonged to a kind master,
and because he had business acumen, Father was put in charge of
his master's finances. He was given an allotment of money for his
own personal investment and managed to earn enough to buy his
freedom. As a means of retaining his services, Caius Ancus
Herophilus, my grandfather, offered his daughter, Drusilla, in mar-

riage. My father had been in love with my mother for a long time and gladly accepted. When my grandfather died, my father inherited his estate through my mother. They had seven children. . . ."

When he had paused, Hadassah's eyes had searched his face. He had known she had seen that he was not finished. So she had simply remained silent, waiting.

Alexander had looked at her, his eyes reflecting an age-old pain. "My father and mother had property, money, and prestige. All the advantages one could desire. And yet, with all of that, I am the only child who survived. My brothers and sisters, one by one, died while still small. And all the wealth, all the prayers and offerings at the temples, all the tears on my mother's face, couldn't change that."

"Is that why you decided to become a physician?"

"Partly. I saw my brothers and sisters die of various childhood illnesses and diseases, and I saw the cost to my parents. But it was more than that. It was also what I felt each time my father took me to the Asklepion to beseech the god's favor. I was helpless in the face of the misery I saw there. There was no evidence of power. Just suffering. And I wanted to do something about it. I've learned since that you can't change very much in this world. I do what I can and try to be content with that." He had reached out to take her hand then. "Listen to me, Hadassah. You'll see things tomorrow morning that will turn you inside out. But we can only bring one patient back with us."

She had nodded. "Yes, my lord."

"I warn you not to have expectations. Whomever we choose has little chance of survival. The slaves you see at the Asklepion are useless to their masters and have been left to die. I've failed more times than I've succeeded in treating them."

"How many times have you done this?"

"A dozen times, maybe more. The first time I tried to treat a slave left at a temple in Rome. I had more money then, and private quarters. But the man died within a week. Still, at least he died in comfort. I lost four more after that and almost gave up."

Her eyes had shone with compassion. "Why didn't you?"

"Because part of my training involved a proper worship of the healing deities. I couldn't walk by those people and pretend they weren't there." He had sighed, shaking his head. "I can't say that my reasons were entirely altruistic. When a student of medicine loses a patient left on the steps of the Asklepion, no one cares.

Lose a freeman of station and you can kiss your future good-bye." A grimace had crossed his face. "My motives are both good and bad, Hadassah. I want to help, but I also want to learn."

"Have any of these patients lived?"

"Three. One in Rome, a Greek every bit as stubborn as my father. And two in Alexandria."

"Then what you did was worthwhile," she had said with a quiet certainty.

Now, though, watching the look on her face, Alexander wondered if he was right to keep doing this . . . and if he should ever have brought Hadassah with him. Despite all he'd said the night before, he could see Hadassah was filled with horror at the sight of so many abandoned slaves on the temple steps.

"*Oh,*" she whispered, coming to a stop beside him, that single word piercing his heart with its wealth of compassion and sorrow.

Alexander looked away, his throat suddenly tight with emotion. After a moment, he spoke, his voice gruff. "Come on. We haven't much time."

He passed by an emaciated gray-haired man and bent down beside one younger. Hadassah followed him toward the marble steps of the Asklepion, but paused beside the man he had passed by. She went down on one knee and felt the old man's fevered brow. He didn't open his eyes.

"Leave him," Alexander called to her as he strode across the courtyard to the steps of the Asklepion.

Hadassah glanced up and watched him quickly pass by two other abandoned slaves. Their masters had not even taken the time to place them on the uppermost temple steps where there was some shelter. This poor old man had been discarded barely a few feet inside the *propylon*. Others nearby lay unconscious, devastated by unknown illnesses.

"We'll find one that might be cured and do what we can," Alexander had told her several times last night, adding a warning. "You'll see many who have fatal illnesses or are simply old and worn out. You must harden yourself to pass by them, Hadassah. We can only bring one back with us, a man with a chance of survival."

She looked toward the glistening marble steps of the pagan temple and counted more than twenty men and women lying on them. Discarded humanity. She looked down at the old man again. He had been abandoned here in the night without even a blanket to cover him.

"Leave him," Alexander called to her sternly.

"We might—"

"Look at the color of his skin, Hadassah. He won't make it through the day. Besides, he's old. One younger has a better chance."

Hadassah saw the old slave's eyes flicker and felt a grief past reasoning. "There is one who loves you," she said to him. "His name is Jesus." The old man was too weak and sick to speak, but as he looked up at her with fever-glazed eyes, she told him the Good News of Christ. She didn't know if he understood or received consolation, but she took his thin hand between hers. "Believe and be saved," she said. "Be comforted."

Alexander looked around grimly at the selection of abandoned slaves before him. Most were too close to death to warrant attention. Glancing back, he saw Hadassah still bent over the dying old man. "Hadassah!" he shouted, commanding this time. "Come away from him." He motioned for her to follow. "See about the others."

She pressed the old man's limp hand against her veiled cheek and prayed, "Father, have mercy on this man." She removed her shawl and laid it over him, her eyes blurred with tears as he gave her a weak smile. "Please, Yeshua, take him up that he be with you in paradise." She rose painfully, helpless to do anything more for him.

Leaning heavily on her walking stick, she crossed the courtyard and went up the steps after Alexander. She started to bend down to another man, but the young physician called out to her not to waste her time with that one either. "He's dead. Look at those others over there."

As she moved laboriously up the steps, she looked at each abandoned man or woman on the white gleaming steps of the Asklepion. She wanted to cry out in anger. More than twenty sick and dying slaves had been left here by their callous masters. Some had already died and would soon be carted away by temple attendants. Others, like the old man, lay half-conscious, without hope or comfort, awaiting death. A few moaned in pain and delirium.

Temple attendants were already moving some—not to care for them, but to get them out of sight so that they might not offend the eyes of early morning worshipers, some of whom had already arrived on plush, veiled litters born aloft by slaves. As the wealthy devotees alighted and walked up the steps, they kept their eyes straight ahead, focusing on the majestic temple rather than on the human suffering before it. They had their own problems to concern them and—contrary to those sprawled about them—the money needed for ceremonial offerings and prayers.

Hadassah bent to another man. She turned him gently and found he was already dead. As she rose, she felt weak and nauseated. So much pain and suffering, and yet only one of these pitiful creatures would gain Alexander's full attention and medical assistance.

God, who is it to be? Whose life will you spare today? She looked around, confused and disheartened. *Who, Lord?*

She sensed someone watching her and turned. Several steps above her lay a large, dark-skinned man, his black, fever-glazed eyes staring at her without blinking. His features were aquiline, and he was wearing a soiled gray tunic.

An Arab.

He reminded her piercingly of the long march from Jerusalem when she had been chained with other captives. Men who looked very much like him had thrown dung at her and the other Jewish prisoners. Men like him had spit on her as she passed by.

This one, Lord? She looked away, her gaze passing again over all the others and coming back to the Arab above her.

This one.

Hadassah labored up the steps toward him.

His fingers worked beads swiftly with each prayer he rasped. To Vishnu.

She lowered herself painfully onto the marble step just below him and put her walking stick aside. She cupped his hand in hers, stilling his futile, repetitive pleas. "Shhh," she said gently. "God hears your prayers." His fingers loosened, and she took the prayer beads and tucked them into her sash for safekeeping should he want them later. She touched his forehead tentatively and assessed his eyes as he gazed up at her. She was surprised at the fear in his eyes. Did he think she was the specter of death beneath her veils? His breathing was labored.

She raised her head and motioned to Alexander. "Over here, my lord!"

Alexander hurried toward her. As he reached them, the man coughed. It came deep from his lungs, wracking his body. Alexander watched small spots of blood stain the pristine marble. "Lung fever," he said grimly and shook his head.

"This is the one," Hadassah said and slipped her arm beneath the man's broad shoulders.

"Hadassah, the disease has already consumed his lungs. I can't do anything for him."

Ignoring him, she spoke to the Arab. "We're taking you home with us. We will give you medicine and food. You will have shelter and rest." She helped him into a sitting position. "God has sent me to you."

"Hadassah," Alexander said, his mouth flattening out.

"This one," she said, and Alexander looked at her sharply. He had never felt such fierce determination from her before.

"Very well," he said and put his hand heavily on her shoulder. "I'll take him." He drew her to her feet and set her aside. Handing her the walking stick, he looked around for help and called to two temple attendants. Eager to have the ill man removed from their midst, they lifted him easily to a rented litter.

Alexander looked at the Arab again. Drugs and time would be wasted on this one.

Hadassah lingered, looking at all the others they had to leave behind to die.

"Come, Hadassah. We must show these men the way," Alexander said. She lowered her head in a way that told him she was weeping silently beneath her veils. He frowned. "I should've left you at the booth rather than bring you to see this."

Her hand whitened on the walking stick as she walked with him. "Is it better to hide from what's happening in the world than to know?"

"Sometimes. Especially when there's nothing you can do to change it," he said, slowing his pace to make it easier on her.

"You are changing it for one man," she said.

He looked at the Arab being carried on the open-air litter. His dusky skin had a faint tinge of gray and sheen of sweat. Deep hollows were beneath his eyes. "I doubt he'll live."

"He will live."

Alexander was amazed at her conviction, but he had learned from past experience to respect what she said. She had knowledge he couldn't fathom. "I'll do what I can for him, but it'll be up to God whether he lives or dies."

"Yes," she said and fell into silence. He knew by the way she limped and held her walking stick that all her efforts were now concentrated on making her way through the crowded streets. He stayed just ahead of her with the litter to his left in order to protect her way. She was tired and in pain. She needed no careless passersby jostling her, and he meant to make sure none did.

When they reached the booth, Alexander placed the Arab on the table to examine him further. Hadassah took the goatskin bottle from the wall hook and poured water into a clay cup. She hung the bottle back on its hook and came to slip her arm beneath the man's shoulders, raising him enough so that he could drink.

"Shall I mark his cup lest we use it by mistake, my lord?"

He laughed. "Now that you've gotten your way in bringing him here, it's 'my lord' again."

"Of course, my lord," she said again, and he heard the smile in her tone.

She lowered the Arab, and Alexander watched her stroke the man's hair back like a mother would. He knew the tenderness that would be in her touch and the compassion that would shine from her eyes. A sudden surge of protectiveness shot through him. The thought that anyone could have wished her dead, could have ordered her sent to the lions, filled him with a fury that startled him.

Abruptly he directed his gaze at the Arab. "Your name," he said.

"Amraphel," he rasped. "Rashid Ched-or-laomer," he finished.

"That is too much name for any man," Alexander said. "We'll call you Rashid." He took the damp cloth Hadassah handed him and wiped the man's sweaty face. "You have no master now, Rashid. Do you understand me? Whoever left you on the steps forfeited all rights to you. I claim none. Your only obligation to me is to do as I say until you are well. Then it will be up to you whether you go or stay and work with me."

Rashid coughed heavily. Alexander stood by, watching him with a grim expression. When the spasm finally passed, Rashid groaned in pain and sank back weakly on the table.

Hadassah came and stood beside the table again. She put her hand on Rashid's chest and felt the steady, strong beat of his heart beneath her palm. *He will live.* The still small voice assured her again of this. God knew how. God knew why.

Relaxing, Rashid put his hand over hers and looked up at her with deep-set obsidian eyes. She smoothed his black hair back from his brow again. "God has not abandoned you."

He recognized the Judean accent and frowned slightly. Why had a Jew taken pity on an Arab?

"Rest. We'll prepare a bed for you."

When it was ready, Alexander helped him into it. He was asleep almost within the moment he was covered with the wool blankets.

Alexander stood with his hands on his hips gazing down at his sleeping patient. "In good health, he must have been a man worth reckoning with."

"He will be again. How will you treat him?"

"With horehound and plantain—not that it'll do him much good at this point in the disease."

"I'll prepare a poultice of fenugreek," she said.

"Frankly, it would be more productive to beseech your god in his behalf."

"I have been praying, my lord, and will continue to do so," she said. "But there are things we can do for him as well."

"Then let's get to it."

9

Rashid did little else but sleep over the next few weeks. His mat was against the back wall of the booth, out of the way. When he was awake, he watched Alexander and Hadassah care for patients. He listened to all that was said and observed what was done.

Hadassah gave him fish, vegetables, and bread soaked in wine twice a day. Though he had no appetite, she insisted he eat. "You will regain your strength." She spoke with such certainty, he obeyed her.

When the long day ended, he watched her prepare the evening meal. She always served him first, then the physician, which surprised him. As he thought proper, the woman served herself only after they had eaten their fill.

Each night he listened as they carried on lengthy discussions of each patient. It became quickly apparent to Rashid that the veiled woman knew more about each man, woman, and child who came to the booth than the physician himself. The physician had heard words; the woman had heard their pain, anguish, and fear. The physician saw each patient as some physical ailment. The woman knew their souls . . . just as she had known his the moment she looked into his eyes. He had felt it when she touched him.

People came more often to see her, but she guided them gently to the physician. Yet Rashid could not help wonder over the weeks that passed if anything the physician did would do any good without her presence.

He looked at Alexander sitting at his worktable nearby, transferring all that Hadassah had written on the tablets onto scrolls, adding what he had done for each patient. When he finished this task, he would take the evening inventory of drugs, making note of what was needed. He would prepare medicines.

And all the while he worked, she sat, hidden beneath her veils on the small stool near the brazier, praying.

It seemed to Rashid that she prayed constantly. Sometimes Rashid heard her humming softly. At times, she would unclasp her hands and spread them, palms upward. Even during the day when she was seeing the sick, there was an air about her that made him think she was *listening,* contemplating something unseen.

Watching her filled him with a sense of peace, for he had seen amazing things happen in this booth over the past weeks. He was convinced that the God of Abraham had touched her with power.

As he improved, he sat on a mat outside and overheard other things. *"She has the healing touch."* More than one person spoke these words to any who would listen. Word about Hadassah and Alexander was spreading, for some who came to see them were not from the narrow streets near the wharf or baths, but from across the city.

A small crowd gathered outside each morning. They could be heard whispering respectfully, waiting for the partitions to be drawn back and the booth opened. Some came because they were sick or injured and needed a physician's attention. Others came to hear Hadassah's stories and ask questions about her god.

A woman named Ephicharis came often with her little daughter, Helena. So, too, did a man named Boethus. He sometimes brought his wife and four children with him. He never left without giving Hadassah coin "for someone in need." And always this offering was given to someone before the day had ended.

One morning, a young woman came to the booth. Rashid noticed her immediately, for she was a lovely finch among a flock of plain brown sparrows. Though she was dressed in a simple brown tunic with a white waist sash and a shawl drawn over her dark hair, her beauty captivated. A woman such as this belonged in silk and jewels.

Hadassah was pleased to see her. "Severina! Come. Sit. Tell me how you are."

Rashid stared at Severina as she moved gracefully among the others. She possessed the radiance of a star shining in the heavens as she took the stool beside Hadassah's writing table and said, "I didn't think you'd remember me. I was here so long ago."

Hadassah covered the woman's hand with her own. "You look in good health."

"I am," she said. "I didn't return to the Artemision."

Hadassah said nothing, allowing her the freedom to say more if she chose. Severina raised her eyes again. "I sold myself as a household slave. The master who bought me is kind, as is his lady. She's trained me as a weaver. I enjoy the work very much."

"The Lord has been good to you."

Severina's eyes filled with tears. With trembling hands, she took Hadassah's and pressed it between hers. "You were kind to me when I came here. You asked me my name. You remembered me. So simple a thing as that and yet important in ways you can't imagine." She blushed. Letting go of Hadassah, she arose. "I just wanted you to know," she whispered and quickly turned away.

Hadassah rose clumsily. "Severina, wait. Please." She hobbled over to where the young woman stood uncertainly on the edge of the circle of waiting patients. They spoke for several minutes while others watched. Hadassah embraced her, and Severina clung to her, then drew back and walked quickly away.

Rashid watched Hadassah's stiff, awkward gait as she made her way back to her stool. He wondered if she was even aware that several patients who sat on the stone-cobbled street waiting to see the physician touched her hem as she passed by.

Each day brought improvement for the Arab. Alexander examined him daily and kept record of the amount of horehound and plantain he gave him, as well as the fenugreek poultices Hadassah bound to his chest. Perhaps these things, as well as the nourishing food and warmth of blankets and shelter, had had a part in saving him from death. But Rashid knew it was more than medicine or shelter that had restored his life. Because of his knowledge, he treated Hadassah with a respect bordering on reverence.

One thing, though, greatly troubled him. One evening he gathered his courage and sought an answer. "Are you his slave, my lady?"

"Not exactly," she said.

Alexander was bent over a scroll on which he was writing. He glanced up at her answer. "She is free, Rashid. Just as you are free."

Hadassah turned toward Alexander. "I am a slave, my lord, and will remain so until legally freed."

Rashid saw that her statement annoyed the physician, for he put down his stylus and turned fully on his stool. "Your masters forfeited all rights to you when they sent you to the arena. Your god protected you, and *I* put you back together again."

"If it was known I was alive, my lord, it would be within my lady's right to demand my return."

"Then she will not know," he said simply. "Tell me her name so that I may avoid her."

Hadassah sat in silence.

108

"Why do you not tell him?" Rashid asked, perplexed.

Alexander smiled wryly. "Because she is stubborn, Rashid. You see every day how stubborn she is."

"If not for her, you would have passed me by on the steps of the Asklepion," Rashid said darkly.

Alexander's brows rose slightly. "I admit that's true. I thought you were near death."

"I was."

"Not near enough, it would seem. You are gaining strength each day."

"I was nearer death than you know. *She* touched me."

His meaning was all too clear, and Alexander smiled wryly at Hadassah. "Clearly he thinks my ministrations had nothing to do with his improvement." He returned to his scrolls.

"Do not credit me with healing you, Rashid," Hadassah said in dismay. "It was not I, but Christ Jesus."

"You have told others that this Christ dwells in you," Rashid said.

"As he dwells in all those who believe in him. He would come to dwell within you if you chose to open your heart to him."

"I belong to Siva."

"We are both children of Abraham, Rashid. And there is only one God, the true God, Jesus, God the Son."

"I have heard you speak often of him, my lady, but it is not the path Siva has chosen for me. You forgive your enemy. I kill mine." His eyes darkened. "As I swear before Siva, I will kill yours if they ever come for you."

She sat in stunned silence, staring through her veils at the dark, proud, rigid face before her.

Alexander glanced back over his shoulder, equally surprised by such fierce vehemence. Turning around, he assessed the Arab. "What position did you have in your master's household, Rashid?"

"I guarded his son until my illness overtook me."

"Then you are a trained soldier."

"From a race of warriors," Rashid said with a proud lift of his head.

Alexander smiled ruefully. "It seems God has not sent me an apprentice after all, Hadassah. He has sent you a protector."

10

Julia stood among the crowd inside the propylon of the Asklepion and listened to the seemingly endless program of poets competing in the triennial festival honoring the god. She had found the earlier game with athletic and gymnastic events more to her taste. This sea of words pouring forth meant nothing to her. She was not a poet, nor an athlete. And she was in poor health. The reason she had come so often to the Asklepion was to attain the mercy of the god. She could not please the deity by literary works or feats of strength and agility. Therefore, she would make a vigil through the long night in order to honor and appease him.

As the sun set, she went inside the temple and knelt before the altar where the sacrifices were made. She prayed to the god of health and physique. She prayed until her knees and back ached. When she could kneel no longer, she lay on her face on the cold marble, arms outstretched toward the marble statue of Asklepios.

Morning came and she was filled with pain in every part of her being. She heard the chorus singing ritual hymns. She arose and stood with the others who had made vigils through the night with her. A priest gave a lengthy speech, but in her exhausted state, little of what he said made any sense.

Where was mercy? Where was compassion? How many offerings and vigils would she have to make to be made whole, to earn restoration?

Weakened from her long vigil, depressed and sick, she sank down and leaned heavily against one of the marble columns. She closed her eyes. The priest droned on and on.

She awakened with a start, someone shaking her. She glanced up, confused, still half-asleep.

"This is not a place to sleep, woman! Arise from here and go home," the man said, clearly annoyed with her presence. From his robes, she knew he was one of the temple wardens.

"I can't."

"What do you mean you can't?"

"I was here all night praying," she stammered.

He took hold of her and pulled her roughly to her feet. "Have

110

you no maid with you?" he said impatiently, assessing the fine linen of the tunic and veils she wore.

Julia looked around for Eudemas. "She must have left me sometime during the night."

"I will summon a slave to take you home."

"No. I mean, I can't go home. I've been praying, praying for hours. Please. Let me enter the *abaton* and receive healing."

"You must go through the purification ceremony and then be washed at the Sacred Well before we can admit you to the abaton, woman. You should know that. And even after that it's up to the god whether you regain your health."

"I will do anything you ask," she said desperately.

He assessed her again. "It is very costly," he said quietly.

"How much?" she said quickly. She saw his eyes move to her gold earrings. She removed them and handed them to him. He tucked them swiftly into the folds of his red silk girdle and looked pointedly at her gold pendant. She removed it as well and placed it in his outstretched hand. His thick fingers closed around it and pushed it hastily into the folds of his red girdle along with her earrings.

"Now will you take me inside?"

"Have you nothing else?"

She looked down at her shaking white hands. "All I have left is this lapis and gold ring my father gave me when I was child."

He took her hand and looked at it. "I will have it," he said, letting go of her.

Tears blurring her eyes, she twisted the ring until she was able to pull it from the little finger of her right hand. She watched him tuck it away with the earrings and pendant. "Follow me," he said.

He left her in a purification chamber, where she was told to remove all her clothing. She had always been proud of her body. Now as this servant washed her, cleansing her body in preparation for entering the Sacred Well, she was ashamed and embarrassed. Revealed were the festering ulcers and strange purple-red bruises that were evidence of her mysterious, malignant disease. When the loose white garment was held out to her, she grasped it and drew it on quickly, covering herself from prying, curious eyes.

Julia entered the chamber that protected the Sacred Well and saw others waiting ahead of her. She looked away from a woman with *mentagra,* a terrible skin disorder. She fought a wave of repulsion at the ugly skin eruptions on the woman's face and watched a man with swollen joints enter the sacred pool. He went into a spasm of violent coughing as the attendants began to lower him, and they had to wait for it to end.

The next to enter the pool was an obese woman who was trembling violently. Attendants sang ritual hymns and then repeated incantations as each applicant of the god's favor went down the steps into the water. One after another, each with some disease or deformity, entered the pool.

When it came Julia's turn, she couldn't concentrate on the words being chanted or sung. All she could think about was the woman with mentagra entering the sacred waters just ahead of her. She had watched as the attendants lowered the woman until she was submerged in the murky pool. Now she was to enter the same water that had washed over those revolting eruptions.

The hands of the attendants took hold of hers firmly, helping her down the slippery steps. She fought panic as they leaned her back, the water cold against her back and creeping up around and over her, covering her face. She wanted to scream, but she held her panic inside, pressing her lips together, holding her breath. Down, down, she went into the cloudy water of the Sacred Well, sulfur burning her eyes even though they were closed.

She was lifted up again, and it took all her willpower not to shake free of the attendants and clamber frantically up the opposite steps and out of the polluted pool. She gave those helping her a false, tentative smile, but their attention was already focused on the man behind her, who was now entering the sacred waters.

Shivering, she entered the next chamber, where she discarded the sodden white smock and put on a loose white tunic. Another attendant led her down a long open corridor to the abaton, a sacred dormitory adjacent to the Asklepion, where she would be "incubated" for the night. In front of it was the sacred pit of snakes. Priests poured libations into the writhing mass of churning reptiles, chanting and praying aloud to the gods and spirits of the underworld.

Julia entered the abaton. Though she had no appetite, she ate the food and drank the wine they brought to her. Perhaps it had drugs in it that would bring on the healing dreams. She lay down upon the sleeping bench and prayed again. She knew if she dreamed that dogs licked her body or snakes crawled over her, it would be a sign that Asklepios had favored her and would heal her. So she prayed that the dogs and snakes would come to her, though the very thought of either terrified her.

Her eyelids felt heavy, her body weighted. She thought someone had entered the room, but was too tired to open her eyes and look. She heard a man's voice, speaking softly, invoking the gods and spirits of the underworld to come to her, to heal her of her afflictions. Her body became heavier and heavier as she sank down into a dark pit. . . .

Snakes were beneath her, thousands of them in all sizes, squirming and twisting together in a terrifying mass. Boa constrictors and tiny asps, small harmless snakes she had seen in the villa garden in Rome, and poisonous cobras with their spreading capes. Their split tongues darted in and out, in and out, closer and closer, until they flicked against her flesh, each touch like fire until her body was being consumed by it.

She struggled, crying out, and awakened.

Someone was in the shadows of her small cell, speaking to her in a low voice. She strained to see who it was, but her vision was distorted, her thoughts clouded.

"Marcus?"

The form did not answer. Disoriented, she closed her eyes. Where was she? She breathed deeply and slowly until her mind cleared slightly, and she remembered. The abaton. She had come for healing.

She started to cry. She should be happy. The snakes had crawled over her in her dream. It was a sign from the gods that she would get well. And yet she couldn't still the voice of doubt that echoed in her mind. What if the dream meant nothing? What if the gods were mocking her? Her chest ached as she tried to stop sobbing.

Turning her head, she saw the shadowy figure still standing in the dark corner of the cell. Had Asklepios come to her? "Who are you?" she whispered hoarsely, afraid, yet hopeful.

He began to speak in a low, strange voice, and she realized he was chanting. The voice droned on, the words making no sense to her. She grew drowsy again and struggled against sleep, not wanting to dream of the snake pit. But she could not withstand the effects of the drugs she had been given, and she sank into darkness. . . .

She heard dogs barking and moaned. They were coming closer, closer, faster and faster. She was running across a hot, rocky plain. When she looked back, she saw the dogs coming in a pack, racing across the ground toward her. She stumbled and fell, clambered back to her feet, panting, her lungs burning as she tried to run faster. They came on, barking wildly, fangs bared.

"Someone help me! Someone help—!"

She stumbled again, and before she could get up, they were on her, not licking her diseased flesh but tearing at it with their sharp fangs. Screaming, she fought them.

She awakened with a cry and sat up on the narrow bed. It was a moment before her breathing slowed down and she fully realized it had only been a dream. No shadowy figure loomed in the dark corner. She covered her face and cried, afraid to go back to sleep again. And so she waited through the long, cold hours until darkness began lifting.

A temple warden came to her at daybreak and asked what she had dreamed. She told him in as much detail as she could remember and saw he looked troubled.

"What's wrong? Is it a bad omen? Won't I get well?" she asked breathlessly, near tears again. Her stomach quivered, warning of near hysteria. Clenching her hands, she fought against it.

"Asklepios has sent a good sign," the warden assured her calmly, his face once again devoid of emotion. "Many snakes, many dogs. It is unusual. Your prayers have found great favor with our most high god."

Julia felt vaguely uncomfortable with his interpretation. She had seen something in his eyes, something terrible and unsettling. She was certain that now he was telling her what she longed to hear. Still, she couldn't help but ask, "Then I will be well again?"

He nodded. "In time, Asklepios will restore your health."

"In time," she said bleakly. "How much time?"

"You must show more faith, woman."

And then she knew. "How do I show Asklepios that I have enough faith for him to heal me?" she said, trying to keep the bitter cynicism out of her voice. She knew what was coming. She had heard it often enough from the priests of half a dozen other gods whose favor she had sought and failed to secure.

The warden raised his head slightly, his eyes narrowing. "In vigils, in prayer, in meditation, and in votive offerings. And when you are well, you must show the proper gratitude in worthy gifts."

She looked away from him and closed her eyes. She had no strength for lengthy vigils and no heart for prayer and meditation.

The wealth she had once thought enough to keep her in luxury for a lifetime had dwindled to almost nothing, siphoned off by Primus. He had stripped her of most of her estate and then vanished from Ephesus. Perhaps, like Calabah, he had simply boarded a ship and sailed away to Rome, where he would find a far more exciting life than watching her die slowly of some unnamed illness.

She had learned only a few days ago that she had barely enough money left to live in simple comfort. She could spare little for the kind of votive offerings to which the warden alluded: gold replicas of the internal organs that pained her. It wasn't pain as much as it was a spreading weakness . . . the constant fevers, the nausea and sweats, spells of trembling, and the oozing sores in her secret places all drained her to the point of exhaustion.

"Why don't you kill yourself and have done with it?" Primus had said during what she later realized was their last conversation before he abandoned her. "Put yourself out of misery."

But she wanted to live! She didn't want to die and be in darkness for the rest of eternity. She didn't want to die and face whatever unknown horror awaited her.

She was afraid.

"I have very little money," she said, looking back at the warden, who sat silently waiting for her to say something. "My husband has taken most of my estate and left me. I haven't enough to have votive offerings made of gold or silver or even brass."

"A pity," he said without feeling. He rose. "Your clothing is on the shelf. Please leave the tunic behind."

She was stunned by his indifference.

Alone again, she sat on the couch, too tired and despondent to feel anything. She rose after a long time, removed the white garment she had been given, and put on her own fine blue linen tunic. She touched her earlobes and throat where her last pieces of gold jewelry had been and let her hands drop to her sides. She took up her blue shawl with the elegant, expensive, embroidered flower trim and draped it over her head and shoulders.

Tipping her chin slightly, she walked out into the corridor. Several attendants stopped her and asked how her night had gone, if the gods had answered her prayer. Smiling, she lied and said she was healed of her affliction.

"Asklepios be praised!" they said one after another.

She walked quickly across the courtyard and through the propylon to the people-thronged street beyond. She wanted to be home. Not in her villa here in Ephesus. She wanted to be back in the villa in Rome, a child again. She wanted to return to the times when her whole life stretched out ahead of her, brilliant and beautiful as the colors of dawn, fresh and new, full of potential, full of opportunities.

She wanted to start over. If only she could, how differently she would do things, how differently things would have turned out!

She had thought Asklepios would give her that. She had thought her offerings, her vigils, her prayers would earn that for her. And he had sent the snakes. He had sent the dogs.

And yet she knew, deep within, that it was all for naught. Helpless rage filled her. "Stone! That's all you are! You can't heal anyone! You're nothing but cold, dead stone!" She bumped into someone.

"A curse on you, woman! Watch where you're going!"

Bursting into tears, Julia ran.

11

The *Minerva* landed in Caesarea Maritima at the beginning of the warming of spring. Though the city was built by a Jewish king, Marcus found it as Roman, both in appearance and atmosphere, as the Eternal City in which he'd been reared. Four centuries before, this same site had been settled by Phoenicians who built a small, fortified anchorage called Strato's Tower, honoring one of their kings. The anchorage had been expanded and modernized by Herod the Great, and he named his new city in honor of Emperor Caesar Augustus. Caesarea had become one of the most important seaports in the Empire and the seat for Roman prefects governing Palestine.

Herod had rebuilt the city with his eyes on Rome, borrowing mightily from the conquered Greeks. Hellenistic influence showed strongly in the amphitheater, hippodrome, baths, and aqueducts. There was also the temple honoring Augustus, as well as the statues to various Roman and Greek gods that continued to so enrage righteous Jews.

Marcus was well aware that conflicts had often arisen between the Jewish and Greek people of the city. The last bloody rebellion had been sparked ten years before, only to be crushed by Vespasian and his son Titus before they had marched on against Jerusalem, the heart of Judea. Vespasian had been pronounced emperor here in Caesarea and had promptly elevated the city to a Roman colony.

Despite the iron grip of Rome upon the city, Marcus sensed that unrest remained an undercurrent as he walked through the narrow streets. Satyros warned him against entering certain sections of the city, and it was to those very sections that Marcus went. These were Hadassah's people. He wanted to know what made them so stubborn and determined in their faith.

He wasted no time in contemplating the violence that might befall him at the hands of zealots or *sicarii*. He was on a quest to find Hadassah's god, and he wouldn't find him in the Roman baths and arenas or in the homes of fellow Roman merchants.

The information he needed lay in the minds of these Jewish patriots who had the same stubbornness he had sensed in Hadassah.

Within three days of his arrival, Marcus had purchased a strong desert horse, supplies for his overland journey, and an itinerary showing roads, *stationes,* and *civitates,* all with distances between. After a day of studying the map, he rode away from Caesarea and headed southeast for Sebaste, in the district of Samaria.

Marcus reached the city early in the afternoon on the second day. He had been told beforehand that the ancient Jewish city vied in grandeur with Jerusalem before the destruction. He spotted it long before he reached it, for it was high on a hill. From his conversations with Satyros while sailing from Ephesus on the *Minerva,* Marcus knew Sebaste to be the only city the ancient Hebrews founded. Built by King Omri over nine hundred years before, Samaria—as it had previously been called—had served as a capital for the kingdom of Israel, while Jerusalem was capital for the kingdom of Judah.

The city had a long and bloody history. It was here that a Jewish prophet named Elijah had slaughtered two hundred Baal priests. Later the dynasty of King Ahab and his Phoenician wife, Jezebel, was overthrown by a man named Jehu, who slaughtered the worshipers of Baal and then turned the god's temple into a latrine. But the bloodshed had not ended there.

Over the centuries, Samaria was conquered by the Assyrians, Babylonians, Persians, and Macedonians. Finally, a Hasmonean leader by the name of John Hyrcanus I made the city part of a Jewish kingdom again. But less than two centuries later, Pompey took the city for Rome. Caesar Augustus gave Samaria to Herod the Great as a gift, and the Jewish king promptly renamed it "Sebaste," Greek for "Augustus."

As Marcus rode through the gates into the city, he saw again the heavy stamp of Roman and Greek influence. The populace was a mingling of races: Roman, Greek, Arab, and Jew. He found an inn near the marketplace, or what was called an inn. Actually, it was little more than a protected courtyard with booths along the inner walls and a fire in the center. Still, it was shelter.

After a visit to the baths, he returned to the inn and asked questions of the proprietor, a thin, shrewd-eyed Greek named Malchus.

"You're wasting your time looking for the Jews' god. Even they dispute among themselves as to which mountain is *the* holy mount. Those in Sebaste say Mount Gerizim is where Abraham took his son to be sacrificed."

"What do you mean 'sacrificed'?"

"The race of Jews began with a man named Abraham, who was told by their god to sacrifice his only son, a son he had in his old age and who was promised him by this same god," Malchus said, pouring wine into Marcus' goblet.

Marcus gave a mirthless laugh. "So he killed his own from the beginning."

"They don't see it that way. The Jews believe their god was testing their patriarch's faith. Would this Abraham choose to love God more than his only son? He passed the test, and his son was spared. It's considered one of the most crucial events in their religious history. Abraham's obedience to his god is what made his descendants 'the chosen people.' You'd think they'd know where it happened, but somewhere along the line the location came into dispute. It's either Moriah to the south or Gerizim within walking distance of here. It didn't help matters that the Jews in Jerusalem look upon those here in Samaria as a tainted race."

"Tainted by what?"

"Intermarriage with Gentiles. You and I are Gentiles, my lord. In fact, anyone not born a direct descendant of this Abraham is a Gentile. They're adamant about it. Even those who embrace their religion aren't considered true Jews, not even after they've been circumcised."

Marcus winced. He'd heard what circumcision entailed. "What man in full possession of his senses would agree to such a barbaric practice?"

"Anyone who wants to adhere to the Jewish Law," Malchus said. "The problem is the Jews can't even agree among themselves. And they hold grudges longer than any Roman. The Jews in the districts of Judea and Galilee hate those here in Samaria, and it's got to do with whatever happened centuries ago," he said. "There was a temple here once, but it was destroyed by a Hasmonean Jew named John Hyrcanus. The Samaritans haven't forgotten that, either. They've got long memories. There's a lot of bad blood between them, and the rift between them grows wider as time goes by."

"I'd think worshiping one god would unite a people."

"Ha! Jews are splintered into all kinds of factions and sects. You've got the Essenes, the Zealots, the Pharisees, and the Sadducees. You've got Samaritans, who proclaim Mount Gerizim the holy mountain, and Jews in Judea who're still praying at what remains of their temple walls. Then you've got new sects cropping up all the time. These Christians, for example. They've lasted longer than most, though the Jews have driven almost all of them out of Palestine. There are still a few determined to stay and *save* the rest. I'll tell you, where there are Christians in Palestine, you can be sure there'll be a riot and someone will get stoned."

"Are there Christians here in Sebaste?" Marcus said.

"A few. I don't have anything to do with them. It's not good for business."

"Where would I find them?"

"Don't get anywhere near them. And if you do, don't bring any into my inn. Jews hate Christians worse than they hate the Romans."

"I thought they'd have a common ground. The same god."

"You're asking the wrong man. About all I know is the Christians believe the Messiah has already come. His name was Jesus." He laughed derisively. "This Jesus, who was supposedly their anointed one of God, came from some little dunghill in Galilee named Nazareth. Believe me, nothing good comes out of Galilee. Ignorant fishermen and shepherds, mostly, but certainly not a Messiah like the one the Jews are expecting. The Messiah is supposed to be a warrior-king who comes down from the heavens with a legion of angels. The Christians worship a Messiah who was a carpenter. What's more, he was crucified, though they claim he arose from the dead. According to this sect, Jesus fulfilled and, thereby, abolished the Law. There's enough in that claim to keep a war going forever. If there's one thing I've come to know in twenty years of living in this miserable country, it's this: A Jew isn't a Jew without *the Law*. It's the air they breathe."

Malchus shook his head. "And I'll tell you something else. They've got more laws than Rome, and they're adding to them all the time. They've got their Torah, written by Moses. Then they've got their civil and moral laws. They've even got dietary laws. Then they've got their traditions. I swear Jews have laws about everything, even how and where a man can relieve himself!"

Marcus frowned. Something Hadassah had once said about the Law flickered like a small flame in his mind. She had summed up the entire Law in a few words for Claudius, Julia's first husband. He had written it down onto one of his scrolls and then read her words to him. What had they been?

"I need to find out," Marcus muttered to himself.

"Find out what?" Malchus said.

"What the truth is."

Malchus frowned, not understanding.

"How do I get to Mount Gerizim?" Marcus said.

"Just walk out that door and you'll see two mountains, Mount Ebal to the north, Mount Gerizim to the south. Between them is the pass to the valley of Nablus. Abraham came through there to their 'Promised Land.'"

Marcus gave him a gold coin.

Malchus' brows lifted slightly as he turned it in his fingers. The Roman must be very rich. "The road'll take you through the town of Sychar, but I give you fair warning. Romans are hated throughout Palestine, and a Roman traveling by himself is asking for trouble. Especially one with money."

"I was told a Roman legion guards these roads."

Malchus laughed without humor. "No road is safe from sicarii. And they'd sooner slit your throat than listen to any plea for mercy."

"I'll be on the watch for zealots."

"These men aren't zealots. Zealots are like those who committed suicide on Masada a few years back. They preferred death to slavery. You can respect men like that. Sicarii are something else altogether. They see themselves as patriots, but they're nothing more than murderous bandits." He pushed the gold coin into the fold of his grimy girdle. "You've picked a foul country to travel in, my lord. There's nothing here to recommend it to a Roman."

"I came to find out about their god."

Malchus gave a surprised laugh. "Why would anyone want to have anything to do with their god? You can't see him. You can't hear him. And look what's happened to the Jews. If you ask me, you ought to stay well away from their god."

"I didn't ask you," Marcus said in clear dismissal.

"It's your life," Malchus muttered under his breath and went to see to his other patrons.

Malchus' wife placed a clay bowl of stew before Marcus. Hungry, he ate and found the mixture of lentils, beans, and grain with honey and oil satisfying. When he finished, Marcus rose and found his booth against the wall of the open courtyard. His horse had been given hay and grain. Nudging the animal aside, Marcus rolled out his bed and lay down for the night.

He awakened every time someone stirred or got up. Two travelers from Jericho drank wine, laughed at jokes, and talked far into the night. Others, like a retired soldier and his young wife and child, settled early.

Marcus awakened at daybreak and set off for Mount Gerizim. He rode through the town of Sychar late in the afternoon. Eager to reach his destination, he didn't stop but continued up the mountain. He stopped at a Jewish shrine to ask questions, but hearing his accent and noting his dress, the people avoided him. He rode a little farther, hobbled his horse, and set off on foot to reach the top.

What he found there was a magnificent view of the hill country of the Jewish Promised Land.

But there was no sign of a god. Not that he could see. Frustrated, he cried out against the emptiness around him. "Where are you? Why do you hide from me?"

He spent the night staring up at the stars and listening to a wolf howl somewhere in the valley below. Hadassah had said her god spoke to her in the wind, and so he strained to hear what the wind had to say to him.

He heard nothing.

He spent all the next day waiting and listening.

Still nothing.

He started down the mountain on the third day, famished and thirsty.

A shepherd boy was standing near his horse, feeding the animal green sprigs from the palm of his hand. Scattered around the hillside were sheep grazing.

Marcus strode down the slope. With a cold look at the boy, he unlooped the goatskin water bag from the saddle and drank thirstily. The boy did not retreat but watched him with interest. He said something.

"I don't understand Aramaic," Marcus said tersely, irritated that the boy hadn't taken himself off to tend his sheep.

The young shepherd spoke to him in Greek this time. "You are fortunate your horse is still here. There are many who would steal him."

Marcus' mouth curved sardonically. "I thought Jews had a commandment against stealing."

The boy grinned. "Not from Romans."

"Then I'm glad he is still here."

The boy rubbed the velvety nose. "He is a good horse."

"He'll get me where I'm going."

"Where are you going?"

"To Mount Moriah," he said and then after a brief hesitation, added, "to find God."

The boy looked up at him in surprise and then studied him curiously. "My father says Romans have many gods. With all of them to choose from, why do you look for another?"

"To ask questions."

"What sort of questions?"

Marcus looked away. He would ask God to his face why he had allowed Hadassah to die. He would ask him why, if he was the almighty Creator, he had created a world so full of violence. Most of all, he wanted to know if God even existed. "If I ever find him, I'll ask him about many things," he said heavily and glanced back at the boy. The small shepherd studied him with dark pensive eyes.

"You will not find God on Mount Moriah," the boy said simply.

"I've already looked on Mount Gerizim."

"He is not on a mountaintop, like your Jupiter."

"Then where will I find him?"

The boy shrugged. "I don't know if you can find him in the way you want."

"Are you telling me this god never shows himself to man? What about your Moses? Didn't your god appear to him?"

"Sometimes he appears to people," the boy said.

"What does he look like?"

"He's not always the same. He came as an ordinary traveler to Abram. When Israelites came out of Egypt, God was before them, a pillar of cloud by day, a pillar of fire at night. One of our prophets saw God and wrote he was like a wheel within a wheel and had the heads of beasts and shone like fire."

"Then he changes form, like Zeus."

The boy shook his head. "Our God is not like the gods of the Romans."

"You think not?" Marcus gave a cynical laugh. "He's more like them than you know." His grief rose, gripping him. A god who loved his people would have reached down from the heavens to save Hadassah. Only a cruel god could have watched her die.

Which are you?

The boy looked at him solemnly but without fear. "You are angry."

"Yes," Marcus said flatly. "I am angry. I'm also wasting time." He unhobbled the horse and mounted.

The boy moved back as the animal pranced. "What do you want of God, Roman?"

It was an imperious question from so small a boy, and was said with a curious blend of humility and demand. "I'll know when I face him."

"Perhaps the answers you seek can't be found in something you can see and touch."

Amused, Marcus smiled. "You have big thoughts for a small boy."

The boy grinned. "A shepherd has time to think."

"Then, my little philosopher, what would you advise?"

The boy's smile faded. "When you face God, remember he is God."

"I'll remember what he's done," Marcus said coldly.

"That, too," the boy said almost gently.

Marcus frowned slightly, studying the boy more intently. His mouth curved wryly. "You're the first Jew who's spoken to me man-to-man. A pity." Turning the horse, he started down the hill. He heard the jingle of bells and glanced back. The boy was walking across the grassy hillside, tapping his belled staff on the ground. The sheep responded quickly, gathering closer and following him as he headed toward the western slope.

Marcus felt something strange move within him as he watched the boy with his sheep. An aching hunger. A thirst. And suddenly, he sensed an unseen presence . . . a vague hint of something, like a sweet, tantalizing aroma of food just beyond his grasp.

Reining his horse in, he stopped and stared after the young shepherd for a moment longer, perplexed. What was it about him that was different? Shaking his head, Marcus gave a self-deprecating laugh and urged his horse on. He had spent too much time on the mountain without food and drink. He was turning fanciful.

He continued at a brisk pace down the mountain and headed south for Jerusalem.

12

Hadassah awakened to someone banging on the outer partition of the booth and calling for help. "My lord physician! My lord! Please. We need you!" She sat up, struggling from sleep.

"No," Rashid said, moving quickly to intercept her. "It is late, and you must rest." He stepped around her to push the partition aside, determined to silence and chase off the intruder. "What do you want, woman? The physician and his assistant are asleep."

"My master sent me. Please. Let me speak to him. My mistress' time has come, and we learned her physician has left Ephesus in disgrace. My mistress is in great difficulty."

"Be off with you. There are other physicians at the baths. This booth is closed."

"She will die if she doesn't get help. You must awaken him. He must come. I beg you. Please. She is in terrible pain, and the baby won't come. My master is rich. He will pay whatever you ask."

"Rashid," Hadassah said as she drew her veils down over her face. "Tell her we will come."

"You have just lain down to rest, my lady," he said in protest.

"Do as she says," Alexander told him, already up and checking his instruments, adding several to his leather carrying pack. "Bring the mandragora, Hadassah. If it's as bad as it sounds, we may need it."

"Yes, my lord." She added several other drugs to the box besides the mandragora. She was ready before he was, and, taking up her walking stick, she limped to the partition. Rashid blocked her way, and she put her hand on his arm. "Let me speak with her."

"Do you not need rest like any other?" he said and glared at the slave girl outside. "Let her go elsewhere."

"She has come to us. Now move aside."

Mouth tight, Rashid yanked the partition back. Hadassah went outside. The slave girl drew back from her, her face pale in the moonlight. Hadassah understood her trepidation, for she had seen it often enough. The veils made many people nervous. She tried to ease the slave girl's anxiety. "The physician is coming," she said gently. "He is very knowledgeable and will do all he can for your mistress. He's packing what he needs."

"Oh, thank you, thank you," the girl said, bowing several times and then bursting into tears. "My lady's pains began yesterday afternoon and grow worse and worse."

"Tell me your name."

"Livilla, my lady."

"And the name of your mistress?"

"Antonia Stephania Magonianus, wife of Habinnas Attalus."

Alexander had appeared. "Magonianus? Surely not Magonianus the silversmith?"

"The same, my lord," Livilla said, clearly distressed at the slightest delay. "We must hurry. Please. We must hurry!"

"Lead the way," Alexander said, and Livilla set off quickly.

Rashid yanked the partition closed with one hand and followed. "You cannot keep up," he said walking beside Hadassah.

She knew he was right, for already pain was shooting up her bad leg. She stumbled once and gasped. Rashid glowered at her with an expression of grimness as he reached out to take her arm. "Do you see?"

Alexander glanced back and saw her difficulty. He stopped and waited for her to catch up.

"No," she panted. "Go without me. I will come as quickly as I can."

"She should not be coming at all," Rashid said in annoyance.

Hadassah shook his hand off her arm and limped after Livilla, who was standing at a corner and calling back to them to hurry. Alexander fell into step beside her. "Rashid is right. It's too far and too hard on you. Go back. I'll have Magonianus send a litter for you."

Gritting her teeth against the pain, Hadassah scarcely heard him. All of her attention was on the frightened slave girl urging them to hurry.

Rashid swore in his own language and caught Hadassah up in his arms. He strode up the hill, still muttering under his breath.

"Thank you, Rashid," Hadassah said, her arm around his neck. "God sent her to us for a reason."

They followed Livilla through the maze of dark city streets and reached a large shop facing the Artemision. One glance told Hadassah who they were coming to see. Magonianus. The silversmith. The idol maker.

Rashid carried her through the shop to the residence behind.

"This way," Livilla said, panting from exertion and running for a marble staircase. Somewhere above them a woman screamed. *"Hurry!* Oh, please, hurry!"

Rashid followed her into a room on the second floor and stood looking around, Hadassah still in his arms. Alexander was right behind him and halted just inside the door with the same reaction. The lavish surroundings were stunning. The room was resplendent with color. Murrhine glass glistened, and Babylonian coverings draped the east wall. Two murals bespoke of a wealth far removed from the small booth on the street outside the public baths. One covered the west wall and displayed sprites dancing in a forest while two lovers were entwined together in a bed of flowers. Another on the south wall displayed a hunting scene.

Hadassah, however, saw nothing but the young girl writhing on the bed. "Put me down, Rashid."

Rashid obeyed, staring in amazement at the conspicuous evidence of Magonianus' prosperity.

Hadassah limped to the bed. "Antonia, we're here to help you," she said and laid her hand against the girl's damp forehead. She was no older than Julia when she had first married. Across from her was a gray-haired man much like Claudius, holding her small white hand between both of his. His weary face was pale and beaded with perspiration. Antonia cried out again as another contraction was upon her, and a look of agony etched his exhausted face. "Do something for her, woman. Do something!"

"You must be calm for her, my lord."

"Habinnas!" Antonia cried, her blue eyes widened in fear as she looked up at Hadassah. "Who is she? Why is she covered in veils?"

"Don't be afraid, my lady," Hadassah said gently, smiling down at her, though she knew Antonia couldn't see her face. It was best that she couldn't, for the dreadful scars would frighten the girl even more. "I have come with the physician to help with your lying in."

Antonia began to pant again and then moan. "Oh . . . ohhh . . . ohhhh, Hera, have mercy."

As Hadassah stroked the girl's forehead gently, she saw an amulet around her neck. She had seen many such amulets over the past months. Some, made of stone or hare's rennet, were meant to make childbearing easier. Others, like this one, were to stimulate fertility. She took the smooth oval hematite in her hand and saw, engraved on one side, a serpent devouring its own tail. She knew without turning it over that on the other side would be an engraving of the goddess Isis and a scarab beetle. Also engraved in minute detail were an invocation in Greek and the names of Oroiouth, Iao, and Yahweh. Wearers believed the combination of Greek, Egyptian, and Semitic motifs and words would bring magical powers. Untying it, she set it aside.

"I'm going to die," the girl said, rolling her head back and forth. "I'm going to die."

"No," Habinnas said in agony. "No, you're not going to die. I won't let you. Even now, the priests are making sacrifices in your name to Artemis and Hera."

Hadassah leaned closer. "Is this your first child, Antonia?"

"No."

"She's lost two others," Habinnas said.

"And now this one won't be born." She began to pant, one hand raking the damp blanket while her other whitened on her husband's hand. "It pushes and pushes, but it won't come. Oh, Habinnas, it hurts! Make it stop. Make it stop!" She screamed, her body curling in agony.

Habinnas held her hand with both of his and cried.

Still distracted by the opulence of his surroundings, Alexander crossed the room and removed perfume bottles and unguents from an ivory table. He glanced around again at the shining Corinthian bronze bed with its Chinese silk veiling, at the intricate pattern of various colors of marble on the floor, and at the large ornate brazier and gold lamps.

As Alexander methodically laid out oil, sea sponges, pieces of wool, bandages for the newborn, and surgical instruments, he wondered why a man of Magonianus' obvious wealth would send a slave to the public baths for a commoners' doctor. Another thought came to him in the wake of the first, a grim realization that filled him with misgivings. If he failed to save Magonianus' young and clearly beloved wife, he would be driven from the city, his reputation as a physician destroyed.

"I should have listened to you," he said under his breath to Rashid.

"Say you can do nothing and leave."

Alexander gave a soft mirthless laugh and glanced toward the bed. "I would not be able to pry Hadassah away from her now."

Antonia's screaming subsided, and Hadassah spoke quietly to her and to the distraught Habinnas. "May Asklepios guide me," Alexander said and approached the bed.

"We will need hot water, my lord," Hadassah said to Habinnas.

"Yes. Yes, of course," Habinnas said, prying his hand free of his young wife's grasp.

"Don't leave me," Antonia said, sobbing. "Don't leave—"

"He won't leave you, my lady," Hadassah said, taking her hand. "He's sending Livilla for water."

"Oh, it's coming again! It's coming," Antonia moaned, her back arching. "I can't bear it! I can't bear it anymore. . . ."

Habinnas didn't return to the bed but stood with his fists pressed against his temples. "Artemis, almighty goddess, have mercy on her. Have mercy."

Hadassah placed one hand on Antonia's forehead and found her skin hot. Antonia held her breath, her eyes filling with tears as her face reddened. The cords in her neck stood out, and the tears ran from her eyes. She gritted her teeth and let out a deep moaning cry. Her hand tightened until Hadassah thought her own would be crushed.

When the contraction eased, Antonia sank back exhausted, sobbing. Hadassah's eyes blurred with tears, and she stroked the girl's forehead, wishing she could comfort her more. She glanced back at Alexander. "What can we do?" she whispered, but he merely stood watching grimly.

"Make it stop," Antonia whispered hoarsely. "Please, make it stop."

When Alexander said nothing, Hadassah leaned down. "We will not leave you," she said softly and dabbed the sweat from Antonia's forehead with a cloth.

"I must examine her," Alexander finally said. When Antonia tensed, he spoke quietly, explaining what he was doing and why. Antonia relaxed, for his hands were gentle. Her ease was short-lived, for another contraction was upon her. She groaned in agony as it built. Alexander did not remove his hands from her until she sank back, weeping. He straightened, and the look on his face filled Hadassah with anxiety.

"What's wrong?"

"The child is in the wrong position."

"What can you do?"

129

"I can perform an operation, take the baby out through her abdomen . . . but there are risks. I'll need Magonianus' permission to do it." He left the bedside.

Hadassah was filled with doubt as Alexander spoke to Habinnas Attalus Magonianus in a voice too low for her to hear.

"No!" Magonianus suddenly said in alarm. "If you cannot guarantee me she will survive, I will not permit it. She is what matters to me, not the babe. I will not allow you to risk her life!"

"Then there is only one other thing I know to do—" Alexander broke off, glancing at Hadassah as though hesitant to continue. Then, his face drawn and tense, he looked again at Magonianus and spoke quietly. Hadassah saw the older man's face turn even whiter, and he shook his head as though dazed.

"Are you sure? You can do nothing else?" Alexander shook his head, and Magonianus nodded slowly. "Then do what you must. But, by the gods, do it quickly so she doesn't suffer more."

Heart pounding, Hadassah looked at the instruments Alexander took from his leather carrying case. Her stomach knotted. She watched as he had Rashid move the table to the foot of the bed. He glanced up at her. "Give her a strong draft of white mandragora, and then go outside. Rashid will assist me."

"Mandragora will put her to sleep."

"It's best if she is asleep for what I have to do." Alexander placed a hooked knife, a decapitator, a cranioclast, and an embryotome near at hand.

Hadassah rose and blocked his way. "What do you mean to do to her that you would send me from the room?" she whispered, her hand on his arm as she looked at the fearsome instruments.

He leaned close, speaking in her ear. "She will die if I don't remove the child."

"Remove it?" she said weakly. She looked at the surgical instruments again and realized with a sickening jolt that he meant to dismember the child and extract it from the womb. "You can't do this, Alexander."

He caught hold of her arm and drew her firmly aside. Holding her in front of him, he spoke in an earnest whisper only she could hear. "Would you have them both die, Hadassah? The child is wedged inside her. Do you understand? The way it's positioned, it *can't* be born."

"Turn the child yourself."

"I can't," he said firmly. He held his hands out for her to see how large they were. "Can you?"

"You can't do this, Alexander."

"I don't like it any more than you do," he said in a low, fierce voice, his eyes full of desperation. "But there's nothing else to be done. Besides, the child is probably already dead. She's been lying in for two days. The mother is more important than the child."

"They are both important in God's sight."

"Go outside and wait until I call for you. I know you've no stomach for this part of medicine. It's best if you don't have to stand and watch. You can tend her afterward."

He started to step past her, but she caught his arm in a surprisingly strong grip. "Please, Alexander!"

"If you have a suggestion, Hadassah, I'll listen. Otherwise, stay out of the way. She can't wait." Seeming to confirm his words, Antonia cried out again.

Hadassah could see Alexander was not eager to do what he had said, but he had set his mind on what he thought must be done to save Antonia. She shook her head. "We must pray."

"Prayer isn't going to save that girl! I know what has to be done."

Hadassah knew only too well the low value placed upon a baby's life. Even when a child was born, there was a high chance of death. So high, in fact, that no law forbade the burial of an infant within the city walls, nor was a name given for the first week or more. Infants were disposed of in villa gardens and tossed into rubbish heaps. There was even a custom of placing a newborn infant in the foundation of a new building!

Hadassah glanced at Habinnas and knew she would gain no help from him. His only concern was for his young wife.

Seeing her glance at the idol maker, Alexander grasped her arm in a painful grip. "I can't let that girl die, Hadassah. Do you have any idea who this man is? He's one of the wealthiest men in Ephesus. He eats at the table of the proconsul. If his wife dies in my care, my medical career is *over*. Do you understand? *Over!* Finished before it's even begun. I'll have to leave the city and hope I can start somewhere else."

Hadassah met his eyes unflinchingly. "Do not be so eager to destroy a human life. Ask for help from the one who created Antonia *and* her child."

Alexander drew back. He could not see her face behind the

131

veils, but he heard the conviction of her words. "I beseech him then, and you. Call upon your god. I beg you to do so," he said in a hushed voice. "But pray hard and *fast,* and may he hear you quickly because I can't give you any more time than it will take me to get everything ready for the surgery." He turned from her, a cold fear taking hold of his heart. If there was any other way to save Antonia, he would take it. But time had left him no choice. He would have to cut the child in half and crush its skull in order to extract it from the girl—and if he didn't do it carefully and soon, she might die. No one would care that he hadn't been brought here until the last moment. The blame would fall on him.

As Alexander returned his attention to his instruments, Hadassah's heart cried out in anguish. All of Alexander's faith was in his own knowledge, in what other masters had taught him. And that was not enough.

Hadassah returned to Antonia. Another contraction had already begun, and she was whimpering pitifully, her hands twisting in the damp linens as the pain increased. She had no more strength to even scream. "My baby," she moaned. "Save my baby."

"O God, please . . . ," Hadassah said and placed her hands on Antonia's distended abdomen. Her lips moved, though no sound came as she cried out to the Lord for his intervention.

O God, you are the Creator of this woman and child. Save them both! Turn things aright that they both might live. Turn things aright that Alexander will not do what's in his mind to do and bring sin upon himself. Please, Jesus, let them see your power and your love.

Antonia gave a deep cry, and Habinnas started toward the bed. "Leave her alone! You're hurting her more!"

Rashid stopped him. Habinnas fought to free himself, and Rashid slammed him up against the mural of sprites, uncaring how rich and powerful he was.

At the sound of Antonia's moans, Hadassah wept. "Please, Jesus, oh please," she whispered, moving her hands in a gentle caress over the child held captive in the womb. "Please, Lord, hear us. Please have mercy on her and her child. Turn the babe aright and bring him forth."

The child moved.

Hadassah left her hands lightly on Antonia and felt the baby turn, slowly, smoothly, as though invisible hands had gently taken hold of him. She wept harder, filled with joy, and her tears dripped onto the taut skin.

Antonia cried out again, but differently this time, and Alexander, standing close by with the hooked knife, saw what was happening and dropped it.

Habinnas had stopped shouting and fighting against Rashid's hold. "What's happening?" he cried.

"The baby has turned," Alexander said, unable to keep the excitement from his voice. There was no time to place Antonia in the birthing chair. He braced himself with one knee on the end of the bed and leaned forward. Another contraction had already begun, and as it did, the babe slid smoothly from Antonia's body into his hands. She gave a gusty exhalation and sank back.

Alexander laughed, looking down at the child in his hands. "You've a son, Magonianus!" he said with a mixture of awe and relief. "Come take a look at him," he urged as he cut the cord and tied it.

Hadassah stepped back, trembling violently, enraptured by what she saw.

Rashid released Habinnas, and the idol maker stood motionless for a moment, hearing the cry of his newborn son. Livilla was there to take him from Alexander.

"A son, Habinnas," Antonia rasped, exhausted. "I've given you a son. . . ." She tried to rise enough to see her child, but hadn't the strength to do so. She sagged against the damp bed, her breathing slowed and relaxed, her eyelids closing.

After a brief glance at the squalling child in Livilla's arms, Habinnas knelt down beside the bed. Seeing the blood on the sheets, he buried his head in his wife's neck. His shoulders shook. "Never again. I swear. Never again will you go through this."

"Tend to the child," Alexander said to Hadassah, massaging Antonia's abdomen so that her body would expel the placenta. "I'll see to her."

Livilla put the child in her arms and drew back from her, eyes wide. She was shaking noticeably, and Hadassah frowned slightly, wondering what was wrong with the slave girl.

Hadassah washed the baby carefully in a basin of warm water. Then she placed him gently on soft linen and rubbed his body all over with salt to prevent any infection. Remembering how her mother had wrapped Leah, she did likewise. Murmuring to him, she wrapped the infant tightly so that he was perfectly firm and solid, like a small mummy. She took a small strip of white linen and bound his head, passing the shawl under his chin and across his forehead in small folds. Then she lifted him, secure and warm in his swaddling clothes, and carried him to his mother.

Habinnas rose at her approach. "Livilla will take him to his wet nurse."

"He will not be given to a wet nurse. He needs his mother," Hadassah said and leaned down. "Antonia," she said softly, brushing the girl's brow. "Your son." Smiling sleepily, Antonia shifted slightly, and Hadassah laid the infant down beside her. Antonia gave a soft, gasping laugh of joy as the baby's mouth closed on her nipple. Her expression fell after a moment.

"I have no milk," Antonia said, blinking back tears and struggling against exhaustion.

Hadassah stroked her cheek gently. "Don't worry. You will." Already Antonia's eyes were drifting closed.

The room was very quiet. Hadassah continued to stroke Antonia's cheek, giving thanks to God for sparing her and the child. She felt joy swelling within her and longed to sing praises as she had once done, but the scars she bore from the lion's attack in the arena had done more than disfigure her. Ensuing infections had taken most of her voice. Yet, she knew it didn't really matter. God had heard her prayer. He now heard the singing of her heart.

Blinking back tears, she raised her head. Habinnas Attulus Magonianus stood across the bed from her, staring at her. She saw in his eyes what she had seen in Livilla's a moment before— fear.

Alexander stepped back from the bed, having finished binding Antonia. He gave instructions to Livilla concerning her mistress' care. Turning from Magonianus' stare, Hadassah approached, only to have Livilla bow deeply. Hadassah told her to change the infant's swaddling clothes once a day. "Wash him carefully and rub him again with salt. Then wrap him as you saw me do. Do not give him over to a wet nurse but allow his mother to tend him."

"It shall be as you say, my lady," Livilla said, bowing again.

Habinnas spoke to another servant. He left his wife's bedside and approached Alexander and Hadassah as they packed up unused instruments and medicines. "I do not even know your name."

Alexander introduced himself, but hesitated when Habinnas

looked pointedly at Hadassah. "My assistant," he said, withhold-
ing her name for a reason he couldn't quite grasp. He looked at
Rashid. "We are finished here," he said. "You may take her
back."

As Rashid bent and caught Hadassah up in his arms, Alexander turned to Magonianus again, ignoring Hadassah's soft protest
as the Arab carried her from the room. "How is it a man of your
position sent for a physician who practices outside the public
baths?" Alexander said, curious, but also wanting to distract
Habinnas' attention from Hadassah.

"Cattulus removed himself from Ephesus," Magonianus said,
and Alexander recognized the name of a prominent physician.
Cattulus was reputed as one of the finest physicians in the city
and treated only those of wealth and position. "I learned of his
disgrace when it was too late to make other arrangements,"
Habinnas said grimly. "I sent my wife's slave to find help. How
she came to find you, I don't know, but I thank the gods that she
did."

"God sent her to us," Hadassah had said on the way here.
Alexander frowned. Had he?

"Make sure she is warm," he said, nodding to Antonia. "She
will need rest. I'll return tomorrow and see how she's doing."

"Will she come back with you?" Habinnas said, nodding
toward the doorway through which Rashid had carried Hadassah.

"Not unless you wish it," Alexander said cautiously.

"Yes. I wish to know more about her."

Alexander straightened, his leather carrying case securely
under his arm. "What is it you wish to know?"

"I saw what she did with my own eyes. The woman has great
power. Who is she? What god does she serve?"

Alexander hesitated again, unsure of the unease he felt stirring
within him. Might this man move in the same social circles as
Hadassah's masters? If so, would revealing her identity put her in
danger? Whoever had owned her had sent her to die in the arena.
If they learned she was still alive, would they take possession and
send her there again?

"Who is she?" Habinnas asked again.

"If she wishes to reveal herself to you, she will do so," Alexander said and started for the door. A servant stood to one side of it,
a small cedar box in his hands.

"Wait," Habinnas said. He took the box from the servant and held it out to Alexander. "Payment for your services," he said.

The box was heavy.

"See that the physician reaches home safely," Habinnas told the slave and then ordered another to have a sleeping couch brought in so that he could stay close to his wife and son.

Alexander went outside, gave directions to his booth to Habinnas' four litter bearers, then stepped into the luxurious box. As the slaves lifted the litter, he closed the thin privacy curtains and leaned back wearily into the soft cushions. Though exhausted, his mind was whirring.

Tonight had been momentous! Just how momentous filled him with disquiet.

He reached the booth before Rashid and Hadassah. With a twinge of conscience, he realized he hadn't even looked for them on the way. He entered the booth and put his instruments and medicines away. Sitting at his writing table, he mixed soot and water and wrote on his scroll the events that had just occurred. Leaning back slightly, he looked at what he had written with dissatisfaction:

> *Hadassah laid her hands upon Antonia's abdomen and wept. As she did so, her tears fell upon the woman, and the child turned and came forth.*

Bottled tears were often used as a curative. Was there healing power in Hadassah's? Or had it been her touch that had brought on the miracle? Or had it been the words she spoke silently to her god?

Someone kicked the partition, and Alexander rose and pulled it back. Rashid entered, Hadassah in his arms. She was asleep. Rashid lowered her gently to the beddings on the floor near the back of the booth and covered her carefully. He rose and turned to Alexander. "She must rest."

"It's almost sunrise," Alexander said. "Patients will be gathering outside soon."

His jaw set. "You must send them away."

Alexander's mouth tipped at his tone. "Are you sure you were a slave, Rashid, and not a master?" He held up his hand and added, "You are right." He took a writing tablet and wrote a short message on it. "Put this outside on the ledge. We will hope those who come can read."

Rashid read it.

"Does it meet with your approval?" Alexander said dryly.

"Yes, my lord."

When Rashid came back inside, Alexander nodded toward the small cedar box on the counter. "Take a look," he said, sprinkling sand on his notes.

Rashid opened it. He took one of the gold coins out and turned it in his fingers. An aureus. "A fortune," he said.

"Habinnas prizes his wife's life very highly. There's enough there to rent an apartment and buy more supplies." His mouth flattened. "I have a feeling we will be needing both soon."

Rashid put the coin back in the box and closed it. "Yes, my lord. Tonight opened a new path. Hadassah touched that woman and brought the child forth. Magonianus saw. He will tell others . . . and those others will come."

Alexander nodded grimly. "I know." He poured the sand back into the small bowl. "As long as her compassion was limited to commoners or slaves like you, we've had no problem other than more patients than we can handle. Now there's danger."

Rashid's gaze darkened. "Magonianus moves in exalted circles."

"Yes, as do the masters who sent Hadassah to die in the arena," Alexander said, seeing Rashid fully comprehended the threat. He rolled the scroll and tucked it into a cubicle above the writing table. "As Hadassah said, legally she still belongs to those who purchased her."

"You are also in danger for harboring her, my lord."

Alexander hadn't considered that. "There's that, too, I suppose. The problem is what do we do now? She has a valuable gift, and there are many who need it." The thought of what could happen if Hadassah's owners discovered she was alive propelled Alexander from his stool. He paced in frustration. "I'm not about to give her back to anyone who sent her into the arena to die, no matter their reasons!"

"Find out their names, and I will kill them."

Astonished, Alexander stared at him and saw the dark fierceness in the Arab's eyes. "You leave me in no doubt you could do such a thing," he said, appalled. He shook his head. "There are sides to your character that worry me, Rashid. I'm a physician,

137

not an assassin. I strive to save life, not take it. In that, Hadassah and I are alike."

"I will protect her, whatever the cost."

"Hadassah wouldn't approve your means of protection. In fact, it would cause her tremendous grief."

"She need not know."

"She would know. I don't know how, but she would." He looked at Hadassah, lying asleep on the mat. "She's a strange one. She can see into people and know things about them. She says it's only because she listens and looks, but I think it's more. I think her god reveals things to her." She had curled on her side like a child. He stepped over and gently removed the veils, exposing the disfiguring scars. Gently he touched her marked face, careful not to awaken her. "The fact that she's alive is a testimony to her god's power. My abilities as a physician wouldn't have been enough." Straightening, he looked at Rashid. "Perhaps we should leave it to her god to go on protecting her."

Rashid said nothing.

Alexander looked at the fathomless face. "Do you know why she covers herself?"

"She is ashamed."

Alexander shook his head. "She has not one particle of vanity in her. She covers her scars because they disturb others. No other reason than that. People see the mark of the lion on her. They fail to see what it means."

He bent down and smoothed back the tendrils of hair. His heart ached for her. From the moment he had seen her walk into the middle of the arena, he had been drawn to her. She was like the slaves at the Asklepion: cast away and forgotten, her life meaningless in the scheme of things. And yet her sweetness and humility were like a beacon to Alexander's heart—and to many others. Scarred and broken, Hadassah had a resilience that defied reason. Sometimes the love she expressed to a patient by a light touch or softly spoken word pierced him. It was the love he wanted to show . . . the love he seemed to lack.

He cared. Hadassah *loved*.

He shook his head in wonder. How was it possible for anyone who had been through what she had suffered to be the way she was?

"I've never known anyone like her, Rashid," he said, rubbing a strand of dark hair between his fingers. "I will do nothing that would displease her." He was startled to realize that his voice was shaking with the intensity of his emotions, and he straightened quickly. He looked at the Arab, staring hard into his dark eyes. "Nor will you."

"I have sworn to protect her, my lord."

"Then protect her, but do so in a manner pleasing to Hadassah and not yourself."

"My life belongs to her. Because of that, I can't let someone take hers."

Alexander's mouth tipped. "She would say your life belongs to her god, just as hers does." He let out his breath and rubbed his neck wearily. "Don't ask me for answers. I haven't any. Perhaps we are only borrowing trouble. Nothing may come of tonight, neither opportunity nor threat. Let's get some sleep. We can face whatever comes much better with some rest."

But rest was elusive.

Alexander lay awake, thinking, going over and over the night's events in his mind. Wonder over what had happened mixed with a troubling confusion when he considered the intensity of his feelings at the thought of Hadassah being in danger. He tried to tell himself that it was only natural he be worried. After all, Hadassah was a capable and valuable assistant. But something deep inside told him there was much more to it than that.

Finally someone knocked on the partition and called out an appeal in Hebrew. Alexander recognized a few words and knew it was not him for whom the man called, but Hadassah. Apparently, Rashid was having equal difficulty sleeping, for he rose swiftly and opened the partition just enough to speak to the intruder upon their sleep.

"You fool! Can't you read?"

"I must speak with Rapha."

"The physician has left the city and will return tomorrow."

"Rapha. I want to speak to Rapha."

"She's not here. Go away! There are other physicians at the baths. Take your trouble to them." He shut the partition firmly and lay down on his bed again, his face rigid as he saw Hadassah had been awakened.

She sat up, rubbing her face. She grimaced as she looked toward the crack of light coming through the partition. "It's morning."

"No," Rashid lied. "The moon merely shines."

"So brightly?"

"Go back to sleep, my lady. There is no one to disturb you."

"I heard someone—"

"You heard no one," he urged gently. "You were dreaming you were back in Judea."

She rubbed her face, then raised an eyebrow at him. "If I was dreaming, how is it you know they spoke in Hebrew?" She reached for her veils.

Alexander got up. "I'll look," he said, fully aware she couldn't ignore someone's plea for help no matter how badly she herself needed rest. He stepped over her and went to the partition. Peering out the crack, he saw a man walking away dejectedly. "There's no one standing outside," he said truthfully.

"You're sure?"

"Absolutely." He went to the back of the booth, where he took down a skin bag. Pouring water into Hadassah's small clay cup, he added a portion of mandragora and took it to her. "Drink this," he said, holding the cup to her lips. "You must rest or you'll be no good to anyone. I'll awaken you before I open the booth."

Thirsty and exhausted, she drank. "What about Antonia?"

"Antonia is sleeping as you should be. We'll go and see her tomorrow." He covered her again and remained hunkered down beside her until the drug took effect. As soon as she drifted to sleep, he returned to his own mat.

Rashid sat watching Hadassah.

"Rest, Rashid. She won't wake up for hours."

The Arab reclined. "Did you hear what the Jew called her?"

"I heard. What does it mean?" Rashid told him. Alexander thought for a long moment, then nodded in satisfaction. "I think we have our answer."

"Answer to what?"

"How to protect her. Henceforth, Hadassah won't be known by name, Rashid. She'll be known by the title just given her. She'll be known as Rapha."

The healer.

13

Marcus rode south for Jerusalem, following the road through Mizpah. He continued on to Ramah, where he stopped to purchase almonds, figs, unleavened bread, and a skin of wine. People withdrew from him. He saw a woman gather her children close and hurry them inside a small clay house like a hen protecting her brood of chicks against a predator.

He understood when he saw Jerusalem.

As he rode toward it, he felt the pall of death over the land. All Rome had talked about the conquest and destruction of Jerusalem. It had simply been another uprising successfully crushed by Rome's legions. Now he saw for himself the annihilation of which Rome was capable.

Crossing the arid valley, he was staggered by what he saw. Where once a great city had stood were broken-down walls and buildings, blackened remains of burned homes—it was a land stripped bare of life. In a wadi behind a mount were tangles of bleached bones, as though thousands had been tossed heedlessly into the pit and left unburied. Two strategic towers had survived the demolition and stood like lone sentinels in the rubble.

Jerusalem, the "Dwelling of Peace," was peaceful indeed. It had been reduced to an open graveyard.

Marcus made camp on a small hillside beneath a scraggly olive tree. Looking over the small valley, he could see the shattered remains of Jerusalem's ancient walls. He slept fitfully, disturbed by the echoing silence of so many dead.

He awakened at the sound of hobnailed sandals on rock. He rose and saw a Roman legionnaire coming toward him.

"Who are you and why are you here?" the soldier demanded.

Marcus curbed his annoyance and gave his name. "I've come to see the house of the god of the Jews."

The legionnaire laughed once. "What's left of it is up there on that hill. They call it Mount Moriah, but it's nothing when compared to Vesuvius. You won't find much left of the temple. We've torn it down and razed it for materials to rebuild barracks and the township you see over there."

"Were you with Titus during the siege?"

The legionnaire looked at him enigmatically. "I was in Germania. Under Civilis."

Marcus studied the man more closely. Civilis had rebelled against Caesar and fought with the Germanic tribes during that brief uprising. Domitian had commanded the legions that brought the frontier back to order. Civilis had been brought to Rome to die and one out of every ten men under his command had been put to the sword in the field. Apparently the rest had been sent to duty stations throughout the Empire. Judea was considered the worst.

"Decimation has a way of restoring one to loyalty," the soldier said, looking squarely into Marcus' eyes. "Sending me here made sure of it." His mouth twisted in a bitter smile.

Marcus stared back at him, unafraid. "I came to see the temple."

"There is no temple. Not anymore. Titus' orders were to tear it down stone by stone until nothing was left." His mouth tipped. "We left one section of wall." He looked at Marcus again. "Why are you so interested in the temple?"

"Their god was supposed to dwell in it."

"If there ever was a god here, there's nothing left of him now." The soldier's gaze swept across the stretch of devastation. "Not that Rome will ever convince the Jews. They still come here. Some of them just wander through the ruins. Others stand by that cursed wall and weep. We send them away, but they still come back. Sometimes I think we should tear the whole thing down and crush every stone to dust." He let out his breath and looked at Marcus again. "Nothing will come of it. There aren't enough men left in all Judea to make any serious trouble for Rome. Not for generations."

"Why did you tell me you were part of Civilis' rebellion?" Marcus asked.

"As a warning."

"A warning against what?"

"I've fought campaign after campaign for twenty-three years so that men like you could recline on comfortable couches in Rome and live a life of ease and safety." His hard mouth curved sardonically, his hard eyes flicking over Marcus' expensive tunic and brass and leather tooled belt. "You've the stamp of Rome all over you. Take warning. I won't raise a finger to save your neck. Not here in this place. Not now."

Marcus watched him walk away. Shaking his head, he picked up his mantle and put it around his shoulders.

He left his horse hobbled on the small mount and went into the ruins. As he picked his way through the fallen stones and gutted buildings, his thoughts were focused entirely on Hadassah. She had been here when the city lay under siege. She had been hungry and afraid. She had been here when Titus broke through. She had seen thousands put to the sword and crucified.

And yet, never once had he seen the look in her eyes that he had just seen in those of a Roman soldier.

She had given the small insignificant coins of her *peculium* to a Roman woman who had no money for bread. And she had given it freely, knowing the woman's son had been a legionnaire who had taken part in the destruction of her homeland.

She had lost everyone here, father and mother, brother and sister. Somewhere among these broken-down buildings and the blackened rubble lay the forgotten bones of those she had loved.

The Jews believed their god had promised that Abraham's descendants would become as numerous as the stars in the heaven. The multitude had been reduced to the thousands, and those scattered across the Empire, yoked to Rome.

Marcus looked around him and wondered how Hadassah had survived at all.

"God has not deserted me." Her words echoed in his mind.

"Here is the evidence, Hadassah," he whispered, the dry hot wind stirring up dust around him.

"God has not deserted me."

Marcus sat on a block of granite. He remembered clearly the first time he had seen her in Rome. She had been standing among other slaves Enoch had brought back from the market—men of Judea, emaciated of body and broken of spirit. And she had stood among them, small, thin, shaved bald, eyes too large for her face . . . eyes clear of animosity, but full of fear. He had been struck by her frailty then, but hadn't felt pity. She was a Jew, wasn't she? Hadn't her people brought destruction on themselves by civil war and insurrection?

Now, here, he saw Roman retribution.

Did any people deserve so great a devastation as this? He hadn't cared then. Without thought of what a slave girl had been

143

through, he had looked at her and seen nothing to interest him. He had said she was ugly, unaware of the beauty within her, the gentle spirit, her capacity for love and loyalty.

She had been a child during the fall of Jerusalem. As a child, she had seen thousands die of bloody civil war, starvation, annihilation. Men. Women. Children. How many thousands had she seen nailed to crosses around this city? How many more had she walked beside on the journey north to arenas and slave markets?

And still, with evidence of the physical trauma she had suffered and the yoke of slavery around her neck, there had been a sweetness in her face that day in the villa garden. A sweetness that remained unchanged even to that day when she had walked out into the sunlight of the arena, her arms spread.

"God will never desert me. . . ."

He groaned and put his head in his hands.

Sitting here in this desolate place, he could believe her god had delivered her from certain death as a child. Why then had he abandoned her later when her love of him had been even stronger?

Looking up at the holy mount, Marcus' mind whirred with questions. He felt strangely connected to this landscape of devastation. In a sense, it reflected the devastation of his own life when he lost Hadassah. The light had gone out in his life, even as it had gone out in Jerusalem. With her, he had felt alive. In her, he had known hope. Near her, he had tasted joy. She had awakened in him a yearning that tore his soul open, and now he was left bleeding in the aftermath. Wounded. Lost.

He clenched his hands. He shouldn't have *asked* her to become his wife. He should've taken her into his home and made her so. Had he done it, she would still be alive.

Around him, heavy silence lay like a shroud over the ruins of Jerusalem. He could almost hear the screams of the dying . . . the weeping of thousands echoing across the valley.

He heard someone crying now.

Marcus listened and then rose and went toward the sound.

An old man stood weeping before the scarred remains of the temple's last remnant of wall. His palms and forehead were pressed against the cold stone, his shoulders shaking with sobs. Marcus stood behind him and watched with a sense of inexplicable sorrow and shame.

The man reminded him of faithful Enoch back in Rome, steward of the family villa. Marcus' father had been tolerant of all religions and had allowed his slaves to worship whatever god in whatever manner they chose. Enoch was a righteous Jew. He followed the letter of the Judaic law. Following the letter of the Law was the very foundation of his faith, the rock on which his religion was built. Yet, Enoch had never had the opportunity to make the necessary sacrifices his laws demanded. Only here, in Jerusalem, would that have been possible. Only here could Enoch have given the appropriate offering to the chosen priesthood to sacrifice on the consecrated altar.

Now, nothing was left of that hallowed altar.

Pax Romana, Marcus thought, watching the old man grieving for what was lost. Judea was finally at peace, and that peace was built upon blood and death. What cost peace?

Had Titus known how great was his victory over the Jews? Had he realized how complete his triumph? He had torn away from them more than buildings; he had ripped the very heart out of their religion.

The people could go on studying the laws. They could go on prophesying in their synagogues. But for what purpose? To what end? Without the temple, without the priesthood, without the sacrifices for the atonement of sin, their religion was empty. It was finished. When the walls of the temple came tumbling down, so, too, did the power of their almighty unseen god.

"Oh, Marcus, beloved, God cannot be contained in a temple. . . ."

Groaning, Marcus pressed his hands over his ears. "Why do you speak to me like this?"

The old man heard and turned. When he saw Marcus, he hurried away.

Marcus moaned. It was as though Hadassah stood beside him among the ruins of this ancient city. Why did the echo of her words come so vividly to life here in this place of death and destruction? He spread his arms wide. "There's nothing here! Your god is dead!"

"You can't contain God in a temple."

"Then where is he? *Where is he?*" Only the sound of his voice echoed off the remnant of wall.

"Seek and ye shall find . . . seek . . . seek . . ."

Marcus left the shadow of the war-scarred wall and picked his way among the rubble until he found the center of the temple. He stood upon a large half-buried boulder and looked around.

Was this the same rock on which Abraham had laid his son Isaac for sacrifice? Was this the inner sanctuary, the Holy of Holies? Had it been here that the covenant was made between God and Abraham?

Marcus looked out over the hills. Somewhere out there Jesus of Nazareth had been crucified, outside the gates of the city but within sight of the place where the promise had been given. "God sent his only begotten Son to live among men and be crucified for our sins . . . . through this Christ, all men can be saved and have eternal life," Satyros, the ship captain, had said.

Was it coincidence that Jesus of Nazareth had been crucified during Passover? Was it coincidence that the beginning of the end for Jerusalem had begun during the same celebration?

Thousands had poured into this city for celebration—and been trapped here by civil war and Titus' legions. Had everything that happened been by chance, or was there a plan and a message to all mankind?

Perhaps if he rode to Jamnia, he would learn something from the leaders of the faith. Satyros had told him a Pharisee named Rabbi Jochanaan had become the new religious leader and had moved the Sanhedrin there. As quickly as the idea came to him, Marcus dismissed it. The answers he needed would not come from any man but from God himself, if God existed. And he wasn't sure who he was looking for anymore. Did he search for Adonai, God of the Jews, or Jesus of Nazareth, whom Hadassah had worshiped? Which one did he want to face? Or were they one and the same, as Satyros said?

A hot wind blew across the ruins, stirring up dust.

Bitterness filled Marcus' mouth. "She chose you over me. Wasn't that enough?"

No still, small voice spoke to him in the wind. No echo of the words Hadassah had spoken to him. Bereft, Marcus' throat closed. Had he really expected an answer to come from thin air?

Stepping off the slab of dark stone, he kicked a blackened chunk of marble aside and headed back. When he reached the small slope, he sat beneath the shade of the olive tree, hot and frustrated, soul-weary.

He would find no answers here within this dead city.

Perhaps if he saw it from the outside, he would understand

why this place was so special to the Jews' faith. He wanted to understand. He had to.

Removing the hobbles, he mounted his horse and rode toward the hills. For the next three days, he traveled through the wadis, across the valleys, and along the hillsides, looking at Jerusalem from all angles. Nothing commended it.

"O Lord God of Abraham, why did you choose this place?" he said, bemused and unaware he was inquiring of a god in whom he claimed no belief. The hills of Jerusalem were unfit for agriculture, possessed no valuable mineral deposits, held no strategic military importance. It was fully eight miles to the nearest trade route. "Why here?"

"The promise . . ."

"'On this rock will your faith be built . . . ,'" he said aloud, not remembering where he had heard it. Was it something Satyros had said to him, or something he imagined?

Abraham's rock, he thought. A rock of sacrifice. That was all Jerusalem had to commend it.

Or was it?

He didn't care anymore. Maybe he hadn't come to find God at all. Maybe he had just come to this place because Hadassah had been here and he was drawn to it for that reason alone. He wanted to walk where she had walked. To breathe the air she had breathed. He wanted to feel close to her.

As night came, he wrapped himself in his mantle and lay down upon the earth to rest. Sleep came slowly and with it confusing dreams.

Press on . . . press on . . . a voice seemed to whisper. His questions wouldn't be answered here.

He awakened abruptly and saw a legionnaire standing above him, silhouetted against the rising sun. "So, you're still here." The mocking voice was familiar.

Marcus rose. "Yes. I'm still here."

"Bethany is two miles east, and there's a new inn. You look as though you could use a good night's sleep."

"Thanks for the advice," Marcus said wryly.

"Find what you're looking for?"

"Not yet, but I've seen all of Jerusalem I need to see."

The legionnaire's smile verged on insult. "Where to now?"

"Jericho and the Jordan Valley."

"There's a company riding out to patrol that road in about two hours. Ride with them."

"If I wanted company, I'd hire it."

"The death of one fool can cost the lives of many good men."

Marcus' eyes narrowed coldly. "Meaning?"

"Rome frowns upon the murder of its citizens, no matter how they dare the fates."

"On my head be the fault of whatever happens."

"Good," the man said with a half smile. "Because I've performed all the crucifixions I intend to in my lifetime. Put your head in a lion's mouth, expect to have it taken off." He started to walk away and then turned and looked back at Marcus, his hard face oddly perplexed. "Why are you here?"

"I'm looking for the truth."

"The truth about what?"

Marcus hesitated and then gave him a self-deprecating smile. "God." He expected the soldier to laugh at him.

The legionnaire looked at him for a long moment, then gave a single, slow nod and walked away without a word.

Marcus rode east toward Qumran. The "city of salt" lay on high ground near the Dead Sea and had once been inhabited primarily by a Jewish sect of holy men called Essenes, who studied and worshiped there. With the threat of invasion, the holy men had departed, hiding their precious scrolls as well as themselves in the caves of the Judean wilderness, leaving the city to Roman troops.

When Marcus reached the junction, he took the fork heading northeast for Jericho. He rode along a deep wadi cut by water erosion into the arid slopes that descended toward the Jordan Valley.

The sun rose hot and heavy, pressing down on him with each hour that passed. Pausing, he removed his mantle and loosened the skin bag from his saddle. He drank deeply and squirted some of the water over his face.

His horse blew out suddenly and sidestepped.

A lizard probably startled him, Marcus thought, leaning down to pat him and whisper soothing words.

Something moved at the edge of his sight, along the rim of the wadi. He studied the spot carefully but saw nothing. Turning slightly in his saddle, he looked all around cautiously. Somewhere close by, a soft cascade of rocks trickled down the steep incline of the wadi. Marcus assumed it was another goat like the others he had seen a few miles back.

He leaned down to secure the skin water bag to his saddle, just as a rock came flying at his head. The horse let out a high-pitched whinny and backed sharply, and Marcus quickly straightened in the saddle.

Four men leaped up from their hiding place along the rim of the wadi and ran toward him. Swearing, Marcus tried to get control of his horse. One of the men scooped up a rock and armed his sling as he ran. Marcus ducked as another rock flew past his head. The horse reared sharply, and Marcus barely held his seat as one of the men reached him and tried to drag him off.

As the horse came down, two robbers went for the bridle. Marcus kicked one man in the face, knocking him back. Another leaped. Dodging, Marcus let the momentum take the man across the saddle and flipped him off the horse.

Terrified, the horse let out another high-pitched whinny and reared again, lifting one man off the ground and breaking the hold of the other. Someone grabbed Marcus from the side. Jabbing his elbow into the attacker's face, Marcus sank his heels into the horse's flanks. The animal leaped forward, riding straight for another sicarius in front of him. The man managed to dive to one side out of the way, then, coming to his feet, he swung his sling.

Pain exploded in Marcus' head as the stone struck its mark. His fingers loosened on the reins, and he lost his balance. He could hear the legionnaire's words echoing around him: *"Put your head in a lion's mouth, expect to have it taken off."* He felt hands on him, dragging him from the saddle. He tried to fight them off, but it was no use. He hit the ground hard, the breath knocked out of him. As he gasped for air, one of the sicarii kicked him in the head, another in the side. A final kick to his groin consumed him in fiery pain, and he slid gratefully down a funnel of darkness.

He roused far too soon.

"Stinking Roman pig!" someone said and spit on him.

In a haze of pain, Marcus felt hands yanking in a frenzy at his possessions. Someone pulled the gold pendant from around his neck. Another dragged off his belt, taking with it the gold aurei hidden within it. They picked him over like vultures. When he felt one of them trying to slide the gold signet ring his father had given him from his finger, Marcus clenched his fist. A backhanded blow was delivered to the side of his head. He tasted blood and fought for consciousness. His fingers loosened, and he felt his father's signet ring stripped from him.

Voices came through the crushing fog.

"Don't cut him yet. The tunic is good linen. Get it off him first."

"Hurry up! I hear a Roman patrol coming."

"The tunic will bring a good price."

"Do you crave being nailed to a cross?"

The tunic was stripped from him.

"Dump him in the wadi. If they find him, they'll come looking for us."

"Hurry up!" one of them hissed, and they grasped his heels and dragged him.

Marcus groaned as rock tore his bare back. They dropped him near the edge. "Hurry up!" One man began to run while the one who remained drew a curved knife.

"Roman *raca*," the man said and spit in Marcus' face. He saw the blade come down and instinctively rolled. He felt the knife slice along his ribcage as he fell over the edge of the wadi. He hit a narrow ledge, then rolled and slid down the jagged bank. The man above him cursed roundly. The others were shouting from a distance. The sound of hooves beat against the earth.

Groaning, Marcus clawed for a handhold. The searing pain in his side took away his breath. As he looked up toward the ledge, his vision doubled and blurred, the world spinning around him. Fighting nausea, he lay helpless, halfway down the steep bank of the wadi, wedged against an outcropping of rocks.

The sound of horses came closer.

Marcus tried to call out, but the words came out in a deep groan. He tried to pull himself up, but fell back and slid a few more feet down the steep incline.

The horses were on the road just above him.

"Help me . . . ," he rasped, fighting to stay conscious. "Help me . . ."

The sound of hooves receded and a cloud of dust drifted down into the wadi.

Silence fell. No bird sang. No breeze rustled the meager grass or brittle brush. There was only the sun beating down on him, an orb of hot, merciless light.

And then there was nothing.

Hadassah arranged the small amphoras, vials, and boxes on the shelf while Rashid and Alexander carried in an examining table. She had been thinking of Marcus all morning. She closed her eyes, wondering why unease filled her. She had not glimpsed him since that day he had bumped into her before the baths. Why was he so strongly in her mind now?

God, wherever he is, whatever he is doing, watch over him and protect him.

She returned to her work and tried to concentrate on putting the drugs and medications in the proper order. Alexander and Rashid had gone out again, and she could hear them talking as they went down the steps.

The money Magonianus had given Alexander for the safe delivery of his son was already spent on renting these grander, more spacious quarters closer to the center of Ephesus and the medical school where Phlegon taught.

"It's a risk, I know," Alexander said when he told Hadassah of his decision the morning after Antonia's baby had been safely delivered into the world. "But I think we're going to need better accommodations for our patients."

"The patients you've served near the baths won't come there."

"They might, and if they don't, others will. Friends of Magonianus."

"And have they more need than the others?"

"No," Alexander said, "but they can pay, and I need money to further my studies."

"What of Boethus and his wife and children? What of Ephicharis and Helena?"

"We're not deserting them. I'm sending messages to all the patients we've seen and telling them where we can be found should they need us further."

Hadassah was dismayed at the haste with which he was making decisions—and the direction those decisions were taking him.

He tipped her face tenderly. "You must trust me, Rapha."

She drew back slightly. "Why do you call me that?"

"It's what people are calling you."

"But it is the Lord who—"

He put his fingertip over her lips. "Performed the miracle. Yes, I know you believe that. Then believe it was the Lord who provided the name."

"For what purpose?"

"To protect your identity from those who've tried to destroy you. Magonianus moves in the circles of the wealthy and powerful. It'd help if you told me the name of the family who owned you, so we could avoid them. Since you won't . . ."

She turned her face away, but he turned it back again, lifting her chin and looking into her eyes. "Hadassah, you're too important to me now. I won't risk losing you."

Her heart took a startled leap. *Important in what ways?* she wondered, searching his eyes.

"What you did last night . . ."

"I did nothing," she said insistently.

"You prayed. God heard and did as you asked."

She saw clearly his thinking. "No. You can't manipulate God, Alexander. Don't ever think it. You can't pray in hopes of getting what you want. It's God's will that prevails. It was God who saved Antonia and her son. God, not I."

"He heard you."

"No more than he hears you," she said, her eyes brimming with tears.

He cupped her face. "That may be so, and if it is, he hears me thanking him now for bringing you into my life. I was afraid for you last night. So was Rashid. And then the answer came as clearly as someone shouting at the partition." He laughed. *"Rapha.* So simple. And so shall you be called." He saw her concern. "Set your mind at rest."

But everything happened so quickly, she could scarcely think.

What Alexander and Rashid had suspected would happen, did. When they had arrived at Magonianus' residence late that afternoon, they had been immediately ushered into Antonia's chambers. She was already receiving company. The sleeping infant had been cradled in the new mother's arms while three women hovered, whispering, laughing, and admiring him. Magonianus stood by with the proud airs of a new father.

He had seen them first and put his hand on his young wife's shoulder. "They are here, my love."

Everyone had turned toward them and fell silent. Alexander's hand had tightened beneath Hadassah's arm as they approached the bed. Hadassah had felt the intent curiosity of the three women and lowered her head slightly as though they could see beneath the veils.

"Rapha and I have returned to see how you are, my lady. You are looking well," Alexander had said, grinning down at Antonia.

"She is indeed well." Magonianus' eyes had been shining.

Antonia had smiled up at him and then looked at Hadassah. "Thank you," she whispered and held the baby out slightly. "Will you hold him?"

Hadassah had taken the child carefully in her arms. "O Lord, bless this child. Keep him well and raise him up to be your child," she had murmured, touching the soft, velvety cheek. His head moved slightly, and the tiny mouth worked as though nursing. She gave a breathless laugh.

"Marcus . . ."

The soft whisper of his name had filled her mind and heart. Was it only because she held a newborn child in her arms and knew she might have borne one with him? Tears had welled in her eyes, and she had handed the child back to his mother. "He is very beautiful."

Oh, Marcus, I still love you. I still love you so much.

Marcus . . . Marcus . . .

Father, it wasn't your will that I fall in love with a man who rejects you, was it? Help me to forget him. How can I serve you wholeheartedly when I long for him? You know the deepest desires of my heart. O please, Lord, remove this burden from me. . . .

But now, as she put away the healing drugs and herbs in the new quarters, the soft whisper came again, insistent, not to be set aside.

Marcus . . . Marcus . . . Marcus . . .

She felt the call and pressed her fist against her heart.

O Lord, be with him. Watch over him and protect him. Put angels around him. O Father, let him know your mercy. . . .

Alexander carried the small writing table up the steps. He bumped the edge of it into the doorway, banging his fingers. He muttered a curse under his breath and carried his clumsy burden into the room and set it down with a thump.

Hadassah was on her knees, her head bowed, her hands pressed against her heart.

Rashid entered behind him with a painted screen. He saw her, too, and looked at Alexander in question. Alexander shrugged.

They quietly went about the work of putting things in their proper places.

Suddenly Rashid nudged Alexander, a look of fear in his dark eyes. Alexander turned his head and felt a prickling sensation down his spine.

Still kneeling in the same position, Hadassah was bathed in a stream of sunlight.

14

"Taphatha, we must hurry or we won't make Jericho before dark!" Ezra Barjachin called back over his shoulder to his daughter. He switched his donkey's side. Following on a smaller donkey, Taphatha obeyed his command but tapped the beast's haunches so lightly it continued its leisurely pace. "Beat that lazy beast with your stick, Daughter! Don't pet him with it."

Biting her lip, Taphatha applied a heavier hand, and the animal quickened its pace.

Ezra shook his head and turned around again, gazing nervously at the road ahead. He should not have bought the donkey. It was small and far too tame, but he had thought it perfect for his grandson, Shimei. Now, however, the animal's placid nature was jeopardizing their safety. They would have moved faster with him leading this animal while Taphatha rode.

He looked up the road ahead. Robbers hid in these hills, awaiting hapless travelers. Ezra swatted the donkey's side again, and the animal broke into a trot up the incline. He would feel safer once they reached the rise of hills and could see down the descending slopes to Jericho. Here the road was desolate, the sun hot, the risk of attack hovering over him like the carrion birds he saw up ahead.

He glanced back at Taphatha, hoping she hadn't seen the birds. She tapped the gentle beast again. In another moment, he knew she would pity the donkey and lead rather than ride him. "We must hurry, Daughter." He should never have listened to his brother Amni and brought her on this trip. As the eldest and most successful of the family, Amni had always intimidated him.

Now Taphatha was back on this lawless road with him, and the journey was a pointless disaster. Not only had no marriage agreement been reached, but familial ties had been severed. It was unlikely Amni would ever forgive him or Taphatha for the debacle that had occurred.

What could he have done differently? Had he ignored Amni and left Taphatha at home, would everything have come out as he had hoped? What if she had married Adonijah? Would disaster have come from such a union?

He conceded that without Taphatha there, the matter of her marriage would have been settled easily—had Amni been reasonable and Adonijah less insistent on his way.

Ezra looked around again. He had worries enough trying to arrange a secure future for Taphatha. Now he had the added burden of worry about robbers accosting her and stripping her of her virtue.

Adonijah had never been his first choice of a husband for Taphatha. His first choice had been Joseph. The son of a potter, of the tribe of Benjamin, Joseph had been wholeheartedly devoted to God. But Joseph was gone. Roman soldiers had arrested him a year ago and taken him outside the city walls and crucified him.

Taphatha was fifteen now, a full year older than her sister had been when she married. God had already blessed his daughter Basemath with a son and daughter. Surely God would bless Taphatha even more, for she was devoted to the Lord.

He must find a good husband for her and assure her future happiness, as well as the continuation of his own bloodline and heritage. So many had died in Jerusalem. So many others had ended up in Roman arenas. A precious few had been sold as slaves to Roman masters and were now scattered over the conquered territories.

God had promised that Abraham's offspring would be as great in number as the stars. Barely a handful remained, and that grievous number was being sifted still. Vespasian had put forth a decree that all descendants of David be killed, and for that reason alone, Isaac had been nailed to a cross.

God, why have you forsaken us? What will become of my youngest daughter?

In all Jericho, Ezra did not know one man good enough for her. Many claimed to be Jews, but they interpreted the Law according to their own lusts. A few good men of strong faith were still unfit because of intermarriage. Bartholomew would be perfect for Taphatha. Like her, he was devout and strong in the spirit of the Lord. Unfortunately, his father was a Greek. Josephus was another who had approached Ezra several times. He was a good man, but his grandmother had been a Syrian.

Sinking deeper into depression, Ezra tapped his donkey again. He had been so certain that Taphatha's future would be settled by this journey. He had been sure that when Amni saw her beauty, her gentle spirit, her purity, he would want her for his son. What father would not? And he had been right.

"She is wonderful," he had said quietly, "but Adonijah insists upon seeing her for himself. I'll advise him, of course. She is quite lovely."

When Adonijah joined them, he scarcely looked at Ezra, giving only a cursory greeting. Handsome, possessed of a proud bearing, his gaze had fixed upon Taphatha in surprise, and a small smile had touched his mouth. While he studied her, Amni had boasted of his son's acumen in matters of religion and business. Satisfied with what he saw, Adonijah had approached her boldly. Amni had been amused when his son took Taphatha's chin and raised her head. "Smile for me, Cousin," he had said.

And then Ezra's daughter, who had never once disobeyed him nor given him grief, had stepped back from Adonijah and said very clearly, "I will not marry this man, Father."

Adonijah's countenance had darkened noticeably. "What did you say?" he had commanded with mockery.

She had looked straight into his eyes. "I will marry no man who treats my father with disdain or who ignores the counsel of his own." And with that said, she had fled the room.

Ezra turned cold again thinking of it.

"Your daughter is a fool!" Amni had shouted, outraged and insulted.

Ezra looked between his brother and nephew, mortified with embarrassment.

"Go and speak with her, Uncle," Adonijah had said haughtily. "It's unlikely my fair cousin will find a better opportunity than this one."

Ezra had spoken with her.

"It would be madness to marry such a man, Father," she had said, weeping. "He looks upon you as beneath him because his purse is heavier. He refuses the counsel of his own father and looks upon me like a heifer for his pagan sacrifice. Did you see his face?"

"He is very handsome."

She shook her head, her face in her hands. "He is so proud."

"Taphatha, he is of our tribe, and there are not many of us left. Amni is a righteous man."

"What is righteous about him, Father? Was there kindness in

his eyes? Did he greet you with respect? Did your brother wash your feet or kiss you? And what of Adonijah when he entered the room? Did he speak to you with the respect due an elder? If they cannot love you, they can't love God."

"You judge them too harshly. I know Amni is proud. He has some right to be. He has made a fortune for himself. He—"

"Adonijah looked at me, Father. He *looked at* me. Not into my eyes, not once. It was as though he was . . . touching me. I was cold into my very bones."

"If you don't marry Adonijah, what am I to do for you, Taphatha?"

She had thrown herself on the ground before him, her forehead on his feet, her shoulders shaking. "I will stay with you, Father. I will care for you. Please, don't give me to this man."

Her tears had always been his undoing. He went to his brother and told him there would be no marriage. "I offered your daughter a great honor, and she dares insult us. Take her and get out. I will have nothing more to do with you or any member of your family."

As Ezra had lifted Taphatha onto the donkey, Amni had shouted at him from the doorway. "Your daughter is a fool and so are you!"

It had taken every ounce of self-control he had not to respond in kind. He had looked at Taphatha, and she smiled at him, her eyes clear.

Perhaps he was a fool. Only a fool would be on this accursed road.

The heat of midday beat down upon him. His mouth was set in grim lines as he urged the donkey on. He knew he must place his trust in the Lord. The Lord would provide Taphatha with a righteous husband, a husband of her own tribe.

But don't wait too long, Lord. We are so few.

He glanced back and saw Taphatha walking, the lead rope in her hand. "Daughter, what are you doing?"

"It's very hot, Father, and the poor animal is weary from carrying me." She ran up the road toward him. "Besides, I'm tired of riding," she said cheerfully.

"You will tire soon enough in this heat," he said, dabbing the sweat from his forehead with the sleeve of his robe. There was no use in insisting she ride. Besides, the donkey needed no urging now that she held the rope.

"What do you suppose they're circling, Father?"

"What?" he said in alarm and looked around for robbers leaping from the rocks.

"Up there." She pointed.

As he lifted his head slightly, he saw the vultures again. "Something died," he said flatly. *Or was killed*, he added to himself. And it could be them next if they didn't get out of these hills and down to Jericho.

Taphatha kept watching the birds flying their slow, graceful circles.

"A goat probably fell into the wadi," Ezra said, trying to allay her concern. He whipped the stick on his donkey's side, hurrying its pace as they came nearer.

"Goats are very surefooted, Father."

"Perhaps it was an *old* goat."

"Maybe it isn't a goat at all."

The vultures were almost overhead. Ezra's fingers tightened on the stick. He glanced up again and frowned. They would not still be circling had their prey died. They would be feasting upon it. What if it was a man?

"Why me, Lord?" he muttered under his breath and then motioned sharply to Taphatha. "Stay away from the ledge. I'll look." He slid from the donkey's back and handed her the rope.

He walked to the edge and looked down into the wadi. He saw nothing on the floor of it but rock and dust and some scraggly bushes that would be washed away during the first rains. He was about to step back when he heard the trickle of rocks. He looked to his left and down along the steep cut in the bank.

"What is it, Father?"

"A man," he said grimly. Stripped and bleeding. He looked dead. Ezra looked for sure footing and started down. Now that he had seen him, he couldn't ride on without finding out if he was alive or dead. "Why me, Lord?" he muttered again, sliding down a few feet and moving cautiously along a rocky surface until he could descend again without sending a cascade of rocks over the man. Glancing up, he saw his daughter on her hands and knees, leaning over the edge. "Stay back, Taphatha."

"I'll get the blanket."

"We probably won't need it," he said under his breath.

As he came closer, he saw the man had been slashed along the side. The open wound was swarming with flies. His skin was reddened from exposure, both eyes were blackened and swollen shut, his lip was split, he was covered with bruises and scrapes. Sicarii must have beaten him, stripped him of everything he owned, and dumped him in the wadi.

Full of pity, Ezra knelt on one knee, but as he leaned over him, he realized the man's hair was cropped short. *A Roman!* Closer examination revealed a pale band of white around the first finger of his right hand where a signet ring had been. Ezra drew back and stood up.

Staring down at the wounded man, Ezra struggled against the rising heat of animosity. Romans had destroyed his beloved Jerusalem, the bride of kings. Romans had crucified Joseph and obliterated his daughter's chances of having a secure and happy future. A Roman foot was on the neck of all Jews.

"Is he alive, Father?" Taphatha called down to him.

"He's a Roman!"

"Is he *alive?*"

The man moved his head slightly. "Help me," he rasped in Greek.

Ezra winced at the pain in that voice. He bent down again, his gaze moving over the purpling bruises, the deep gash, the burned and abraded skin . . . and his animosity evaporated in a warm wave of compassion. Roman or not, he was a man.

"We won't leave you," he said and called up to his daughter. "Tie the water bag to the rope and lower it. My cloak as well." She disappeared from the edge momentarily and then returned. He caught hold of the water bag and untied it. She pulled the rope up and sent the cloak down next while two donkeys stood at the edge, peering down at him.

He tipped the Roman's head up and let a few drops of water drip into his mouth. Pouring a small amount of water into his cupped hand, Ezra cooled the man's sunburned face. The Roman moved slightly and groaned in pain. "Don't move. Drink," Ezra said in Greek and held the mouth of the water bag to his lips. The Roman swallowed the precious liquid. Some of it ran down his chin and neck onto his scraped chest.

"Attacked . . ."

"You're not out of danger yet, and you've put me and my daughter in it along with you," Ezra said grimly.

"Leave me. Send the patrol back."

"You'd be dead by then, and I'd have to answer to God." He lay the cloak over the man.

"Drop the rope," he called up to Taphatha and caught it as it slithered down the incline to him. The man had passed out again. Ezra used the precious moments to wrap the cloak firmly around him and tie a makeshift harness.

Lord, help me, he prayed and began to pull the man up the incline. *I'm too old for this. How am I going to get him up to the road?*

"Father, you'll hurt him more bringing him up that way," Taphatha called down.

"He's unconscious again," Ezra said, gritting his teeth as he put his back into the chore of pulling the man a foot at a time. He stopped to get his breath. "A pity you aren't a small wiry man, Roman. Then I could hoist you over my shoulder." Clenching his teeth, he started again.

A cascade of rock and dirt nearby made him glance up sharply. "What are you doing, Taphatha. Stay on the road."

"He's too heavy for you." She had his donkey by its rope. The other followed. "It'll be easier to take him down into the wadi, Father. If he was attacked up here, the robbers may be waiting somewhere along the road."

"You can't get down here. It's too steep."

"Yes I can."

He watched her lead his donkey down a diagonal cut. The small donkey followed docilely. How she had managed to find a place to take the animals safely into the wadi, he didn't know. Bracing himself a foot at a time, he began to slide the Roman down, foot by foot, toward the floor of the wadi.

As soon as Taphatha reached the bottom, she left the animals and came up to help her father. One look at the Roman's battered face and her eyes filled with tears. She grasped the other side of the harness and helped Ezra. When they reached the bottom, Ezra unlooped the water bag from his shoulder and lifted the man's head so he could drink again.

The Roman's hand grasped his wrist. "Thank you," he rasped.

"Lie still. My daughter and I will make a litter out of what we can find," Ezra told him.

Marcus lay wreathed in pain, listening to the man and his daughter speaking Aramaic. They came back and struggled to lift him onto the litter they had made, and he blacked out briefly. He drifted between a dark netherworld and agonizing consciousness. One eye was swollen shut, but he could make out blurred images from the other. The eroded walls of the wadi rose above him on both sides. Each jarring bounce laced his body with pain, but he was spared the brilliant glare of sunlight as they kept to the shadows of the cliffs.

A sea of pain rolled over Marcus. As he floated toward darkness, he could hear Hadassah whispering, *"Yea, though I walk through the valley of the shadow of death, I will fear no evil; for You are with me. . . ."*

15

"You're doing too much, my lady," Iulius said to Phoebe, shifting the bundles he was carrying as they walked the narrow alleyway near the docks. "You can't keep on this way."

"I'm a little tired today, Iulius. That's all."

The slave's mouth tightened. She was wearing herself out trying to take care of the sailors' widows and their children. She arose at dawn, worked until midmorning, and then called for him so she could take clothing and food to needy families. By the time she returned to the villa in the afternoon, she was exhausted and faced with hours of evening chores she had set out for herself. It wasn't uncommon to find her asleep at her loom.

"You can't clothe and feed everyone, my lady."

"We must do what we can," she said as she looked up at the shabby tenement they were passing. "There are so many in need, Iulius." She saw women hanging old garments out to dry, while below them ragged children played soldiers in a street splattered with night soil. Phoebe recognized several of the boys and greeted them warmly.

Iulius saw all that she did. "The poor will always be with us, my lady. You can't take care of them all."

Phoebe smiled at him. "Do you reprimand me, Iulius?"

He shifted the heavy bundle again. "Your pardon, my lady. Far be it from me to reprimand my owner."

Her smile faded at his obdurate manner. "You know very well I wasn't reminding you that you're a slave, Iulius. You may have your freedom right now if you so wish it."

His face reddened. "My lord Decimus would not have wished me to leave you."

"You mustn't remain out of duty to me, Iulius," she said, though the thought of losing him saddened her. She relied on him in so many ways. She trusted him completely and couldn't imagine completing all she needed to do each day without his assistance. And he was a good companion.

Iulius' knuckles whitened. How had a woman of forty-six remained so naive? How could she not be aware that he loved her? Sometimes he was sure she must know how he felt, and then she would say something like this that proclaimed she didn't have the slightest notion of his need to be near her. He would far rather be a slave at her side than a freeman away from her.

"As a slave, I am bound to you and free to serve in whatever way you need," he said. "As a freeman, I'd have to leave your household."

"I'd never ask you to leave."

"If I remained, you'd no longer be looked upon as a woman of unquestioned virtue."

She frowned for a moment, and then, as she comprehended his meaning, she blushed. "People would never think. . . ."

"Ah yes, they would. You've lived in the world, my lady, but you've never really been part of it. You've no conception whatsoever of the evil that's in man's mind."

"I'm not a fool, Iulius. I know evil is loose in the world. And that's all the more reason we must strive for good. We *must* help these people."

"You can't help them all."

"I'm not trying to do the impossible. The women I help had husbands who worked for Decimus or Marcus. I can't turn my back on them when they're in need."

"What of Pilia and Candace? What of Vernasia and Epaphra? Did their husbands work for Lord Decimus or your son?"

"There are exceptions," she conceded. "I heard of their difficulties from the others."

"You can't take care of the whole world."

"I'm not trying to take care of the whole world!" she said, taxed. Why must he plague her today when her physical resources were so weakened? She wasn't merely tired, she was drained. Utterly. And there was so much to do, so many to see, and so little time.

Iulius held his silence.

Phoebe glanced up at him after a long moment and saw his stony expression. He was exasperated with her. She smiled tenderly. "You used to fuss over Decimus the same way you now fuss over me."

It was not the same at all. "It is not in my nature to bow and scrape."

"I've never asked it of you."

"No, my lady."

"I'm not a child, Iulius."

He said nothing.

"Don't be annoyed with me, Iulius. Please. I wish you could understand. . . ."

"I do understand, my lady," he said more gently. "You spend every waking moment serving others so you'll have no time left to think about—"

"Don't say it."

He winced inwardly at the pain he heard in her soft voice. He hadn't meant to hurt her.

"I can't change some things, Iulius," she said, her voice choked with emotion. "Here, I can."

Two little girls sat in a doorway across the street, playing with a dirty rag. One saw her. "Lady Phoebe!" The girls ran across the street to her, faces beaming with bright, elfin smiles.

"Hello, Hera," Phoebe said, laughing in delight at their warm greeting.

The little girl held her doll up so Phoebe could see it. "My mama made it for me," the girl boasted. "She said you gave her a new tunic and so she made me this baby from her old one. Isn't she beautiful?"

"She's a very pretty baby, Hera," Phoebe said, still struggling against the tears that had come far too quickly at Iulius' words. Was he right? Did she drive herself from morning to night so she could forget Decimus was gone and that her own children were lost to her as well. "What's her name?"

"Phoebe," the child said with a grin. "I named her after you, my lady."

"I am very honored."

"Good morning, Lady Phoebe," someone called from above. Phoebe glanced up and waved. "Good morning, Olympia. I saw your son a few minutes ago. He looks very well now."

"Yes," Olympia laughed. "The medicine you brought worked wonders. He and his friends have been playing legionnaires all morning."

Phoebe pushed Iulius' words from her mind and entered the tenement. She'd come to visit a widow whose husband had been lost at sea. The woman had three small children. Phoebe saw her own problems were paltry in comparison; hers were matters of the heart, not survival.

As she entered the small room, the children gathered around

her, tugging at her tunic and competing to be heard. Laughing, Phoebe gathered the smallest in her arms and sat down with the child on her lap while the mother put an extra piece of wood on the brazier.

Iulius set his burdens down and scooped beans, lentils, and grain from one sack into a basket. He dispensed enough to last the family for a week while listening to Phoebe put the woman at ease and talk of children and womanly things. She set one child down and took another, until each had received an embrace and moment in her arms. It was clear the children adored her.

His mouth flattened as he thought of Marcus, so caught up in his own pain that he failed to see the suffering he caused his own mother. And when was the last time Julia had bothered to visit her?

Phoebe gave the woman a new shawl and a small pouch of coins. "This is enough to pay your rent and provide you with a few essentials."

The young woman began to weep. "Oh, my lady, how can I ever repay you?"

Phoebe cupped her face and kissed one cheek and then the other. "It will not always be like this, Vernasia. When your circumstances change for the better, help someone as I've helped you. That will be thanks unto God."

Phoebe and Iulius left the tenement apartment and walked down the narrow, stinking alley to another tenement closer to the harbor. Prisca lived on the top floor. Her husband had died several weeks before, and Phoebe had been told of the old woman's dire circumstances by a woman who had sought her out.

"I have heard of how you help widows, my lady. I know of one old woman who needs help desperately. Her name is Prisca. Her son sailed on the *Minerva* two months ago and won't be back for a year or more. Her husband worked thirty-three years caulking ships, and he died on the deck of one a few weeks ago. She's lived in the same apartment for twenty years, but now she's unable to pay the rent, and the landlord's going to cast her out in the street. I'd help her if I could, but we've hardly enough to feed our own family. I don't know what'll become of that poor old woman if someone doesn't help her. Please, my lady, if you can . . ."

Phoebe had grown very fond of Prisca. The old woman was amusing. The hardness of life hadn't embittered or cowed her. She sat by the small window, "taking in the air" and watching the activity in the streets below. She was in full possession of her mental faculties, taking in the news of what went on in Ephesus and imparting her own ironic wisdom concerning it. She was too old to worry about propriety and treated Phoebe with the affection and frankness she might have reserved for her own daughter, had she ever had one.

Phoebe tapped at the door and entered when she heard Prisca call out to come in. The old woman was sitting by the open window, her forearm resting on the frame as she peered out. Smiling, Phoebe crossed the room and bent down to kiss her cheek.

"How are you today, Mother Prisca?"

"As well as an old woman of eighty-seven can expect." She captured Phoebe's chin as one would a child and studied her with a slight frown. "What's the matter?"

Phoebe drew back slightly from Prisca's scrutiny and forced a smile. "Nothing's the matter."

"Don't tell me nothing's the matter. I'm *old*. I'm not a doddering fool. Now, why are you upset?"

"I'm not upset."

"Tired *and* upset."

Phoebe took the old woman's hand and patted it as she sat upon a chair Prisca kept close by for her visits. "Tell me all you've done since last I saw you."

Prisca glanced up at Iulius and saw the way he watched his mistress, as though she was a precious Corinthian vase about to be shattered. "Very well, change the subject," she said somewhat testily. "I finished the shawls and gave them to Olympia. She delivered them to the women you mentioned."

"That's wonderful. How did you ever finish them so quickly? Iulius only brought you the wool last week."

"Save your accolades. What else does an old woman have to do with all this time on her hands?" She stood. "Would you like a cup of *posca?*" The drink, enjoyed by the poor and soldiers, was a refreshing mixture of cheap wine and water.

"Thank you," Phoebe said. She took the cup and smiled as Prisca poured another for Iulius. Prisca took her seat again, sighing as she relaxed once more.

Phoebe remained an hour. She enjoyed hearing Prisca retell the tales her son had told her from his voyages.

"Decimus always returned home from the sea tanned and full of life," Phoebe said wistfully. "I used to be jealous of the allure travel had for him. When he was younger, he was so hungry to explore, to open new trade routes, to know what was happening in the farthest reaches of the Empire. Sometimes I'd see this look on his face and I'd feel like an anchor."

"He loved you, my lady," Iulius said quietly.

Quick tears came unexpectedly, and she looked away to hide them. Embarrassed by the stillness that fell in the room, she rose. As she turned with a smile, she saw the way Prisca watched her. "I'm sorry," she murmured, seeing the old woman's eyes were filled with tears as well.

"Don't be sorry." Prisca gave a snort. "I'd rather see your honest pain than a brave front."

Phoebe winced. She bent and kissed the woman's withered, wrinkled cheek. "You're a very difficult old lady, do you know that, Prisca?"

"Because I'm not blind and deaf?"

"I'll see you in a few days."

Prisca patted her cheek. "Send me more wool."

On the walk back to the Valerian warehouses, Phoebe said nothing. Her mind was filled to overflowing with memories of Decimus and Marcus and Julia. She wanted to push them away because they brought with them only anguish. She had to accept and not dwell on her losses; she had to go on with what God expected. Love one another, Jesus had told his disciples, and that's what she was trying to do. Her work was to take care of all those she could with the resources she had available to her.

Past and future were out of her hands. One was finished and couldn't be undone. The other was beyond imagining. She didn't want to imagine it. She couldn't. The pain of losing Decimus was enough. Facing the fact that both her children's lives were in shambles was too much. She only had this moment, and she must fulfill it worthily. Of what use was it to allow herself regret and grief, to ponder endlessly what she might have done differently? Could she have changed the courses of Marcus' and Julia's lives? Could she?

When she had accepted Jesus as her Savior, she had taken his yoke upon her. Now she must be worthy. Love one another, he'd told his apostles and disciples. Love one another, not in word but in deed.

Didn't that mean *do something* for others? Surely her work was the will of God.

The litter was waiting at the warehouse. Iulius handed her in and she sank back into the cushions, exhausted. She needed to rest on the ride home so she would be able to make preparations for tomorrow. But rest would not come.

The villa was quiet as she entered. This was the part of each day she dreaded most, coming home to an empty home. She looked across the peristyle to the door of her lararium but turned away. She knew she should pray, but she was too tired even to think.

She went up the stairs and along the open corridor to her bed-chamber. She removed her shawl and went out onto the balcony that overlooked Ephesus. At dusk, the city gleamed with colors as the sun struck the Artemision. It was a beautiful structure, amazing in its grandeur. Thousands were lured to the altars of Artemis, clinging to empty promises.

Did Julia still go there?

"I brought you something to eat, my lady," her maid said from behind her.

"Thank you, Lavinnia," Phoebe said, not turning around. She had to stop thinking about Julia. What good did it do to go over and over the past, trying to see where she had gone wrong? The last time she had gone to see her daughter, she had been ushered into the triclinium by Primus.

"She's not feeling well this evening," he had said, but it was all too clear Julia was drunk. When Julia saw her, she hurled such shocking insults and accusations at her husband that Phoebe was rocked with mortification. Never had she heard anyone speak as her daughter had. Primus stood by with a pained expression, apologizing for her behavior, all of which only seemed to incense Julia more. She cursed him. Ashamed and heartsick, Phoebe had left. Every time she thought of going back, something prevented her. Sometimes it was only a strong sense that she must leave Julia alone to find her own way home.

Julia was lost to her, and so was Marcus. Remembering the purpose of his quest, she wondered if she would ever see him alive again.

She tried to turn her thoughts away from the plight of her own children and concentrate on the needs of the widows she would see tomorrow. She had done everything she could for Marcus and Julia. Dwelling on the past only defeated her chances for changing the future. She had to help those she could and let go of those she couldn't.

But they were her own children. How could she let go? How could she bear to see the anguish they caused themselves?

Alone and lost in her own sense of failure, Phoebe clutched the iron railing and wept. Somehow she had failed them. She hadn't loved them enough or taught them what they needed to know to survive in the world. And what could she do about it now? She felt helpless and hopeless.

"I am defeated, Lord. What can I do? O God, what can I do?"

She trembled, her mind in tumult. She pressed her fingertips to her aching temples, remembering Julia running down from the gardens and leaping into her father's arms when he'd come home from a long trip. She could almost hear her joyous laughter as Decimus swung her up high in the air and then held her close, telling her what a beautiful little girl she had become in the months he'd been gone.

Later, that same daughter had screamed she hated him and wished him dead.

O Jesus, what can I do for my child? What can I do? O God, show me what to do!

A strange weakness came over her, and she sank down. She clung to the railing with her left hand, trying to prevent herself from falling. Sitting on the balcony floor, she leaned heavily against the iron bars. She wanted to call out for her maid, but when she opened her mouth, only an unintelligible sound came. She wanted to pull herself up again but found she had no feeling in her right arm or leg. Fear filled her until all she could hear was the sound of her own heart beating in her ears.

The sun sank slowly, its rosy warmth against her back.

Someone tapped at the door of Phoebe's chambers. "My lady?"

The door opened slowly, and the maid peered in. Frowning slightly, she entered and crossed the room to where she had placed the tray of food earlier. Nothing had been touched. Lavinnia straightened with the tray and glanced toward the bed. Seeing no one in it, she looked around the room again and then toward the balcony.

Uttering a cry, she dropped the tray. The crash reverberated through the household. "My lady!" Lavinnia cried out, hurrying to Phoebe. Throwing herself onto her knees, she bent over her mistress. "My lady! *Oh!* My lady!"

Iulius charged into the room and saw the maid weeping hysterically as she bent over Phoebe on the balcony. He ran to her. "What's happened?" He pushed the girl aside so he could lift Phoebe from the cold tiles.

"I don't know! I came in to get the tray and saw her lying here."

"Be quiet, girl!" He carried Phoebe to her bed and laid her down gently. Her eyes were open and they shone with fear. She lifted her left hand weakly, and he grasped it. "Get some blankets," he said and heard the maid hurry from the room.

"You've worked too hard for too long, my lady. You'll rest now and be better in a few days," he said with an assurance he was far from feeling. He was cold with fear for her. He stroked her forehead and wondered if she understood what he was saying. Her face was slack on one side, her eyelid and mouth drooping. She made sounds, but they were beyond recognition. The more she tried, the more distraught she became. Unable to bear it, he put his fingers against her lips.

"Don't try to talk now, my lady. Rest. Sleep."

Tears ran down across her cheeks. She closed her eyes.

Lavinnia returned with blankets. Others followed her into the room, servants who loved their mistress and were afraid for her. "Gaius has gone for a physician," Perenna, the downstairs maid, said. A young man brought more wood for the brazier and set it closer to the bed. The laundress, cooks, and other servants all crowded into the room and stood about the bed, grieving as though Phoebe Valerian were already dead.

The cook's son, Gaius, brought the physician straight up the stairs and into Phoebe's bedchamber. Iulius told everyone to leave and then stood by watching the man examine her.

"What's wrong with her, my lord?" Iulius said after the examination.

The physician didn't answer. Stepping away from the bed, he looked at Iulius. "Are you in charge here?"

"Yes, my lord."

The physician shook his head. "Nothing can be done."

"What is it? What's happened to her?"

"A god has touched her and caused a brain seizure. She doesn't even know what's going on around her."

171

"You won't help her?"

"I can't help her. It's in the hands of whatever god has placed his hand on her." He started toward the door, but Iulius blocked his way.

"You're a physician. You can't just walk away and leave her like this!"

"Who are you to question me? I know far more about these matters than you do and I tell you there's nothing that can be done for her. You have two choices. You can try to feed her and keep her alive in hopes the god or goddess who did this to her will relent and remove the curse. Or you can leave her alone and allow her to die with dignity."

"Die with dignity?"

"Yes. And I'd advise you to do that. Be merciful and put some of this in her drink," he said and held out a small vial. When Iulius didn't take it, he set it on the small table near the bed. "You can let nature take its course," he said, "but, in my opinion, that would be the ultimate cruelty." He looked toward the bed. "She's of little use to herself or anyone else in this state. If she had a choice, I'm sure she would choose to die."

Alone with Phoebe, Iulius sank down on a stool beside the bed. He looked at Phoebe lying so still and pale, completely helpless. Her eyes were closed. The only sign that she was alive was the gentle rise and fall of her chest.

He thought of how hard she worked to help others, the hours she spent preparing for the coming day. Would she want to live like this?

Could he bear life without her?

Iulius took the small vial in his hand and looked at it. The doctor's conviction about her condition rang in his ears. He had to think of *her*, of what she would want. But after a moment he set it back on the table. "I can't do it, my lady," he said in a choked voice. "I'm sorry. I can't let you go."

Reaching over, he took her left hand and pressed it between both of his.

16

"Put the tray over there," Alexander said to the servant who entered the bibliotheca, not even glancing up from the scroll he was studying. He tapped his finger on the parchment in frustration. "I've been over and over these records, Rapha, and I'm still no closer to knowing what's wrong with her. The baths and massage didn't do any good. She's as uncomfortable now as she was a few weeks ago."

Hadassah stood near the windows, looking out over Ephesus. They were a long way from the booth near the baths. She could see the Artemision from here, its magnificent facade enticing masses into the dark environs of pagan worship. She was uncomfortable in this place, too close to the steps of that foul but beautiful temple. She remembered Julia dressing in her red finery and setting off to seduce the famous gladiator, Atretes. Oh, what tragedies had come of that! What other sorrows befell those who bowed down to Artemis and other false gods and goddesses like her?

"Are you listening, Hadassah?"

She glanced back at him. "I'm sorry. . . ."

He repeated himself. "What do you think?"

How many times had they been over this same conversation? Sometimes she was so tired and disheartened, she could weep. Like now, when her mind was elsewhere. Why was Marcus so much in her thoughts of late?

"Hadassah?"

"Perhaps you're too busy treating symptoms and neglecting the possible cause."

"Specifics," Alexander said. "I need specifics."

"You say you've found nothing in your physical examinations of Venescia to explain the severity and persistence of her many ailments."

"That's correct."

"Then what do you know about her?"

"She's rich. I know that. Her husband is one of the proconsul's advisers." Hadassah turned toward him, and he looked at the

173

blue hue of the veils that covered her scars. When his financial circumstances had changed for the better, he had purchased new tunics and veils for her, but she had gone on wearing the gray. Finally, exasperated, his temper had erupted.

"What stubbornness is this you have that keeps you attired like a specter of death? Has God something against colors that you must look like a veiled raven? You look more like a servant of the underworld ready to pole someone's way across the river Styx than a healer!"

Of course, he had immediately regretted his outburst and apologized. And the next morning she had appeared in the blue dress and veils she now wore. He had been embarrassed, his face hot. Something within him was changing subtly toward her, and he wasn't sure what it was or what it meant.

Patients often gave her gifts of money. She didn't dissuade them, but accepted it with murmured thanks and then simply dumped the coins in a box and left it forgotten on a shelf. The only time she opened it was before she visited the patients they had treated near the baths. She poured the contents into a pouch and took it with her. When she returned, it was always empty. However, time was becoming more precious these days as his practice grew and demands upon her increased.

"Did you hear me, Hadassah?" he said, perplexed at her pensiveness this evening. Was she praying again? Sometimes he could tell simply by the quietude that surrounded her.

"I heard you, my lord. Do you think Venescia's wealth has something to do with her illness?"

Tired, Alexander tried to curb his impatience. It was dusk, and he had seen more than twenty patients today, most with simple complaints that were easily remedied. Venescia was different. And her husband was important. A misdiagnosis could mean the death of his career.

There were days when he wished he had stayed in the booth by the baths.

"You're leading me again, but not telling me where," he said. "Just say what you think and stop expecting me to come to the right conclusions on my own."

She turned and looked at him. "I don't know what the right thing is to do," she said simply. "You're a physician and you want *physical* answers. All I know about diet is what I remember from the Pentateuch, and you've already written that down. All I know about drugs I learned from you. All I know of massage and rubbing techniques I learned by watching you."

"Pray then, and tell me what God says."

Hadassah's hands clenched. "I do pray. I pray all the time. For *you.*" She turned away again. "And others . . . ," she added after a moment.

Was Marcus all right? Why did she have this persistent nagging inside her to pray for him? And what of Julia? Why was she on her mind so much lately?

Lord, I pray and pray and still have no peace about them.

"So Venescia's problem isn't physical," he said, doggedly searching for treatment. Hadassah said nothing. Maybe she was thinking the problem over. Alexander took some meat from the platter and poured himself some wine. "All right. We'll look at this logically. If it's not physical, it's mental. Maybe she *thinks* an ailment into being." He chewed the tender beef and swallowed. "Maybe the answer is to have her change her thinking."

"Will you ever change yours?"

He raised his head and looked at her standing by the windows. Something in her stance made him sense her sadness. He frowned slightly. Crossing the room, he put his hands on her shoulders. "I believe everything you've told me, Rapha. I swear it. I *know* God exists. I know he's powerful."

"Even the demons believe, Alexander."

His hands tightened as he turned her to face him. Filled with an inexplicable fury, he swept the veils from her face so he could see her eyes. "What are you saying? That I'm a demon in your eyes?"

"I'm saying your knowledge is all in your head, and that's not enough. Saving knowledge is of the heart."

"I want *saving* knowledge," he said, mollified, thinking again of Venescia. "What do you think I've been asking for all this time we've been together?"

Hadassah shook her head. His hands dropped from her shoulders, and she sank down on a stool.

Alexander went down on one knee before her and put his hands on her knees. "I believe, Rapha. I say all the prayers I've heard you say exactly the same, and still I never have the answers I need. Tell me where I'm going wrong."

"Maybe you receive no answers because you're asking for the

wrong things." She put her hands over his. "Maybe what you really desire is God's power and not his revealed wisdom."

Alexander let out his breath. "I'd take either one if it would help that woman get well. That's all I want, Rapha, to heal people."

"It's what I want, too, only in a different realm. God comes first."

"I only know the realm of reality. Flesh and bone. The earth. Reason. I have to deal with those things I know best."

"Then think in those terms. Life is like a pond, and every decision and act we commit, good or bad, is a pebble flung into it. The ripples spread in widening circles. Perhaps Venescia suffers the consequences of the choices she made in her life."

"I've thought of that. I told her to abstain from sexual relations with men other than her husband, and she's already abstaining from wine and lotus."

"You still don't understand, Alexander. The answer isn't in *removing* things from your life or *adding* more rules to follow. The answer is giving your life back to the God who created you. And he's every bit as real as flesh and blood, the earth, *reason*. But I can't make you see that. I can't open your eyes and ears."

He sighed heavily and stood. He rubbed the back of his neck and went back to his scrolls. "Unfortunately, I don't think Venescia is looking for God, Rapha."

"I know," Hadassah said quietly.

Venescia was like so many of the patients that had come to Alexander and her since Antonia had been delivered of her child. They came looking for magic cures and quick recoveries. Some were pale and thin, addicted to vomiting one rich meal so they could partake of another. Others complained of trembling muscles while their breath reeked of wine and their skin was yellow with jaundice. Men and women alike practiced a life of promiscuity and then wanted to be cured of ulcers on their genitals or noxious discharges. The appeal was so often the same: Make me comfortable so I can go on doing whatever I want to do.

They wanted sin without consequences.

How do you bear us, Lord, when we are so stubborn and foolish? How do you bear us at all?

And then there was poor Alexander, empathetic to their pain and suffering, striving to be a master physician, yearning for concrete answers to all the ills of mankind.

Remedies, he always thought in terms of remedies! Avoid the midday sun, the morning and evening chill. Be careful not to breathe the air near marshes. Observe the color of your urine. Exercise, sweat, take lots of cleansing baths, get a massage, read aloud, march, run, play. Be cautious of the cut of meat, the type of soil your foods were grown in, the quality of water, and freshness of food.

None of them, not even he, seemed to realize they weren't just physical beings, that God had left a mark upon them by the simple fact of his creation. They preferred their idols, tangible, possessing capricious characteristics like themselves, easily understood. They wanted something they could manipulate. God was inconceivable, intangible, incomprehensible, unexploitable. They didn't want a life of self-sacrifice, purity, commitment, a life of *Thy* will be done, not mine. They wanted to be master of their own life, to have their own way, and be answerable to no one.

And you allow it, Father. You absolutely refuse to violate our free will. O Lord, blessed Jesus, sometimes I wish you would reach down and take hold of us and shake us so hard there would be no one able to deny you—that every man, woman, and child would bow down before you. Forgive us, Lord. Forgive me. I am so discouraged. I saw you at work in those near the baths, but here, Lord, I only see pain and mulish struggle. Father, I see Julia over and over again in their faces. I see her same unquenchable, wanton hunger. Strengthen me, Lord. Please strengthen me.

"I'm going to tell Venescia and her husband that she'll need to find another physician," Alexander said, rolling up the scroll.

Hadassah looked up in surprise. "What reason will you give them?"

"The truth," he said simply. "I'll tell them you believe her illnesses are of a spiritual nature. I won't contend against God." He shoved the scroll into one of the many cubbyholes in the large shelf above the desk. "Perhaps I'll recommend Vitruvius. He'd contend against anything."

"Don't send her to a diviner, my lord. Please."

"Where do you suggest I send her?"

"Leave that up to her."

Someone tapped on the door, and Alexander called for them to come in. Rashid entered. "There's a young man downstairs who was sent to find Rapha. He said his mistress has been struck down by a sudden, strange paralysis. I wouldn't have bothered you, my lord, but when he told me her name, I thought it best to advise you."

"What is her name?"

"Phoebe Valerian."

Hadassah's head came up sharply. Rashid glanced at her. "You know this name?"

"Everyone knows the name," Alexander said. "Decimus Andronicus Valerian was one of the wealthiest and most powerful merchants in Rome. According to legend, he started his enterprise here in Ephesus and then moved to the more lucrative hills of Rome, where he flourished. I heard he returned with his family a few years ago to die of a wasting illness. Last I heard, his son, Marcus Lucianus, had taken the reins of the holdings. Was it the son who sent this servant?"

Hadassah's heart beat wildly.

"He didn't say who sent him," Rashid said. "I came to you, my lord, because I know Valerian is a name far more powerful than Magonianus."

Alexander raised his brows. "Then his message was in the manner of a summons."

"No, my lord. He *pleads* as though his life depended on it."

"Valerian. I'm not sure I want to be involved with someone so powerfully connected," Alexander said, thinking of his current dilemma over Venescia. He had trouble enough with her. Could he afford to add more risk?

"Tell him we will come, Rashid," Hadassah said and rose.

Surprised, Alexander protested. "We should think about this!"

"Either you are or you are not a physician, Alexander."

Hadassah didn't recognize the servant. He was young and handsome, his skin swarthy. He was the sort of slave Julia would purchase, not Lady Phoebe. "What's your name?"

"Gaius, my lady."

She remembered him then as a young boy who'd worked in the kitchen.

"Rashid," Alexander said, "call for the litter."

"That won't be necessary, my lord," Gaius said, bowing. "There is one waiting for you outside."

They were carried swiftly to the Valerian villa in the most exclusive section of Ephesus. Alexander lifted Hadassah from the litter and carried her up the marble steps. Another slave had been watching for them and opened the door to greet and usher them in. "This way, my lord," the young woman said and hurried toward another marble stairway. Alexander glanced into the peristyle and thought it was one of the most beautiful and restful he had ever seen.

He carried Hadassah up the steps and lowered her when they reached the upper corridor. She swayed slightly. He caught her hand to steady her. It was ice cold. "What's wrong?" he demanded. She shook her head and took her hand from his, preceding him down the corridor and into the bedchamber.

She recognized Iulius at once. He had been Decimus' personal servant, and she had had little discourse with him. He sat beside Phoebe's bed, his face lined with worry. The slave girl spoke softly to him, and he rose and came toward them. Bowing deeply, he said, "Thank you for coming, my lord." He bowed again to her. "Rapha," he said, and there was great respect in that single word—and great hope as well.

Hadassah looked toward the bed and the woman lying upon it. She walked slowly toward it, each step bringing back piercing memories. Phoebe's hair lay against the cushions. Her skin was pale, almost translucent.

While questioning Iulius, Alexander examined Phoebe. Iulius told him how one of the servants had found her lying on the tiles out on the balcony, how she uttered strange sounds and couldn't move anything but her left hand.

While they talked and Alexander worked, Hadassah stood close by studying Phoebe intently. Her face was lax, her mouth sagging slightly, one eye dull. She muttered garbled words at Alexander once as he examined her.

"She was working very hard, my lord," Iulius went on. "Too hard. She spent every day down at the tenements near the docks visiting sailors' widows. She'd be up late at night weaving cloth for tunics."

"I'll need to speak with her son," Alexander said, drawing up her eyelid and leaning closer to study her.

"He sailed for Judea some months ago. There's been no word from him since."

Hadassah's heart sank. Judea! Why would Marcus want to go to that war-torn country? Yet a pang came as she remembered the flower-splashed hillsides of Galilee.

Alexander put his head against Phoebe Valerian's chest, listening to her heartbeat and breathing. "Has she any other children?" he said, straightening.

"A daughter."

"Here in Ephesus?"

"Yes, but they don't see one another," Iulius said.

Alexander stood and moved away from the bed. Iulius followed.

Hadassah moved closer to Phoebe. She saw a chain around her neck and a small medallion lying against her white skin. Leaning down, she took the small medallion and turned it in the palm of her hand, expecting to see one of the many gods or goddesses Phoebe had always worshiped in her lararium. Instead, she found the engraving of a shepherd holding a lamb over his shoulders.

"*Oh!*" she breathed softly, and warmth and thanksgiving spread through her. Phoebe's eyes moved, one seeming to focus in confusion on her veils. Hadassah leaned down closer and looked into Phoebe's face, studying her intently. "You know the Lord, don't you?"

Alexander spoke with Iulius a few feet away. "She's suffered a brain seizure."

"That's what the other physician said," Iulius said. "Can you help her?"

"I'm sorry, I can't," Alexander said flatly. "There's nothing anyone can do. I've seen a few cases like this before, and all you can do is make her comfortable until it's over. Mercifully, I don't think she's aware of what's going on around her."

"And if she is?" Iulius said in a choked voice.

"That's a possibility too painful to think about," Alexander said grimly. He glanced across the room and saw Rapha leaning down over the woman, something clutched in her hand as she spoke softly to the woman in the bed.

Iulius saw as well and returned to the bedside. He looked at Hadassah uneasily. "That's very important to her."

"I hope so," she said quietly. She raised her head, looking through the blue veils at Alexander and Iulius. "What gods does she have in her lararium?" Iulius tensed at her question, and he said nothing. "You can tell me the truth without fear, Iulius."

He blinked, startled that she knew his name. "None," he said, believing her completely. "She burned her wooden idols over two years ago. The other physician said a god had put his hand on her. Is that what you think is wrong? That one of the gods she disposed of has put a curse on her?"

"No. The God your mistress serves is the only true God, and he does all things to good purpose for those who love him."

"Then why has he done this to her? She loves him, Rapha. She'd exhausted herself in service to him, and now the physician says there's nothing that can be done, that I should let her die. The other physicians said the same thing. One even left poison to end her life quickly," he said, nodding toward the colored vial on the table near the bed. "What can I do for her, Rapha?" His face was lined with despair.

"Don't lose hope. She breathes, Iulius. Her heart beats. She lives."

"But what of her mind?" Alexander said from where he stood, annoyed that she was giving hope where there was none. "Is a person truly alive whose mind no longer functions?"

She looked down at Phoebe. "Leave me alone with her for a while."

Iulius, eager for a miraculous cure, withdrew immediately. Alexander, who had seen what God could do, still clung to reason and doubted in supernatural intervention. "What are you going to do?"

"Speak with her."

"She can't understand you, Rapha, nor can you understand her. I've seen cases like this before when I was studying under Phlegon. Her mind is confused. She is beyond reach. She will decline physically and then die."

"I think she understands a great deal, Alexander."

"What makes you say that?"

"Look into her eyes."

"I did."

She put her hand on his arm. "Let me speak with her alone."

Alexander looked toward the bed and then back at Hadassah. He wanted to ask her what she intended to do, what words she intended to utter.

"Go, please, Alexander."

"I'll be right outside the door." He grasped her arm. "Whatever happens, I want the details later."

As he left the room, a servant closed the doors behind him, shutting Hadassah alone in the room. She came closer to the bed.

"My lady . . ."

Phoebe heard the gentle voice above her and felt the slight dip in the wool-stuffed mattress as someone sat down on the bed beside her. The voice was husky and low, unfamiliar. "Do you know who I am?" it said, and she rolled her eyes toward the sound and tried to focus. All she could make out was a blue cloud of veils. "Don't be afraid of me," the woman said as she began to lift the concealing layers that hid her.

When Phoebe saw the scarred face, she felt a wave of pity and sadness. Then she looked into the young woman's eyes. Oh, the dark, luminous eyes, so gentle, so calm. She knew them so well. Hadassah! But how could this be? She tried to speak, but the words came out garbled and unintelligible. She tried harder. Tears filled her eyes. She moved her left hand sluggishly.

Hadassah grasped it, pressing it against her heart. "You do know me," she said and smiled down at her. "Oh, my lady, you are well."

"Haa . . . daaa . . ."

Hadassah stroked Phoebe's forehead, soothing her. "The Lord is good, my lady. I've been discouraged these past weeks, and now I see by you that his Word doesn't go out and come back empty. You've opened your heart to him, haven't you?" She felt Phoebe's hand squeeze hers weakly. Hadassah kissed it, tears of joy pouring down her cheeks.

"Don't lose hope, my lady. Remember that you rest in him, and he loves you. When you came to him, he poured out blessings upon you. He promises his continued blessing. I don't know why this paralysis has come upon you, but I do know Jesus has not abandoned you. He will *never* abandon you, my lady. This may even be his way of drawing you closer to him. Seek his face. Listen to him. Remember who he is, our comforter, our strength, our counselor, our healer. Ask what his will is for your life. He hasn't taken you home for a purpose. He will reveal that purpose to you. It may be that God has done this thing in order to give you a greater commission than one you might have assumed for yourself."

Hadassah felt Phoebe's fingers bear down weakly on hers. Hadassah put both of her hands around Phoebe's as though in prayer. "I will pray that God reveals his love for you in ways that will give you new purpose."

"Mar . . ." Tears rolled down Phoebe's temples into her graying hair.

Hadassah's eyes filled with tears. "I have never stopped praying for Marcus." She leaned down and kissed Phoebe's cheek. "I love you, my lady. Surrender to the Lord completely, and he will lead you."

She rose from the bed and covered her face with the veils. She went to the doors and opened them. Iulius and Alexander were right outside the door, as well as several servants. Filled with excitement and joy, she laughed. "Come in, please."

Iulius strode to the bed. He stood staring down at his mistress, and his shoulders drooped. "She's no better," he said flatly. "I thought. . . ."

"Look into her eyes, Iulius. Her mind isn't confused. She understands you perfectly. She's not lost to us, my friend. Take her hand."

He did so and drew in his breath as Phoebe's fingers weakly pressed his. He leaned down and looked into her eyes. She closed them and then opened them. "Oh, my lady . . . !"

Hadassah looked at Alexander and saw his grim stance. She wondered what thoughts were going through his mind.

"What do we do now, my lord?" Iulius asked him. "What do I do to take good care of her?"

Alexander gave him instructions on how to prepare nutritious foods that would be easy for her to eat. He told Iulius that he or one of the servants should move Phoebe regularly. "Don't let her remain in the same position for too many hours a day. She'll develop pressure sores and bruises that would only aggravate her condition. Massage her muscles and work her arms and legs gently. Beyond that, I don't know what to tell you."

Hadassah sat down on the bed and took Phoebe's other hand. Phoebe moved her eyes until they focused on her, and Hadassah saw that her eyes shone.

Hadassah rubbed her hand. "Iulius will take you out onto the balcony each day that the weather is good so you can feel the sun on your face and hear the birds sing. He knows you understand, my lady." She raised her head. "Talk to her, Iulius. There'll be times when she'll be discouraged and frightened. Remind her that God loves her and he's with her and no power on earth can take her from the palm of his hand."

She looked at Phoebe Valerian again. "You have some movement, my lady. Find ways of telling Iulius what you need and what you're feeling."

Phoebe closed her eyes and opened them again.

"Good," Hadassah said. She lightly brushed Phoebe's cheek with the back of her knuckles. "I'll come back to visit when I can, my lady."

Phoebe closed her eyes and opened them again. They filled again with tears.

As Hadassah rose, she took the vial from the small table. She held it out to Iulius. "Throw this away."

Iulius took the vial and hurled it through the open doors to the balcony, where it shattered upon the tiles. He bowed low. "Thank you, Rapha."

She returned the bow gravely. "Thank God, Iulius. Thank *God*."

Alexander said little on the ride back to the new apartments. He helped Hadassah out of the litter and braced her as she limped toward the door. Rashid had seen them from above and was waiting for them. He lifted Hadassah and carried her up the steps and into the main chamber. He gently lowered her to her feet. She limped over to a couch and sat down, rubbing her bad leg.

Alexander poured a small draft of wine and handed it to her. She removed her veils and sipped.

"What possible life can that woman have, imprisoned in a body that won't function?" he said, allowing his anger to vent. He poured himself a goblet of Falernian wine. "It would be better if she died. At least then, her soul would be free rather than trapped in that useless shell of a body."

"She is free, my lord."

"How can you say that? She can hardly move, let alone walk. She can't utter an intelligible word. Everything she says comes out meaningless gibberish. She can move her left hand and foot and blink her eyes. And it's not likely she will ever again be able to do more than that."

She smiled. "I was never more free than when I was locked in the dungeon waiting to be sent into the arena to die. God was there in the darkness with me, just as he is with her now."

"What use is she to herself or anyone else?"

She raised her head, her dark eyes flashing. "Who are you to say whether she is of use? She is *alive!* That is statement enough." Her anger quieted, and she tried to reassure him. "God has a purpose for her."

"What possible purpose has anyone in her condition? And what sort of life will it be, Rapha?"

"The life God has given her."

"Don't you think it'd be more merciful to end her suffering than allow her to linger in her present condition?"

"You said once that it's God who decides whether a man lives or dies. Have you changed your mind? Would you now say it's up to *you* or some other physician to decide whether she lives? Murder is not an act of mercy, my lord."

Heat filled his face. "I'm not speaking of murder, and you know it!"

"Indeed, you are, though you would try to cloak it in other words." She spoke with quiet conviction and sadness. "What else can you call ending someone's life before God's time?"

"I don't consider that a reasonable question, Rapha."

"What is a reasonable question?"

"One that doesn't involve celestial interpretation that is beyond the ability of any man to answer." His mouth tightened. "Perhaps we should talk of something else."

"Not a sparrow falls from the sky without God knowing. He already knows the moment and reason for Phoebe Valerian's death. Nothing is hidden from God." She rested the small clay cup on her lap, knowing what she had to say would hurt him. "Perhaps you aren't even aware of the deeper reasons you have for wanting to end her life."

"And what reason might that be?"

"Convenience?"

His face reddened. "You would say that to me?"

"She will be completely dependent upon others to care for her physical body. That requires great compassion and love, Alexander. Iulius has that. You have no time for it."

He was seldom angry, but her words stirred a fury within him. "Have I ever lacked for compassion? Hasn't my sole desire been to learn all I can in order to help people?"

"What of those you turn away?"

"I only turn patients away I know I can't cure."

"Have they less need of your love?"

He sensed no condemnation in her words, yet felt the sharp slice of them in his heart. "What am I supposed to do, Rapha? Take on everyone who asks me for help? What would you have me do?"

185

Setting her cup aside, she rose and limped across the room. She stood before him and said simply, "This" and put her arms around him. She said nothing more, and her sweet embrace made his heart ache. He felt her hand move on his back, rubbing softly, comforting, and all the anger and confusion left him. His eyes smarted. He closed them and put his arms around her, resting his cheek on the top of her head. He let out his breath slowly.

"Sometimes I'd like to ring your neck, you frustrate me so much," he said gruffly.

She laughed softly. "I know exactly how you feel."

Grinning, he drew back and cupped her face, lifting it. "What would I do without you, Rapha."

Her amusement died. She took his hands in hers and squeezed them. "You would have to learn to trust the Lord."

Alexander felt dismay as she released his hands and limped slowly toward the door. Suddenly, unaccountably, he knew he was alone. He knew he would eventually lose her. He didn't know how or why, he just *knew.*

Something had happened tonight that he couldn't define. Had God shown her another path? For the first time in his life, he wished he owned her, that he could claim legal, personal possession of her and keep her by his side permanently.

He frowned, wondering at this unease he felt, and then remembered his suspicions when Rashid had brought word that a servant from the Valerian household was waiting below. Hadassah's head had come up as though struck by a bolt of lightning.

Sudden understanding flowed into him, and he looked at her in horror. "You knew her, didn't you, Hadassah? You didn't just know *of* Phoebe Valerian, you had personal knowledge of her." His heart beat heavily. "It was the Valerian family who owned you, wasn't it?" Fear filled him, fear for her sake—fear for his sake and the thought of losing her. "What did you do during that time you were alone with her? Hadassah!"

She left the room without answering him.

But Alexander already knew what she had done. Hadassah had removed her veils. She had revealed herself to a member of the very household who had tried to have her killed.

"By the gods . . . !" he said under his breath, raking his hands through his hair.

Why hadn't he asked her if she knew the Valerians before he had taken her there? He had known from the beginning there were risks. Now he had put her in danger. And for what? To witness another miracle of healing? No! He had taken her along with him because he was *proud* of her abilities, *proud* she was his assistant. And what had his insufferable pride accomplished?

A helpless desperation flowed over him. *God, protect her! I've been a fool! I've put her in mortal danger. I've exposed her to the family who tried to kill her once already.*

What if the woman regained her voice? What then? *God,* he prayed fervently, hands clenched, *keep that woman's tongue confused. Keep her silent!*

Sitting down, he cursed himself.

Hadassah entrusted herself to God, but he couldn't be so trusting. To lose Hadassah would be to lose everything. He was only just beginning to understand that, only beginning to face what she meant to him. Maybe he had to put all scruples aside and take the matter into his own hands. Besides, the woman was better off dead. He winced, thinking of what Hadassah had said. But he had to be rational.

One visit to Phoebe Valerian and he could make sure Hadassah would be out of danger for good. Once Phoebe Valerian was dead, he would make sure Hadassah never went near another Valerian.

Suddenly Hadassah's words echoed in his mind. *Convenience.* Was convenience reason enough to kill someone? No. But what about protecting the life of another? What of *retribution?* The Valerians had tried to murder her by sending her into the arena to face the lions. What of *vengeance?*

He shuddered, realizing the course of his thinking. He remembered Hadassah bending over Phoebe Valerian. Everything about the way she stood and spoke revealed the love she had for that woman. How was it possible?

He clenched his teeth. There were any number of ways he could protect Rapha from the Valerians.

But that wasn't the real problem.

How was he going to protect Hadassah from herself?

17

Ezra Barjachin threw his hands into the air in frustration. Why must his wife go to pieces now when he needed her to stand firmly beside him? "I know he's a Roman! You don't have to tell me!"

"If you knew, why did you bring him into our house? Why have you done this terrible thing to us?" Jehosheba wailed. "Everyone knows! They saw you enter the gates of the city. They watched you bring that man up the street and into our house. I can feel their hot eyes boring through the walls. They will not let you enter the synagogue after this!"

"What would you have had me do, Jehosheba? Leave him in the wadi to die?"

"*Yes!* It's no less than a Roman deserves! Have you forgotten Joseph? Have you forgotten the others who died in Jerusalem? Have you forgotten the thousands carried off into slavery to Gentile dogs like him?"

"I've forgotten nothing!" He turned away in futility. "Your daughter wouldn't let me leave him."

"*My* daughter? So you lay the blame at my door even when I wasn't there. She's *your* daughter, her head always in the clouds. You should both come down to earth! You take our daughter to arrange a marriage for her and what happens? You come back and tell me your brother threw you out and said he never wants to see you again! And to make matters worse, you find a Roman along the road and drag him home with you!"

"I tried to leave him at the inn, but Meggido wouldn't accept him. I even offered to pay."

She burst into tears. "What will the neighbors say?"

Taphatha stood listening on the steps to the roof, where she and her father had carried the Roman. She had remained until he slept. The long, painful ordeal of the journey to Jericho had been very difficult on him. She was thankful it was over. She was thankful he was alive.

She was also thankful he could not hear what her mother was saying.

The only sound now was her mother weeping. She came down the last steps. Her father looked at her, distraught and helpless, and shook his head in frustration.

Taphatha went and knelt before her mother. "Mama, the neighbors will say Father remembered the Scriptures. God desires mercy, not sacrifice."

Jehosheba raised her head slowly, her cheeks streaked with tears. She looked into her daughter's face and wondered at her. How had Taphatha come to possess such a beautiful, sweet spirit?

It couldn't have come through me, Jehosheba thought ruefully, for she knew well that she was rebellious and doubting. Nor could it have come through Ezra, who was enmeshed in a constant struggle against circumstances. Jehosheba's lips tightened— circumstances he often brought upon himself.

She cupped Taphatha's cheek and shook her head sadly. "They won't remember that at all. They'll remember Jerusalem. They'll remember Joseph. They'll remember *Masada.* And because they remember, they will turn their backs on us because we have given shelter to a Roman, a Gentile, and thereby defiled our home."

"Then we will remind them of what God says, Mama. Have mercy. You mustn't worry so much about what others say. Fear God. It is the Lord we must please."

Jehosheba smiled bleakly. "We will remind them," she said, doubting it would do any good. Besides, what choice had they now? The damage was done.

Taphatha kissed her cheek. "I'll fetch some water."

Ezra watched her take up the large earthen jar and go out the door into the sunlight. She slipped her feet into her sandals and, balancing the jar on her head, started down the street. He went to the open door and leaned against the frame, watching Taphatha. "Sometimes I think God has called our daughter to bear witness to him."

"That's hardly comforting when you consider what happens to prophets."

Her words struck him and he closed his eyes, resting his head on the doorframe, near the *mezuzoth.* He knew the words contained in the small rectangular stone cases by heart. He could recite each of the Ten Commandments and the Holy Scriptures, all written so carefully on parchment so that they could be stored in the mezuzoth, fastened to the doorframe of his house. He believed those Scriptures and promises with all his heart . . . and

yet a few words from this woman could pierce him with a stran-
gling doubt. Had he endangered his daughter by helping the
Roman? Had he endangered them all?

Help me, Lord God . . ., he prayed as he turned and looked
back at his wife. Raising his hand, he kissed it and laid it over a
mezuzah before coming back inside. "I couldn't just leave him to
die, Jehosheba. God forgive me. I did think about it."

Her face softened. "You're a good man, Ezra." She sighed.
"Too good." She rose and returned to her work.

"As soon as the Roman is well enough to travel, he will go."

"What's the hurry? The damage has already been done!" She
looked toward the steps to the roof. "Did you put him on the bed
in the tabernacle?"

"Yes."

She flattened the dough with several hard whacks. It was just
like Ezra to give the best bed away. Well, as far as she was concerned, when the Roman left, he could roll up that defiled bed
and take it with him.

18

Marcus awakened to the sound of a town crier. He could hear the man clearly, calling out his announcements in Aramaic from a nearby rooftop. He tried to sit up, then sank back with a gasp of pain, his head throbbing.

"You will feel better in a few days," a woman said.

He heard something rinsed in water, and he sighed as a cool cloth was placed over his forehead and eyes. He made a sound in his throat. "Robbed . . . horse . . . money belt." He gave a low, harsh laugh of contempt. His split lip stung. His jaws hurt. Even his teeth hurt. "Even my tunic."

"We will give you another tunic," Taphatha said.

Marcus was aware of the resonance of the girl's voice, her accent. "Are you a Jew?"

"Yes, my lord."

Her words pierced him, bringing back memories of Hadassah. "A man helped me."

"My father. We found you in the wadi and brought you here."

"I thought all Jews hated Romans. Why would you and your father stop to help me?"

"Because you needed help."

He remembered hearing the Roman patrol on the road. He had heard others pass by above him speaking Greek. If they had heard his call, they had not tarried to find or help him.

"How is he doing, Daughter?" a man's voice said.

"Better, Father. His fever is down."

"That is good."

Marcus felt the man draw near. "I was warned not to travel alone," he said dryly.

"Wise counsel, Roman. Heed it next time."

Despite the pain in his lip, Marcus smiled wryly. "Sometimes a man can't find what he's looking for with others beside him."

Taphatha tipped her head, curious. "What are you looking for?"

"The God of Abraham."

"Haven't you Romans gods enough of your own?" Ezra said sardonically. His daughter looked up at him in silent plea.

"You aren't willing to share yours?" Marcus said.

"It would depend on your reasons for wanting to do so." Ezra gestured Taphatha to move away and hunkered down to remove the cloth and rinse it again himself. He didn't want his daughter to spend too much time with this Gentile. He laid the cool cloth over the Roman's face.

Marcus moved again and drew in a hissing breath through his teeth.

"Don't try to sit up yet. You may have a few cracked ribs."

"My name is Marcus Lucianus Valerian." His name roused no comment, no questions. "The name means nothing to you?"

"Is it important?"

Marcus uttered a laugh. "Apparently not important enough."

Ezra glanced at his daughter. "Go and help your mother, Taphatha."

She lowered her eyes. "Yes, Father," she said meekly.

Marcus listened to the sound of her footsteps as she went to the stairway. "Taphatha," he said. "A sweet name."

Ezra's mouth tightened. "You were fortunate, Marcus Lucianus. You lost your possessions and suffered scrapes and bruises, but you are alive."

"Yes. I'm alive."

Ezra noticed the dismal way the Roman uttered the words and wondered at the reasons behind it. "My wife and daughter applied salt and turpentine to your wounds. The cut in your side is sealed with pitch. You should heal in a few days."

"And then be on my way," Marcus said, his mouth curving faintly. "Where am I?"

"In Jericho. On my roof."

Marcus listened to the crier calling out his announcements across the neighborhood. "Thank you for not leaving me in the wadi to die."

Ezra frowned at the humility of those words and relented slightly. "I am Ezra Barjachin."

"I am in your debt, Ezra Barjachin."

"Your debt is to God." Annoyed at the trouble the Roman had brought upon his household, he rose and left the roof.

Marcus dozed, awakening periodically to sounds rising from the street. Taphatha came back and gave him a thick gruel of lentils. He was hungry enough that it tasted good. He hurt too much after eating to make conversation. Her hands were gentle as she readjusted the blankets over him. He caught the scent of her skin—a mingling of sun, cumin, and baked bread—just before she left him alone again.

Night came, bringing with it a blessed coolness. He dreamed he was adrift on the sea. He could see no shoreline, only a vast, endless blue all the way to the horizon.

He awakened as the sun rose. He could hear children playing on the street. Carts passed. The crier shouted again in Aramaic, then in Greek. The swelling around his eyes had gone down enough that he could open his eyes. His vision was slightly blurred. When he tried to sit up, he sank back, overwhelmed by a wave of dizziness.

Ezra came up to the roof. "I have brought you something to eat."

Marcus tried to sit up again and groaned.

"You must not push yourself, Roman."

Marcus submitted to being fed again. "What difficulties have I made for you by being here?"

Ezra didn't answer. Marcus looked up at the solemn, bearded face framed by two long curls of hair. He suspected the man was already suffering from repercussions and heartily regretting his act of kindness.

"What do you do to make a living, Ezra Barjachin?"

"I am a *sopherim,*" he said solemnly. "A scribe," he explained when Marcus frowned, not understanding. "I copy the Holy Scriptures for the phylacteries and mezuzoth."

"The what?"

Ezra explained that phylacteries held strips of parchment on which were written four select passages, two from the book of Exodus and two from Deuteronomy. These parchments were enclosed in a small square black calfskin case and fastened on the inside of the arm nearest the heart, between the elbow and shoulder, by long leather straps. Another phylactery was tied to the forehead during prayers.

A mezuzah, he explained further, was a container on the doorframe of a Jewish home. Inside it was a small piece of parchment on which were written two passages from Deuteronomy and marked with "Shaddai," the name of the Almighty. The parchments were replaced after time and a priest would come to bless the mezuzoth and the household.

Having finished his meal, Marcus sank back onto the bed. "What Scriptures are so important you have to wear them on your arm and head and post them on your door?"

Ezra hesitated because he was not sure he should share Scripture with a Gentile dog of a Roman. However, something compelled him.

"'Hear, O Israel: The Lord our God, the Lord is one! You shall love the Lord your God with all your heart, with all your soul, and with all your strength. And these words which I command you today shall be in your heart. You shall teach them diligently to your children, and shall talk of them when you sit in your house, when you walk by the way, when you lie down, and when you rise up. You shall bind them as a sign on your hand, and they shall be as frontlets between your eyes. You shall write them on the doorposts of your house and on your gates.'"

Marcus listened intently as the words flowed from Ezra. His voice was full of reverence. He spoke the Scriptures precisely, but in a way that made it clear they were written in his heart and not just ingrained in his head after years of copying them.

"'You shall fear the Lord your God and serve Him, and shall take oaths in His name. You shall not go after other gods, the gods of the peoples who are all around you (for the Lord your God is a jealous God among you), lest the anger of the Lord your God be aroused against you and destroy you from the face of the earth. . . .'" Ezra went on, his eyes closed. When he finished reciting the Scriptures for the Roman, he fell silent. No matter how often he said or heard them, those words were like music to him. They sang in his blood.

"No half-measures," the Roman said grimly, "or God will wipe you off the face of the earth."

Ezra looked at him. "God blesses those who love him with all their heart."

"Not always. I knew a woman who loved your god with all her heart." He fell silent for a long moment. "I saw her die, Ezra Barjachin. She didn't deserve such a death. She didn't deserve to die at all."

Ezra felt a pang within his own heart. "And so you look to God for answers."

"I don't know if there are any answers. I don't know if there is a god such as the one you believe in and she served. He's in your heart and head, but that doesn't mean he's real."

"God is real, Marcus Lucianus Valerian."

"For you."

Ezra pitied him. The Roman had been beaten more than physically. And in the wake of Ezra's pity came the first flicker of hope he had felt since seeing Joseph crucified. Many enemies had come against God's chosen people. Some had conquered them because Israel had sinned against the Lord. Jerusalem, bride of kings, had fallen to other nations. But when the people turned back to God, God went before them, destroying their enemies and restoring his people to the Promised Land. Assyria, Persia, and Babylon had put Israel to the sword and in turn been called to judgment. Just as Assyria, Persia, and Babylon had fallen, so too would Rome fall. Then the captives would return to Zion.

The Roman spoke, shattering his dream with a single question. "What do you know about Jesus of Nazareth?"

Ezra recoiled. "What makes you ask me about *him?*"

"The woman of whom I spoke said Jesus was God's Son come down to earth to atone for the sins of man."

A chill washed over Ezra. "Blasphemy!"

Marcus was surprised at the vehemence of that single word. He started at it. Perhaps he shouldn't ask questions of this Jew.

"Why do you ask me this question?" Ezra said harshly.

"I apologize. I only wanted to know. Who do you say Jesus is?"

Heat poured into Ezra's face. "He was a prophet and healer from Nazareth who was tried and judged by the Sanhedrin and crucified by Romans. He was killed over forty years ago."

"Then you reject him as your Messiah?"

Ezra stood up, agitated. He glared down at the Roman, resenting his presence, resenting his reasons for being here, resenting the unrest in his own household, his own mind. And now this question!

Why did you give me this man, Lord? Do you feed the doubts I've had over the years? Do you test my faith in you? You are my God and there is no other!

"I've angered you," Marcus said, squinting against the sunlight. Even with blurred vision, he could see Ezra's agitation in the way he moved away. How many other pitfalls would he face in conversing with this Jew? Why hadn't he kept silent? Why hadn't he waited to ask another, someone knowledgeable but uninvolved and objective? This man clearly was not.

Ezra stood with his hands on the wall of the roof. "It isn't you who angers me, Roman. It's the persistence of this cult. My father told me long ago that Jesus told his followers he came to set a man against his father, a daughter against her mother, and a daughter-in-law against her mother-in-law. And so he did. He set Jew against Jew."

He had set Ezra's own father against his uncle.

"Do you know any Christians?"

Ezra stared down into the street, flooded with painful memories. "I knew one."

He remembered his father's brother coming to this very house when he was a boy. He had been hard at work, practicing letters while his father and uncle talked. He had listened intently, curious about the man called Jesus. He had heard many things said about him. He was a prophet, a poor carpenter from Nazareth with a band of followers who included fishermen, a tax collector, a zealot, and a supposed harlot who had been demon-possessed. Whole families followed him. Some said he was a miracle worker. Others, a revolutionary. Ezra had heard that Jesus had cast out demons, healed the sick, made the lame walk and the blind see. His father had insisted it was hysteria, rumor, false claims.

Then Jesus, the supposed Messiah, was crucified. Tried and judged by his own people. Ezra's father had commented only that he was glad the debate over the man was over. And then . . .

"I have brought you good news, Jachin," his uncle had said all those years ago. "Jesus has risen!"

Ezra could still remember the incredulous, cynical look on his father's face. "You are mad. It's impossible!"

"I saw him. He spoke to us at Galilee. Five hundred people were there."

"That can't be! It was someone who looked like him."

"Have I ever lied to you, Brother? I followed Jesus for two years. I knew him well."

"You only thought you saw him. It was another."

"It was Jesus."

His father argued vehemently. "The Pharisees said he was a troublemaker who spoke against the temple sacrifices! Don't deny it! I heard he turned over the tables and drove the moneychangers out of the temple with a whip."

"They were cheating the people. Jesus said, 'My house is a house of prayer, and you have turned it into a den of robbers.'"

"The Sadducees said he disclaimed heaven!"

"No, Jachin. He said there is no marriage in heaven, that men will be as angels."

Back and forth they went, his father contending with his uncle. As time passed, Ezra saw the gap grow between them—his uncle, calm, filled with joy and assurance; his father, frustrated, afraid, growing more enraged.

"They will stone you if you go about telling this story!"

And so they had.

"If you proclaim this Jesus is the Christ, I will take up the first stone against you myself!"

And so he had.

"Such blasphemy is an affront to God and his people," his father had said later to Ezra, and then nothing more was ever said.

After all these years, the one thing that stood out the most clearly in Ezra's mind were his uncle's words. They had echoed over and over down through the years. "Jesus has risen. He is *alive*. Death, where is your sting?" He could hear his uncle's joyous laughter. "Don't you realize what this means, Brother? We are *free!* The anointed one of God has finally come. Jesus *is* the Messiah."

He had tried for years to squelch those words, but still they rang, "The Messiah has come . . . the *Messiah* . . ."

And now, here was a pagan, an idol worshiper, a despicable *Roman* dog whose very presence was turning Ezra's household upside down and inside out, asking the one question that had always terrified Ezra most: "Who do *you* say Jesus is?"

Why, Lord? Why do you bring this upon me?

The truth was that Ezra didn't know who Jesus was. He was afraid to think on it, but, in his heart, he had always wondered. He had hungered and half-hoped, but been too afraid to find out for himself.

His uncle's body had not been placed in a tomb. He had been crushed to death beneath the weight of the stones and left to rot in a pit outside the city walls. A terrible fate for any man. All because he believed in Jesus.

After his uncle's violent death, not one word had been uttered about him or about Jesus of Nazareth. It was unspoken law from that day forth: neither man had ever existed, neither name was ever to be uttered again. And so it had remained for twenty-three years.

Ezra had thought his father had completely forgotten what happened. Until that day, when Ezra had been sitting near his father's deathbed.

His father had given Amni, Ezra's brother, a blessing. The time was short. Amni stood and withdrew slightly, waiting for death to come. Ezra knelt and took his father's hand, wanting to comfort him. His father turned his head slowly and looked at him. Then he whispered the unsettling words. "Did I do right?"

The words hit Ezra like a blow to his stomach. He knew instantly of what his father spoke.

"Answer him! Tell him yes," his mother pleaded. "Give him peace."

But Ezra couldn't.

Amni had spoken instead, vehemently. "You did the right thing, Father. The Law must be preserved."

And still Ezra's father looked at him. "What if it was true?"

Ezra had felt something near panic stir within him. He wanted to speak. He wanted to say, "I believed him, Father," but Amni stared at him coldly, as if compelling him to answer the same way he had. His mother stared at him, too, waiting, frightened, unsure. He couldn't even breathe, let alone speak.

And then it was too late to say anything at all.

"It is over," his mother said softly, almost relieved. She leaned down and closed his father's eyes. His brother left the room without a word. A few minutes later, the paid mourners began to wail and scream outside.

In the years that followed, with the hardship of making a living for himself and his wife and children, Ezra forgot what he had felt at his father's bedside. He forgot in the intensity and demands of his work. He forgot in his love of being among his friends in the synagogue. He forgot in the safe boundaries of his existence.

And still . . . the question remained. And so he pushed it far back in his mind where it couldn't intrude or complicate his life. Only infrequently did it return to him—in his dreams.

"Who do you say I am, Ezra Barjachin?" a soft voice would say, and Ezra would find himself facing a man with nail scars in his hands and feet. "Who am I to you?"

And now, that strange sensation he had felt so long ago returned, powerful, compelling, stirring something within him he was afraid to contemplate, terrified to face. His heart raced, like wings beating within his breast. He felt as though he was on a precipice, about to fall over—or be caught up.

O Lord God. Help me.

What if it was true?

19

Taphatha blushed when Marcus looked at her. His dark brown eyes had an intensity that made her stomach tighten and her pulse race. Several days before, he had asked her if he frightened her. She denied it, but later she wondered if fear wasn't part of what she felt, fear of her growing fascination with a Gentile—a Roman, no less.

Marcus Lucianus Valerian was unlike any man she had ever known. Though he was gentle, she sensed he could be cruel. At times she would hear him say things to her father that were alarmingly cold and cynical. Yet, she sensed about him a terrible vulnerability. He was like a man driven before a wind, striving against forces impossible to comprehend, challenging them nevertheless, tempting his own destruction, almost eager for it.

Once she had overheard Marcus speak to her father of a woman he had known who had loved God. Taphatha knew intuitively it was love for that woman that still consumed Marcus' thinking. Whatever he was seeking had to do with her.

What would it be like to be loved so obsessively by a man like Marcus Valerian? He had said the woman died, and yet he hadn't given her up. She was with him every moment, even moments like now, when he looked at Taphatha so intently.

Taphatha wondered what he was thinking. Often these days she found herself wishing he would forget the woman he had loved and lost, and love her instead. Sometimes she struggled against a hunger to be with him on the rooftop, to hear his voice, to look into his eyes. She wondered now what it would be like to have Marcus Valerian reach out to her . . . and these feelings *did* frighten her.

Marcus was forbidden. From the time she could remember, her father had taught her that disaster came from disobeying the Lord, and the Lord clearly forbade intermarriage with Gentiles. It was true, many Gentiles had become proselytes, were circumcised, and became Jews, but this would never happen with Marcus. He said he was searching for God, but there was an edge to his questions. The wall around his heart was almost palpable.

What was he really hoping to find?

Her father didn't want her spending too much time with Marcus. She understood why, yet circumstances had thrown her together with him, for her mother would not even go onto the roof. "I will serve no Roman," she said on the first day Marcus had been brought into the house. And so, during the days that followed, when her father was at his writing table, Marcus' care fell to Taphatha.

And each time she came up onto the rooftop, she felt more drawn to him and thus, more vulnerable.

His steady gaze made her body warm.

"You're very quiet today," Marcus said and smiled at her as he took the bread from her hands. His fingers brushed hers lightly and sent a rush of heat through her. She knew the touch was an accident but couldn't help but catch her breath softly. She lowered her eyes, embarrassed by her reaction to him. "What's wrong, little one?" His question merely made her heart beat faster.

"There's nothing wrong, my lord," she said, striving for normalcy, dismayed by the nervous tremor in her voice.

"Then why won't you look at me?"

She lifted her head and forced herself to study him. The swelling on his face was gone, but the flesh around both eyes was deep purple and streaked with yellow. As soon as he had been well enough to get up and move about the roof, she had noted his proud bearing and his strength. And she had felt sure that his handsome features had probably turned the heads of many women before her. Now he smiled again—a slow curve of his lips that made her stomach drop.

Realizing she was staring at his mouth, she blushed and lowered her eyes. What would he think of her?

Marcus leaned his hip back against the roof wall. "You remind me of someone I once knew." Hadassah had been embarrassed by the least of his attentions, just as this young girl was.

Taphatha raised her head again and saw the pained expression on his face. "Was she very beautiful?"

"No," he said with a sad smile. "She was plain." Marcus gently reached out and tipped her chin. "Little Taphatha, you are very beautiful. You'd have all the men of Rome groveling at your feet for a single smile. The women would pine with jealousy."

Taphatha felt a strange sense of pride in the way he assessed her. She knew she wasn't plain, nor was she blind to the way men looked at her when she walked to the well. Sometimes she wished to be plain so men wouldn't look at her as Adonijah had. Yet, it pleased her that Marcus thought she was beautiful.

Marcus touched the smooth, flawless skin of Taphatha's cheek. How long had it been since he had touched a woman or was even aware of one as he was aware now? His fingers glided down over the rapid pulse in her throat. He took his hand away. "Hadassah was not beautiful in the way the world sees beauty," he said. "It is your innocence and gentleness that reminds me of her."

His face became shadowed again, and, though he looked at her, she knew he was thinking of someone else. She spoke quietly. "You must have loved her very much, my lord."

"I still love her," he said heavily and looked away. A muscle jerked in his jaw. "I'll never stop loving her until I take my last breath."

His words saddened her more than she wanted to admit. "Did she love you that much, Marcus Lucianus Valerian?"

His mouth curved bitterly. He looked down at the girl again. Hadassah had been about Taphatha's age when he had realized he was falling in love with her. He remembered how Hadassah's dark eyes had seemed to hold all the mysteries of the universe in them. Just as Taphatha's now did. Watching her, he noticed other things as well. Her cheeks were flushed. Her brown eyes held a soft glow. It would be easy, too easy, to take advantage of her.

"You and I will never talk of love, little Taphatha. It's a subject best left alone between a Roman and a Jew."

Mortified with embarrassment, Taphatha was too ashamed to speak. She had thought her feelings for him were secret and hidden, but now it was clear she had made a complete fool of herself. Marcus read her as easily as her father read the Scriptures and he felt nothing for her. Cheeks on fire, tears burning her eyes, she turned to flee the roof and him.

Marcus caught hold of her shoulders. "The last thing I want to do is hurt you," he said roughly. He felt her trembling, and his hands tightened. She was far too enticing for a man's peace of mind. He turned her around. Seeing her tears, tears he knew he had caused, he wanted to hold and comfort her. And that was the last thing he could allow himself to do.

He was too conscious of her awareness of him. She was awakening physically, like a flower bud opening, succulent and sweet. He had once enjoyed taking advantage of moments such as these, fulfilling his baser needs for pleasure. But Taphatha, daughter of Ezra Barjachin, was not Arria or a women such as she. She was like Hadassah.

Too much like Hadassah.

Marcus took his hands from her. "Another day or two and I'll be leaving."

Taphatha caught her breath and looked up at him, forgetting her embarrassment in her desire to have him stay. "You won't be ready to travel that soon, my lord. Your ribs must heal. Your strength hasn't fully returned."

"Nevertheless," he said, his mouth firm. He was more worried about her heart than his ribs. "It's too comfortable here on this rooftop." It was too heady a feeling having a beautiful young girl look at him the way she did now, tempting him to fall in love again. Loving Taphatha would be as hopeless as loving Hadassah had been.

"Father will dissuade you."

His smile was rueful. "I think not."

Ezra came up to the roof as evening fell. Marcus saw he wore his phylacteries and knew he had come to pray. Marcus went on with his exercises, slow movements designed to stretch and strengthen unused muscles. Surreptitiously, he watched Ezra walk about the roof, his lips moving, his hands lifting now and then. Sometimes he would stop and raise his head as though seeking the warmth of the setting sun. Then he would begin to walk again, speaking silently to his god. Ezra didn't prostrate himself or kneel as Hadassah had done in the villa garden in Rome. Yet Marcus sensed his love for his god was as deep as hers.

Tired and in pain, Marcus eased himself down onto the bed beneath the canopy. He poured himself some water and drank.

Ezra stopped at the wall nearest the booth where the Roman reclined. He looked at the brilliant reds and oranges of the sunset. "Taphatha told me you intend to leave within a few days."

"I'd leave tomorrow if I could arrange it," Marcus said grimly. "I've caused your family enough grief without prolonging the situation unduly."

"Do you speak of my wife or my daughter?"

Marcus glanced up sharply and hesitated. "Both," he said after a moment. "Your wife has confined herself below while I'm on your roof, and Taphatha . . ." Ezra turned his head slightly.

Marcus felt the impact of his eyes. His mouth flattened. "Your daughter is very beautiful, Ezra. And very, very young."

Ezra said nothing for a long moment. He stared up at the stars. "Until you're fully recovered, you are welcome to stay."

Marcus' mouth curved sardonically. "Are you sure that's wise?"

Ezra turned and looked at him squarely. "Because my daughter is beautiful, and for the first time in her life she has looked upon a man with favor?"

Marcus hadn't expected such calm frankness. His admiration of Ezra deepened. "There is that," he said with equal bluntness. "It would be better if she didn't come up on the roof. I'm a Roman, remember?" His smile was full of self-deprecation. "A raving beast, by Jewish standards." His smile fell away. "Besides, my presence in your household has undoubtedly caused you no end of trouble with your people, not to mention your own wife. You would have been wise to leave me in that wadi."

"Better to have trouble with man than trouble with God."

Marcus gave a soft laugh of derision. "God," he said under his breath, and a sharp pain shot up his side. He had overtaxed himself. "You're a good man, Ezra, but a fool." He leaned back slowly and stared bleakly at the canopy. "You should have dumped me at an inn."

"No one would take you."

Marcus began to laugh and then sucked in his breath as the pain licked across his ribs. Gritting his teeth, he tried to think of something besides the pain.

Ezra sat down on the roof. He untied the phylacteries and held them in the palms of his hands. "All men are fools in some way," Ezra said. "Men want what they can't have."

Wincing, Marcus pushed himself until he was sitting upright. He studied the deepening lines around Ezra's eyes. "What can't you have, old man?" Whatever it was, he would give it to him at the first opportunity—a better house, animals, luxuries. He could give Ezra Barjachin anything he wanted. Why shouldn't he? If not for Ezra, he'd be dead. His body would be rotting away in that foul wadi.

Ezra clutched the phylacteries tighter. "I cannot be like Enoch." With a rueful smile, he looked at Marcus Valerian and wondered why he was sharing such deep feelings with an unbeliever, and a Roman at that.

"Who is Enoch?"

"Enoch walked with God as a man would walk with a friend. Others saw God. Adam. Moses. But only Enoch had a heart that so pleased God that he was caught up into heaven without ever tasting death." He looked at the velvety deep blue of the evening sky. "That is what I pray for."

"Not to taste death?"

"No. All men taste death. It's a natural part of life. I long for a heart that pleases the Lord."

Marcus' face became rigid. "Hadassah wanted to please God and look what it got her, old man. Death." His eyes darkened. "What does this God of yours want from you other than every drop of your blood?"

"Obedience."

"Obedience!" Marcus spat the word. "At what cost?"

"Whatever the cost."

Yanking back the overhang of the canopy, Marcus stood abruptly. A sound of pain hissed from his lips, and he gripped his side. He uttered a short, foul expletive and went down on one knee, light-headed. He swore again, even more vilely than the first time.

Ezra watched him with a strange swelling of pity.

Marcus raised his head, his face ravaged by pain. "Your god and hers sound one and the same. Obedience to his will no matter what the cost." His pain incensed him. "What manner of god killed a girl who loved him more than anything else in the world, even her own life? What manner of god sends his own son to die upon a cross as a sacrifice for mistakes of others?"

Ezra was pierced by his words. "You speak of Jesus."

"Yes. *Jesus.*" He said the name like a curse.

"Tell me what you've been told about him," Ezra said. "Only do so quietly."

Marcus poured out the story Satyros had told him on the voyage. Ezra had heard his father speak of Saul of Tarsus, at first in glowing terms and then in fury and derision.

"If this Christ had the power to do miracles, why does he let his believers die?" Marcus said. "First his disciples, and now hordes of others. I've seen them burned alive in Rome. I've seen them cut down by gladiators. I've seen them eaten by lions. . . ." He shook his head, wanting to shake the memories out of his mind.

"What else did this Satyros tell you about Jesus?"

Marcus raked his fingers through his hair. "Why do you want to know this now? You said yourself he was a false prophet."

"How do we fight what we don't understand?"

What Ezra said was true. Marcus needed to know and understand his adversary.

"All right. I was told this Jesus was betrayed by a friend for thirty pieces of silver. He was deserted by his own disciples before his trial for crimes he hadn't committed. He was hit, spit upon, wounded, and beaten. Does that sound like the son of a god to you? He was crucified between two thieves while people hurled insults at him and the guards cast lots for his clothing. And while he was dying, he prayed for them. Prayed that his father would forgive them. Tell me what kind of a god would allow all that to happen to him or his son, and even worse to come on those who followed after."

Ezra didn't respond. He could not. He was filled with a numbing chill that struck to his very core. He stood and went to the roof wall, clasping it. After a moment, he looked at the heavens. The Roman's words had brought the prophecies of Zechariah and Isaiah ringing in his ears. Closing his eyes tightly, Ezra prayed. *Deliver me from my doubts! Show me the truth!* What came was a conviction so swift and startling, he swayed.

"So they weighed out for my wages thirty pieces of silver . . . 'Throw it to the potter'—that princely price they set on me."

His fingers pressed into the plaster as he remembered the old prophecy. And then another came.

"He was oppressed and He was afflicted, yet He opened not His mouth; He was led as a lamb to the slaughter. . . ."

Ezra could see words he himself had copied onto the scrolls, counting each letter, rechecking over and over for accuracy. Every jot and tittle had to be exact.

"And they made His grave with the wicked—but with the rich at His death. . . ."

Ezra's mind cried out in anguish. *But, Lord, wasn't the Messiah supposed to be like King David, a warrior sent to save his people from the oppression of Rome?*

The answer came swiftly. *"He poured out His soul unto death, and He was numbered with the transgressors, and He bore the sin of many, and made intercession for the transgressors."*

Ezra lowered his head and closed his eyes tightly, his heart breaking. He didn't want to remember those Scriptures, for they had never made sense to him. He tried not to remember them now, but suddenly, inexplicably, they came like trumpets. Words rushed and swelled, pouring over him like a flood, until he could hardly breathe beneath the onslaught.

"He was wounded for our transgressions, He was bruised for our iniquities; the chastisement for our peace was upon Him, and by His stripes we are healed. All we like sheep have gone astray. . . ."

And then, as though the deepest corners of his mind had been given light, Ezra remembered a day long ago when the sky had gone dark at noon and the earth had trembled violently. He had been but a small boy when it had happened. He saw himself sitting on a mat in a rented house in Jerusalem, where his family had gathered for the Passover. His mother was laughing and talking with the other women while preparing food. And suddenly everything went dark. A great roaring sound came from the skies outside. His mother screamed. He screamed, too.

Now, lifting his head, Ezra opened his eyes, stared up at the stars, and said aloud, "'And it shall come to pass in that day,' says the Lord God, 'that I shall make the sun go down at noon, and I will darken the earth in broad daylight.'"

The words of Amos.

Had the prophet spoken of God using Assyria in bringing judgment against Israel, or had his words held a deeper meaning? Had Amos also been given a warning of what would happen when the Messiah came to save his people?

"Jesus has risen!" his uncle had said all those years ago. And what Ezra had felt upon hearing those words came back to him now. Fear. Wonder. Excitement. *Awe.*

What if it was true . . . ?

Ezra stared a moment longer at the heavens. His heart beat within him, and he felt as though he had just awakened from a long nourishing sleep and was seeing the world clearly for the first time.

"Jesus has risen! I have seen him!"

Excitement filled him. He came back and sat down before Marcus again.

"Tell me *everything* about this woman you once knew. Tell me everything she ever told you about Jesus of Nazareth."

Marcus saw the fever in his eyes. "Why?" he said, frowning. "What does it matter?"

"Just tell me, Marcus Lucianus Valerian. Tell me *everything*. From the beginning. Let me decide for myself what matters."

And so Marcus did as he was asked. He gave in to his deep need to speak of Hadassah. And all the while he talked of her, he failed to see the irony in what he was doing. For as he told the story of a simple Judean slave girl, Marcus Lucianus Valerian, a Roman who didn't believe in anything, proclaimed the gospel of Jesus Christ.

THE MOLDING

20

Julia poured herself another goblet of wine. It was so quiet in the villa. She was so lonely she even missed Primus' caustic wit and vicious gossip. At least he had served to distract her from other disturbing thoughts about her life and approaching fate.

No one came to see her anymore. She was sick, and everyone she knew avoided her because of it. She understood all too well. Illness was depressing. It was tedious and boring. Only those suffering wanted to discuss it. She remembered several friends who had become ill. She had avoided them just as others now avoided her. She hadn't wanted to hear a chronicle of pain and symptoms. She hadn't wanted to face the fact that she was mortal. Life was too short to waste on someone else's tragedy.

Now she was in a tragedy of her own.

Julia lifted the goblet to her lips and sipped. She wished she could get so drunk she wouldn't be able to think about the future or *feel* the present. She would just drift on a sea of wine-sodden tranquility. No pain. No fear. Time without regrets.

Once she had dined on lotus. Now, she had to drink posca. However, enough of even the cheap wine and she would feel nothing at all.

No one cared. Why should they? She didn't care. She had never cared. Not about any of them. She had just been pretending to enjoy herself.

Julia gave a brittle laugh that echoed in the chamber. Then she fell silent again, staring morosely into her goblet, wishing she could drown in the rusty-colored wine.

She felt hollow inside. Maybe the ravages of her disease were eating away parts of her that had once been there, unseen but essential parts. Life was a cruel joke. She had possessed everything she needed to be happy: money, position, beauty, complete freedom to do whatever she wanted. Hadn't she taken control of unfortunate circumstances and overcome them by her own will?

So why was life now so unbearable? What had she done wrong?

Her hand trembled as she raised her goblet again, swallowing

211

the bitter wine while trying to swallow the feelings that rose in her. She felt as though she was choking.

She would not think of anything unpleasant today. She would think of things that made her happy.

What had made her happy?

She remembered how she had always run to her brother, Marcus, when he came home to the villa in Rome. He had teased her and pampered her and adored her. Blinking back tears, she forced herself to remember that he had broken his promise to love her no matter what she did. She reminded herself that when she most needed him, he had turned his back on her.

Pushing Marcus from her mind, she began to chronicle the relationships in her past: her father and mother, Claudius, Caius, Atretes, Primus, Calabah. Every name roused regrets and anger, resentment and self-pity—all followed by self-defense and self-justification. No one had a right to tell her how to live. No one! Yet that's what everyone had always tried to do.

Her father had expected her to be who he wanted her to be rather than who she was. Claudius wanted another wife like the one who had died. He had been a fool to chase after her when she had run away one night. It wasn't her fault he fell off his horse and broke his neck. Caius had been cruel. He had used her body and her money for his own pleasures and then, when circumstances turned against him, he had beaten and blamed her. Caius had poisoned her life. What better retribution could she have made than to poison him in return?

Her heart ached as she thought of Atretes. Atretes, oh, most beautiful of men . . . how she had loved him. Never had there been such a gladiator. He had looked like a shining god to her with his perfect features and blazing blue eyes and his beautiful, powerful body. Throngs of women had wanted him—and men, as well—yet all Atretes had wanted was *her*. At least until she had chosen to protect herself against his complete dominance by refusing his offer of marriage, making instead a marriage of convenience with Primus. Then even Atretes, whose plebeian barbaric morality had defied reason, had deserted her.

She frowned as images of the past swirled in her mind. If she had it to do over again, what would she have done differently? How could she have changed anything and retained control over her own life?

One by one, in each case and with each person, Julia sat in the judgment seat, acquitting herself of all blame. Yet, the niggling doubt remained and fed upon her heart: Was it the things done to her that had made the course of her life, or was it things she had done to herself?

She sipped again, trying to dull the pain in her breast. It only intensified.

If she hadn't married Primus, everything might be different now. She might still have Atretes. Hadn't he bought a villa for her? Hadn't he wanted her to be his wife?

She thought of the child she had borne him, and the pain deepened, raw and cold, gripping her heart. She could still hear the faint echo of a soft, helpless cry and her own words coming back to haunt her. *"Put him on the rocks. Let him die."*

She closed her eyes tightly, her knuckles whitening on the wine goblet. It wasn't her fault. Atretes had said he hated her. He had said he didn't want the child. He had said he wouldn't claim it as his own. What else was she supposed to do with it?

Hadassah had entreated her. *"Look at your son, my lady."*

Atretes' son.

Her own son.

She moaned, struggling to press the emotions down into the deepest recesses of her being where she could forget them. The pain within her became heavy and unbearable.

It was all Calabah's fault. Calabah with her cunning lies, her mastery at manipulation. *"You can forget about it now. It's over and done with. Put it behind you."* Calabah's words echoed in Julia's mind. Over and over she heard Calabah, with her seductive words, reminding her that every man Julia had ever known had hurt her . . . Calabah with her seductive reassurance that no man could possibly understand and love a woman the way another woman could.

"With me, you'll always have your freedom. You can do whatever you want."

Calabah with her empty promises. Calabah, a woman who embodied a stone tomb.

"I'll always love you, Julia. I'll never try to make a slave of you the way a man would."

But a slave she had become, in ways she had never fathomed possible. A slave to others' expectations, a slave to her own passions . . . to circumstances, to fear.

A slave to *guilt*.

Groaning, Julia rose from her couch. Her stomach lurched, and she gritted her teeth against the rising nausea. Perspiration broke out on her pallid skin. Swaying, she set the wine goblet down and leaned against a marble pillar to steady herself. The nausea subsided slightly.

A stream of sunlight poured into the peristyle. How she hungered for warmth. She walked out into it and lifted her head to feel the sun on her face. She was filled with a deep, aching longing. She stood in the warmth, wanting it to soak in through her skin and warm her from the inside out. Sometimes she was so cold even the hot waters of the tepidarium were not enough to warm her. Sometimes she thought the coldness emanated from her very heart.

Hugging herself, she closed her eyes and saw amber, reddening heat against her eyelids. Patterns moved. She didn't want to see anything more than that. She didn't want to think about anything or feel anything other than this one single moment in time. She wanted to forget the past and not be afraid of the future.

Then the light was gone.

Shivering, she opened her eyes and saw that the ray of sunlight was now obscured by a cloud. Sadness welled up inside her until she felt she was suffocating beneath the weight of it.

Inexplicably, she felt like a frightened child desperately in need of her mother. Only three others were in the villa with her now, all slaves: Tropas, a Greek cook; Isidora, a household servant from Macedonia; and Didymas, the Egyptian handmaiden she had bought after Eudemas had run away.

Was it only two years ago that she had had a household of servants at her beck and call? She had once owned four Ethiopian litter bearers, two bodyguards from Gaul, a handmaiden from Britannia, and two others from Crete. There had been more servants when Calabah had lived in the villa, all beautiful young women from the farthest reaches of the Empire. Primus had had his own retinue of male servants, all except three of whom he had sold before deserting her. He had taken the handsome lute player from Greece and a brutal mute Macedonian with a hard face. She hoped the Macedonian had slit Primus' throat and dumped him overboard to become food for the fish. What a conniving, insidiously evil man he had been. Worse than Caius by far.

Over the past few months, she had been forced to sell most of her own slaves. She no longer had aurei for luxuries, let alone a plenitude of denarii for the barest of essentials. She had had to resort to whatever means she had to raise money. With only three slaves left to wait on her, life was looking increasingly grim.

Feeling weary, she decided to retire. Leaning heavily on the marble banister, she went up the stairs slowly. Her head was spinning from the wine. She staggered along the upper corridor and entered her bedchamber.

Didymas was tying back the thin netting over her sleeping couch. Julia saw the stiffening in her shoulders as she entered the room. She had whipped her two days ago for shirking her duties.

"Did you wash the floor as I told you to do?"

"Yes, my lady."

"And put fresh linens on the couch?"

"Yes, my lady."

Julia was annoyed by Didymas' placid tone. She saw no evidence of animosity in the girl's shuttered expression, but she sensed it. She needed to be put in her place. Julia looked around the room, searching for something to criticize. "There are no flowers in the vases."

"The vendor wanted two sesterces for lilies, my lady. You only gave me one."

"You should've bargained with him!"

"I did, my lady. He had many customers and wouldn't come down in price."

Julia's face reddened in shame. Many customers. And every one of them had more money than she. "The room is depressing without flowers."

Didymas said nothing, and her servile silence depressed Julia even more. The servants her family had owned in Rome had always served with warmth and affection. They had never been coldly withdrawn, holding grudges when they were properly and rightly disciplined. She remembered some had even laughed as they went about their duties.

She thought of Hadassah. Swaying, Julia grasped the doorjamb, leaning heavily into it. She didn't want to think about Hadassah. The decline of her own life had begun with that wretched girl. If not for her, nothing would be as it was.

Blinking back tears, she looked at Didymas' expressionless face. The slave girl stood where she was. She would do nothing to help until commanded to do so. Somewhere in the defenseless recesses of Julia's mind, a betraying realization came. Hadassah wouldn't have waited. She wouldn't have stood staring at nothing, face stony, her entire being silently screaming her animosity. Hadassah would have come to her and put her arms around her.

Julia looked at the rich trappings of the room and felt its barrenness. She didn't want to enter it. "I'm going out today," she said flatly.

Didymas stood silent, waiting.

Julia glared at her. "Don't just stand there! Lay out my blue palus and bring me a basin of warm water."

"Yes, my lady."

Dejected, Julia watched her handmaiden find the blue palus and place it on the couch. She pushed her hair back from her face and entered the room with as much dignity as she could muster, ignoring Didymas as she left the room to fetch the water.

Clutching the edge of her marble vanity table, Julia sat down heavily. She stared into the shiny metal surface of her mirror and saw reflected there a pale thin face with dark circles beneath large brown eyes. The dark hair was in disarray as though the stranger she stared at hadn't bothered having it brushed or combed for days. How long had it been?

She picked up a tortoiseshell comb and began to work it through the tangles. Finally, giving up, she decided to wait for Didymas to return. When she did, Julia rose and washed her face. As she dabbed her cheeks with a cloth, she sank down once again on the chair before the mirror and commanded Didymas to comb her hair.

Julia winced at the first tug of the comb and turned on the servant in a rage. "Stupid girl! Hurt me again and I'll send you to the lions. I did it once before, in case you didn't know. And I'll do it again!"

Didymas' face whitened. Gratified to have cowed the slave, Julia turned around and lifted her chin. "Now, do it properly."

Hands shaking, Didymas worked with tedious caution.

After a few minutes, Julia felt worse than before. The slave girl's fear was more depressing than her animosity. Lifting her eyes, Julia looked at Didymas' pale, tense face. The girl's eyes flickered, and Julia felt her work even more slowly. Disheartened, Julia looked away.

"Your hair is very lovely, my lady."

Julia took a strand of dull, dark hair and wound it around her finger. She knew the words for what they were. Empty flattery. "It used to shine," she said bleakly.

"Would you like me to brush some scented oil into your hair, my lady?"

So deferential now with the threat of the arena hanging over her head. "Yes, do that," Julia said tersely, glaring at her in the mirror. "Make it shine again by whatever means we have available."

Didymas' hands shook as she poured a few drops of oil into her palms, rubbed them together, and then worked the oil gently into Julia's hair and scalp. Sighing, Julia relaxed slightly, for the massaging felt good. "Braid it into a crown," she said.

Didymas did as commanded. "Are you pleased with it, my lady?" she said when she was finished.

Julia studied the effect critically. The coiffure that had once made her look like a queen now made her look austere. "Eudemas used to weave pearls into my hair," she said.

"There are no pearls, my lady."

"I didn't ask you to remind me!"

Didymas took a step back, her eyes reflecting her fear.

Julia regretted saying anything about the pearls. What did the servants think of her circumstances? Did they whisper among themselves and gloat over her reversal of fortune? They were only concerned with their fates, not hers.

"What is there in the jewelry box?" Julia said imperiously.

Didymas opened the box and studied the contents. "Three glass-bead necklaces, my lady, and some crystals."

"I must have more left than that," Julia said impatiently. "Bring it here." She snatched the box from Didymas and put it on her lap. Sifting through the contents, she found nothing more than what Didymas had said. She took an amethyst crystal from the box and held it in the palm of her hand. She had bought it long ago in Rome from an eastern magus who had set up a booth in the marketplace. Her friend Octavia had been with her. Last she had heard, Octavia's father, deep in debt, had committed suicide. What had become of Octavia? Julia wondered. Was she still giving away her favors to whatever gladiator would accept them? Or had she finally found a man of her own station who was fool enough to marry her?

Julia held the amethyst in her hand. What had the man told her about it? Hadn't he said the crystal had some sort of healing quality? She slipped the chain around her neck and held the crystal tightly in her hand.

Asklepios, let it be so.

"See what you can do with the beads," she said, and Didymas undid her hair. She braided it again, weaving the glass beads into the strands this time. Julia studied the finished effect and sighed. "That will have to do."

"Yes, my lady," Didymas said.

"You may go."

"Yes, my lady." Didymas bowed low and hurried from the room.

Julia picked up a pot of white lead and smoothed some of it beneath her eyes to erase the dark shadows. How much would it take to erase the darkness beneath her eyes now? She worked expertly and set it down again, taking up a pot of red ocher. She added a final touch of kohl to her eyelids and then stared at her reflection.

She looked presentable. But only presentable. Once she had been beautiful. Everywhere she had gone, men had stared at her in admiration. Women had envied her dark brown eyes and creamy skin, her full red mouth, high cheekbones, and sleekly curved body. Now her eyes were glassy, her skin sallow, her mouth red, but painted so. The high aristocratic cheekbones jutted with the prominence of ill health.

Forcing her lips into a smile, she tried to instill some life into her face, but the image in the mirror became a caricature. She looked what she was: a woman who had lost all innocence.

Turning away from her reflection, Julia rose. Unwinding her toga, she dropped it on the floor and took up the blue palus. Didymas had put the silver belt out for her, and Julia hooked it. It hung loosely about her waist. How much weight had she lost since the last time she wore it?

"Didymas!"

The girl came quickly at her summons. "Fix this belt and put on my sandals." Didymas adjusted the silver belt and put it on Julia again. Then she knelt and put the silver sandals on Julia's feet. "The pale blue shawl," Julia said coldly and held her arms out. Didymas brought it to her and arranged it expertly over her shoulders.

Julia took a coin from her money box and held it out to Didymas. "Tell Tropas to rent a litter for me."

"He will need more money than this, my lady."

Julia felt the heat rise into her face and slapped the girl. "Give me the coin!" She snatched it back, shaking with anger and resentment. "I'll walk," she said with a jerk of her chin. "It's a beautiful day and it's not that far to my mother's villa." She put the coin in the box and slammed the lid, putting her hands on top of it. "I know exactly how many coins are in this box, Didymas. If even one is missing when I return, I'll hold you to account. Do you understand?"

"Yes, my lady." The girl stood placid, her face reddened with the print of Julia's hand.

"While I'm gone, air out this room and find some flowers for the vase by my bed. Steal them if you have to. Or trade favors for them. I don't care what you do to get them, but *get them!* Do you understand?"

"Yes, my lady."

"I can't bear this dreary place."

She walked to the main thoroughfare and rested in one of the pretty vine-covered marble fana. The street was crowded with people on their way to and from the Artemision. Closing her eyes, she rested her head against the marble pillar and listened to the hum of life passing her by. She was thirsty, but hadn't thought to bring any money with her, not even a copper to buy a cup of watered wine from one of the street vendors.

She rose and went on.

It had been weeks since she had had any word from her mother. Usually she received a message through one of her mother's servants: "Would you care to come for the evening meal?" A cordial invitation from a dutiful mother. Julia always sent polite regrets. Yet now she realized how she had grown to count on those invitations. Even though she had refused them, they represented a last gossamer line of connection with her mother and her past life.

Perhaps now that connection, too, was broken.

She had to know.

Having rested, she rose and went on. When she reached her destination, she paused at the base of the stone steps. Julia looked up at the formidable structure of the beautiful villa. Her father had never needed to count the cost of anything, and this house set into the hillside bespoke wealth and position. It was not unlike the villa Marcus owned not far away. Naturally, his was a little closer to the center of the city and hub of commercial activity. How many *emporiums* did her brother own now? Two? Three? Undoubtedly more than the last time she had spoken with him.

Gathering her courage, Julia went up the steps. She was breathless when she reached the top and knocked on the door. When no one answered, she knocked again, her heart beating rapidly within her breast. What would her mother say to her after all this time? Would she be glad she had come to pay a call? Or would that pained look of disillusionment and disappointment seep into her expression?

She recognized the slave who opened the door, but couldn't put a name to him. Her father had purchased him shortly after arriving in Ephesus. "Lady Julia," he said in surprise, and she stepped past him, entering the antechamber. As she looked around, the feeling of homecoming weighed heavily on her.

"Tell my mother I've come to see her. I'll wait for her in the peristyle."

He hesitated, a strange look on his face.

At his hesitation, she lifted her chin imperiously. "Did you hear what I said to you, slave? Do as you're told."

Iulius didn't move, amazed at the young woman's arrogance and insensitivity. "Your mother is unwell, my lady."

Julia blinked. "Unwell? What do you mean 'unwell'?"

He wondered if she was concerned about her mother or simply annoyed with the inconvenience to her. "She cannot move or speak, Lady Julia."

Julia glanced up the stairway in alarm. "I want to see her. Now!"

"Of course," he said, gesturing for her to proceed up the stairs as she wished. "She's on the balcony that faces the harbor. I will show you the way in case you don't remember."

Sensing a reprimand, she glared at him. She wanted no reminders of how long it had been since she had entered this house. "I know where it is."

Julia entered her mother's bedchamber and saw her mother outside on the balcony. She was sitting in the sunshine near the railing. Julia crossed the room quickly and went out through the archways. "Mother? I'm here," she said. Her mother didn't turn to her in happy greeting, but sat unmoving. Nervous at such a lack of welcome, Julia came around in front of her.

Julia stared, stunned at how her mother looked. How was it

possible for anyone to change so much in only a few weeks? Her
hair had gone white, and her hands were veined. Her face sagged
on one side, and her mouth hung slightly open. Despite all this,
someone had taken great care to comb her hair and dress her in a
white palus. She looked so pitifully dignified.

Fear filled Julia. What would she do without her mother? She
glanced at the servant. "How long has she been like this?"

"The seizure came upon her forty-six days ago."

"Why wasn't word sent to me?"

"It was, my lady. Twice."

Julia blinked and tried to remember when she had last received
an epistle from her mother. Hadn't someone come one evening
several weeks ago? She had sent them away. Of course, she had
been drunk—understandably so, for she had just learned the full
details of her financial situation and Primus' perfidy. Another messenger had come a week later, but she had been ill that time and
not emotionally able to receive words that might rouse intense
feelings of guilt. Calabah had always said guilt was self-defeating.

"I don't remember any messengers."

Iulius knew she was lying. Lady Julia had never been a good
liar. Her face became pinched, and she would look away as the
words were uttered. He felt sorry for her, for she looked frightened and distressed. He wanted to believe her concern was for
Phoebe, but he was almost certain it was for herself. "She knows
you're here, my lady."

"Does she?"

"I'm sure she's happy you've come."

"Happy?" She gave a bleak laugh. "How can you tell?"

Iulius didn't answer. His mouth tightened. Why had the girl
come? Had she no deep feelings for her mother? She stood staring
down at her. The look on Julia Valerian's face annoyed him. He
thought what a delight it would be to pitch her off the balcony
into the street below. But knowing Julia Valerian, she would, like
a cat, land on her feet and have him sent to the arena.

He hunkered down beside Phoebe's chair. "My lady," he said
gently, wishing heartily that he had better news for her. "Your
daughter Julia has come to visit with you."

Phoebe's hand moved slightly. She tried to speak, but the
sound that came from her lips was little more than a deep garbled
groaning. A drop of saliva glistened on her lips.

Julia drew back, repulsed. "What's been done for her?"

He glanced up and saw the look of disgust on Julia's face. He rose, standing between the girl and her mother. "All that can be done."

"Will she improve?"

"Only God knows."

"Meaning she won't." Julia released a soft, defeated breath and turned away, staring out across the city toward the harbor. "Now what will I do?"

Phoebe tried to speak again. Julia closed her eyes tightly, hunching her shoulders at the pathetic sound of it. She wanted to press her hands over her ears and shut out the sound completely.

Iulius understood what Phoebe wanted.

"I will leave you alone with her, my lady," he said grimly. "It would be kind of you to speak to her," he told Julia and left the balcony.

Julia kept staring out across the city through eyes now blurred with tears. Speak to her, he had said. Not that her mother could possibly understand anything in her condition. Not now.

"You were my last hope, Mother." She turned and looked down at her sadly. "Oh, Mother . . ." With a soft cry, she went down on her knees, put her head in her mother's lap, and wept. She clutched the soft linen of her mother's palus. "It's not fair! It's not fair all the things that've happened to me. And no one's even left to care anymore what suffering I have to endure. And now, you, like *this*. I tell you, the gods are against me."

Phoebe's hand fluttered slightly, her fingers lightly brushing Julia's hair.

"Oh, Mother, what will I do now? What will I do?" Her mother tried to speak again, but Julia couldn't bear the garbled sounds that made no sense. Her mother sounded mad. Julia lifted her head and saw the tears that streamed down her mother's cheeks. With a cry, she fled.

She almost ran across the balcony and out of the room. When Iulius tried to intercept her, she ordered him out of her way and hurried down the steps and out the door.

She wandered the streets of Ephesus. Though the sun was shining, she felt an oppressive darkness around her. She was hungry but had no money to buy bread. It was dusk when she returned to her own villa. Didymas greeted her dutifully and took her shawl. Julia entered the triclinium. Exhausted, she reclined on one of the couches. The room pulsed with cold silence.

Tropas brought in a tray. He set it before her with his usual ceremony and poured her a full goblet of posca. She said nothing to him, and he left the room. She stared at the meal he had prepared for her: one small roasted dove, a thin loaf of grainy bread, and a wrinkled apricot. A bitter smile curved her mouth. Once she had dined on the richest delicacies the Empire could offer, and now, this was her feast.

She picked the meat from the dove until only the small bony carcass remained. Dipping the bread in the wine, she ate it as well. She had fallen so low that even this pauper's meal tasted good to her.

A small knife lay on the tray. She picked it up and toyed with it, her thoughts turning to Octavia's father. Perhaps she should cut her vein as he had done and end this slow, painful fall into complete ruin. She was going to die anyway. The unnamed disease was slowly sapping her strength and eating her up inside. Better to die quickly with a little pain than to linger and suffer unknown agonies.

Her palms began to sweat. The hand holding the knife trembled. She positioned the blade over the blue lines that ran beneath the pale flesh of her wrist. Her hand shook harder. "I must do it. I must. There's no other way. . . ." She closed her eyes, trying desperately to gather the courage to end her own life.

With a soft moan, she leaned forward, the knife dropping from her fingers. It clattered to the marble floor, the sound echoing out into the peristyle.

Curling up on the long couch, Julia covered her face with her trembling hands and wept.

21

Marcus stood on the roof with Ezra Barjachin for the last time. Though his strength had not fully returned and his wound was not fully healed, he felt driven to continue his quest. He had informed Ezra last night that he would leave this morning, requesting clothing for his journey with a promise to repay him.

"Accept these as a gift," Ezra said and presented Marcus with a new seamless, ankle-length tunic, a sash of colorful striped cloth, a heavy mantle to serve him as a cloak and bedding, and a pair of new sandals.

Marcus was deeply touched by the Jew's generosity and kindness and was even more determined to see that Ezra was properly recompensed for his inconvenience. He had asked Taphatha to find him a Roman messenger. He gave the man a letter and promised him payment when he arrived at his destination. It took some convincing, but the messenger finally agreed to ride to Caesarea Maritima on trust and contact Marcus' representatives. As soon as they read his instructions and saw his signature, Marcus knew they would send what he demanded and all would be done as he instructed.

Marcus looked at the older man standing by the roof wall. Ezra wore the *tallis* draped over his head, and Marcus knew he was praying. He felt a mingling of impatience and envy. The older man was as disciplined and tenacious as Hadassah had ever been. Would he share the same fate? What good were all his prayers? What good had hers ever been?

And why had Ezra become so hungry to learn about Jesus?

Marcus had been surprised at how intently Ezra had listened to every bit of information he could relate of what Hadassah had said about the man she had worshiped as a god. Marcus hoped telling Ezra would bring the truth to light. Perhaps this learned Jew would see the impossibilities and discrepancies of the strange story of a homely carpenter-turned-magician who proclaimed himself the Son of Adonai and who, some claimed, had arisen from the dead.

But something strange had transpired on the rooftop over the past few days. Marcus had witnessed a change in Ezra. Subtle, indescribable, yet undeniable. Marcus couldn't put words to it. He only sensed it with his inner being. It was as though he was with someone completely different from the Ezra Barjachin who had found him in the wadi half-dead.

Marcus looked at Ezra, studying him. The older man was gazing distractedly into the street. He had to know for certain. "You believe Jesus is your Messiah, don't you, old man?"

Ezra lifted his head and looked at the heavens. "It is as you say."

"As *I* say? Don't credit me with that story. I didn't say Jesus was your Messiah, or God, or anything other than a man. I told you what Hadassah believed he was."

"Yes, but with every word you spoke, I remembered the Scriptures' foretelling of him." He looked at Marcus. "My uncle was stoned because he believed Jesus was the Messiah. On his last visit here, I overheard him tell my father what Jesus said to those close to him, 'I am the Way and the Truth and the Life. The only way to the Father is through Me.'"

"Any man alive could say that."

"Only one can fulfill it. In the midst of his suffering, Job said, 'Surely even now my witness is in heaven, and my evidence is on high.' Man needs someone to speak for him before the Lord. Job said also, 'I know that my Redeemer lives, and He shall stand at last on the earth.' A redeemer who sacrificed himself for our sake. Only God himself is pure and without sin, Marcus. I believe Jesus is the Redeemer I've been waiting for all my life."

"Think with reason. You've waited so long for your Messiah you want this Jesus to be the one. But what stand did he take other than to die on a cross between two other criminals?"

"He presented himself as the Passover Lamb. He was sacrificed as an atonement for the sins of all mankind."

"You're saying he gave up his life and became a symbol."

"No, not a symbol. *Truth*. I believe he did arise from death. I believe he is God the Son."

Marcus shook his head. Was it possible that all he had said to make this man see the fallacy in Hadassah's faith had only convinced him it was true? "Why? How can you?"

"You have told me many things over the past few days, Marcus. Events I remember from my childhood. I was a boy when Jesus came into Jerusalem and was crucified. Words were said, and I overheard. To add to that, I have read and copied the Scriptures from the time I was a boy. It is my craft. Your testimony and the Word of God and what I remember of those times have confirmed what is in my heart. Jesus *is* the pathway to almighty God. Only through him will I find what I've been hungering for all my life."

"And what's that?"

"A personal relationship with the Lord."

"Be careful what you wish for, old man. Jesus is the pathway to death. Believe me. I know. He will demand your life's blood."

"He can have it."

Marcus looked away, disturbed. What had he done to him? He should never have spoken. He tried to block out the memory of Hadassah standing in the center of the arena. "I hope what you have come to believe will not prove to be the death of you."

"Why do you harden your heart against God, Marcus Valerian? Who do you think it was that led me to you on that road from Jerusalem?"

Marcus gave a brittle laugh. "It was the vultures who led you to me. Remember?" He saw Ezra wanted to say more and held up his hand. "But let's not argue about something over which we can never agree." He didn't want his last conversation with Ezra to end in anger. "It is time I left. I want to walk as long as possible before nightfall."

"So be it."

Ezra walked down the steps and out of the house with Marcus. He accompanied him all the way to the city gates. And then he blessed him. "May the Lord shine his face upon you and give you peace, Marcus Lucianus Valerian."

Marcus grimaced at the blessing. "I've much for which to thank you, Ezra Barjachin, and I fear what I've given you will cause you great harm." He extended his hand.

Ezra clasped his arm. "You have given me a gift beyond price."

Marcus' mouth curved wryly. "You are a good man. For a Jew."

Well aware Marcus meant no insult, Ezra laughed. "Perhaps one day you will overcome your Roman blood," he said in kind.

The casual words struck Marcus like a blow, for they unwittingly brought to his mind an image of himself laughing and cheering as men and women died for no other reason than entertainment for the mob.

Ezra saw his anguish and understood. "Your Hadassah is alive, Marcus."

"She's dead," Marcus said with flat clarity as he withdrew his hand. "I saw her die in an Ephesian amphitheater."

"Life is far more than we see with our eyes. Your Hadassah is with God, and God is eternal."

Pain clutched Marcus' heart. "I wish I could believe it."

"In God's time, perhaps you will."

"May your God protect you," Marcus said and smiled slightly. "And find a good, strong man for Taphatha."

Ezra stood at the gate and watched Marcus walk down the road. He was filled with a deep compassion for the tormented young Roman and wondered what would happen to him. Turning toward home, Ezra prayed that God would place a hedge of protection around Marcus as he traveled.

Jehosheba glanced up from her work as Ezra entered the house. "Perhaps now that *he* is gone, everything will return to normal."

"Nothing will ever be the same again," Ezra said.

"Bartholomew walked Taphatha home from the well yesterday afternoon. He said she hardly spoke to him." She pressed her lips together. "She never had trouble finding words with that Roman you brought into our house."

"She will have the man God intends for her."

She dropped the garment she was repairing into her lap and looked up at him. "And who will that be?"

"You worry too much, woman," he said and ladled water into a clay cup.

"You used to worry more about Taphatha than I." Her eyes flickered with uncertainty. "What's happened to you over the last few days?"

"Wondrous things," he said and drank.

She frowned in annoyance. "What *wondrous* things?"

He set the cup down. Soon he would tell her, but not now. "I need time to sort through what I have learned before I can explain in a way you will understand."

"I am such a fool? Tell me, Ezra. While you're sorting through whatever it is you've learned, will you work at your booth again?"

Ezra didn't answer. He stood in the open doorway and looked down the street. Taphatha was coming from the market, a basket balanced on her head. Bartholomew was walking beside her. He was a good and persistent young man.

Ezra had not told his daughter Marcus was to leave this morning. He supposed it was the coward's way out. Her feelings for Marcus had become more and more apparent with each day. And Marcus Valerian's attraction for her had been noticed as well. It was to the young man's credit that he had left when he did. A lesser man would have remained to take advantage of a beautiful girl's infatuation.

But what was he to do now?

Jehosheba came to stand beside him. "Do you see how she ignores him? And all because of a Roman," she said bitterly, but when she raised her head and looked at him, Ezra saw the chagrin in her expression. "What will you say to her?"

"I will tell her Marcus Lucianus Valerian has gone."

"And good riddance," she said as she turned away. "It would have been far better if he had left sooner." She sat down and took the worn garment again.

Taphatha paused and spoke briefly with Bartholomew. She turned toward the house again, and Bartholomew stood watching her go the last bit of distance. Clearly dejected, he turned away and started down the street again.

"Good morning, Father," she called cheerfully as she came the last bit of the way. Lowering the basket from her head, she kissed his cheek and entered the house.

"How is Bartholomew?" Jehosheba said, keeping her eyes on her work.

"He is well, Mother."

"So are others," she muttered under her breath.

Taphatha took the fruit from the basket and placed it in the clay bowl on the table. "He said his mother is already preparing plum *hamantashen* for the *mishlo'ah manot* this year."

"I haven't even begun my preparations for Purim," Jehosheba said dismally. "Other things have interfered." Her gaze flickered accusingly at her husband.

"I'll help you, Mother. We have more than enough time to prepare the gifts for the poor and food packages for our friends." She selected two perfect apricots and started for the steps to the roof.

"He's gone," Ezra said.

Taphatha stopped and turned. She stared at him with alarm. "He can't be!" she said, blinking. "His wounds aren't fully healed."

"Healed enough," Jehosheba muttered.

"He left this morning, Taphatha."

She ran up the steps to the roof. When she came down again, Ezra thought she would run after Marcus. She even took a few steps toward the door and then stopped. Her shoulders sagged, and with a soft cry, she sank down onto a stool. Her eyes filled with tears. "He did not even say good-bye."

Jehosheba clutched the worn garment in her hands and studied her daughter. She looked up at Ezra, beseeching him.

To do what? he wondered.

"He said he would go," Taphatha said tremulously, tears slipping down her cheeks. "He said it would be better if he did."

"A pity he didn't go sooner," her mother said dismally.

"I hoped he would stay forever."

"To what end?"

"I don't know, Mother. I *hoped*."

"Hoped what, Taphatha? That a Roman would agree to be circumcised? That a Roman might become a Jew? You must think, Daughter."

Taphatha shook her head and looked away, her face pale with misery. Jehosheba started to say more, but Ezra shook his head, silencing her before she did. Her own eyes were filled with tears and accusation as she looked at him. He knew what she was thinking. It was his fault Taphatha had fallen in love with a Gentile. It was his fault she was suffering. He shouldn't have brought Marcus Valerian into their home.

But if he hadn't, he might never have come to know the truth.

Having no words to spare his daughter her pain, Ezra remained silent. After a moment Taphatha rose and fled to the roof.

"You couldn't say something?" Jehosheba said in accusation, her cheeks pale and tear streaked.

"Whatever I say will only hurt her more."

Jehosheba dumped the garment she was sewing into a basket and rose. "Then I will—"

"No, you won't. Sit down, woman, and leave her be."

Wide-eyed, Jehosheba sat.

Taphatha carried out her duties over the next few days. She said very little. Jehosheba went to the market and visited with the other women. Ezra returned to his parchments, ink, and pens. He felt a restlessness and hunger and spent more and more time on the roof during the evening hours, praying for direction.

He was waiting, but he knew not for what.

A Roman advocate came from Caesarea Maritima seven days after Marcus' departure. The man was richly dressed and accompanied by eight well-armed guards. With great ceremony, he presented Ezra a letter and gestured for two guards to set a strongbox upon the table.

Confused, Ezra peeled off the wax seal and unrolled the scroll. The epistle stated that the bearer of the letter, one Ezra Barjachin, could sail at any time to any destination on any ship owned by Marcus Lucianus Valerian. He was to be given the best accommodations and treated with the highest respect and honor.

"How can this be?" Ezra said, stunned. "Who is he that he can say these things?"

The advocate laughed. "Do you not know who was under your roof, Jew? Marcus Lucianus Valerian can do whatever he pleases. He is a Roman citizen and one of the richest merchants in the Empire. He owns emporiums in Rome, Ephesus, Caesarea Maritima, and Alexandria. His ships sail as far as Tartessus and Brittania."

Jehosheba sat down heavily on her stool, her mouth agape.

The advocate opened the strongbox, revealing its contents. "For you," he said with a grandiose sweep of his hand. It was filled with gold aurei.

Stunned, Ezra drew back from it.

"The difference between a Roman and a Jew," the advocate said haughtily, casting a disdainful look around the simply furnished room. Having finished his assignment, the advocate walked out of the house. The soldiers followed.

Ezra looked into the box again. Unable to believe his eyes, he picked up a handful of golden coins and felt the weight of them in his hand.

Jehosheba rose, trembling. She stared into the strongbox and clutched Ezra's sleeve. "There is enough here to live comfortably for the rest of our lives! We can buy a bigger house. We can have servants. You can sit by the city gates with the elders. Your brother Amni will never look down his nose upon you again!"

Taphatha stood silently, her wide, dark eyes upon her father.

"No," Ezra said. "God has another purpose for this money."

"What purpose? He has blessed you for your righteousness. He has given you wealth to enjoy."

Ezra shook his head. "No," he said again and dropped the coins back into the box. "This is for his work."

"Have you gone mad? Haven't you listened to the Pharisees? God *rewards* the righteous."

"No one is righteous, Mother. Not even one," Taphatha said softly. "Only the Lord himself is righteous."

Ezra smiled at her, his heart expanding at her words. He nodded, his eyes shining. She would understand and believe when he told her the Good News. "We will wait upon the Lord."

"Yes, Father. We will wait upon the Lord."

Ezra closed the lid of the strongbox and locked it.

22

Marcus walked north within sight of the banks of the Jordan River. He passed through Archelais, Aenon, and Salim and then walked northwest toward the hill country. In each village, he paused to ask anyone who would speak with him if they remembered a girl named Hadassah who had gone with her family to Jerusalem and not returned after the destruction. No one had ever heard of her.

He left wondering if the people to whom he spoke told him the truth. Often the courteous demeanor with which he was first greeted changed instantly to wariness and hostility when he spoke. His accent was marked. He could see the change come in their eyes and knew what they were thinking. Why would a Roman dress as a Jew unless he had some hidden scheme to trap them by their words?

After days of wandering, he entered a small village named Nain in the hills of the district of Galilee. He stopped at the marketplace and purchased bread and wine. As had happened before, he was assumed to be a Jew until he spoke and his accent was recognized. However, this time the merchant was blunt rather than apprehensive, straightforward rather than withdrawn.

"Why are you dressed as a Jew?" he said, openly surprised and curious.

Marcus told him of being robbed on the road to Jericho and of being rescued by Ezra Barjachin. "These were a gift from him. I wear them proudly."

The merchant nodded, seemingly satisfied with his answers but still curious. "What are you doing here in the hill country of Galilee?"

"I'm looking for the home of a girl named Hadassah."

"Hadassah?"

"Have you heard the name before?"

"Maybe. Maybe not. Hadassah is a common enough name among Jewish girls."

Marcus was not satisfied with his answer. He described her in as much detail as he could.

The merchant shrugged. "Dark hair, dark brown eyes, slight build. Your description would fit any one of a hundred girls. Was there something remarkable about her?"

"*She* was remarkable." An old woman was standing in the shade of the stall. Marcus could tell she was eavesdropping on his conversation with the merchant. Something about her expression made him direct his next question to her. "Do you know of a girl named Hadassah?"

"It is as Nahshon says," the old woman said. "There are many Hadassahs."

Dejected, Marcus started to turn away when the old woman spoke again. "Was her father a potter?"

He frowned, trying to remember, then glanced back at her. "Maybe. I'm not sure."

"There was a potter who lived here. His name was Hananiah. He married when he was advanced in years. His wife's name was Rebekkah. She bore him three children—a son and two daughters. One of the girls was named Hadassah. The other was Leah. The son was called Mark. They went to Jerusalem and never returned."

The merchant looked impatient with her. "The Hadassah of whom you speak may not be the same one."

"Hadassah claimed her father was raised from the dead by Jesus of Nazareth," Marcus said.

The merchant glanced at him sharply. "Why did you not say this in the beginning?"

"Then you know of her."

"The Hadassah you seek is the same one," the old woman said. "The house where her family lived has been closed up since they went to Jerusalem for Passover. We heard they all died there."

"Hadassah lived."

The old woman shook her head in amazement. "An act of God," she said reverently.

"She was a timid child," the merchant said. "One would think it would be the strong who survived. Not the weak."

Leaning heavily on her cane, the old woman studied Marcus intently. "Where is Hadassah now?"

Marcus looked away. "Where did she live?" His question met with a long silence. He looked at the old woman again. "I must know," he said heavily.

The woman studied him, and her lined face softened. "Hananiah's house is down that street, on the east side, fourth from the end."

Marcus turned away.

"Roman," she said gently, "you will find no one there."

He found the house with ease and was amazed at how small it was. The door had been left unlocked. It creaked as he pushed it open. As he entered the dim interior, cobwebs caught at him. He brushed them aside. The place had the dry smell of disuse and abandonment.

He glanced around at the small main room. There were no steps to the roof in this house, only a door at the back that opened into a bedchamber. A bare platform bed was built into the clay wall.

Marcus crossed the room and lifted the small bar on the window doors and pushed them open. Sunlight streamed in and, along with it, a blast of warm air that set particles of dust dancing in the stream of light. Stepping back, Marcus turned and saw the sun shone in upon a potter's wheel. He went to it and turned it. The wheel moved stiffly, protesting years of disuse.

Leaving it, Marcus ran his hand over the dusty, roughhewn table. He sat on one of the five stools and looked slowly around the room. There was a yoke and two water buckets near the front door. Other than that, there were a few clay jugs and bowls. Little else. Certainly nothing of value.

Closing his eyes, he breathed in deeply, his hands flat on the rough surface of the table. Hadassah had grown up in this house. She had slept in this room, eaten at this table. His fingers spread on the gritty surface, thinking her hands had touched it. He wanted to capture her essence, to be close to her.

Instead, fear filled him.

He couldn't remember the details of her face anymore.

He tried desperately to grasp his memories of her, but they were fading, blurring her image in his mind. He covered his face and tried to remember, to put her features together. All he could see now was a faceless girl on her knees in his father's villa garden, her hands raised toward the heavens and God.

"No." He groaned, digging his fingers into his hair and holding his head. "Don't take what little I have left of her." But no matter how he pleaded or how hard he tried, he knew she was slipping away from him.

Exhausted and depressed, Marcus looked around. He had come so far. And for what? For this? He closed his eyes and laid his head on his arms.

23

Didymas entered the bedchamber and came out onto the small balcony where Julia was sitting with a cool cloth pressed over her forehead.

"What is it?" Julia said, annoyed by the slave girl's presence.

"A man is here to see you, my lady."

Julia's heart took a small leap. Had Marcus returned? Perhaps he had finally come to his senses and decided they had only one another. Though she knew it was improbable, knew she shouldn't hope, she felt hope rise anyway. Her fingers trembled as she continued to press the cool wet cloth against her throbbing forehead. She was afraid to reveal her face to Didymas' scrutiny. Didymas would no doubt secretly relish her struggle, and even more so, her pain.

"Who is it?" Julia said with feigned indifference. She had had no visitors in weeks. Who among her supposed friends would come to see her as she was now?

"His name is Prometheus, my lady."

"Prometheus?" she said blankly, her heart dropping as a wave of disappointment poured over her like cold water. "Who is Prometheus?" she demanded in irritation. The name was familiar, but she couldn't place it.

"He said he's a slave of this household, my lady. He asked first for Primus. When I said the master was no longer in Ephesus, he asked to speak with you."

With a shock, Julia remembered who he was. "Prometheus!" Primus' catamite! What was he doing here? He had run away almost four years ago. Why would he come back now? If Primus were here, he would either kill the boy on the spot or, far more likely, suffer anew from his foul passions for him. What was *she* supposed to do with him?

She thought quickly. With Primus gone, Prometheus must know he was placing his life in her hands. He might not be aware of the two maids she had sent to the arena in Rome, but he had been here when she sent Hadassah to the lions. He was also more than aware she had always been repulsed by his position in the household. She had mocked Primus' passion for him and looked upon Prometheus himself as something less than a trained dog.

Her head throbbed. "Why does he come back now?" The cool cloth she held over her eyes did little to ease the pain.

"I don't know, my lady. He did not say."

"I wasn't asking you, you fool!"

"Do you wish me to send him up to you, my lady? Or shall I send him away?"

"Let me think!"

Julia stared, unseeing, past the balcony railing, reflecting briefly on the past. Prometheus had been very fond of Hadassah. In fact, it was Prometheus' admiration for the slave girl that had roused the terrible beast of jealousy and hatred in Primus. Julia further remembered it was much of this that brought on so many of her own troubles. Sometimes, late at night, Prometheus would sit with Hadassah in the peristyle, and they would talk. Primus said her little Jewess was seducing the boy, but Julia knew there had never been that kind of relationship between them. Her lip curled. Hadassah had been too *pure* for that. Yet, no matter how innocent the discourse between Hadassah and Prometheus, trouble had come from it.

What a fool he was to come back! She could do whatever she pleased with him. Slaves who ran away and were captured were often thrown to the dogs in the arena. She could think of far worse things to do to him.

The echo of roaring lions filled her mind, and she gripped her head, moaning softly. "What does he want?"

"He didn't say, my lady."

"Did you ask?"

"I didn't think it my place."

She didn't want to think about the past. Prometheus would only be a reminder. "Send him away."

"Very well, my lady."

"No, wait!" she said. "I'm curious." What would possess a runaway slave to return to a master or mistress who would more than likely order him tortured and killed? Surely he must know what she would like to do to him. Upon hearing Primus was gone, he had probably taken a wiser course and fled the villa as soon as Didymas left the antechamber.

"If he's still waiting below, send him up," she said. "I'm curious to hear what he has to say for himself."

Julia was surprised when, a few minutes later, Didymas escorted him into the bedchamber, then came to the balcony to tell her "Prometheus, my lady" in a voice devoid of emotion.

"I wish to speak with him alone," she said, lowering the cloth from her eyes and gesturing impatiently. Didymas hurried from the chamber.

Taking a deep breath, Julia tossed her cloth aside and rose from her couch. She snatched up a robe and put it on as she entered the bedchamber.

Prometheus stood in the middle of her room. She glanced at him, expecting him to prostrate himself before her or plead tearfully for mercy. Instead, he stood silent, waiting. Her brows rose.

Besides his grave dignity, his appearance was very changed. He was taller than she remembered, and he had grown more handsome over the past few years. He had been a mere boy when Primus bought him from the slavers in the booths beneath the arena stands. Now, he was a handsome young man of fifteen or sixteen, his hair cut short, his face clean-shaven.

"Prometheus," she said, drawing out his name with dark meaning. "How nice of you to return." She saw no fear in his face and wondered at his calmness.

"I've come to beg your forgiveness, my lady, and ask that I may return to serve you."

Stunned, Julia stared at him. "Beg my forgiveness and return?"

"Yes, my lady. I'll serve you as you wish, unless you deem otherwise."

"By *otherwise,* you mean if I should decide to have you killed?"

He hesitated and then said softly, "Yes, my lady."

She was amazed at his attitude. Clearly, he was in no doubt of his highly precarious situation, but he seemed unafraid. Or perhaps he was as good a hypocrite as the ones who performed in the theater.

She smiled faintly. "Serve me as I wish? Considering your previous position in my household, that's an interesting proposition." Her glance flickered over him. He blushed and lowered his head. She was surprised more by that than anything else. Surely all the time he had spent serving Primus' various aberrant passions had obliterated all modesty.

Her mouth curved in a mocking smile. "Do you not realize you broke poor Primus' heart when you so cruelly deserted him? He was madly in love with you."

Prometheus said nothing.

"You should be ashamed to have treated your master so unkindly," she said sardonically, enjoying his discomfort. "You should be groveling."

Prometheus didn't move.

Strangely, he intrigued her. And it had been a long time since anything had distracted her from her illness.

"Did you ever love him?" She saw the boy swallow convulsively and knew she was plumbing emotion below the surface. "Look at me and answer truthfully. Did you ever *really* love Primus, even for one tiny little instant? Answer me!"

"No, my lady."

"What did you feel for him?"

He raised his eyes and looked at her. "Nothing."

She gave a laugh of pure satisfaction. "Oh, how I wish he could hear you say that." She saw the small frown that crossed his forehead. Her pleasure faded. Did he think *her* cruel to say that? What about all she had suffered at Primus' hands? Didn't Primus deserve to suffer as well? He should have suffered more!

She turned away and walked to the table that held the jug of wine. "For all Primus' politic charm and public gaiety, Prometheus, he is a vicious and vindictive man who uses people for his own ends. He sucks them dry and then leaves the empty husks behind." Her throat closed. "But you should know all about that, shouldn't you?" she said in a choked voice.

She left the jug untouched and turned to look at Prometheus again. Her mouth curved into a bitter smile.

"I was glad when you ran away, Prometheus. Do you know why? Because it hurt Primus. Oh, it hurt him terribly. He grieved over you as one would grieve over a beloved wife who betrayed him." She gave a bleak laugh. "For a little while, he understood how I felt when Atretes deserted me." She looked away, wishing she hadn't spoken of her lover. The merest mention of his name brought a rush of pain and sense of loss. "Not that Primus was ever sympathetic."

Regaining control, she looked at Prometheus again, head high. "Do you want to know something else, slave? You became my one small defense against Primus' innumerous cruelties later on."

Prometheus looked troubled. "I'm sorry, my lady."

He sounded sincere. "For him?" Her mouth curved bitterly. "You needn't be. He found a means of getting his revenge."

"For you, my lady."

His grave sincerity dazed her briefly. He spoke as though he was indeed sorry. "Sorry?" she said, taking defense in her intellect. For what reason? Her eyes flashed. "Oh, I'll bet you're sorry, Prometheus." She tilted her head back slightly, studying him coldly. "You're sorry now because you know what I can do to you."

"Yes, my lady. I know."

It was a simple statement, uttered with complete acceptance. He wasn't afraid to die.

Just as Hadassah hadn't been afraid to die that day she walked out onto the sand.

Julia blinked, trying to flee the memory. "Why did you come back?"

"Because I'm a slave. I had no right to leave."

"You could be a thousand miles from Ephesus by now. Who would know if you were slave or free then?"

"*I* would know, my lady."

She wondered at his answer, for it made no sense to her at all. "You were foolish to return. You know very well I despise you."

He lowered his eyes. "I know, my lady. But it was right that I return, whatever the consequences."

She shook her head. Crossing the room, she sat down weakly on the end of her sleeping couch. Cocking her head to one side, she studied him. "You're very different from what I remember."

"Things have happened to change me."

"So I can see," she said with a mocking laugh. "For one thing, you've completely lost your mind."

Amazingly, he smiled. "In a manner of speaking, I gave it away." His eyes shone with an inner, unfathomable joy.

Julia felt her spirits lift slightly just looking at him. A strange, soulful hunger filled her. Struggling against it, she studied him from head to foot and back to head again. She liked what she saw. He was like a marvelous work of art.

His smile died at her intimate perusal, and his cheeks deepened in color.

"You are embarrassed," she said in surprise.

"Yes, my lady," he said frankly.

How was it possible, after all he had done with Primus, that he could be so sensitive? She was touched. "I'm sorry to stare, Prometheus, but it's clearly evident the gods have been very good to you. Beauty and good health." Her smile grew wistful. "The gods have not been so kind to me."

"Can nothing be done for you, my lady?"

His question was clear acknowledgment of her sad physical state. She didn't know whether to be angry at his impudence or thankful she didn't have to try to keep up a false front. She shook her head slightly. Anger took strength, and she had little to spare.

"I've tried everything," she said, amazed at her own frankness. She spread her hands and shrugged. "As you can see, nothing has done much good."

Prometheus looked at her openly then, assessing her in a way that made her want to weep. "Do they say what's wrong with you, my lady?"

"One said it was a wasting illness of some kind. Another said it was Hera's curse. Another said it's the Tiber fever that comes and goes."

"I'm sorry, my lady."

There it was again. He was sorry. For her! How pathetic she must be that even a lowly slave should feel pity! Chilled, she stood and drew her robe more tightly around her.

She walked toward the balcony, concentrating on moving with grace and dignity. Marcus once had said she walked like a queen. She stopped beneath the archway and turned to face him. Lifting her chin slightly, she forced a smile, a cool smile full of womanly awareness.

"You are very beautiful, Prometheus. Well built. Strong. Very male. I might find interesting use of you." Her words were calculated to cut him, and she saw they did. His wounds must still be very raw that she could manage it so easily. Or had she become as adept at wounding others as Calabah and Primus? The thought disturbed her greatly. She had expected to feel in control of the situation. Instead, she felt ashamed.

She let out her breath softly. "Do not look so distressed," she said gently. "I merely wanted to see your reaction, Prometheus. I assure you, my interest in men has long since waned. The last thing I want or need right now is another lover." Her mouth curved wryly.

Prometheus was silent for a long moment. "I can serve in capacities other than—"

"For example?" she broke in wearily.

"I could be a litter bearer, my lady."

"If I had a litter."

"I could be a message carrier."

"If I had someone to whom I wanted to write a letter." She shook her head. "No, Prometheus. The only thing I need now is *money*. And the only thing I can think to do with you is take you down to the slave market and have you auctioned off. There are any number of men like Primus in this city who would pay most handsomely for a young man who received the specialized training you did."

His silence was like an anguished cry in the room. She felt it. She saw it, too. His eyes were moist. He didn't speak, but she knew he wanted to plead. Yet, he stood silent, rigid with self-control. Oh, how he must wish he had never returned.

Something long forgotten was awakened within her. Compassion stirred soft wings within her breast. She felt his anguish and, for the briefest moment, shared in it. He wanted to run away again, and who, least of all her, could blame him?

"You have no liking for that fate, do you?" she said very quietly.

"No, my lady," he said, voice trembling.

"Would you rather I sold you to the editor of the games? They would make a gladiator out of you."

He looked defeated. "I won't fight."

"Surely you can fight. You look strong enough. They would train you before sending you into the arena. You would have a chance of survival."

"I didn't say I can't fight, my lady. I said I *won't*."

"Why not?"

"It's against my religious beliefs."

She stiffened, torturous memories of Hadassah returning to haunt her again. Why now? She clenched her hands. "You would fight if your life depended on it!"

"No, my lady. I would not."

She looked at him again, closely, and insight came. He was exactly like Hadassah. "Did the gods send you here to torment me?" Her head began to throb again. Pain blurred her vision. She gave a soft cry. "Ohhhh . . ." She pressed her hands against her temples. "Why do you come to me now?" She couldn't think past the pounding in her head. Feeling faint and struggling against nausea, she stumbled across the room and sank down on the end of her sleeping couch. "Why did you come?"

241

"To serve you."

"How can you serve me?" she said with biting sarcasm.

"I will serve you however you need, my lady."

"Can you cure me of this affliction?" she cried with bitter mockery.

"No, but I've heard of a doctor in the city . . ."

She clenched her hands into white fists. "I've seen so many doctors, I'm sick of them! I've been to every temple there is! I've prostrated myself and pled for mercy before a dozen idols. I've impoverished myself with buying votive offerings from bloodsucking merchants. What good has it done me? What good, I ask you! *What good?!*"

He came closer, speaking gently. "This doctor of whom I have heard is said to have an assistant who has worked miracles."

She gave a cynical laugh and looked up at him. "How much does a miracle cost these days?" Her lips twisted bitterly. "Take a look around you, Prometheus. Is there anything of any real value left?" She looked around the barren room herself, ashamed. "All I have left is this villa, and it's already encumbered by debt." Even as she revealed the facts to him, she wondered why she admitted her utter humiliation to a slave.

"What is your life worth to you, my lady?"

Her anger evaporated at his question, fear taking its place. She looked up at him again and was filled with misery. "I don't know. I don't know if my life is worth anything at all. No one cares what happens to me. I don't even know if I care anymore."

Prometheus went down on one knee before her and took her cold hand in his. "I care," he said very quietly.

She stared at him, amazed. She wanted desperately to grasp hold of the hope he offered her, and, for one brief instant, she almost did. Then she was afraid to believe him. After all, why should he care? She had never been kind to him. In fact, she had always treated him with disdain and disgust. It made no sense that he would care about her now. What if this was some terrible trick . . . ? She felt fear gnawing at her.

Out of her fear came anger.

Oh, she knew why he cared! She could almost hear Calabah's voice echoing in her head, reminding her of the way things really were. "Naturally, he *cares*," she would say. "He's worried about his own skin." The echo of Calabah's dark, mocking laughter rang in her ears.

Julia removed her hand from his. "How touching," she said brittlely, glaring down at him. She stood shakily and moved away, head high, heart racing, as she allowed anger to rule her thinking. But she did not have the strength to sustain her anger, and it quickly gave way to despair, and despair to self-pity.

"Don't think I believe you. Not for a minute," she said, her back to him. "No one cares," she whined, her lip trembling. "You're just like all the rest. Smiling and pretending when you really hate me and wish I was dead. Every time Didymas walks into this room, I can see the look in her eyes. I know what she's thinking. She'll dance on my tomb." Perhaps she would have her killed before that day came!

She turned and saw he was standing again. His expression was solemn but still not afraid. She looked at him for a long moment, oddly comforted by his calmness. How long had it been since she had felt that way?

"I will keep you," she said finally, wondering even as she said it why she was doing so. What was she going to do with him? What good was he to her?

A flicker of relief crossed his face. "Thank you, my lady."

"I'll have to think about your duties. But not right now." She trembled with weakness. Perspiration beaded her forehead, and she felt sick. She put her hand out. "Help me to my bed."

He did so, lifting her feet gently onto her sleeping couch.

"I'm so cold," she said, shivering. "I can't seem to get warm anymore."

Prometheus covered her with a blanket. Without her telling him what to do, he took a dry cloth and gently dabbed the beads of perspiration from her brow. "I'll add wood to the brazier, my lady."

"There isn't any wood." She avoided looking at him, ashamed of her poverty. How far she had fallen since he had first known her.

Prometheus added another blanket.

Julia plucked at it. "Do you think you could find this physician of whom you spoke?"

"Yes, my lady. He has become well known in the city. It shouldn't be too difficult to find him."

"Go, then, and see what he says." She watched him stride toward the open doorway. "Don't come back if you don't succeed in speaking with him. I'm afraid what I would do to you. Do you understand?"

"Yes, my lady."

She saw that he did. "You may go, and may the gods go with you." He went out the door. She sank back in dejection.

Perhaps Prometheus would have better luck with the gods than she did.

24

Alexander sank onto the soft cushions of his new couch and let out his breath in a long, drawn-out sigh of exhaustion. "If anyone else comes, Rashid, send them away."

"Where is Rapha?"

"She's writing the treatments into the log. She'll finish soon."

"Do you want to eat now, or will you wait for her?"

Alexander opened one eye and looked at him drolly. "I'll wait for her."

"Very good, my lord."

His mouth curved slightly as he closed his eye again, intending to doze until Hadassah came.

A servant entered. "My lord, a young man is downstairs asking to speak with you."

Alexander groaned. "Didn't he read the sign? No patients until tomorrow morning."

"He can't read, my lord."

"Then read it to him."

"I did, my lord."

"Tell him to come back tomorrow."

Rapha entered the room, and he propped himself up. He could tell how tired she was by the way she limped. She sank down onto the couch opposite him and put her walking stick aside. Her shoulders drooped, and she rubbed at her bad leg.

"I'll tell Andronicus you are ready to dine," Rashid said and left the room.

Alexander rose. "I'm eager to see what Andronicus has prepared this evening," he said, grinning at her. "The man is a genius with food and I'm starving. Here. Let me help you." He braced her back, and she gasped in pain as she reclined. "You've overdone it again." He took hold of her bad leg and carefully straightened it. She caught her breath again. "Sitting for long periods of time makes the muscles cramp." He began to knead her leg gently.

"I needed to finish making the entries."

"We'll hire a scribe to do it." He bore down with his thumbs

245

and saw her fingers whiten on the cushion. "You need a good soak in the calidarium."

"Tomorrow, perhaps."

"Tonight," he said firmly. "As soon as we finish eating."

Rashid entered with a large silver tray on which were displayed two succulent partridges artfully arranged in a nest of cut fruit and greens. The aroma made Alexander's stomach cramp with hunger and his mouth water.

Rapha gave silent thanksgiving and lifted her veils. The partridge was so perfectly roasted that she was able to remove a leg with ease. It was delicious. She had been so intent on her work that she hadn't realized how hungry she was. As she ate, she watched Alexander in amusement. He was obviously enjoying the meal.

Alexander finished one partridge leg and removed another. "Clementia left another pouch of coins for you this afternoon," he said, tearing the meat from the bone with his teeth.

Hadassah's eyes lifted in dismay. "I told her not to do that."

Swallowing the meat, he wagged the leg at her. "Don't make your usual objections. She's grateful to you. Giving you a gift makes her happy. What harm is there in that? Orestes did the same thing." He took another bite.

Frowning, she took another bite of partridge. She was troubled. She hadn't objected to Orestes' gift because she had known of a need for the money at the time. Now, cut off by the overwhelming number of patrons and amount of work, she had had little time to find those in need—and a surfeit of gold coins was piling up in her money box.

Alexander saw she was distressed. He shouldn't have told her about Clementia. Not until she finished eating. He knew the expensive gifts and pouches of money bothered her, and he knew why. He thought her reasons foolish. "Their gratitude belongs to God," she often said, but he saw nothing wrong in her receiving the bounty.

A week ago, she had entered the antechamber, and a man had bowed down to her. Alexander had never seen her angry before. "Get up!" she had cried out, and the man had jumped to his feet in fright.

"Rapha," he had said gently, trying to intercede, but she had turned on him as well.

"Am I a god that he should bow down to me?"

She had limped toward the man, who drew back from her, his face pale with fear. She had held out her arm. "Touch me," she said. The man had raised his hand, but it had been clear he didn't dare to do what she told him. She took his hand firmly and placed it on her arm, putting her own hand over his. "Flesh and blood. Never, never bow down to me again. Do you understand?" The man had nodded, but as she turned away, Alexander saw the look on his face.

Alexander had seen the same look in others' eyes as well. The man revered her.

"Think of the money as a fee," he said now, trying to calm her concerns.

"You know very well Clementia already paid the fee you named. Let her take her offering to God."

"You're making too much of this," he said, only to be interrupted as the servant entered again. "What now?"

"The man said he will wait, my lord."

Alexander's mouth tightened. Rain was pounding on the roof tiles. "So be it," he said, determined to enjoy his meal.

"Who will wait?" Hadassah said.

"Someone who wants to speak to me."

"It's raining."

"I told him to come back tomorrow. If he insists on waiting, he can get wet!"

"Who is he?"

"I don't know." He tossed a leg bone onto the platter in annoyance.

"Is he ill?" she said to the servant.

"No, my lady. He looks very healthy."

"Does he seem upset?"

"No, my lady. He's very calm. When I told him he would have to wait until morning, he thanked me and sat down by the wall."

Annoyed, Alexander split his partridge in half. Why couldn't people understand that physicians needed rest just like any other human being? He could feel Hadassah looking at him in silent appeal. "Obviously, it's not urgent," he muttered.

She still looked at him.

"It's a warm rain, Rapha."

Amazing how silence could speak volumes.

"Very well!" he said, resigned. He gave a slight wave to the servant. "Invite the wretch in and let him dry off in the antechamber."

"Yes, my lord. Will you speak with him tonight?"

"No. I'm too tired." He saw Hadassah start to rise. "Don't even think about it!" he said in a tone that eliminated argument.

Rashid moved closer to her couch. Hadassah glanced up at him and then looked back at Alexander with a rueful smile.

"You're not going to do anything more today except eat that bird and go to the baths."

She saw he meant it and reclined again.

"The man can wait," Alexander said to her and then looked at his servant again. "If the brazier is still lit, add fuel. And give him a dry tunic."

"Yes, my lord."

He looked at Hadassah. "Satisfied?"

She smiled at him. "He might be hungry." She broke her partridge in half and held one part up toward the servant. "And he'll need a bedroll since he must wait through the night."

Alexander gave a nod. "Let it be done as she says."

Prometheus was surprised when the servant opened the door to him and said he could come inside and wait. A fire had been prepared, and he was given a towel and dry tunic. The servant left and then came back a short while later with a tray on which was half a roasted partridge, bread, and a pitcher of fine wine. A big, dark-skinned man gave him a bedroll. "The physician will see you in the morning," he said. "You may sleep here."

Giving thanks to God, Prometheus marveled at the delicious meal. Warmed by the fire in the brazier and the good wine, he stretched out on the bedroll. He slept comfortably for the night.

The big Syrian prodded him awake in the morning. "Get up. The physician will speak with you now."

Prometheus followed him up the stairs and down a corridor into a bibliotheca. A young man stood behind a writing table, reading a scroll. He glanced up as Prometheus entered behind the servant. "Thank you, Rashid," the man said, and the Syrian left. "What is it you wanted to speak with me about?"

Prometheus was surprised to be speaking to so young a physician. He had expected someone elderly, of long experience. "I've come to plead with you for the sake of my mistress. She is gravely ill, my lord."

"There are many physicians in the city. Why do you come to me?"

"She's seen many physicians, my lord. She has been to priests. She's given votive offerings to numerous gods. I was told by her maid that she spent a night in the abaton."

Alexander found himself curious. "How does her illness manifest itself?"

Prometheus told him all he had observed.

"Can she be brought here?"

"I'd have to carry her, my lord, and though she doesn't weigh a great deal, it's a long distance."

Alexander frowned. "Very well," he said. "I have people to see today, but I'll find time to come and examine her this evening. Where does she live?"

Prometheus told him.

Alexander's brows flickered. "Hardly the neighborhood of the impoverished," he said dryly, wondering why she couldn't have a litter carry her.

"Her illness has impoverished her, my lord."

"Oh," he said and gave a nod. The young man turned to leave. "One moment," Alexander said. "Make sure she understands I make no promises. If I can help her, I will. If I can't, her fate will be left in the hands of the gods."

"I understand, my lord."

"I hope I can help her."

"Thank you, my lord," Prometheus said. "May God bless you for your kindness."

Alexander's brows rose. He glanced up again as the slave left the room.

Hadassah entered. She paused in the doorway, looking after the young man. "Who was he?"

Alexander glanced up. "That was the young man who wanted to speak with me last night. Remember?" He gave her a wry smile. "The one to whom you sent half your partridge."

"Yes, my lord, but what was his name?" Though she hadn't gotten a good look at him, he seemed familiar.

He shrugged, returning his attention to the scroll. "I didn't ask his name."

Later that night, Alexander would have grave cause to wish he had.

25

Marcus heard a knock on the door. Ignoring it, he continued to lie on the mat and stare at the beamed ceiling. Sunlight shone in through several breaks. The house was already in disrepair. Another few years of rain and weather and the roof would begin to crumble. How many years before the wind and storm destroyed it completely?

The knock came again, louder this time, insistent.

Irritated, Marcus rolled to his feet. He crossed the dim chamber with its dusty columns of light. Perhaps the intruder would have the good sense to depart before he reached the door. He opened it and found the old woman who had spoken to him in the marketplace. She was leaning heavily on her walking stick.

"So," she said, "you are still here."

"So it would appear," he said tonelessly. "What do you want?"

She considered him from head to foot. "Why do you take up residence in the house of the dead?"

He flinched as though she had struck him in the face. He had come to feel close to Hadassah, not be reminded she was dead. His hand whitened on the door. "Why do you bother me, old woman?" he said, glowering down at her.

"This house doesn't belong to you."

Who but an old woman near death would dare challenge a Roman for taking possession of a deserted house? His mouth curved into a hard smile. "Have you come to try to throw me out?"

She put both hands on her walking stick and set it before her. "I've come to find out why you're here."

Annoyed, he stood silent.

She stared back. "What do you hope to find in this place, Roman?"

"Solitude," he said and slammed the door.

She knocked again, three hard raps.

"Go away!" he shouted at the closed door and sat down at the table. He raked his fingers through his hair and held his head in his hands. She knocked again, three more hard raps. Marcus swore under his breath.

"*Go away!*"

She spoke through the closed door. "This is not your house."

Marcus set his jaw, his heart beating with hard, angry thumps. "Tell me the name of the owner and I'll buy it!" A long moment passed, and he let out his breath, thinking she had given up and left.

Rap. Rap. Rap.

He slammed his fist on the table and rose. Throwing open the door, he glared down at her again. "What do you want, old woman? Tell me and then leave me in peace."

"Why are you here?" she said with dogged patience.

"That's *my* business."

"This is *my* village. I was born here eighty-seven years ago. And this house belonged to a man I knew and respected." She looked him in the eyes. "I don't know you."

Marcus was stunned by her audacity. "This wretched *country* belongs to Rome! I can take what I want, and I want this house." Even as he spoke, he heard the arrogance ringing out in every word that came from his lips. His eyes fell away from hers. "Just go away," he rasped and started to shut the door.

She lifted her walking stick and hit the door with the end of it. "I won't go away until I have an answer that satisfies me. Why are you here?"

Weary, Marcus considered her for a long moment, trying to think of an answer that would satisfy her and send her on her way. He could think of none. How could he? He wasn't even sure why he was here anymore. The emptiness of the house crushed his spirit.

"I don't know," he said bleakly. "Satisfied?" He turned away and went back into the house. Hearing the scrape of her walking stick, he turned and saw she had followed him inside. "I didn't invite you in," he said coldly.

"The same one who invited you in, invited me," she said testily and planted herself several feet inside the door.

Sighing heavily, he ran his hand through his hair and sank down at the table again. He said nothing more. She was silent so long, he glanced up. She was looking slowly around the room.

"I haven't been in this house since they left," she said and looked up at the light coming through the roof. She shook her head sadly. "Hananiah would have repaired those breaks." She looked at him again and waited.

Marcus met her steady gaze in obstinate silence.

"I already know the answer to my question," the old woman said finally. "You're here because of Hadassah. What happened to her?"

"If I tell you, will you go away?" he said dryly.

"I might."

"She was murdered. In an Ephesian arena."

The old woman came closer. "Why should the death of one more Jew matter so much to a Roman?"

His eyes flashed. "She was a handmaiden in my father's house."

"And for that reason alone, you travel so many miles to see where she lived?" She smiled.

Unable to bear her scrutiny, Marcus rose and walked to the window. Sighing, he stared up at the hot, blue sky. "It's a private matter, old woman."

"Not so private that the whole village doesn't know of it."

He turned. "What do they know?"

"That a Roman came looking for the home of Hadassah. And, now that he's found it, he's closed himself up in it as one would close himself up in a tomb."

Stiffening, he stared at her in anger. "What matter my reasons to anyone? Let them go about their own business, and leave me to mine."

"My legs grow tired. Ask me to sit."

"I'd rather ask you to leave!"

Sighing wearily, she leaned more heavily on the walking stick. "I suppose I must suffer your inhospitality."

Marcus' only reply was a rude snort.

"Of course, it would be too much to expect even a small act of kindness from a Roman."

"Oh, very well! Sit! And after you've rested, *go.*"

"Thank you," she said, a glimmer of humor lighting her expression. "How can I resist such a gracious invitation?" She eased herself onto the stool. She was silent for a long time, studying him. He grew uncomfortable.

"Is this your Jerusalem, Roman?"

"What do you mean?"

"Is Nain your holy city? Are you here on a pilgrimage to honor a slave you loved?"

Her question dissolved his anger and roused anew his grief. He sat heavily on the bench beneath the window. Struggling against the emotions surging up in him, he leaned back against the wall. "Why don't you leave me in peace, old woman?"

"What peace will you find here in this house? The peace of death?"

He closed his eyes. "Leave."

She remained, rooted to the stool. "How long since you've eaten?"

He gave a bleak laugh. "I don't remember."

She rose with difficulty. "Come with me. I'll give you something to eat."

"I'm not hungry."

"I am. Come with me and we will talk about why you're here."

"A kind offer I regret to refuse."

"You regret a great deal, don't you?" Her dark eyes pierced him. "Was it because of you Hadassah died?"

Marcus came to his feet. "You press too hard."

She leaned upon her walking stick and looked at him somberly. "What will you do? Throw a poor crippled old woman into the street?" She smiled faintly at his look of consternation. "I'm too old to be afraid of anything." She tapped her stick lightly, reminding him of the shepherd boy in the hills. "Come with me, Roman, and I'll tell you all I remember about Hadassah."

It was a calculated comment and he knew it. "How well did you know her?"

She walked laboriously to the door and paused there, the sunlight at her back so he couldn't read her expression. "I knew her from the moment of her birth until the day she left with her family to go to Jerusalem for Passover." She walked out into the sunlight.

Marcus followed her out into the street and measured his pace with hers. A few doors down the street, she entered another house much like the one they had just left. He stood at the open doorway and peered in at the interior. Everything was clean and in its place.

"Come inside," she said.

"Your house will be defiled if I enter it."

She gave a surprised laugh. "You know something of our law."

"Enough," he said darkly.

"If our Lord ate with tax collectors and harlots, I suppose I can eat with a Roman." She pointed to a stool. "Sit there." Marcus entered and sat. Breathing in the aroma of cooking food, his stomach growled. She pushed a small bowl of dates toward him. "Take as many as you want." He set his mouth, watching her. She had planned this ahead.

Stooping before the burning coals, she ladled heavy gruel into a wooden bowl and set it before him. She ladled a smaller portion for herself and sat down opposite him. She pushed a basket toward him and uncovered the unleavened bread it held.

"You said you would tell me about Hadassah."

"Eat first."

Mouth grim, Marcus broke the bread and dipped a portion into the gruel. After one taste, he gave in to his hunger. She filled a clay cup with wine and put it before him. When his bowl was empty, she filled it again, then sat down and watched him eat. "Were you fasting or starving yourself to death?"

"Neither."

She finished her own small portion. Noting his empty bowl, she raised her brows slightly. "More? I have plenty."

He shook his head, then gave a bleak laugh of self-mockery. "Thank you," he said simply.

She stacked the two bowls and set them aside. Rising stiffly, she made her way across the room and gave a soft groan of relief as she sat down on some worn cushions. "My name is Deborah." She looked at him and waited.

"Marcus Lucianus Valerian."

"Hadassah had an older brother named Mark. Hananiah began his training as a potter when he was very young, but he said Mark showed great talent. Hananiah saw himself as a simple potter. Mark was an artist." She nodded toward a shelf cut into the thick clay wall. "He made that urn when he was twelve."

Marcus glanced up and saw that the boy's work rivaled what he had seen in Rome.

"Mark was fifteen when they left for Jerusalem."

Marcus studied the urn with a sense of sadness. If he had shown such promise at twelve, what might the boy have achieved had he lived? "A pity he died so young."

"A pity for us. A blessing for him."

Marcus glanced at her darkly. "You call death a blessing?"

"Mark is with the Lord, as are his mother and father and sisters."

A swift arrow of pain struck his heart. "Would you think it a blessing if I told you Hadassah was torn to pieces by lions? Would you think it a blessing if I told you people *cheered* as she died?" His own sister among them.

"You are very angry, Marcus Lucianus Valerian. What is at the heart of it?"

He clenched his teeth. "I came here to hear about Hadassah, not talk about myself."

She folded her hands in her lap and gazed at him enigmatically. "There is little to tell. Hadassah was a quiet girl who did what was asked of her. There was nothing remarkable about her. She was timid. Every time Hananiah took his family to Jerusalem, you could see that child was terrified. Her faith was not very strong."

"Not strong?" He gave a harsh, incredulous laugh.

She studied him. "Not as I remember her." When Marcus gave no explanation, she shrugged. "Hadassah would have been happy to stay in this village her entire life, to marry, have children, and never venture farther than the shores of the Sea of Galilee, which she loved. She was comfortable in the security of family and friends and those things familiar to her."

"All of which her god stripped from her."

"So it would seem."

He put both hands lightly around the clay cup on the table before him. "Who were her friends?"

"Girls and boys of her own age. None to whom you can speak."

"Why not? Because I'm a Gentile?"

"Because her family wasn't the only one that didn't return from Jerusalem. There are many empty houses in our village."

Marcus winced. He was ashamed. Ashamed of his manner toward the old woman. Ashamed he was a Roman. He stood and walked to the open doorway. He stared out at the dirt street. A soft wind was stirring the dust. A woman walked down the street, a large jug balanced on her head as her children skipped alongside her. An old man sat outside his house, his back against the wall.

"What was Hadassah like when you knew her?" the old woman asked from behind him.

He lifted his gaze to the clear sky. "The first time I saw her I thought she was just as you say: unremarkable. Half-starved. Her head had been shaved. Her hair was just growing back. She had the biggest brown eyes I've ever seen."

He turned and looked at the old woman. "She was afraid of me. She shook every time I came close to her. In the beginning. Later, she said things to me that no one would have dared." He remembered how she had come to him in Claudius' gardens and pleaded for the lives of the slaves. And how, at the same time, she had pleaded for him.

"Please, Marcus, I beg of you. Don't bring the sin of innocent blood upon your head."

He closed his eyes. "I'd look for her and find her in the garden at night. On her knees. Sometimes on her face." He opened his eyes again, his face tightening. "Always praying to her unseen god. Her *Christ.*"

He said the word like a curse.

A muscle jerked in his jaw. "Later on, even during the day, I'd know just by the look on her face that she was praying. As she worked. As she served." He shook his head. "You said she had little faith, but I tell you, I've never known anyone with a more stubborn faith than hers. No amount of logic would dissuade her. Not even the threat of death. Not death itself."

Tears spilled from the old woman's eyes, but she was smiling. "The Lord refined her."

Her words roused Marcus' deepest anger. "Refined her into what? A worthy sacrifice?"

Deborah looked up at him. "For his good purpose."

"Good purpose? What good was there in her death? Your god of old was content with the blood of lambs." He gave a harsh, mirthless laugh. "You want to know why Hadassah died? Because his son isn't content with the old sacrifices. He wants the blood of his believers!"

Deborah raised her hand slightly. "Sit, Marcus. Be still and listen."

He sat on the stool and put his head in his hands. "Nothing you can say will make a difference." Yet the soul-hunger within Marcus weakened his resolve to hold his anger as a shield. He felt tired, spirit-spent.

Deborah spoke gently, as to a child. "If a centurion ordered a legionnaire to go into battle, would he not go?"

256

"Hadassah wasn't a soldier."

"Wasn't she? Rome builds armies to take land and people captive, to expand the boundaries of the Empire to the farthest reaches of the known world. But Hadassah was a soldier in another kind of army, one that fights a spiritual battle to free the human heart. And in that war, God's will prevails."

"She lost her battle," he said hoarsely, seeing in his mind's eye Julia gloating as Hadassah faced death.

"You're here."

Deborah's softly spoken words struck hard. Marcus scraped the stool back and stood. "Have you any more wisdom to impart?"

Old Deborah looked up at him placidly and said no more.

Marcus returned to the deserted house. Furious, he kicked the door shut and swore he wouldn't open it to anyone again.

26

Hadassah entered Julia's house in silence. She had known the moment Alexander led the way up the street where she was and to whose villa she was going. She recognized the feeling swelling in her belly, for she had had long acquaintance with it. *Fear.* Yet, she knew God's hand was in this, and so she prayed as Rashid carried her up the marble steps and Alexander knocked on the door that she would know what God willed of her when the time came.

A young servant woman opened the door. Hadassah didn't recognize her. The girl's eyes fixed upon Hadassah even as she greeted Alexander with grave respect. The servant drew back as they entered, bowing as Rashid carried Hadassah into the antechamber.

Distressed, she whispered for Rashid to put her down. He obeyed and held his arm out for her to use as support. "This way, my lord," the slave girl said, flustered and not even daring to look at Hadassah again. She walked quickly toward the stairs.

Hadassah looked around the bare antechamber. She recalled that there had been two marble statues of nymphs in this room, one on each side. Now only the potted palms remained, and they were dying for lack of care. The walls had once been covered with Babylonian tapestries. They were now bare. The marble pedestals that had held Corinthian vases filled with flowers were also gone.

Leaning heavily on Rashid's arm, Hadassah limped toward the stairs. When she reached them, Rashid swept her up in his arms again.

"What's wrong?" he growled close to her ear as he carried her up the steps.

"Nothing," she said, glancing down into the peristyle as he carried her up the steps. The fountain was still running, but around it was a thick layer of dirt clouding the tile murals.

The girl tapped lightly at the bedchamber door, and a young man opened it. Seeing his face, Hadassah recognized him immediately. Prometheus. He had been her only friend in this household.

"My lord," Prometheus said in grave greeting, obviously

258

relieved and pleased to see Alexander. He bowed. "Please, come in." He drew back, his arm extended toward the center of the room. "Lady Julia is resting." He looked at Hadassah as Rashid carried her past, his expression one of curiosity rather than awe or recognition.

Hadassah's fear vanished the moment she saw Julia lying on the bed. Shocked by her appearance, she gasped softly. Rashid stopped.

Prometheus passed them and went to the bed. Bending down, he touched Julia's shoulder. "My lady, the physician has come." She roused. Putting her hand out, she allowed him to help her sit up. Pushing the damp tendrils of hair back from her pale face, she looked across the room with bleary eyes. Clinging to Prometheus' arm, she rose clumsily.

"Oh!" Hadassah said, a catch in her throat. "Put me down, please."

Rashid knew in that instant they were in the lion's den.

"Rashid," she said.

He set her on her feet as she asked, but caught hold of her arm with unyielding fingers. "Do not get close to her."

Hadassah didn't hear him. She had eyes only for Julia. She was dressed in a faded red robe, her hair braided in a crown. She looked so thin and ill as she held her hand out, as regal in bearing as ever, to Alexander. He bowed over it as he would a young queen. "My lady," he said gently.

"Would you care for some wine?"

"No, thank you, Lady Julia."

"It's just as well. What I have to offer isn't very good," she said, and Hadassah knew she had been drinking heavily. Julia turned her head and looked at her. "Is this the famous Rapha?" There was a tinge of mockery in her tone.

"Yes," Alexander said. He saw that Hadassah stood a good distance from the bed and Rashid had firm hold of her arm as though keeping her there. He frowned slightly and glanced at the Arab's dark, set face. Sudden alarm swept through him at the look on Rashid's face. What was wrong? He caught the Arab's eye and gave a faint raise of his brows. Rashid looked back at him fiercely, then his gaze flickered from Lady Julia to Rapha. He looked at Alexander again and jerked his head toward the door.

Alexander's heart dropped.

"My servant told me about you," Julia said, looking at the veiled woman. "It is said you can perform miracles."

Hadassah took a step toward her and winced as Rashid's fingers bit into her arm.

"Miracles only occur for those who are deemed worthy," he said, his voice darker than Hadassah had ever heard it.

Julia smiled brittlely and looked at Prometheus. "What did I tell you?" The vulnerability Hadassah had glimpsed an instant before was now replaced by an implacable coldness. Julia looked at Alexander. "And how much will it cost me to have the great Rapha dispense her healing touch upon my poor unworthy body?"

Alexander felt a sudden, deep surge of dislike.

Hadassah pulled her arm from Rashid's grasp and limped toward the bed.

"Rapha! Do not!" Alexander said, afraid she would remove her veils as she had for Phoebe Valerian. The girl on this bed was like a malignancy.

Julia, not understanding, backed from her, eyes wide with fear. Hadassah held out her hand. Julia blinked, staring at it. She raised her eyes and stared at her in question, trying to see what was behind the veils. She started to reach out, but just before their fingers brushed she drew her hand back sharply. "You have not told me what I must pay," she said haughtily, her hand a fist against her chest.

"Your soul," Rashid said darkly at the same time Hadassah said, "Nothing."

Julia looked between them in confusion. "Which is it?"

"I thought you called for a physician," Alexander said with forced humor. He stepped into the gap between Julia and Hadassah. Taking Julia gently by the arm, he turned her toward her bed. "Let me examine you and see what the trouble is. You may have your servant present if you so wish."

"I don't care," Julia said dismally, having long ago lost all sense of modesty.

Hadassah limped toward the bed. "You may go, Prometheus."

Prometheus glanced at her sharply.

Julia's face paled. "How did she know his name?"

"Rapha knows many things," Rashid said. "She can look into the soul."

Hadassah turned sharply. "You may go also, Rashid."

He lifted his head slightly, eyes dark and steady on Julia Valerian.

"Why does he look at me like that?" Julia said, her voice trembling slightly. "As though he'd like to kill me."

"Go!" Hadassah said.

Rashid's expression did not change. "I will go, but I will not go far."

Julia trembled as she watched the Arab turn and leave her room. "I've never laid eyes upon him before tonight, and he stares at me with such hatred I can almost feel it!"

"It's your imagination, my lady," Prometheus said soothingly, but he, too, wondered at what was happening.

"Just keep him out of here," she said nervously, then gave her full attention to Alexander and Hadassah. "Do you want me to remove my clothing?"

"Not yet." Alexander gestured for her to sit on her bed. He set a stool close and sat down. He began by asking questions about her illness, listening with such acute attention that she relaxed and let all her troubles spill forth, from Calabah's defection to Primus' perfidy. She took his silence for understanding and his nods for empathy.

Alexander felt neither.

"And after all that, he stripped me of all my money before he deserted me." She sniffed and rubbed her nose with the back of her hand.

She talked for a long time. Alexander allowed her to go on and on, though he already suspected what was wrong with her. A brief examination would confirm the matter in his mind. He sat and listened, wondering what the relationship had been between this incredibly self-centered young woman and Hadassah. Lady Julia's bitterness grew as she talked, but along with it came a clear picture of the extent of her own immorality.

Finally, she had exhausted herself. "Is there anything else you want to know?"

"I think you've told me enough," he said quietly. "Remove your robe."

Julia did so without the least compunction. She drew the faded red garment back off her shoulders. With a faint smile, she watched Alexander's face to see if there was the least glimmer of admiration. There wasn't.

Alexander studied her from head to foot, but nothing more

showed on his face than intense clinical interest. "Lie down please."

Julia's self-confidence waned. She did as he told her, seeming ill at ease. "I used to have a beautiful body."

Hadassah moved closer to the bed.

The examination took a long time and reduced Julia to tears of pain and mortification. Alexander was methodical and thorough. He had a strong stomach, but once the extent of Julia's disease was revealed, he struggled to hide his repugnance. "You may cover yourself again."

She did so quickly, unable to look at him.

Leaving the bedside, Alexander crossed to a basin. He washed his hands carefully. Pouring the water into a potted plant, he filled the basin and washed again.

Hadassah limped closer and touched Julia on the shoulder. She jerked slightly and glanced up. "Oh," she said, sighing in relief. "I'll be healed now, won't I?"

"Only God heals, my lady."

"God?" A glimmer of fear crossed her face. "Which god?"

Alexander spoke before Hadassah could. "Which god do you worship?" he said, drying his hands quickly as he walked back to the bed.

"Any one you say I should. I've been faithful to Artemis and Asklepios. I've given offerings to a dozen others."

Alexander put his hand beneath Hadassah's elbow and applied enough pressure to move her aside.

Julia looked between them, fear shining in her eyes. "Do you know what's wrong with me?"

Alexander dropped the damp cloth onto a small table. "You have a venereal disease," he said bluntly. "A very virulent variety that I've never seen before." He shook his head. "Perhaps if I'd seen you sooner . . ."

"Sooner? Are you saying nothing can be done?"

He glanced at Hadassah. "Other than prescribe salves to soothe the eruptions as they occur, no. There isn't anything I can do."

Julia blinked, her face going white.

"I'm sorry," he said. The words came out flat, emotionless.

"You don't sound sorry at all!" Julia stared at him for a long moment, and then her face convulsed. "What's the matter?

Haven't I enough money? Is my name not grand enough? Who are you to say no to me!"

In all his experience, Alexander had never taken such a deep dislike to anyone as he did to this young woman. It wasn't simply due to realizing she was a member of the family who had sent Hadassah into the arena. He had never met anyone so saturated with herself. Many of her symptoms bespoke of a life of dissipation and self-indulgence. She had the pallor and emaciation of a lotus-eater—one who used the fruit for its drugging qualities—and her breath smelled strongly of cheap wine. Her sexual exploits were beyond the commonest decency. He wondered if there was anything this young woman hadn't done and felt certain there wasn't.

For over an hour she had talked about herself, her ailments, her grievances, her pain, her suffering. Yet she saw none of what was happening to her as consequences of her choices, of her lifestyle, of seeking pleasure at every altar known to mankind. And her words rang discordant. Wasn't it her right to find pleasure, to enjoy life the way she chose? What was wrong with it? Ah, and she wanted him to hand her a cure so she could go on doing whatever she pleased. She didn't care about his career, his principles, his feelings. She demanded he make her well when it was by her own hand that she was sick unto death.

Alexander felt no pity for such a woman as this.

All he could think of was Hadassah, body torn and racked with pain, suffering months of convalescence. Never once had she uttered a complaint or cast blame on anyone. A day did not pass, nor ever would, that she would not be in pain because of the injuries she had suffered in the arena, and the scars she bore destroyed any chance for a normal life.

And here, this sick and sickening young woman cried out for help, not in humility, but in demand—and she herself was the cause of all of it.

"It's not fair! It's not my fault I'm sick!"

"Isn't it?" Alexander put his instruments into his carrying case.

"Give me something to make me better! I know you can find a cure if you put your mind to it."

"I've many patients."

"I don't care about your patients. What do they matter in the face of *my* suffering?"

The sound of Julia's strident voice raised the hair on the back of his neck.

Hadassah limped over to him and put her hand on his arm. "Alexander."

He heard the gentle appeal and reacted with anger. "Don't even ask it!"

"Please."

"Do you hear nothing?" he whispered fiercely.

"I hear the voice of someone lost."

"And not worth finding. No," he said again, firmly. The contrast between the two young women hardened his heart and set his mind.

"Won't you even consider—"

"I've examined her, Rapha. You touched her. That's all we can do."

Julia dissolved into tears.

"Alexander, please listen to me . . . ," Hadassah began.

He closed his case firmly and picked it up. "I can't afford to listen to you," he hissed. "I'm not going to risk my reputation and career on someone I know is going to die." His words were loud enough for Julia to hear—and cruel enough to silence her.

Hadassah turned toward the bed, but he caught hold of her arm and headed her for the door. "Rashid!" At Alexander's nod, the Arab strode across the room, caught Rapha up in his arms, and carried her out.

Prometheus entered the room and watched them go. He saw Julia weeping on the bed and looked at Alexander. "You can do nothing?"

"The disease has taken too firm a hold."

Outside in the cool night air, Alexander breathed deeply. The atmosphere within Julia Valerian's villa had been oppressive. It reeked of corruption.

He walked alongside Rashid as he carried Hadassah down the steps. She made no protest. Rashid set her gently inside the litter and adjusted the cushions for her comfort. Alexander was afraid of what she would say to him within the privacy of the curtains.

She would only plead for that despicable young woman, and no one could touch his heart with pleading like Hadassah. He decided not to give her the opportunity. "I'll walk," he said and drew the curtains closed, shutting her inside the litter. "Go," he commanded the bearers.

Tonight, he would not listen. Tonight, mercy sat ill with him.

The bearers lifted Hadassah within the litter and bore her down the street.

Rashid fell into step beside Alexander. "Her servant told me she is the daughter of Phoebe Valerian. Her father is dead. She has a brother named Marcus. He left Ephesus some months ago."

"By all the gods, Rashid. I put her head right into the lion's mouth, didn't I?"

"Rapha must have known."

"Why didn't she say something?"

It was a question neither man could answer with any sense of satisfaction. Neither understood her. She never ceased to amaze and perplex them.

"The Valerian woman is dying, isn't she?" Rashid said, staring straight ahead as he walked.

"Yes, she's dying." Alexander glanced at the stony-faced Arab. "A matter of mere months, I would guess."

"First the mother. Now the daughter."

He nodded and looked ahead again. "It does make one wonder if God is striking the Valerians down one at a time for what they did to Hadassah." He wondered if Hadassah would interpret what was happening that way. She said Christ Jesus was the embodiment of love. Would a god of love take such vengeance?

Rashid was thinking of other things. "Will her death be painful?"

"And slow."

Rashid's stony face relaxed. "Good," he said. "Justice is served."

27

Marcus awakened beneath a beam of sunlight through the high window. He winced as pain shot through his head. Groaning, he rolled away from the light and bumped into the potter's wheel. Swearing, he pushed himself up and leaned against it.

His mouth was dry, his tongue thick. He saw the wineskin he had purchased the night before lying flaccid on the floor. Each beat of his heart drove shafts of pain through his head. Even running his fingers through his tousled hair hurt.

A soft breeze stirred the dust around him, and he noticed that the door stood open. He thought he remembered closing it the night before, but then, he didn't remember much of anything clearly.

Except the dream.

Closing his eyes, he tried to recapture the precious bits and pieces of it . . . Hadassah sitting with him on a bench in the peristyle of the villa in Rome . . . Hadassah with the lyre in her hands, singing softly of a shepherd. In his dreams, she was vivid, clear. He could see her face, hear her voice, touch her. Only when he was awake did she elude him.

As she did now.

Swearing softly, he gave up. He pushed himself to his feet and stumbled across the room. Nauseated, he leaned heavily on the table and looked around the room for another wineskin. He saw the old woman instead, sitting in the shadows beneath the window.

"You!" he said and sat down heavily on the stool. He put his head in his hands again. The throbbing pain was excruciating.

"You don't look well, Marcus Lucianus Valerian."

"I've had better mornings."

"It's afternoon."

"Thank you for the insight."

She chuckled. "You bring back memories of my husband during Purim celebrations. According to our traditions, he would drink until he couldn't tell the difference between 'cursed is

266

Haman' and 'blessed is Mordecai.' Ah, but the next day, he would look like you do now. Pinched white. A tinge of green."

He rubbed his face, hoping if he said nothing she would go home.

"Of course, he drank as part of a joyous holiday. You drink to forget."

His hands stilled. He lowered them slowly and glared at her. "Why do you keep coming back here?"

"I brought you a jug of water. Drink some and then wash your face."

He was annoyed that she spoke to him as though he were a boy she was reprimanding, but he rose shakily and did as she said. Perhaps when he finished doing as she asked, she would leave. He drank a cup of water and poured some into a basin. When he finished washing his face, he sat at the table again. "What do you want this time?"

Undaunted by his rudeness, she smiled. "I want you to walk in the hills and see the spring lambs and lilies of the field."

"I'm not interested in lambs and lilies."

She used her walking stick to stand. "You won't find Hadassah's spirit in this house, Marcus." She saw his pained grimace, and her expression softened. "If you've come to Nain to be close to her, I'll show you the places she enjoyed most. We'll start with a hillside at the east side of the village." She walked toward the door.

Tilting his head, Marcus squinted his eyes at her. "Must I suffer your company along the way?"

"By the looks of you, I don't think you could outrun me."

He gave a bleak laugh and winced.

She stopped on the threshold. "Hadassah liked lambs and lilies."

Marcus sat stubbornly at the table for a long moment. Then he rose. He snatched up the heavy robe from the floor, shook the dust from it, and went after her.

People looked at them strangely as they passed through the village. He supposed they were a strange pair, an old woman with her walking stick and a Roman suffering the aftereffects of his night of drunken indulgence. She stopped twice, the first time to buy bread, the second, a skin of wine. She made him carry both.

"They don't trust you," she said when they left the marketplace.

"Why should they? I'm a Roman." His mouth twisted cynically. "I'm a serpent in their midst. Spawn of the devil."

The hills were new green, the sky blue. Patches of wildflowers splashed color on the slopes. Deborah stopped and set her walking stick before her, leaning on it as she gazed upon the hills. "We can carry water from the well and tend our gardens. Hard work for little gain. But one night's rain from God brings forth *this.*"

"You're like her," Marcus said heavily. "Seeing God in everything."

"You see no power in what's before you? No splendor? No miracle?"

"I see rocky hills with some new grass. A flock of sheep. A few flowers. Nothing extraordinary."

"The most ordinary things of life are extraordinary. The sunrise, the rain—"

"Just for today, old woman, speak to me of other things than God. Or better yet, don't speak at all."

She gave a soft grunt. "Nothing is important in this world except as it pertains to the Lord. That's why you're here, isn't it?"

"What do you mean?"

"You're looking for him."

"I looked. He doesn't exist."

"How is it possible to hold such anger against something you don't believe in?" she said and continued along the path.

Speechless, Marcus glared after her in frustration. He noted that walking seemed to ease the soreness of her joints. She removed the shawl from over her head and lifted her face as though the sun felt good to her.

He caught up and walked alongside her. "I *don't* believe in God," he said vehemently.

"What do you believe in?"

Mouth grim, he stared straight ahead. "I believe in right and wrong."

"Have you lived up to your standard?"

He winced, a muscle jerking in his jaw.

"Why don't you answer?"

"It was wrong that Hadassah died. I want to find a way to set things right again."

"And how will you accomplish that and live up to the highest standard you've set for yourself?"

Her words pierced him, for he didn't know what to say. Looking back on his life, he wondered if he'd ever had a standard. Right had always been what was expeditious; wrong, not attaining his goals, not getting what he wanted when he wanted it. For Hadassah, life had been clear. For Marcus, nothing was clear. He was in a fog.

They reached the top of a hillside. In the distance, he knew, was the Sea of Galilee.

"It is not far," old Deborah said. "Hananiah often took his family down to Capernaum and along the shores to Bethsaida-Julias." She paused, leaning on her walking stick. "Jesus walked the same roads."

"Jesus," he muttered darkly.

She raised her hand and pointed north toward the far end of the sea. "On a hillside over there, I heard the Lord speak." She lowered her hand to her walking stick again. "And when he was finished, he took two fish and broke a few loaves of bread and fed five thousand people."

"That's impossible."

"Nothing is impossible for God the Son. I saw it with my own eyes. Just as I saw him raise Hananiah from the dead."

Her words raised gooseflesh on his spine. He gritted his teeth. "If he was the Son of God, why did his own people turn him over to be crucified?"

Tears filled old Deborah's eyes. "Because, like you, we expected God to be something other than what he is."

He frowned, studying her profile. She was silent for a long time before she spoke again.

"Two hundred years ago, the Maccabean overthrew the Seleucid ruler Antiochus IV and reconsecrated our temple. The name 'Maccabee' means hammer or extinguisher. When the Maccabeans regained power and entered Jerusalem, the people rejoiced by waving palm fronds." Tears slipped down her aged cheeks. "And so we did again when Jesus entered Jerusalem. We thought he was coming in power, as the Maccabees had. We cried out, 'Blessed is he who comes in the name of the Lord.' But we did not even know him."

"Were you there?"

She shook her head. "No. I was here in Nain having a child."

"Then why do you weep as though you had part in his crucifixion? You had no part in it."

"I'd like nothing better than to think I would have remained faithful. But if those closest to him—his disciples, his own brothers—turned away, who am I to think I'm better than they and would have done differently? No, Marcus. We all wanted what we wanted, and when the Lord fulfilled *his* purpose rather than ours, we struck out against him. Like you. In anger. Like you. In disappointment. Yet, it is God's will that prevails."

He looked away. "I don't understand any of this."

"I know you don't. I see it in your face, Marcus. You don't want to see. You've hardened your heart against him." She started to walk again.

"As should all who value their lives," he said, thinking of Hadassah's death.

"It is God who has driven you here."

He gave a derisive laugh. "I came here of my own accord and for my own purposes."

"Did you?"

Marcus' face became stony.

Deborah pressed on. "We were all created incomplete and will find no rest until we satisfy the deepest hunger and thirst within us. You've tried to satisfy it in your own way. I see that in your eyes, too, as I've seen it in so many others. And yet, though you deny it with your last breath, your soul yearns for God, Marcus Lucianus Valerian."

Her words angered him. "Gods aside, Rome shows the world that life is what man makes of it."

"If that's so, what are you making of yours?"

"I own a fleet of ships, as well as emporiums and houses. I have wealth." Yet, even as he told her, he knew it all meant nothing. His father had come to that realization just before he died. Vanity. It was all vanity. Meaningless. Empty.

Old Deborah paused on the pathway. "Rome points the way to wealth and pleasure, power and knowledge. But Rome remains hungry. Just as you are hungry now. Search all you will for retribution or meaning to your life, but until you find God, you live in vain."

Marcus did not want to listen, but her words penetrated, causing him unrest. "One of our Roman philosophers says our lives are what our thoughts make of it. Perhaps therein lies the answer to how I'll find peace for myself."

She smiled at him—a tolerant, half-amused smile. "King Solomon was the wisest man who ever lived, and he said something similar hundreds of years before Rome existed. 'For as a man thinketh in his heart, so is he.'" She looked up at him. "On what does your heart dwell, Marcus Lucianus Valerian?"

Her question shot straight through his soul. "Hadassah," he said hoarsely.

She nodded, satisfied. "Then let your thoughts dwell upon her. Remember the words she said. Remember what she did, how she lived."

"I remember how she died," he said, staring out at the Sea of Galilee.

"That, too," the old woman said solemnly. "Walk in her ways and see life through her eyes. Maybe that will bring you closer to what you're looking for." She pointed down the hill. "That's the path she always walked with her father. It'll take you down to the road and on to Gennesaret, and then to Capernaum. Hadassah loved the sea."

"I'll see you back to Nain."

"I know my way. It's time you found yours."

His smile was pained. "You think you can evict me that easily, old woman?"

She patted his arm. "You were ready to go." She turned away and started back along the path they had followed together.

"What makes you so sure?" he called after her, annoyed that he had been so easily led.

"You brought your coat with you."

Bemused, he shook his head. He watched her go back along the path and realized she had bought the bread and wine for him, for his journey.

He sighed. She was right. There was no going back for him. He had stayed as long as he could bear in the house where Hadassah had lived as a child. All he had found there was dust and despair and memories that were like ashes in his mouth.

Marcus looked north. What hope had he of finding anything different along the shores of the Sea of Galilee? But then, hope had never been a part of this quest. Anger had. But somehow, along the way, his shield of anger had been stripped from him, leaving him defenseless. Emotions in turmoil, he felt naked.

She loved the sea, Deborah had said. Perhaps that was enough reason to go on.

He started down the hill, following the same path Hadassah had.

28

Alexander slammed his goblet of wine down, sloshing the red fluid onto the table. "She was the one who sent you to the arena, and now you're telling me you want to go back to her?"

"Yes," she answered simply.

"Over my dead body, you will!"

"Alexander, you said long ago I was free to do as I will."

"Not something this stupid. Didn't you listen to her? She's eaten up with bitterness. There isn't a remorseful bone in her body for anything she's ever done."

"You don't know that, Alexander. Only God knows her heart."

"You're not going back, Hadassah. That woman forfeited all rights to you the moment she handed you over to the editor of the games."

"It doesn't matter."

Alexander surged to his feet and paced in angry frustration. "I can't believe you're even thinking of this." How could he reason with such thinking?

"Try to understand, Alexander. She needs me."

He faced her. "She needs you? *I* need you. Our patients need you. Julia Valerian has servants. Let them take care of her."

"I am her servant."

"No, you aren't," he said adamantly. "Not anymore."

"Her mother and father purchased me in Rome to be Julia's handmaiden."

"That was a long time ago."

"Time doesn't change my obligations. I am still legally bound to her."

"You're wrong. In case you weren't aware, a price must have been paid for you. A few copper coins! That's how much she valued you. Not even a day's wage for a common laborer." He was angry more with himself than her, for he should have seen this coming. Foolishly, he hadn't thought her sense of compassion and mercy would extend to a woman who had tried to have her murdered.

Over the past week, since they had seen the Valerian woman,

Hadassah had refused everything but unleavened bread to eat and water to drink. She spoke with few patients, spending most of her time in prayer. Alexander thought he had understood. Of course she would be upset after seeing the woman who had sent her into the arena. Of course she would withdraw, perhaps even be afraid. He had even wondered briefly if she felt a sense of satisfaction in seeing how Julia Valerian was now suffering but was ashamed to admit it.

Not once had it occurred to him that she could or would put it all aside and *want* to go back.

"I fail to comprehend you," he said, trying to regain his own calm and find reason so he could argue her out of her decision. "Are you punishing me because I won't take that woman on as a patient?"

"No, my lord," she said, surprised that he would think it.

"I can't take her on, Hadassah. You know the laws in Ephesus. When a patient dies, the physician is held responsible. It's the worst kind of arrogance and madness to take a case you know is terminal. You saw the sores and lesions."

"I saw," she said very quietly.

"Then you know the disease has spread throughout her whole body."

"Yes, my lord."

"There's nothing I can do for her other than keep her drugged up to the end so she'll feel little pain. She's going to die, and there's nothing anyone can do about it. You touched her. You know." He saw his words disturbed her. "And don't give me that look. I know you say you have no healing power other than what God performs through you. Very well. I believe you. But when you took her hand, did anything happen?"

She lowered her head. "No," she said softly.

"Has it occurred to you that the entire Valerian family is under the curse of God for what they did to you?"

She looked up at him again, his suggestion clearly stunning her. "Each one is precious in God's sight."

"Some more than others."

"No! The Lord is impartial."

"The Lord is just," he said vehemently, thinking Julia Valerian was getting what she deserved. He wasn't going to stand in God's way. "I'm not going to forfeit my career and the chance of helping countless others in some vain attempt to save a woman who deserves everything that's happening to her."

"Who are you to judge?"

"Your friend! The one who received you from Charon. Remember? The one who sewed you back together! The one who I—" He broke off suddenly, stunned at what he had been about to say: *The one who loves you!*

"You would take credit that I'm alive?"

"Yes!" he said, exasperated. Grimacing, he gave a wave of his hand. "No!" Letting out his breath, he rubbed the back of his neck and turned away from her. "Partially."

She was quiet for a long moment. "You've told me more than once you believe the Lord has his hand upon me."

He faced her, desperation filling him. She was slipping away from him. He could feel it. "Yes. I believe God kept you alive so you could teach me."

"And for no other reason?"

"The reasons all stem out of that. Don't you see? If not for what you've taught me, what would've happened to Severina and Boethus and Helena and a hundred others who came to us at the booth outside the public baths? Where would Magonianus' wife and child be now if not for you? How many others are there in this city who need the gifts your god has given you?"

His words didn't dissuade her. "It's a matter of honor that I return to Julia."

"What honor? There's only foolishness in putting your life back in the hands of a woman so decadent and corrupt she's being eaten alive by the fruits of her choices. I suspect she's done things so vile you couldn't even comprehend them."

Hadassah had lived with and served Julia for seven years. She knew a great deal more about her than Alexander ever would. A part of her had wanted to think back on those things, to hold those memories like a shield against the softening of her heart. But she knew she mustn't. To dwell on the sins of Julia's life would not please God. Far worse, it would keep her from doing his will.

"I gave my word before the Lord."

"The Lord gave you to *me*."

She smiled gently. "Because he knew when the time came, you would release me."

"No, I won't release you," Alexander said. She sat quietly looking at him. He let out his breath. "You're not thinking clearly. The instant you remove your veils and she sees who you are, she'll have you tossed to the lions again. And then what will you have accomplished other than your own death?"

She lowered her eyes. "There is that risk."

"A risk you needn't take."

She looked up again, the uncertainty he had sensed in her completely gone. "Great opportunity demands great risk."

"Opportunity! Opportunity for what?"

"If it be God's will, to lead her to salvation."

Amazed, Alexander could only stare at her. "Why would you want her, of all people, to be saved from anything?" He saw tears well in Hadassah's eyes, and his eyes widened in disbelief. She meant what she said. Could she really be that naive?

He went to her and took her hands. "I will never understand you," he said hoarsely. "Anyone else would want to stand by her bed and watch her die for what she did. Yet, you . . . you *grieve* for her."

"She was a child once, Alexander. Full of joy and sweetness. The world has done things to her."

"No more than what she's done to herself and others."

"That may be," Hadassah said sadly, "but what I ask to do is so much less than what was done for me."

His hands tightened around hers. "I can't let you go." She was far too valuable to the lives of others . . . to him . . . while Julia Valerian was worthless in his sight.

"I can't listen to you, Alexander. I must listen to the Lord."

Her conviction baffled him. "Did God tell you in so many words to go back to her?"

"My heart tells me."

"What about your head?"

She smiled. "I have thought it through."

"Not enough." He cupped her scarred cheek. "Your heart has always been as soft as mush, Hadassah. That woman is as hard as stone." He spread his hand over the jagged ridges that disfigured her face, hoping she would remember the lions and who it was that had sent her to face them. He looked into her eyes and saw she did. "You're needed here," he said, thinking she would now see reason.

When she didn't speak, he drew her into his arms, holding her close. His heart beat with a fierce protectiveness . . . and something more. Something he would not acknowledge. For if he did so, if he uttered the words pounding in his head, and then lost her, he would not be able to bear it. He spoke, his voice choked with emotion. "I'll keep you safe. So will Rashid."

She drew back from him. "Neither of you understand. I already have a Protector."

"Yes, and God placed you here, with me, and he sent you Rashid, bloody-minded as he is. So listen to us!" He cupped her face, staring intently into her eyes. "I'm not going to let you throw your life away on someone like her."

She took his hands from her face and held them tightly on her knees. "Each one of us is precious in God's sight, Alexander. He counts the very hairs on your head." She let go of him and rose.

"If you're telling me he sees Julia Valerian as precious as you, I can't believe it!"

She touched the green fronds of a palm. "Do you remember when you took me to the Asklepion to see the ceremonies there?"

"Yes. What about it?"

"There was an ensign carried before the procession of priests. A tall pole on which snakes were entwined."

"Serpents on a standard. Yes, I know."

"Your seal ring bears the same symbol."

"Yes. It identifies me as a physician."

"Just as the engraving you had carved on the door of this house."

He frowned slightly. "Does that disturb you?" Of course it must. Why would she bring it up now unless it did? He should have explained. "I suppose it seems sacrilegious to you, but I don't worship the ensign. I only use it to make known what I am—a physician. People see the serpent on a standard and identify it with the sacred snakes of Asklepios, the god of healing and medicine."

Pensive, she lowered her hand from the frond. "When God brought the Israelites out of Egypt, he delivered up the Canaanites to be destroyed. Then our people set out from Mount Hor by the way of the Red Sea to go around the land of Edom."

"What are you trying to tell me with this story?"

She went on as though she hadn't heard him. "The people were impatient because of the journey. They spoke against God, and the Lord sent serpents among the people. Many died because of them."

"I imagine that turned them around again."

She looked at him. "Yes. They realized they had sinned. They went to Moses and asked him to intercede with the Lord, to ask that he would remove the serpents from them, and Moses did. The Lord told Moses to make a fiery serpent and set it on a standard. Moses obeyed his command. He made a bronze serpent and set it on the standard, and it came about that if a serpent bit any man he had only to look at the bronze serpent to live."

Julia Valerian forgotten, Alexander's curiosity was roused. "Perhaps the origin of the standard of Asklepios is the same as that of the Lord."

"I don't know," she said, not denying the possibility. What God gave to man, man corrupted. "The first time I saw the standard, I remembered the history my father taught me. And I tell you now what he told me. The people saw their sin, they repented, they looked upon the standard God had given them, they *believed* in his power to restore . . . and they lived."

He was perplexed.

She saw his confusion, recognized his resistance. *Help me, Lord,* she prayed and then went on. "My father heard Jesus say that just as Moses lifted up the serpent in the wilderness, even so the Son of Man would be lifted up."

He thought then he understood what she was saying, though not her reasons for it. "You speak of his resurrection."

"No. I speak of his crucifixion. He was nailed to a cross and set up before all mankind. He *is* the standard."

He went cold. "Why do you tell me this?"

"To help you understand why I have to go back to Julia."

His anger returned full force. "To be crucified this time? To be nailed to a cross instead of thrown to the lions?"

"No, Alexander. To take the standard of the Lord and place it before her."

Filled with fear for her, he stood and came to her, his mind seeking desperately for the argument that would sway her to sanity. Gently, he took her hands in his. "Listen to me, Hadassah. Think longer on this. You're accomplishing great things here with me. Look how far we've come from that mean little booth outside the public baths. Look at what you've been able to do for others. People revere you."

She pulled away. "What has been accomplished is of the Lord's doing, not mine—"

"I know that," he said, trying to interrupt.

"It is his name that must be glorified. Not the name of *Rapha*."

He frowned. "I didn't realize it bothered you so much to be called by that name."

"I am not the healer, Alexander. Jesus is Rapha," she said with tears in her eyes. "How many times must I tell you?" She placed her hand against her heart. "I am an ordinary woman who loves the Lord. That's all I am."

"And has not your Lord anointed others with the healing touch? Even I have heard of Jesus' apostles who, by a mere touch, could heal the sick."

"I am not an apostle, Alexander. Jesus ascended before I was born."

"Then how do you explain the things that have happened through you? You may not believe in yourself, but people believe in you."

She moved away from him. He realized his error the moment the words were uttered, and he tried to retract them. "I didn't mean to say they see you as a god." She turned. Her look drove him to honesty. "All right! A few do see you in that way, but you've done nothing to encourage them to do so. You have no reason to feel guilty."

"It's not guilt I feel, Alexander. It's sorrow."

He knew he was making a mess of it.

She spread her hands. Her smile was filled with tenderness. "You knew this day would come."

He closed his eyes. He shook his head, wanting to deny it. She was putting her life at risk, and *he* was shaking. He looked at her and wondered. How could she be so fearless? How could he let her go?

"I don't want you to go, Hadassah," he said quietly, then smiled weakly. "I didn't realize how much I'd come to need you."

"You don't need me, Alexander. You have the Lord."

"The Lord can't sit and talk with me. He can't look at me with dark, fathomless eyes and lead me to find the answers I need. He can't stir my imagination with a word, my heart with a touch—"

"He can do all of that, Alexander, and more."

He shook his head. "I don't know him like you do. I need you to speak to him for me."

His words grieved her heart. "I've become your stumbling block."

"Never," he said fiercely, going to her. "Never," he said again and reached out to pull her into his arms. He embraced her, keeping silent, knowing whatever he would say at this point would be fruitless and possibly hurtful.

Oh God, if you hear me, if you are there, protect her! Please, do not take her from me forever. . . .

"How long will you stay with her?" he said gruffly.

"Until the end."

"Hers or yours?" he said, his mouth twisting sardonically.

And she answered softly, having weighed all possibilities: "Whichever comes first."

29

Mother Prisca sat straight backed upon the couch Iulius had carried on the balcony for her. In all her eighty-seven years of life, she had never been more nervous. She had known Phoebe Valerian was an important and wealthy lady, but somehow she had been able to put aside position within the confines of her own poor tenement room. Here, in this beautiful villa with its grand views of the harbor and Artemision, she could not forget or ignore the social class chasm that yawned between them.

A slave girl brought a tray with an arrangement of fruit and delicacies. She leaned down, holding it before Prisca, and smiled encouragement. Prisca shook her head.

Iulius saw her tension, recognized it for what it was, and tried to put her at ease. "Please, Mother Prisca, be at home with us. How many times have you given us refreshment? And now you would deny us the pleasure of serving you?"

Mother Prisca shot him a look, then took a peach. "Satisfied?" She held it gently in her lap on the folds of her threadbare palus as though it were something too precious to eat.

Phoebe mumbled something, and Iulius bent down to her. Her good hand lay in her lap on a small copper plate. She tapped on it, and Prisca watched as the man listened intently. "Hera," he said and glanced at Mother Prisca. "How is the child Hera?" Mother Prisca looked at Phoebe in surprise, her gaze flashing to Iulius in question. Nodding, he smiled. "Lady Phoebe can't speak or move, but she understands what is happening around her."

His words filled Prisca with a deep sense of pity and sadness. Hiding her feelings, she looked at Phoebe and tried to renew the old camaraderie she had felt toward the younger woman. "The little girl is fine. She still plays with her dolls in doorways. She asked why you hadn't come lately, and I told her you were not well." She ran her fingers lightly over the soft skin of the peach, remembering the child's tears.

"Olympia and her son are doing well," she went on. "She has found work at an eatery. Vernasia has decided to marry again. The man works in your son's emporium and lives in the same tenement she does. I don't think she's done with grieving for her young husband, but she can't support herself, now can she? Caius is older, past taking risks. He works on land. He'll take care of her and her children, and maybe he'll finally have a few of his own."

Phoebe listened hungrily to each word about what was happening in the lives of the widows she had visited. When Prisca finished speaking, she sat silent and ill-at-ease. Phoebe saw the sadness etched deeply into the dear old woman's face and wanted to reassure her. She tapped on her copper plate, using the code she and Iulius had painstakingly worked out. She knew he would understand and convey her message.

"'The Lord has not forsaken me,'" Iulius said for her.

Tears sprang into Prisca's eyes. She set the peach aside and rose stiffly. Bending down, she took Phoebe's hand between hers. "That may be, child, but it grieves me to see someone as young as you like this. Better that it had happened to an old woman like me who's lived all the years she cares to live." She kissed Phoebe's hand and pressed it for a moment before laying it down again. She turned away to go.

Phoebe tapped.

Iulius put his hand out, and the old woman waited, looking at him curiously. "Yes, my lady," he said to Phoebe. He took a cloth and laid it on the couch where Prisca had sat. He put her peach on it and added all the fruit from the platter as well. Tying the corners of the cloth, he handed it to the old woman.

"Is she fattening me up?" Prisca said gruffly, embarrassed and overwhelmed.

"Eat in good health and pleasure," Iulius said. Phoebe tapped again. He nodded. "Yes, my lady," he said, laughing, and looked at Prisca. "She reminded me to give you more wool."

"Working me to death," Prisca muttered and glowered at Phoebe. "It's only right you give me peaches."

Phoebe's eyes twinkled in response.

Eyes filled with tears, Prisca patted Phoebe's shoulder and headed for the archways into the bedroom. "Can the others come and see her?" she said as Iulius escorted her out of the room and into the corridor to the steps.

"Not too many at once. She tires easily."

Prisca looked around at the grandness of the inner courtyard and fountain. The house was so grand, but so depressingly quiet. "Does she have no children or grandchildren to comfort her?"

"Her son, Marcus, has never married. He is somewhere in Palestine. It's doubtful he will return anytime soon. Her daughter, Julia, has been married several times but has no children. She's here in Ephesus."

"She knows of her mother's condition?"

"She knows, but she has a life of her own."

Prisca recognized a wealth of information in what Iulius didn't say. "She doesn't come to visit with her mother."

"Her mother's condition depresses her. She hasn't been here in some weeks." He was unable to keep the dislike from his voice.

Prisca shook her head sadly. "When they're young, they trample on your toes. When they grow up, they trample on your heart."

Iulius opened the front door for her. "You are the first person who has come to see her, Mother Prisca."

"And I will come again," she said firmly, then went out the door.

Iulius stepped outside. "Mother Prisca, I would ask a favor of you."

"I will grant it if I can."

"Bring Hera with you next time. Lady Phoebe hasn't seen a child since she was struck down."

The old woman nodded and went on.

He returned to the upstairs room. "You've been sitting long enough," he said and took Phoebe up in his arms, carrying her back inside. He laid her gently on her side on her sleeping couch. He talked with her, telling her what was going on in the household and what news had come from the outside world as he massaged her back. "Rest awhile," he said. "I'll bring up your meal." He left the room.

Phoebe knew as soon as he did so that another slave entered and sat close to watch over her should she need anything. She was never left alone. She listened to the birdsong coming from the balcony. Oh, to have the wings to fly away, to be free of the body.

Yet the Lord had kept her here like this for his purpose. Phoebe relaxed, clothing herself in the Lord's promises. Hadassah had been right. She knew what Adonai wanted of her. It had come to her as clearly as words spoken aloud. Gradually, she had given up the inner struggle and surrendered completely to him.

And in those moments, those infinitely precious moments, she did fly free, clear up into the heavens.

Pray, the voice had said softly. *Pray for your children.*

And so Phoebe did, hour after hour, day after day. And so she would for as many years as the Lord would give her to do so.

Lord, I hold Marcus up to you. Lord, turn my daughter's heart . . . Lord, I beseech you. Father, forgive them . . . Abba, take them in hand . . . In the name of your Son, Jesus, I plead . . . O Lord God of heaven and earth, save my children. . . .

30

As dawn tinged the horizon with rose, Hadassah stood on the street below Julia Valerian's villa. She had left Alexander's apartment before dawn to avoid further conflict with him. He didn't understand her determination to return to Julia. He felt it was foolish, wrong—and now that she looked up at the face of the elegant dwelling place, she wondered if he wasn't right.

Fear, her old enemy, returned in strength. Fear had always been Satan's stronghold on her. Even with all the time that had passed, she suddenly felt like the child she had been when she had waited for death among the throng of captives gathered in the Women's Court of the great temple. How had she forgotten what it felt like to be afraid for her life? It filled her now, bringing with it trembling in her stomach and limbs and cold sweat. She could taste it, like the link of a metallic chain in her mouth. And she despaired and doubted.

Why am I back here, Lord? Didn't you rescue me from this life and this woman? Why am I here again? Was I wrong in what you asked of me?

But she knew the answers to her questions before asking him. He had said it over and over. He had lived it. Hadn't her path been set long ago before she had ever met Julia Valerian? God's will be done, whatever it might be. At this moment, in this place, it was a frightening prospect.

Trust me, the still small voice seemed to say over and over. *Trust me.*

Her hand shook as she put it on the gate latch. Her mind filled with the image of Julia's face, twisted grotesquely in hate. She remembered the blows of her mistress's fists and her screams of rage. She remembered being kicked until she lost consciousness. And when she roused again, she had found herself in a dungeon with other Christians, awaiting death.

O Lord, if you would but take this bitter cup from me. . . .

Her fingers whitened on the latch but didn't open it. She could hardly breathe.

"Is this the place, Rapha?" The servant who had carried her

few things moved closer to her. He glanced up at the stone facade above.

Hadassah shuddered slightly, remembering all the vile things she had witnessed in this house. She looked up again. She could change her mind. Even now, if she chose, she could go back to Alexander. God would forgive her.

Wasn't I doing your will there, Lord? Couldn't I remain with him and help the sick?

But as she stared up at the cold stone villa, she knew God had sent her here. Turning away from Julia Valerian now would mean turning away from the Lord, and without him life had no meaning.

Yes, she remembered the dungeon, cold, dank, fetid. Wasn't it there in the darkness that she had truly seen the Light and been warmed by it? Wasn't it there she had found the peace God had always promised her? Wasn't it there that God had truly set her free?

"Rapha?" the servant said, questioning. "Do you want to go back?"

"No. This is the place," she said and opened the gate. Leaning heavily on her walking stick, she went up the steps ahead of him. Her bad leg was aching terribly by the time she reached the door. She took a deep breath and applied the knocker.

No one answered.

"No one is home, Rapha," the servant said, relieved.

Hadassah knocked again, more loudly, and listened for movement within the house.

Silence.

"I will recall the litter." He turned back, stepping down to the step below her. Shifting his burdens, he held his hand out to support her.

"No. I must go in." She was concerned by the lack of response within the villa. Where were Julia's servants? She lifted the latch and pushed. It gave easily, and the door swung open.

"Rapha, no," the servant said, frightened.

Ignoring him, she entered the antechamber and looked around her. "Leave the things by the door."

"But I can't leave you here—"

"Leave them and go. I will be fine."

He stood nervously, looking around. The place had a deserted air about it. Obeying reluctantly, he closed the door behind him and shut her into the silent house.

The tap of her walking stick on the marble tiles echoed into the peristyle. The fountain was still, the water stagnant. She looked into the triclinium and saw faded cushions and a dusty table. The marble statuary was gone, though the east wall was still emblazoned with a mosaic of Bacchus cavorting with some wood nymphs.

Turning away, Hadassah limped to the stairs leading to the upper chambers. When she reached the top, she paused to rest. The pain in her leg was so intense she trembled. She listened again but still heard no one. After a moment the pain eased, and she continued down the open corridor to Julia's chamber.

The door was open.

Her heart fluttered so fast within her breast, it felt like a bird frantic to escape. Standing on the threshold, Hadassah looked in.

Julia was not in the bed.

Hadassah entered the room and saw it was in disarray. It smelled strongly of an unemptied slops basin. Looking out on the balcony, Hadassah saw Julia. She was alone and dressed in a threadbare ankle-length tunic. A breeze molded the tunic to her waif-thin body. She clutched the wall as though for support, and her face was turned toward the eastern hills. Her expression was so utterly forlorn, Hadassah wondered if she was thinking of Atretes. He had once built a beautiful villa for her in those hills, intending to take her there as his wife.

Hadassah remained where she was watching Julia intently, wondering if she was the same or if circumstances had changed her. Julia lowered her head, and the light breeze stirred the dull tendrils of dark hair about her face and shoulders. She looked like a hurt child. Shivering, she wrapped her arms around herself. As she turned away, she saw Hadassah in her veils and started in fright.

"Rapha," she gasped.

Hadassah had never heard her sound more vulnerable.

The fear that had coursed so strongly through Hadassah vanished. She remembered singular moments of sweetness in Julia. She had been a girl of gaiety and passion. Filled with sadness, Hadassah looked at her now—thin, pale, and ravaged by disease.

She limped toward Julia, the sound of her walking stick tapping the tile floor. Julia stared, eyes wide, uncertain.

"Please forgive me for coming unannounced to your chamber, my lady. No one answered the door."

"You are welcome," Julia said formally as she sank weakly onto a couch near the wall and drew a soiled blanket around her shoulders. "And I am alone. Like rats, Didymas and Tropas have deserted the sinking ship." Her mouth twisted sardonically. "Not that they were of particular use to me." She glanced away and said quietly, "I'm relieved they're gone. It saved me the trouble of selling them."

"Is Prometheus also gone, my lady?"

"No. I sent him out into the city to find work." She lifted a shoulder indifferently. "He may or may not come back. He belonged to Primus, not me. Primus was my husband, such as he was." Her gaze lifted to Hadassah's veils, and a small frown flickered over her pale brow. She fidgeted with the blanket nervously. "Why are you here, Lady Rapha? You touched me and nothing happened. The physician said there was no hope." Her chin tipped. "Have you come back to see if your magic will work this time?" Her show of disdain did nothing to disguise the fear and hopelessness that had settled into her features.

"No," Hadassah answered softly.

Julia felt ashamed, but she needed some sort of self-defense and so clung to disdain of others. "Perhaps you aren't the miracle worker everyone says you are."

"No, I'm not."

Anguish settled on Julia's face, and she wrapped her arms around herself again. She looked away. "Then why are you here?"

Hadassah came closer. "I've come to ask if I may stay with you and take care of you, Lady Julia."

Julia's head jerked up in surprise. "Stay with me?" Swallowing, she gazed at the veiled woman, defenseless, her loneliness and vulnerability exposed completely. "I have no money to pay you."

"I ask for none."

"I have no money even to buy bread for you."

"I have money enough to provide for both of us."

Julia stared at her in amazed confusion. "You . . . would provide for me?" she said tremulously. "Why?"

"Because I must."

Julia frowned, not understanding. "You mean the physician changed his mind and sent you here to care for me."

"No. The Lord sent me."

Julia stiffened slightly. "The Lord?" she said in a choked voice. "Which god do you worship?"

Hadassah felt her withdrawal as strongly as if it had been physical. She saw also the wariness and fear behind Julia's careful look. She moved closer and put her walking stick in front of her, using it as support. She knew God called her now to utter the same words she had said to Julia once before, words that had brought wrath and violence, words that had brought a sentence of death upon her.

O Lord, do you test me so soon? And then she felt ashamed. How many times in the past had she failed to speak out before that final night with Julia? *Lord, forgive me. I denied you every time I was silent, every time I let an opportunity pass.*

"I believe that Jesus is the Christ, the Son of the living God."

Silence fell over the balcony. Even the breeze seemed to still. Only Hadassah's words of faith seemed to echo in the air.

Julia shuddered and looked away, her face white and strained. "I tell you truthfully, Rapha. Your god did not send you to me."

"Why do you say this?"

"Because I *know.*"

"How do you know, Lady Julia?"

She looked up at her, eyes wide and full of suffering. "Because if any god has reason to bear a grudge against me, it is this one."

Hadassah was filled with hope by her answer. "There is but one thing I would ask of you," Hadassah said when she knew she could speak without weeping.

"Now it comes," Julia said sarcastically. "Yes. What do you want of me? What price must I pay?"

"I ask you not to call me Rapha."

Surprise filled Julia's face. "And that's all?"

"Yes."

Her eyes narrowed. "Why not?"

"It is a title I've never been worthy to hold. It was a name given me out of kind but mistaken motives."

Julia gazed at her uncertainly. "What do you wish me to call you?"

Hadassah's heart beat wildly. She had thought to reveal herself, but something within her held her back. *O Lord, I am not like the Hadassah of Purim who saved her people. I am so much less than that. Father, show me who I am to her. Give me a name into which I can grow. A name Julia can use with ease.*

And it came to her, like a whisper. She smiled. "I would ask you to call me by the name of Azar."

Azar. Helper.

"Azar," Julia repeated. "It's a pretty name."

"Yes," Hadassah said, feeling a sudden lightness of heart and giving thanks for it. "Azar."

"I will call you by that name," Julia said in agreement.

"Then whether I stay or go is your choice, my lady. I will do as you wish."

Julia sat in silence for a long moment. Full of doubt and distrust, she was afraid to say yes. Why would a *Christian* come to take care of her? What was there in it for her? If Rapha . . . *Azar* knew all she had done, she would turn away. And Julia knew it was only a matter of time until someone told her.

"I don't believe you'll stay," she said. "Why would you? All of Ephesus knows about you. You are much in demand." No one would give up fame and wealth for a life of drudgery and solitude with a dying woman. She wouldn't. It made no sense.

Hadassah came nearer and lowered herself painfully onto a seat facing Julia. "I will stay."

"A few days? A few weeks? A month or two?"

"Until the end."

Julia searched the veils, trying to see the face behind them. She couldn't. Perhaps Rapha . . . Azar . . . whatever her name was, was old. Certainly the labored way she moved and her strangely rasping voice bespoke a woman of substantial years. Maybe that was it. She was tired and needed the rest of caring for one person rather than many. And what did any of it matter if Rapha-Azar would give her word?

"Do you promise?" Julia said shakily, wishing she had a scribe at hand so that an agreement might be put in writing.

"I promise."

Julia released her breath slowly. How strange it was. Two words uttered by a woman she didn't even know, and yet she was certain she could believe her. She could trust her. Perhaps it was in the way Rapha-Azar said those words.

Suddenly, Julia was filled with an inexpressible sorrow. "*I promise.*" She heard another voice speaking those words, saw laughing dark eyes filled with an indulgent affection.

"*I promise. . . .*"

Marcus had once spoken those words to her, and where was

he now? What had his promise meant? Her own brother had lied to her. How could she believe anyone?

With such desperate circumstances, how can you not? a voice seemed to whisper.

Every moment, she lived with fear. Death was a most terrifying fact of life, but what she had feared most was facing it alone. "Oh, Azar," she said, "I'm so afraid." Her mouth worked as her eyes filled with tears.

"I know what it is to be afraid," Hadassah said.

"Do you?"

"Yes. From the time I was a child, fear almost consumed me."

"How did you overcome it?"

"I didn't. God did."

Julia was immediately uncomfortable. She didn't want God mentioned. And she didn't understand. She only knew that any reference to Hadassah's god distressed her. It made her remember things she wanted desperately to forget.

And now, Azar said her god was the same one. "What pathetic irony," she murmured miserably.

"What is?"

"My life is in utter shambles because of one Christian, and now you come and offer to take care of me." Shivering, she closed her eyes. "All I know is I need someone. *Anyone.*"

It was enough.

Yet, from that one statement, Hadassah saw the hard, treacherous road ahead. Thinking as she did, Julia might never turn. And, as Alexander had warned her, Hadassah knew she herself might yet die in the arena. She was absolutely sure of only one thing: God had sent her here for a purpose, and to his purpose she must yield. She could not count the cost.

"I will never leave you, Lady Julia, nor forsake you. Not as long as I draw breath in this body." With that said, Hadassah held out her hand.

Julia stared at it. Face crumpling, she took it and clung to it out of her own need. Beyond that, she could not think.

31

Marcus spent several weeks in Gennesaret, walking the city streets. Dressed in the clothing Ezra Barjachin had given him and mimicking the reverent posturing of those he had observed, he was able to enter a synagogue. He wanted to hear the Scriptures being read and stood on the outer fringes of the gathering to do so. Though he understood no Hebrew, he gained strange comfort in hearing the Scriptures from the Torah. All the while the words flowed over him, he thought of Hadassah. She had spoken, and he had been deaf. Just as then, Hebrew or Greek, Aramaic or Latin, the language was alien to him, for the meaning escaped his grasp.

He heard the music of the language, the haunting call of it, and wanted to understand. He wanted to see and hear and have it sink in. He wanted to know what had drawn Hadassah to God and held her there with such determination and conviction until the end.

Who are you? What are you?

He looked around surreptitiously and saw the devotion and peace in some of the men's faces, the *hope*. In others, he saw mirrored what he felt. Hunger.

I want to know what sustained her. God, I want to know!

The ache inside him grew. Yet he remained, listening earnestly to the men as they discussed in Greek the fine points of Judaic law. Laws upon laws mounted with tradition. Too complicated for him to understand in a few days. Too complicated for a lifetime. Frustrated, he withdrew and wandered along on the shores of the Sea of Galilee, thinking about all he had heard and trying to make sense of it.

Surely life hadn't been so complex for Hadassah. She had been a simple, ordinary girl, not a brilliant scholar or theologian. Everything she had believed had all narrowed down to one truth for her: *Jesus*. Everything she did, everything she said, the way she lived—it all focused on the man from Nazareth.

If only his own life could be so clear.

What was this constant hunger that gnawed at him? It had

291

plagued him even before Hadassah had come into his life. There was no definition for what he felt, no description of that for which he yearned. He had tried everything to fill the emptiness within himself: women, wine, games, money. Nothing was sufficient. Nothing answered the need. The void remained, an affliction of his spirit.

Traveling the short distance to Capernaum, he took lodging in a Greek inn. The proprietor was gregarious and hospitable, but Marcus kept to himself, untouched by the jovial atmosphere. The activity depressed him, and he took to spending evenings at the harbor, watching the fishermen bring in their catches for the day. At night, he watched the blazing torches as the boats glided over black water and fishermen cast out their nets.

A trumpet sounded six times, ushering in the Sabbath, from the roof of a synagogue on high ground that faced a holy city that no longer existed. He watched men and noted the four-corner fringed garment they wore. He had learned that the deep blue thread at one corner was a constant reminder to the wearer to keep the Law.

After a few days he grew restless and walked on to Bethsaida, but after several nights there, he headed east for Bethsaida-Julias. He had heard that Jesus of Nazareth had taught on the hillsides near the small city. But Jesus had been crucified over forty years ago. Would his words still echo on those quiet slopes?

He had thought he could find Hadassah's God in this war-torn land that bore the stamp of Rome, but God eluded him. He wasn't to be found on a mountaintop or in a holy city. God wasn't at the altar stone in the heart of the temple. God wasn't in a deserted house in a Galilean village or even along a lonely path to the sea.

How do I find you?

No answer came.

Oppressed in spirit, Marcus fell into despair.

He could find no peace. He had even lost all sense of purpose. His carefully laid plans had come to nothing. He wasn't even certain anymore why he had come to Palestine. Worst of all, somewhere along the long road, Hadassah had slipped away from him.

He could no longer see her face. He couldn't remember the sound of her voice. Only her love for her god remained clear. He wanted to imagine her here, walking these same shores, a child, happy. Maybe then he'd feel some peace. Yet, his mind betrayed him repeatedly, going back to a clouded vision of a dark-haired girl kneeling in the garden of his father's Roman villa. Praying. Praying for his family.

Praying for *him*.

Why did that one image remain? Why did it so torment him? Why was that one burning light of memory all he had left of her?

Shunning people, Marcus remained in the hills east of Bethsaida-Julias, seeking solitude to clear his thoughts and find her again. He groped for justification for a quest that had lost all focus. The harder he tried to think on these things, the more jumbled his thoughts became, the more confused his mind grew, until he wondered if he was going mad.

His hair and beard grew. He took to following the shepherds with their flocks, standing off in the distance, watching. They took such care with the animals, guiding them to green pastures, making them lie down in the cool shadows to ruminate. The beasts drank from still pools built along the streams and followed the shepherd each time he pounded his staff on the ground. He watched the animals enter into a sheepfold, not bunched together, but one by one, each carefully tended by the shepherd. Some the shepherd anointed, working the oil into the wool about the sheep's eyes and nose. And once inside, safe within the protective walls, the shepherd lay across the mouth of the fold to guard his flock.

Marcus lay upon his own coat and stared up at the heavens, his mind in chaos. Someone had said sometime during his travels that Jesus had been called "the Good Shepherd." Or had it been Hadassah who said it? He couldn't remember. But, oh, the peace to be like one of those dumb sheep, watched over and provided for and protected by a Shepherd whose existence seemed to be simply that, the tender care of his sheep.

Again and again Marcus returned to watch, and still the pain tormented him, worrying his mind like a dog worried a festering wound. His heart was raw. He wanted to resurrect Hadassah in his mind and, each time he tried, remembered her death instead, the violence and horror of it.

Why? His heart cried out. *God, why?*

Without warning, he dreamed again one night, this time of a fiery pit inhabited by tortured beings writhing in the flickering dark light. It became more intense, more vivid, until he could feel the heat and smell the sulfurous smoke surrounding him. Terror filled him, and then a flicker of hope as somewhere far above him, out of sight and reach, he heard Hadassah crying out to him to come to her.

"I can't find you!" he cried out in anguish and awakened abruptly, bathed in his own sweat, his heart pounding.

Night after night the dream returned, torturing him. And then, as suddenly as it had begun to plague his nights, the dream stopped, leaving a void far worse. A yawning darkness surrounded him—and, exhausted, he felt himself fall into it.

Haggard and unkempt, Marcus wished for death, for an end to torment. "I know you're there. You've won! End it!" he cried out to the skies.

Nothing happened.

He went down to the shores of the sea and sat staring out at the rippling water for hours on end. The wind was cold and cut into him, but he scarcely felt it. A vision of himself came to him. It was so clear he might have been standing before a mirror, yet he saw beyond . . . into his soul. He covered his eyes, gripping his head, and heard his sister's words.

"I heard what she said to you! I heard her throw your love back in your face. She preferred her god over you, and you said her god could have her. Well, now he shall!"

Marcus groaned. "No." He held his head tighter, pressing, wanting to crush the words and images from his mind.

"You said her god could have her!"

"O God, no . . . !" If not for him, she would be alive. It was due to his own rash words, words spoken in hurt and anger, that she had been sent to die.

"I did it for you!" Julia had cried that day when Hadassah had walked out on the sand to face the lions. And though he cried out against it, he could no longer turn away. It came upon him like a storm wave, overwhelming. He saw Julia, the sister he had so loved, wild with fury, hands clutching at him and screaming.

"You said her god could have her . . . you said her god could have her . . . you said—"

"No!" he cried into the wind. "I never meant her to die!"

"You said her god could have her. . . ."

The wind came up strongly and Marcus remembered his last words to Hadassah in the upper chambers of Julia's villa: *"Your god can have you!"*

He had wanted her for himself, and when he couldn't have her, he had walked away full of rage and contempt.

And she paid the price.

On his knees, he covered his head. "*I deserved death, not her.*"

With the dark silence came the weight of judgment. He knelt on the shore until the wind died down and stillness fell around him. Digging his hands into the sand, he lifted his face. "I came to curse you, but I am the one who is cursed." No still small voice spoke to him. He had never felt so alone and empty. "Why should you answer me? Who am I? Nobody. What am I? Nothing."

He felt swallowed up by guilt and vomited on the sand in remorse, for he knew he deserved worse for his part in what had happened to Hadassah. He couldn't run and hide from it anymore. "If you are God, take justice. Take justice!"

The soft wind rippled the waters, and a gentle wave washed the shore. He heard the old woman's words again, as though whispered to him over the water.

"*Until you find God, you live in vain.*"

He saw the vanity all his life had been and the bleak, dark nothingness that stretched out before him. He was convicted of his sin. His own life should be forfeit. Despite Julia's part in what had happened, it should've been him that day, standing on the sand. Not Hadassah. She had never done anything deserving of death. But, looking back, he could see the countless times and countless ways he had taken a path deserving of death.

He waited for judgment, but God was silent. So Marcus rose to his feet and judged himself. He proclaimed his guilt and handed down his sentence . . . and walked into the sea.

The cool water lapped about his ankles, his knees, his hips. He threw himself forward and began to swim, straight out toward the depths. The water became rougher and colder. His limbs grew numb. Exhausted, he swam sluggishly, still outward. A wave struck him and he breathed in water. Choking, he instinctively struggled for life even while craving death.

As consciousness began to slip away and the cold enfolded him, he heard his name spoken.

"*Marcus.*"

It came softly from all around him, and then stillness fell as a rising warmth took hold of him.

THE FURNACE

32

Marcus awakened on the shore. Disoriented, he stared up at the stars. *A dream,* he thought, *it must have been a dream.* But why then did his lungs hurt? He pushed the weight of a dry cloak off of him and sat up. The sea breeze caressed him, and he felt the cool dampness of his tunic against his skin. His heart began to beat faster. Goosebumps rose all over his body.

A fire crackled.

Shaking with fear, Marcus turned his head. A man in a long tunic sat on the other side of the flames, cooking a fish. In the flickering light, Marcus thought his garments shone. Never had Marcus seen such a face.

"Are you God?"

"I am a servant of the Lord Most High."

Marcus felt a chill of apprehension. "By what name are you called?"

"Do not be afraid," the man said, and his voice was at once commanding and soothing. "I am Paracletos."

"Where did you come from?"

Paracletos smiled, and his countenance seemed even brighter. "I have come to bring you good news, Marcus Lucianus Valerian. God has heard your prayers."

Marcus began to shake violently. He had asked God to take his life and thought to drown himself when nothing came of it. Was this stranger here now to strike him down in the name of the Lord? Well, it was no less than he deserved. He waited, heart thundering in his ears, sweat breaking out on his skin.

"Rise and eat," Paracletos said, holding the stick with the roasted fish toward him.

Marcus rose slowly and leaned over the fire, sliding the fish carefully from the stick. He sat again and removed the flesh from the bone. It was delicious and melted in his mouth. After the first bite, he realized how hungry he was. Paracletos gave him bread and wine, and Marcus ate and drank until he was replete. It would seem God wanted him to die with a full stomach.

The intensity of Paracletos' gaze burned Marcus' heart. "Many have prayed for you, and their prayers have been heard," he said, "but you must *ask* in order to receive."

Anguish filled Marcus. "By what right do I ask anything?" He knew what he wanted most, but it was impossible. "Can I receive forgiveness from one whose death I caused?"

"In Christ all things are possible."

Marcus shook his head and closed his eyes. He thought of Hadassah. In his mind, he saw her walking out onto the sand, her arms open wide, smiling, singing. Who but God could give her such peace in such circumstances? Who but God could give her the faith she needed? Faith. Where did it come from?

"Ask and you shall receive."

Marcus looked up at him. Deserving nothing, he clenched his teeth. Should he cry out to God to save him now when he had cursed him time after time? Should he plead for mercy when he had given none?

"God gave his only begotten Son that whoever believes in him should not perish, but would have everlasting life."

"The fiery pit is where I belong, not in the heavens," Marcus said hoarsely. "Hadassah lost her life because of me."

"And has found it. God holds it still in the palm of his hand. She will not be taken from him. I tell you this in truth, Marcus Valerian, that neither death, nor life, nor angels, nor principalities, nor things present, nor things to come, nor powers, nor height, nor depth, nor any other created thing, will ever be able to separate Hadassah from the love of God, which is in Christ Jesus our Lord."

Relief and gratitude washed over Marcus.

The man rose and approached him. "Believe in him who sent me. Hear the Good News. He who died has risen again, just as he raised you up from the sea. You asked the Lord to take your life, and so he has."

He put his hand on Marcus' shoulder, and at his touch, Marcus' heart broke. Tears came like the lancing of an ancient, infected wound that had pained him from birth throughout his life. He fell prostrate on the sand and wept.

"Go to Capernaum," Paracletos said. "You will find a man at the gate. Tell him all that has happened to you tonight."

Marcus stood after a long while but saw no one on the beach with him. Could he have dreamed it? He looked and saw, there before him on the sand, a charcoal fire and the bones of a fish.

The hair on the back of his neck prickled and a spilling warmth spread through his body.

Marcus ran into Bethsaida-Julias. "I'm looking for Paracletos," he said, gasping for breath. "Do you know where I can find him?"

"I know of no one by that name," came the repeated answer, nor had any seen a man who fit the description Marcus gave. Surely someone would have heard of such a man.

"Perhaps you've seen an angel," one man mocked.

"Go sleep off the wine!" others laughed.

Marcus took the road to Capernaum, and it was almost dawn when he came near. He saw a man sitting by the gate. People passed by him, but he seemed to be watching the road. Was this the one Paracletos meant? Marcus strode toward him, and the man's gaze fixed upon him intently. Setting aside his feelings of foolishness, Marcus obeyed Paracletos' command and poured out the story of what had happened to him the night before.

"The last thing he said to me was to come to Capernaum and tell all this to the man by the gate. And so I have." He expected the man to laugh and accuse him of being drunk.

Instead, the man's smile shone. "The Lord be praised! I am Cornelius. I was told in a dream that a Roman named Marcus would meet me here. Are you he?"

"I am Marcus," he said hoarsely, adding dryly, "Were you told what to do with me?"

The man laughed. "Oh yes! Come with me!" He led Marcus down to the sea. Marcus followed him into the water in confusion. Cornelius turned to him and put his hand on his shoulder. "Do you believe that Jesus is the Christ, the Son of the living God?"

Marcus felt a moment of fear. Whatever came now would change his life forever. He clenched his teeth and fists, still struggling against himself. Did he believe? Did he?

Tense, uncertain, he knew he had to make a conscious decision. "I believe," he said. "Forgive my unbelief."

The man took firm hold of him and lowered him into the water. "I baptize you in the name of the Father and of the Son and of the Holy Spirit."

The flow of cool water enfolded Marcus, burying him, and then he was raised up into the warmth of the sun. He planted his feet firmly as the man next to him rejoiced in the Lord. Others

301

came running, and all Marcus could do was stand and stare out over the Sea of Galilee, surprised by the joy he felt.

Sudden. Inexplicable. Complete joy.

It hadn't been a dream. He hadn't imagined any of what had happened the night before or been said by the stranger who called himself Paracletos. Yet even more profound was the change he felt within himself now that he had made the decision to believe that Jesus was the Christ, the Son of the living God. He felt cleansed. He felt whole. His blood rushed through his veins with new life, new direction.

Marcus filled his lungs with the crisp air and let it out again, feeling free. He laughed and lifted his eyes to the heavens with a thankful heart. He wept at the same time. Was it really that astoundingly simple? *I believe.*

He glanced at Cornelius eagerly, responding to the new Spirit within him. "What do I do now?"

"You are to return to Ephesus."

The words came like a physical blow.

"What did you say?"

"You are to return to Ephesus," Cornelius said again, frowning slightly.

Marcus stood, dripping wet, feeling as though his heart had been wrenched from him. He stared at Cornelius, a man he didn't know, and wished he had never asked the question. "Why do you tell me this?" he said hoarsely, angry that his joy should be stripped away so quickly.

"These are the words that were given to me. 'Tell Marcus to return to Ephesus.'" Cornelius put his hand on Marcus' arm. "Do you know what the Lord wants of you there?"

Oh yes, he knew. The appalling fullness and mercy of the command struck his heart, but his mind rebelled against it.

"I know," he said grimly.

God wanted him to forgive his sister.

33

"Tell me another story like the one you told me yesterday," Julia said as Azar helped her to the couch on the balcony. "Something exciting and romantic."

Hadassah's heart sank. Over the past weeks she had told Julia many stories that had been told to her as a child. They were stories meant to reveal the attributes of God's love and mercy, but Julia saw no significance other than as entertainment. They didn't touch her heart. Was she always to be this way, wanting distraction from the pain of illness, blind to the truth of life.

She wanted something exciting. Romantic.

Hadassah wanted to shake her and tell her of Sheol and Satan, of Jesus coming again and taking judgment on the world, on *her*. Did Julia want to be among those cast into the fiery pit for all eternity? Was she so blind to the truth that was proclaimed every dawn of every day? Christ is risen. Christ is Lord. Christ reigns. Christ will judge.

"Why are you so quiet?" Julia said.

If you reign, Lord, why am I so defeated?

"Tell me a story, Azar."

Hadassah let her breath out slowly, trying to rid herself of irritation. Julia was no less demanding than she had ever been. Bracing herself, Hadassah helped Julia lie down. She covered her with the blanket and limped to the other couch. She sat down carefully, pain shooting up her bad leg. She stretched it out and rubbed it as she felt Julia watching her and waiting. She tried to think of a story that would suffice.

"It came about in the days when the judges governed Israel, that there was a famine in the land. And a certain man of Bethlehem in Judah went to sojourn in the land of Moab with his wife and his two sons. . . ."

Julia leaned back and closed her eyes, listening to her companion's rasping voice. The story sounded familiar, but she didn't mind. She couldn't remember the details or events and it would serve to amuse her for a while.

"The sons took for themselves Moabite women as wives; the name of one was Orpah and the name of the other Ruth."

Julia opened her eyes in dismay. "Is this the story where her husband dies and the girl goes back to Judah with her mother-in-law and meets some farmer?"

Hadassah fell silent. She clasped her hands tightly in her lap, struggling against the anger that rose within her. "Yes, my lady."

"I've heard it." Julia gave a pained sigh. "But go ahead and tell it anyway. Just make the man she meets a soldier instead of a farmer, and throw in a few battles." When Azar said nothing, Julia turned her head and looked at her, perplexed. She was so still. With the veils hiding her face, Julia couldn't even begin to guess her thoughts. That disturbed her. Had she offended her? "Very well," she said, with pained tolerance. "Tell it however you want."

Hadassah didn't want to tell her the story at all! She shut her eyes and breathed in slowly, disturbed by the anger that rose within her. It was anything but righteous. When she opened her eyes again, she saw Julia was still looking at her.

"Are you angry with me?"

She sounded like a child who knew she had displeased her mother. Hadassah started to deny her anger and changed her mind. "Yes," she said frankly. "I am angry." She didn't know where the admission might lead, but she wasn't sorry she had spoken openly.

Julia blinked. "But why? Because I've heard the story before? I didn't say I didn't like it. It was amusing in its way. I only asked you to change a few details to make it more interesting." She turned her face away and added in a fractious tone, "But you don't have to if you don't want to."

"You may have listened to the story before, but you failed to *hear* it."

Julia's head snapped around again, her eyes glittering with sudden rebellious anger. "I *heard* it. I'm not stupid. I could tell you the whole story myself. The mother was Naomi, who later called herself Mara because she was bitter she lost her husband and two sons. Isn't that correct? And the farmer's name was Boaz. A ridiculous name, if you ask me. Bow-azz. Why not something strong like Apollo? At least then you'd know he was handsome! And Ruth was the *perfect* daughter-in-law, a woman of excellence. 'Woman of excellence!' She was a drudge who did everything her mother-in-law wanted her to do. Glean in the fields, Ruth. Sleep at his feet, Ruth. Marry Boaz no matter how old he is. Give your first child up."

She turned her head away. "The poor girl had no mind of her own," she said with sneering disdain.

"Ruth had a mind of her own. A strong mind and heart, and she gave both to God and was blessed for it."

"That's your opinion."

"The farmer she married made her the great-grandmother of King David. Even Rome has heard of King David," Hadassah shot back.

Julia turned her head again, her mouth curving coolly this time. "Do I detect pride in your voice, Azar? Was that contempt I heard?"

Heat flooded Hadassah's cheeks. She looked at Julia's smug expression and was filled with shame. She *was* proud. She had burned with it at Julia's disdainful words.

"Israel may have had one King David," Julia conceded haughtily, "but Rome has had the great Julius, Caesar Augustus, Vespasian, *Titus*. Didn't that young man reduce ancient Jerusalem to a pile of rubble?"

Hadassah remembered Titus all too well. "Yes, my lady, he did."

At her quietly spoken words, the coldness left Julia's eyes. A frown flickered across her brow, and her mouth softened. "Were you there when it happened?"

"I was there."

Julia bit her lip and looked away again, troubled. "I'm sorry I reminded you of it. Sometimes I say things without even meaning them."

It was surprising words like these that filled Hadassah with confusion about Julia. Was she arrogant and disdainful? Or was she sensitive? Did her abrasive manner merely serve to hide a deeper vulnerability?

Lord, help me. I used to love her like a sister. Now I dislike her so much it's hard to stay in the same chamber with her. I sit and listen to her constant complaints and demands, and I want to scream at her about the suffering she caused me. Help me see her through your eyes, Father.

As she prayed, she began to relax again. Julia was blind and deaf to the truth. She was ignorant. Did one reprove a blind woman for her inability to see? Did one become angry with the deaf for not hearing?

Julia was a lost sheep who had dined on poisonous plants and wandered among the briars. Pursued by wolves, she had entered swift waters that swept her downstream. Like all of humanity, she hungered for what was missing from birth and sought desperately to fill the emptiness within. She had embraced Calabah's lies, given in to Caius' dark passions, allowed her conscience to be seared by Primus' abominable practices, and fallen in love with Atretes, a man filled with violence and hatred. Was it any wonder she was now weighted down by her sin, even dying of it?

Compassion filled Hadassah. Her body warmed with it, and the ache in her leg eased.

"I wanted to tell you the story of Ruth because it's about a woman who was the daughter of an incestuously begun race that embraced pagan practices. Yet she had a heart for God. She chose to leave her homeland and family and follow her mother-in-law. She said, 'Your God will be my God.' God blessed her greatly because of her faith, not just during her own lifetime, but down through generations. We are all blessed through her."

Julia gave a curt laugh. "How are we all blessed through a Jewish woman who died centuries ago?"

"Ruth is named in the lineage of Jesus of Nazareth, the Savior."

Julia's face stiffened at the mention of his name. "I know you believe he is a god, Azar, but does that mean I must?"

Hadassah was filled with sadness at the stubbornness she saw in Julia's expression. "No," she said. "You will believe what you choose to believe."

Julia yanked her blanket higher and clutched it closer. "If Jesus is a god, he's a god with no power." Her hands whitened on the covers. "I knew someone a long time ago who believed in him, and it did her no good at all."

Hadassah closed her eyes and lowered her head, knowing it was of her Julia spoke. Julia didn't sound the least bit regretful, and she found herself wondering if Alexander wasn't right after all. She was in danger here. Maybe it was pride that had brought her to Julia and not the Lord's calling at all. Satan was the master deceiver. She wanted to get up and walk away, to close the door behind her and forget Julia Valerian. She wanted to leave the prideful young woman to her fate. There would come a day when every knee would bow and every tongue confess that Jesus Christ is Lord. Even Julia.

Why did you lead me here, Lord, when she has a heart of stone?

And yet, lead her he had. She wanted to deny it now and couldn't. The sense of purpose had been too strong, too pervasive. It still was. She was the one who was weak and vacillating.

Strengthen me, Lord. Strengthen me for your purpose. I don't know what to do about her.

She lifted her head again and saw Julia staring up at the sky, blinking back tears. "What's wrong, my lady?"

"Nothing."

"Are you in pain?"

"Yes," she said, shutting her eyes tightly. She was in so much pain even a healer, who spent her life around those in pain, couldn't imagine it.

Hadassah rose. "I'll prepare a draught of mandragora for you."

Julia listened to the tap of Azar's walking stick and the slight drag of her foot. She closed her eyes, fighting back the tears. Azar's presence and manner reminded her piercingly of another she had known. It was thoughts and memories of that other that plagued her now, but she knew she could never speak aloud of what she had done. As much as she longed to purge herself, she did not dare. It was useless wanting to relive the past. It was depressing to contemplate the future. Even the present was becoming increasingly unbearable.

Azar was all she had, and Azar was a Christian.

Hadassah. Oh, Hadassah! What have I done?

Julia promised herself she would never tell Azar what she had done to a slave girl who had done nothing wrong but love her. Better to die with guilt than die alone.

Azar returned with the mandragora. Julia drank it eagerly, longing for peace and thinking to find it in drugged oblivion.

34

While Julia slept, Hadassah sat in the peristyle pouring out her heart to God. She hadn't expected the confusing feelings that would be stirred up in her by returning to this villa. Each time a thought came knocking on the door of her mind, she viewed it cautiously. Was it true? Was it honorable? Was it pure or lovely? Was it of good repute? Too many were not, and she pressed them away. Yet, the dark thoughts kept pounding.

It was so much easier to keep her focus on the Lord when she was alone. It was when she was caring for Julia that her armor seemed too thin against the darts that came.

She warred against the thoughts of the past and those feelings now, turning her mind purposefully to praising the Lord. She recounted all those lives he had touched over the past two years. She thanked him for the life of Antonia and her son, for Severina and Boethus, and dozens of others. She prayed for Phoebe and Iulius. She prayed for Marcus, but thoughts of him turned her mind back again to the past. So she prayed for Alexander instead. She hadn't expected to miss him so much.

The front door opened, interrupting her quiet time. She was almost relieved when she saw Prometheus enter. She felt her spirit lighten, for she often sat with him here, listening to him and talking about the Lord. She hadn't revealed her identity to him, but found their previous camaraderie renewed and even heightened. She no longer saw him as a boy in bondage, but as a young man set free.

She watched him stride across the antechamber and enter the peristyle. The look on his face held her silent. He was greatly distressed. He walked to the fountain without noticing her in the alcove. Leaning over, he put his hands on the marbled edge of the well. He swore. Leaning down, he splashed the water over his face, rubbing it around the back of his neck. He swore again. He washed his hands and scrubbed at his face, but it didn't seem to help his plight. He was shaking badly.

"Prometheus?"

His body jerked in surprise, and she saw color mount into his face. His shoulders sagged, giving him a defeated look as he raised his head. He didn't look at her.

"You look upset."

He turned to her. His eyes were bleak. "I didn't know you were there, Lady Azar."

"I'm sorry I startled you."

His gaze flickered away uncomfortably. "How is Lady Julia?"

"She's sleeping. I gave her a draught of mandragora for the pain." Something was terribly wrong and she hoped he would feel free to unburden his mind. "Sit awhile. You look tired."

Prometheus came reluctantly to the alcove and sat opposite her. His gaze fixed on her hands loosely clasped in her lap. "Were you praying?"

"Yes."

The muscle moved again. "I pray all the time. It hasn't done me much good."

"What's wrong, Prometheus?"

He bent forward and raked his hands through his hair. Without warning, he started to cry, not quietly, but with deep wrenching sobs that shook his body.

Hadassah leaned forward and put both hands on his head. "What's happened? How can I help you?" she said, near tears at his distress.

"I thought it was finished," he sobbed. "I thought when I came to the Lord, he'd wash me as white as snow and *forget* my sins."

"He has."

Prometheus raised his head, tears pouring down his cheeks, his eyes blazing with anger. "Then why does the same thing happen over and over again?"

"What do you mean?"

He put his head in his hands again. "You couldn't understand."

"I understand you're discouraged. So am I."

He raised his head, surprised. "*You?* But you're so strong in the Lord."

"Strong?" Leaning back, she sighed. "I'm the weakest of women, Prometheus. Sometimes I don't know what I'm doing here or why I came or what the Lord wants of me or whether I want to do what he wants. Life was much easier with Alexander."

"Lady Julia *is* difficult."

"Lady Julia is *impossible.*"

He gave her a pained smile in understanding and then frowned, distracted by his own problems. He let his breath out slowly. Hands clasped between his knees, he stared at the floor. "No less impossible than I am. I guess some of us just can't be saved."

"You *are* saved, Prometheus."

He gave a bleak laugh. "I thought so." He looked at her, eyes moist and tormented. "I'm not so sure anymore."

"Why do you say this?"

"Because I met a friend today, and he made me aware of it. We talked a long time. I was telling him about the Lord. He was listening to me so intently, and I was so happy. I thought he was going to accept Christ." He gave another bleak laugh and swallowed. "And then he touched me. I knew when he did, it wasn't the Lord he wanted at all."

Hadassah didn't understand. "What did he want?"

"Me." Color crept up his neck into his face. He couldn't look at her. "It all came back," he said grimly. "All the things I've tried so hard to forget." He looked up at the corridor and around at the archways and steps. "I remembered Primus."

Hadassah caught the deep sadness in his voice and wondered about it. Surely he did not miss Primus.

Prometheus leaned back, looking weary and miserable. "I was owned by a master who had a booth under the stands at the arena. You probably don't know what that means."

"I know."

His face reddened. "Then if I tell you that's where Primus first saw me, you'll understand what *he* was." He looked away and was silent for a long time. When he spoke again, the words came clipped and void of emotion. "He bought me. He brought me here to this house."

"Prometheus—"

"Don't say anything," he said in a tortured voice, his eyes haunted. "You understand I was his catamite. You don't understand how I felt about it."

She wove her fingers together, praying for God's wisdom, for she saw Prometheus was determined she understand everything, and she didn't feel prepared to handle it.

"Primus loved me." His eyes filled with tears again. "There were times I loved him, too. Or, at least, had feelings that pointed in that direction." He bent forward again, head down so she couldn't see his face. "My first master was cruel. Primus was gentle. He treated me well. It's all so confusing." His voice became quiet, almost a whisper. "He took care with me, and what he did . . . well, sometimes it felt good."

Revulsion filled Hadassah at what he was telling her, and yet she saw and felt his shame as well. He went very still. "I disgust you, too, don't I?" he said hoarsely.

She leaned forward and took his hands in hers. "We can't control our feelings the way we can our actions."

His hands tightened, holding on to her as though he were drowning. "Neither are easy." He said nothing for a long moment and then began again. "When Celadus touched me, I was tempted." His head sank lower. "I knew if I stayed another minute, I wouldn't leave at all." He let go of her and raked agitated fingers through his hair, gripping his head again. "So I *ran*." He began to cry again. "I couldn't stand up to the temptation and overcome it. I fled like a coward."

"Not like a coward," Hadassah said gently. "Like Joseph when the wife of Potiphar, Pharaoh's captain of the bodyguard, tried to seduce him. You *ran*, Prometheus. The Lord made a way for your escape, and you took it."

"You don't understand, Lady Azar." He looked up at her, his expression strained. "I ran *today*. What if it happens again, and that time the man is as convincing in his arguments and seduction as Calabah was with Lady Julia? What if I'm depressed? What if—"

"Don't be so anxious about tomorrow, Prometheus. Let today's trouble be enough for today. God will not abandon you."

He rubbed the tears from his face. "That sounds so easy," he said in frustration. "You say God won't abandon me, and yet I feel abandoned. Do you know there are Christians here in Ephesus who will have as little to do with me as possible because they know what I was? Some Nicolaitans go to the Artemision several times a week and use the temple prostitutes. Yet, they're not treated the way I am."

She was much aggrieved. "What they do is sin, Prometheus."

"They're with *women*."

"And you think that makes a difference?"

"One man made a point of telling me it's written in the Scriptures that God considers homosexuality an abomination. That I should be stoned to death."

311

"The Mosaic law considered adultery and fornication abominations deserving of death, too. God despises harlotry of any kind, body or spirit." She thought of Julia in the upper bedchamber, dying slowly of a disease she contracted by practicing a life of sin. She thought of her worshiping other gods. Wherein was the greatest sin?

"I see the way some of them look at me," he said. "They don't look at those men that way. Most Christians think I'm beneath contempt, beyond redemption. And after today, I think they may be right."

"No, Prometheus. You're listening to the wrong voice."

He sat up slowly and leaned back. "Maybe I am and maybe I'm not. I don't know anymore. All I do know is sometimes I get lonely, Lady Azar, so lonely I crave the life I had with Primus."

She wanted to weep. "I get lonely, too, Prometheus."

"But you can always go to God, and he hears you."

"He hears you, too," she said tearfully, full of sorrow at what others were doing to him in the name of the Lord. "Don't measure God by man. He *loves* you. He died for you."

"Then why does he put me into temptation over and over again? I thought it was all over, but it's not. I can't close my mind off to the memories no matter how hard I try. Some things are always there to remind me. I find myself thinking my life was a lot less complicated when I wasn't a Christian."

"The Lord doesn't tempt you. Satan does. He waits for the opportune time and knows exactly where you're most vulnerable. For you, it's the physical pleasures you experienced while practicing homosexuality. For those who persecute you, it's pride. They think they're better than you or their sin is less important. God doesn't think as men think, Prometheus."

She took his hands. "It says in Proverbs there are six things the Lord hates, yes, seven are an abomination to Him: a proud look, a lying tongue, hands that shed innocent blood, a heart that devises wicked plans, feet that are swift in running to evil, a false witness who speaks lies, and one who sows discord among brethren. How many of those sins do they commit who put stumbling blocks before you in your walk with the Lord? Don't look to man for understanding or to yourself for what you need. God sees your pain and your struggle, and God will give you the strength to overcome it. God alone can do it."

Prometheus let out his breath slowly and nodded. "I hear the

Lord speak to me through you," he said, greatly relieved. He lifted his head and smiled sadly. "You remind me of someone I once knew. She was one of the reasons I almost didn't come back to this house." His expression softened. "And, in a strange way, she was part of the reason I did."

The Lord moved her heart. Prometheus had dropped his mask of happiness and revealed the struggle within himself. Could she do less?

She withdrew her hands from his. "Prometheus," she said softly and lifted her veils.

He stared at her scars in revulsion and pity, and then his expression changed.

"O God, *God!*" he whispered hoarsely, recognizing her. He fell to his knees and put his arms around her hips, his head in her lap. "You can't know how many times I've longed to speak with you again! You saw how I lived. You knew what I was. And still you loved me enough to share the Good News with me."

She stroked Prometheus' dark hair as though he were still a child. "God has always loved you, Prometheus. It was no accident we met. I never knew if the seeds I planted would take root in you until I saw you again a few weeks ago. Oh, what joy it was to know you'd accepted Jesus into your heart, too."

Her hand stilled on his head. "You've planted seeds, too, Prometheus. Leave your friend to the Lord." She stroked him again, feeling his muscles relax.

"Oh, my lady," he said.

She smiled wistfully. "I just wanted you to know I struggle with the past as much as you." How many seeds had she planted in Julia? And yet none had taken root.

Why, Lord? Why?

Prometheus raised his head and drew back from her, looking into her face. He took her hands and held them tightly. "Don't lose hope. God is good, and he has just shown me he is sovereign." He spoke with complete assurance, his face alight with joy. "You are here, alive. How else could that be except by his will?"

She cried then, her own need for encouragement breaking through the surface of her self-enforced calm.

And Prometheus, restored, rose up to comfort her.

35

Marcus entered his mother's villa without knocking. As he came up the steps, a slave girl saw him and dropped the tray she carried and cried out, "Lord Marcus!" The sound of shattering pottery and crystal echoed across the peristyle. Frightened, she scrambled to pick up the shards of broken glass. "I'm sorry, my lord," she said, her eyes wide. "I'm sorry. I didn't expect to see you."

"A pleasant surprise, I hope," he said, smiling down at her. She blushed. He tried to remember her name and couldn't. She was pretty, and he remembered his father had purchased her shortly after coming to Ephesus. "You've broken nothing of importance."

Iulius came running down the upper corridor. "What's happened? Is anyone hurt?" He saw Marcus and halted. "My lord!"

"It's been a long time, Iulius," he said and held out his hand.

Iulius saw Marcus' seal ring was missing and wondered. He took his master's hand and started to bow over it, but Marcus clasped his as an equal. Surprised, Iulius drew back uncomfortably. Marcus Valerian had never been one for familiarity with slaves, except, of course, with the prettiest young women. "Your journey was successful, my lord?"

"You might say that," Marcus said, smiling. "I've come home a far richer man than when I left." His eyes took on a sparkle of amusement. "I've much to tell my mother. Where is she?"

Iulius was discomforted. What he had to tell Marcus wouldn't come as welcome news. What would the young master do now that he was home? "She rests on the balcony of her bedchamber."

"Rests? At this time of the day? Is she ill? The fevers again, I imagine," he said in dismay. She had had bouts of fever before he left.

"No, my lord. She's not ill. Not exactly."

Marcus frowned. "What exactly?"

"She can't walk or speak. She has some use of her right hand."

Alarmed, Marcus stepped past him and strode down the corridor. Iulius intercepted him before he reached the door. "Please listen to me before you see her, my lord."

"Then speak quickly and to the point!"

314

"Despite the way she appears, she is not without her wits. She understands what happens around her and what is said. We've developed a way to talk with one another."

Marcus brushed him aside and entered the bedchamber. He saw his mother sitting in a chair that was much like a small throne. Her hand lay limply on the arm, her slender fingers relaxed. Her head was back as though she was drinking in the warmth of the sun. His heart stopped racing. She looked well.

It wasn't until he came closer that he saw the physical changes in her. "Mother," he said softly, his heart breaking.

Phoebe opened her eyes. She had prayed so often about her son it didn't surprise her at all when she heard his voice and saw a vision of him standing before her on the balcony. He looked the same, yet different. He was beautiful—the epitome of manly grace and power—but older, his skin bronzed by the sun. "Mother," he said again. When he knelt down before her and took her hand, she knew he was real.

"Ahhh . . ."

"Yes, I'm here. I'm *home*."

She wanted so desperately to throw her arms around him, but all she could do was sit and weep. Her tears greatly distressed him, and she tried to stop them. "Ahhhh . . . ," she said, her right hand fluttering.

"It will be all right now," he said, his own eyes filling.

Iulius came near and put his hand on her shoulder. "Your son has returned."

Marcus noted the personal way Iulius touched his mother. He also saw the look in the man's eyes. The heat of anger rose.

"I won't leave you again," Marcus said, wiping the tears gently from her cheeks. "I'll find you the best physician money can buy."

"The best have seen her already, my lord," Iulius said. "We have not spared expense. Everything has been done that can be done."

Looking into Iulius' eyes, Marcus felt sure the slave spoke the truth. Yet, he was disturbed. It was right that a slave be devoted to his mistress, but the feelings he sensed from Iulius were far deeper than that. Perhaps it was good God had sent him home at this time.

Marcus returned his full attention to his mother, staring intently into her eyes. He saw how she held his gaze with equal intensity. One eye was clear and aware, the other vague and cloudy. "Was I mistaken to think you were a Christian?" he said.

She blinked twice.

"You were not mistaken," Iulius said.

Marcus didn't look away from her. "I was told by a man on the shores of the Sea of Galilee that there were believers who prayed for me. *You* prayed for me, didn't you?"

She closed her eyes slowly and opened them again.

Marcus smiled. He knew the one thing that would give her the greatest solace. "Then know this, Mother. Your prayers have been answered. I found Christ. A man named Cornelius baptized me in the Sea of Galilee."

Her eyes shone with tears again. "Ahhhh," she said, and it was a sigh of praise and gratitude. Her hand fluttered.

Marcus took it and kissed her palm, then laid her hand full against his cheek.

"I have come home, Mother. To you. And to God."

36

For the next several days, Marcus stayed in his mother's company every moment she was awake. He told her about his voyage and meeting Satyros. He related his journey to Jerusalem and seeing the temple ruins and the stone where Abraham may have laid Isaac for sacrifice. He told her about the robbers on the road to Jericho and how Ezra Barjachin and his daughter, Taphatha, had saved his life. He spoke of the old woman, Deborah, in the village of Nain and how she had sent him on his way to the Sea of Galilee. He spoke of the despair and emptiness he had felt and of his attempt to take his own life. And finally, with reverence and awe, he spoke of Paracletos and the Lord.

"I don't know if I drowned, Mother. I know I felt resurrected." He held her hand, which was still delicate and graceful. "And I know now that Jesus is alive. I see his presence in the world around us." He remembered Hadassah saying the same thing to him once. At the time he had thought it foolishness. Now it seemed so clear and inescapable. "I see him most in the hearts of people like Deborah and Cornelius and a dozen others I've met since then. But I saw him long before that." He had seen the Lord in the life of a simple slave girl.

"Ha . . . da . . ."

He lowered his head and put his hand over hers.

"Ha . . . da . . ."

"I remember her, too, Mother. I remember everything about her."

"Ha . . . da . . ."

"I miss her, too."

"Ha . . . da . . ."

He raised his head, struggling against the grief that still hit him at times. "She is with the Lord," he said, wishing he felt comforted by that knowledge. Yet her loss was like a wound that never healed. *Hadassah*. A word that was synonymous with love to him. How could he have been such a fool?

"Ahhh."

"Shhhh," he said, trying to ease his mother's agitation. Her

317

eyes were so intense, almost wild. "We will not speak of her again if it upsets you so much."

She blinked twice.

"She must rest, my lord," Iulius said, ever protective. "The physician said—"

"Yes, you told me." Marcus lifted his mother in his arms and carried her back into the bedchamber. "We'll talk again later," he said, kissing her cheek.

Marcus straightened and looked squarely into Iulius' face. He gestured toward the door. Iulius went out.

The girl who had dropped the tray on his first day home took the seat near the bed to watch over his mother. "Call for me when she awakens."

"Yes, my lord."

Marcus closed the door of the bedchamber behind him. Iulius stood at the railing overlooking the peristyle. Marcus looked at the older man with narrowed eyes. "Exactly what is the relationship between you and my mother?"

Dark color rose into Iulius' face. "I am her slave, my lord."

"Her slave?"

"I've seen to her care since she was struck down."

"And before that?"

Iulius' voice was level. "Don't say anything you'll regret."

Marcus' anger rose swiftly. "Who are you to command me?"

"I grant you that I am your slave, my lord, but I tell you this: If you speak one word that reflects unkindly upon your mother's character, I will strike you as your father would have done and *curse* the consequences!"

Astonished, Marcus stared at him. Iulius knew as well as he that such words were enough to have him crucified. "You've answered my question with your rash words."

"Not rash, my lord. Heartfelt. She is the gentlest of ladies."

He clenched his teeth. "Does my mother love you in the same way you love her?"

"Of course not!"

Marcus was not so sure. He had entered the room several times when Iulius was alone with her. The slave's voice had held a distinct tenderness when he spoke to his mother, and once, when Iulius had lifted her from the chair, she had laid her head upon his shoulder, content.

Marcus was not sure how he felt about their relationship, not sure he had a right to feel anything. Where had he been when his mother needed him? Iulius had devoted every moment to her care, seeing to her every need. He was watchful and protective. Iulius' devotion was not a matter of duty, it was a continuing act of love.

Marcus put his hands on the rail. Suddenly he was ashamed. "I'm jealous by nature," he confessed. "It's not something of which I'm proud."

"You love your mother."

"Yes, I love her, but that doesn't give me an excuse to make accusations against you. Forgive me, Iulius. Without your care, my mother wouldn't be alive. I am grateful to you."

Iulius was amazed at the change in Marcus. There was a new humility in him that he had never seen before.

"You need not be concerned about anything, my lord. To your mother, I am a slave and nothing more."

"You are more to her than that." He had seen the look in his mother's eyes when Iulius spoke with her. He put his hand on Iulius' shoulder. "You are her dearest friend."

37

Days passed. Marcus waited for someone to mention his sister, but no one did. Finally, he became curious and asked how long it had been since Julia visited.

"About six months, my lord," Iulius said.

"Six months?"

"Yes, my lord."

"Does she know of Mother's condition?"

"We would not leave her in ignorance," Iulius said. "We sent word several times, my lord. Lady Julia came once. She was very distressed about your mother's condition."

"So distressed she didn't bother to come again." Marcus uttered a foul word for her. *Forgive her, Lord?* He wanted to strangle her with his own two hands. His heart beat heavily as rage filled him.

Iulius regretted his condemning words, concerned they might not reflect the true state of Julia's affairs. After all, he didn't know why she hadn't returned, and it was far from appropriate for him to make assumptions. He looked for possible reasons behind her neglect. "She didn't look well, my lord."

"She was probably suffering the effects of having been drunk the night before."

Iulius had wondered the same thing at the time but didn't admit to it. "She was very thin."

Marcus looked at him coolly. "You're defending my sister's neglect?"

"No, my lord. My only concern is Lady Phoebe. Your mother waits for her daughter's return."

Marcus looked away, his face set.

"She awaits Lady Julia in the same way she waited for you, my lord."

A muscle jerked in Marcus' cheek. "Thank you for your kind reminder," he said sardonically.

"It might be wise to find out why Lady Julia hasn't returned, my lord."

"I could make an educated guess," Marcus said in biting cynicism. "Calabah was against my sister having anything to do with Mother. She was afraid a little decency might rub off on Julia." He gave a brittle laugh. "I doubt there's much chance of that."

"Calabah Shiva Fontaneus left Ephesus a year ago."

Marcus glanced up in surprise. "That's interesting. What else have you heard about my sister's affairs?"

"Rumor had it Lady Julia's husband also left a few months after you sailed for Palestine. As far as I know, he hasn't returned."

Marcus grew thoughtful. So, poor Julia was deserted. It was no more than she deserved. Hadn't he warned her against Calabah and Primus? He could guess what had happened. Calabah would have used Julia until she grew tired of her, while Primus took whatever opportunity there was to systematically strip Julia of whatever money he could grasp.

What was her situation now?

And why should he care?

Julia had probably come to their mother for help and, seeing there was none, had left. Julia never did like to be around anyone who was ill. He remembered how she had run out of the room when their father had called the family to his deathbed.

Yet, he could not help but wonder.

"You say she looked ill?"

"Yes, my lord."

He was filled with conflicting emotions, the strongest being anger against her. He was intensely aware of what the Lord wanted and equally intense in his struggle against it. He wanted to remember what Julia had done, to have a shield against more tender feelings. She deserved no tenderness. She deserved only judgment.

"Six months," he said darkly. "Perhaps she died during that time."

Iulius was disturbed by the cool indifference in Marcus' voice. Did he truly hope his sister was dead? "And what if she hasn't died, my lord? Your mother would have more peace of mind if she knew Lady Julia was safe and well."

Marcus' face hardened. He knew what Iulius said was true. If his mother had prayed for him, he knew she prayed for Julia.

The prospect of seeing his sister roused the heavy feelings that had lain dormant over the last weeks. The quiet before the storm was over, and the fierce gale of emotion now hit with a vengeance. He had sworn never to see or speak to Julia again. When he had made that vow, he had meant to keep it. Forever. Now he knew he had to put aside his own feelings and think instead of his mother's needs. As for Julia, he could not care less what happened to her.

"Very well," Marcus said grimly. "I'll find out where she is tomorrow."

He prayed to God she was dead and buried and that would be the end of it.

38

Hadassah brushed Julia's hair with slow strokes. She noticed the coin-sized patches of baldness, another manifestation of the venereal disease. Julia had been very agitated today, suffering acute pain from the ulcers. Hadassah had given her a small dose of mandragora and added a special blend of herbs to her bath. Now Julia was drowsy in the afternoon sunlight, at ease. A breeze stirred the vine leaves, bringing with it the strong smells of the crowded city.

Running her fingers down the silky strands, Hadassah began to braid Julia's waist-length hair. When she finished, she laid the braid over Julia's shoulder. "I'll get you something to eat, my lady."

"I'm not hungry," Julia sighed. "I'm not thirsty. I'm not tired. I'm not anything."

"Would you like me to tell you a story?"

Julia shook her head, then glanced at her hopefully. "Can you sing, Lady Azar?"

"I am sorry, my lady. I can't." Infection and trauma had damaged her vocal cords so that she could only speak in a rasping voice. "I can play a lyre."

Julia looked away. "I don't have a lyre. There used to be one in the house, but Primus smashed it to pieces and then burned it." She had been glad at the time, for the instrument had been a reminder of the slave girl who played it and sang songs about her god.

"I'll ask Prometheus to purchase another."

Julia put a trembling hand to her forehead. "Don't waste your money." She gave a sad laugh. How much had she wasted over the past years? When she thought of how much she had had, she could scarcely believe she had come to live like this.

Hadassah put her hand on Julia's shoulder. "It's the fever that makes your head ache, my lady." Prometheus had set a small table beside the couch, on which sat a bowl of scented water and a small stack of rags. Hadassah wet one and wrung it out. She dabbed Julia's face. "Try to rest."

"I wish I could rest. Sometimes I hurt too much to sleep. Other times, I don't want to sleep because I dream."

"What do you dream?"

"All sorts of things. I dream about people I've known. Last night I dreamed about my first husband, Claudius."

Hadassah stroked her forehead and temples. "Tell me about him."

"He broke his neck when he fell from his horse." She relaxed under Hadassah's tender care. She felt like talking about the past today, unburdening herself of it. "He wasn't a very good rider to begin with, and I heard later he had had several goblets of wine before coming to look for me."

Hadassah put the rag aside. "I'm sorry."

"I wasn't," Julia said in a flat voice. "Not at the time. I should've been, but I wasn't."

"Are you now?"

"I don't know," she said and worried her lip. "Yes," she said softly after a moment. "Sometimes." Would Azar condemn her? Julia waited, tense. Azar reached over and took her hand. Julia was so grateful, she gripped the woman's small, sturdy hand tightly and went on. "It was my fault in a way. You see, he was looking for me. I'd gone to a *ludus* to watch the gladiators practice. I was mad for them. One in particular. I'd asked Claudius to take me a dozen times before, but he didn't approve. All he really cared about was his studies about religions in the Empire. And I was bored with all that, bored with him."

She sighed. "I never would have married him if my father hadn't forced me. Claudius was twenty years older than me, but he acted even older than that." She went on, trying to justify her actions, but the more she talked, the more unjustified she felt. Why did what happened so long ago plague her so much now? The incident with Claudius was only one among so many others.

Hadassah put her other hand over Julia's. "You were very young."

"Too young for him," Julia said. She let her breath out softly on a sad laugh. "I think Claudius loved me because I looked like his first wife, but I wasn't anything like her. What a shock I must've been to him after the first few weeks of marriage."

"Do you know what his wife was like?"

"I never met her, of course, but I gathered she was gentle and kind and shared his passion for learning." She raised her head, looking at the veils, thankful she could see no face behind them. "I was none of those things. Sometimes I find myself wishing. . . ." She shook her head and looked away. "It doesn't do any good to wish."

"What do you wish, my lady?"

"That I had been a little kinder, at least."

Hadassah wanted to embrace her, for it was the first time Julia had admitted even a twinge of remorse about anything.

"I don't mean I wish I'd loved him," Julia said. "I never could have loved him, but if I'd been . . ." She shook her head. "Oh, I don't know." She closed her eyes. "There's no use in it, I suppose. I've been told it's useless to dwell on the past, and yet, that's all I seem to have left. Visions of the past."

"Sometimes we have to go back and remember the things we've done and be cleansed of them before we can go on."

Julia looked at her bleakly. "To what purpose, Lady Azar? I can't change what happened. Claudius is dead, and that's that. And it'll always remain partly my fault that he is."

"It doesn't have to."

Julia gave a harsh laugh. "That's exactly what Calabah said."

Hadassah was startled. "Calabah?"

"Yes, Calabah Shiva Fontaneus. Oh, I can tell you've heard of her. Everyone's heard of Calabah." Her mouth curved into a bitter smile. "She used to live here with me. She was here almost a year. She was my lover. Does that shock you?" She yanked her hand away.

"No," Hadassah said quietly.

"Calabah said we don't have to regret the past. All we have to do is set our mind on enjoying the present." She gave a caustic laugh. "I told her about Claudius once. She laughed and said I was foolish to have any regrets." Perhaps she was being foolish now telling Azar so much.

"But you did."

"Did what?"

"Feel regret."

"Briefly, right after he died. Or maybe it was more fear than regret. I don't know. I was terrified someone was going to poison me. Every one of Claudius' servants loved him. He was very good to them." She was quiet a moment, thoughtful. Claudius had been kind to her as well. He had never spoken a harsh word to her despite her lack of manners and decorum as his wife. The realization made her feel ashamed. "Lately, I've been remembering things I said to him, things I wished I hadn't."

She pushed herself up and walked the few steps to the balcony. Leaning on the wall, she looked toward the sea. "I think about Caius, too. My second husband." She could remember the look on his face just before he had died from the poison she had given him. She'd done it slowly, over a period of weeks. It wasn't until the very end that he'd realized . . .

She bowed her head. "What use is there in regret?"

"Regret drives us to repentance, and repentance leads us to God."

"And God drives us to oblivion," Julia finished with a jerk of her chin. Why did Azar always come back to God? "There's a warm wind coming in from the sea," she said, deliberately changing the subject. "I wonder what ships are coming in. My father owned a whole fleet. He brought in merchandise from every port in the Empire." He and Marcus had often argued about what the people wanted. Father said grain for the starving masses. Marcus said sand for the arenas. Marcus had proven right and gained the use of six of Father's ships. With those ships, he had begun amassing his fortune. Marcus was undoubtedly one of the wealthiest men in the Empire by now, while here she lolled in relative penury, dependent upon a stranger's kindness for her very sustenance.

Where was Marcus now? Was he still in Palestine? Did he still hate her?

She could almost feel it across the miles. Wherever he was, whatever he was doing, she knew his hatred for her burned within him. Marcus had always been determined in whatever he set out to do. And he was set upon hating her forever.

Depressed, she turned away. She didn't want to think about Marcus. She didn't want to feel guilty about what she had done. She had only been trying to protect him from himself. Hadassah, a mere slave, had shamed him with her refusal to marry him.

Besides that, Julia thought, *Hadassah caused dissension in my household.* Primus had hated Hadassah because Prometheus' affections were turned from him. Calabah had never really said why she hated the slave girl, but hate her she had. Intensely. Julia remembered her own anger toward the slave but not the root cause of it.

But she would never forget her brother's last words to her

before he left the arena. *"May the gods curse you for what you've done!"*

Shivering, she sat down on her couch again and dragged the blanket around her shoulders.

"You're cold, my lady," Hadassah said. "Perhaps we should go back inside."

"No. I'm tired of being inside." She lay back and curled on her side, looking at Azar expectantly, like a child awaiting a bedtime story. "Tell me another story. Any kind of story. I don't care."

Hadassah began to tell the story of the Samaritan woman at the well. She got as far as Jesus telling her he was the Living Water when she saw that Julia, lulled by the sound of her voice, had fallen asleep. Rising, Hadassah adjusted the blanket over her. She stroked the damp tendrils of hair back from her temple.

When would the stories serve to open Julia's eyes instead of close them? And yet, despite the sick woman's inner blindness, Hadassah felt a flicker of hope. What Julia had said about Claudius had surprised her. It was the first indication that she had regrets or felt even partial responsibility for anything. During the past weeks, Julia had stopped being fractious. Now, her moods were darker and deeper, as though her mind was mulling over the past . . . taking inventory before the end.

Hadassah took up her walking stick and went back into the bedchamber. Setting the stick aside, she tidied the covers on the sleeping couch, then picked up clothing, separating soiled garments from discarded ones. She folded those that were clean and put them away. The rest she left dangling over her arm as she took up her walking stick again and left the room. Julia might eat something when she awakened, and Prometheus would be returning soon.

Holding her walking stick under her arm, she leaned on the railing as she went down the steps. When she reached the bottom, she turned to go through the peristyle to the kitchen at the back of the house.

Someone knocked on the front door.

Startled, Hadassah glanced back. No one had come to see Julia during all the weeks she had been with her. Alexander and Rashid never came at this time of the day and never bothered to knock. They knew she was upstairs with Julia and wouldn't hear, so they entered unannounced.

Hadassah limped to the door and opened it.

The caller had already turned away and started down the steps. The man was tall, strongly built, and finely dressed. Hearing the door open, he turned with an air of reluctance and looked up at her grimly.

Hadassah caught her breath, her heart leaping. *Marcus!*

His dark brown eyes swept her from head to foot. He frowned slightly and came back up the steps.

"I've come to see Lady Julia."

39

Marcus was surprised to see a woman in veils. He looked her up and down, and then frowned when she said nothing. "This house does still belong to Julia Valerian, does it not?"

"Yes, my lord," she said in a rasping voice. Bracing herself with a walking stick, she stepped back so he could enter. He walked by her into the antechamber and was immediately struck by the emptiness of the place. It felt deserted. He could hear the fountain through the archways. The woman closed the door softly behind him, then limped past him, the soft tap of her walking stick echoing in the empty entryway. He found it surprising that Julia would have a cripple in her household. And why the veils?

"This way, my lord," she said, preceding him to the steps.

He noticed the garments over her shoulder and surmised she was the laundress. "Where are the other servants?"

"There are no other servants, my lord. Only Prometheus and I. He's taken work in the city." She placed the garments in a neat pile at the base of the steps.

A cripple and a catamite, Marcus thought with dark humor. How Julia had fallen. Things must be bad indeed. He watched the servant mount the steps. She stepped up with her good leg and brought her crippled one next to it, one step at a time. It was a difficult process, probably a painful one as well. He felt pity, which was quickly overshadowed by curiosity about her foreign attire. "You are Arabic."

"No, my lord."

"Then why the veils?"

"I am disfigured, my lord."

Which, no doubt, bothered Julia. He couldn't imagine his sister even allowing a disfigured servant in the household, let alone near her. A dozen questions rose in his mind as he went up the steps, but he held his tongue. All he needed to know, he would soon learn from Julia.

"She was asleep when I left her," the slave woman said in a hushed voice. Marcus followed her into a bedchamber. He

329

stopped beneath the archways and watched the servant limp out onto the balcony. She went to the couch and bent down, speaking softly so as not to startle its sleeping occupant.

"A visitor?" Julia said drowsily, pushing herself up. She turned slightly and allowed the servant to help her sit up.

Stunned, Marcus took in the change in his sister's physical appearance. Equally shocked, Julia stared at him from hollowed eyes, her face so white she seemed to be carved in marble. She reminded him of the starving Jews who had arrived in Rome after the long, grueling march from their fallen Jerusalem. And remembering that, he was reminded again of Hadassah and what his sister had done to her.

"Marcus," Julia said tremulously and held out her hand. "How nice of you to come and call."

Did she suppose he had forgotten everything?

Marcus remained where he was.

Julia felt his hatred. She had seen the shock in his eyes and been briefly gratified, thinking perhaps now he would feel sorry for her and regret all the cruel things he had said. Now she saw how cold his eyes were, how rigid his stance. She lowered her hand, discomforted at the way he stared at her, his mouth set. Without a hint of mercy in his eyes, he glanced over her, taking in the ravages of her illness.

"It would appear you're ill."

Was he glad of it? She lifted her chin slightly, hiding her hurt. "You could say that, though it shouldn't surprise you." When he raised one brow, she smiled brittlely. "Don't you remember your last words to me?"

"I remember them well, but don't waste time casting blame on me for what's become of you. Look to yourself. The choices you've made have more to do with the condition in which you now find yourself than anything I might have said."

His indifference hurt. "So. You have come to gloat."

"I came to find out why you haven't bothered to visit Mother."

"Now you know."

Marcus stood silent, anger pouring through him at her casual disregard. She didn't even ask how their mother was. He gritted his teeth and wished he hadn't come, for now that he saw how things were with her, he knew his duty and it sat ill with him.

Julia looked up at the veiled woman. "My shawl," she said imperiously and held her arms out slightly so that it could be draped over her. She hoped Azar would forgive her abruptness, but she did have appearances to make. She must salvage her pride in the face of her brother's disdain. Nothing had changed, least of all him.

She put her hand out, and Azar gave her the support she needed to rise from the couch. "Hatred is best met standing," she said, smiling at Marcus coldly. "You may go," she said to Azar.

"I will be outside if you need me, my lady."

Marcus watched the veiled servant limp from the room. "A curious choice for a personal maid," he said as she closed the door behind her.

"Azar is free to come and go as she pleases," she said. She forced her lips into a mocking smile. She needed to strike back at him for hurting her and knew how best to do it. "She's a Christian, Marcus. Don't you find that deliciously ironic?"

Pain flickered across his face.

She saw she had wounded him and held the shawl tightly, trembling despite her resolve. She was sorry she had alluded to the past but justified herself because of his manner toward her. He had hurt her. Did he expect her to stand and take it? "How is Mother?"

"Nice of you to finally ask."

She pressed her lips together, fighting against the force of his judgmental attitude. How he hated her! "And where have *you* been all these months?"

He didn't answer. "Mother will be better when she sees you."

"I doubt that."

"Don't doubt anything I tell you."

"Did Iulius suggest you come? I can't imagine you coming of your own volition." She hugged the shawl around her and went to the wall.

"Iulius has convinced me Mother misses you."

"Misses me?" she said with a harsh laugh. "She doesn't even know me. She sat in that throne he's made for her, drooling and making these horrible noises. I couldn't bear to see her like that."

"You might try thinking about how Mother feels and what *she* needs, instead of always thinking of yourself."

"In her place, I'd want someone to give me a drink of hemlock and end my misery!"

Marcus' dark gaze moved over her thin body and back up to her hollowed eyes. "Would you?"

331

She drew in her breath at what she saw so clearly in his face. She was sick and dying, and he did not care in the least. In fact, she was left in no doubt that he wished her dead. She fought against the tears that burned her eyes. "I never knew you could be so cold and cruel, Marcus."

"I'd have to go a long way to catch up with you." He walked to the wall and rested his arm on it. Glancing at her, his mouth tipped sardonically. "What happened to Calabah and Primus?"

Tilting her head back, she pretended to enjoy the soft breeze. "They left," she said as though it didn't matter.

"How deeply in debt did they leave you?"

"You needn't concern yourself on my behalf," she said airily. He was enjoying her utter humiliation.

"I'm not concerned," he said, looking out at the harbor. "Just curious."

Her hands tightened, steadying herself. "I still have this villa."

"Encumbered with debt, no doubt."

Each word he uttered was a barb. "Yes," she said flatly. "Are you satisfied?"

"It makes things simpler." Marcus straightened. "I'll have your things removed and settle your debts."

Surprised, she looked at him, hoping he had softened toward her after all. His eyes were hard.

"Mother will be relieved to have you under her roof again," he drawled.

Chilled by his expression, she rebelled. "I'd rather remain here."

"I don't care what you'd rather do. Iulius said Mother's mind will be eased if you're there. And so you shall be."

"What good am I to her? I'm sick, though you obviously don't care."

"You're right. I don't."

"I'm *dying*. Do you care now?"

Marcus' eyes narrowed, but he said nothing.

Julia looked away from his hard face and clutched the wall with white fingers. "She has *you*. She doesn't need me."

"She loves both of us, God only knows why."

She glared at him through her tears. "And if I say I won't go?"

"Say no all you want. I don't care. Scream. Rant and rave. Cry. It won't change anything. You have no husband anymore, do you? No father, either. That leaves me with full legal right over you. You won't walk over me the way you've walked over others. Like it or not, I'll see you do whatever I decide. And, for now, I've decided to have you brought home."

Marcus stepped away from the wall. "I'll send someone to pack whatever things you have left and I'll see you have servants to see to your needs." He strode across the balcony.

"I've servants of my own," she called after him.

Marcus stopped and glared back at her, his face white with anger. "I won't have Primus' catamite under my roof," he said between his teeth. "You've always been good at dispensing with servants. Dispense with him. Sell him. Give him away. Free him. I don't care what you do, but don't bring him with you. Do you understand? And as for the other—"

"I want Azar. I *need* her."

"You'll have a servant younger and better able to dash to your beck and call."

Fear filled Julia. The thought of being without Azar's tender mercy was unbearable. "I *need* her, Marcus. Please."

"You've always *needed* a lot, haven't you, Julia? I'll see you have all you *need*." He turned away, striding toward the door.

"I'll beg if you want. Only don't send her away!"

Marcus kept walking.

"Marcus! *Please!*"

Marcus yanked the door and slammed it behind him. He had heard Julia cry too many times before to be softened by her tearful appeal now.

The veiled woman was standing beneath an arch overlooking the peristyle. He crossed over to her and told her briskly of his decision. "Consider yourself free to go wherever you choose," he said. He took a step away, eager to leave and have done with all this.

"I choose to stay with Lady Julia."

Marcus glanced at her in surprise. Perhaps it was another matter that held her. "If there's a problem with money, I'll see you have enough to sustain you for the rest of your life."

"It's not a matter of money, my lord. I'm a woman of independent means."

That surprised him. "Then what reason have you to remain with her?"

"I gave her my word."

"She doesn't keep hers."

"I keep mine."

It was the simplest of answers, and the last one he wanted to hear. "Do as you like," he said angrily and strode down the hall.

Hadassah stared after him. She put her hand over her racing heart and felt she could breathe again. He had appeared so unexpectedly on the front step. Had he sent a message ahead, perhaps she could have prepared herself. And she could've prepared Julia. The thought of being under the same roof with him again filled her with joy and pain.

She went to the door and opened it. Julia was lying on her sleeping couch, weeping. She sat up and held her arms out like a child desperately in need of comfort. "Don't let him send you away. Please!"

Hadassah sat down beside her and held her close. "I'm here."

"Don't leave me," Julia wept. "I'll die if you leave me."

"I won't leave you, my lady." She stroked her hair. "I'll never leave you."

"He hates me. He hates me so much."

Hadassah knew she was right; she had felt it emanate from him the moment he stepped into Julia's bedchamber. She had seen the dark sheen of it in his eyes. "Why does he hate you?" What could possibly have happened to turn Marcus' heart against a sister he had so dearly loved?

Julia closed her eyes, mouth quivering. She drew back, scrubbing at the tears. "I don't want to talk about it. It was all so long ago, you'd think he'd have forgotten by now." She sniffed, tears still coming. She looked up at Azar. "He said I'm to get rid of Prometheus."

Hadassah went cold. "What do you mean, 'get rid of him'?"

"Sell him, do whatever I please. But Prometheus has been kind to me. I don't want to do anything to him. My brother despises him because he was Primus' catamite. Marcus hated Primus. He hated Calabah. And he hates me the same way he hated them."

Hadassah took her hand. "My lady," she said gently, wanting to draw Julia's attention away from herself, "the Lord has given you an opportunity to perform an act of kindness."

Calming slightly, Julia looked at her tearfully. "How?"

"You can free Prometheus."

She thought about it for a moment and frowned. "He's worth a lot of money."

"You'll have no need of money now that your brother is settling your debts and you're returning home."

The way Azar said it, the situation sounded hopeful rather than the last of numerous disasters. Julia chewed on her lip. "I don't know. Marcus probably wouldn't like it." She gave a grim laugh. "But then, why should I care what he thinks when he so obviously doesn't care about me." She looked at Azar, her eyes glittering. "I'll do it. I will free Prometheus."

"Free Prometheus out of gratitude for the kindness he's shown you during your illness, my lady, not to spite your brother. Otherwise there is no blessing for you."

Julia's expression fell. "You're displeased with me."

"Set your own feelings aside and do what is right."

Julia was very quiet for a moment. "I don't know what's right. Maybe I never knew." She looked at Azar and felt the warmth of her spirit. "But I will do as you suggest."

40

Marcus' servants arrived a few hours after his departure. Julia spent the afternoon writing out a proper document of manumission for Prometheus. She presented the scroll to him as soon as he returned from what work he had found in the city. It was a moment before he realized what she had given him. "My lady," he said, overcome.

Julia's smile trembled. "You have been a good and faithful servant, Prometheus. I wish you well." She extended her hand. He took it and kissed it fervently. She had never felt so light of heart. "Go in peace."

Julia saw Azar waiting for him just outside the door. Prometheus seemed about to embrace her but drew back, a glance flickering in her direction. He said something too soft for her to hear and left. Julia sat down weakly on her sleeping couch.

Azar came and sat beside her.

"I did it."

"Yes, you did." Azar put her hand over hers. "How do you feel now?"

"Wonderful."

"You've done a good thing, my lady. The Lord has seen what you've done."

"It's strange," Julia said, bemused. She gave a soft laugh. "I can't remember ever feeling so happy."

"It's more blessed to give than to receive."

She shook her head. "Then I guess I'd better enjoy the feeling for the little while it lasts because I haven't anything to give anymore. It's all been taken away."

"You have a great deal more to give than you realize." She wanted to say more, but one of Marcus' servants came out to them.

"We are almost finished packing, my lady," he said to Julia. "A litter has been arranged for you, and a room has been prepared for your arrival."

Her hand grasped Hadassah's. "Azar is to come with me."

"The litter is only large enough for one."

336

"Then get another!"

"I'm sorry, my lady, but—"

"Never mind," Hadassah said. "It's all right."

"It's not all right! This is just another way for Marcus to punish me. He wants to keep me from having you."

At Hadassah's gesture, the servant left. She turned to her mistress. "I will follow you, my lady. Go and don't worry."

"You promise?" Julia said, eyes wide.

"I already have. Be reassured." She put her arms around Julia and held her for a moment. "I will not be far behind."

As soon as Julia was on her way, Hadassah went to the small alcove in the peristyle where Prometheus said he would wait for her. He rose as she approached.

"I know this is your doing," he said, the sealed document clutched in his hand.

"It's the Lord's doing."

"I've dreamed of having my freedom," he said, sitting down with her, "but now, I'm not certain. I want to be where you are."

"That's not possible, Prometheus. Lord Marcus gave strict instructions."

"Oh," Prometheus said, expression falling. "I understand."

"The Lord has given you this opportunity, Prometheus." She removed a pouch from the folds of her sash. She took one of his hands and placed it on his palm. "A gift to help you start your new life," she said, closing his hand around the small purse of gold coins. She gave him instructions on where to find the apostle John. "Confess your past sins and your present struggle. He will instruct you in all the ways of the Lord."

"How can you be so sure?"

"Oh, I am very sure. John will love you as God loves you. Go to him, Prometheus. If you can't yet fashion your life after Jesus, fashion it after a man who walked with the Lord while he was on this earth. Observe how he continues to do so."

"I will go," Prometheus said, "but what of you?"

"I'll remain with Lady Julia as long as she lives."

"I am grateful to her for my freedom, my lady, but this was one isolated act of kindness after a long list of cruelties. A whim, not a change of character. If she ever finds out who you really are, I'm afraid to think what she'll do to you."

"What real danger do I face, Prometheus? My soul belongs to God. Renew your mind and remember what you have learned.

Nothing can separate us from the love of God which is in Christ Jesus." She touched his face tenderly. "And nothing can separate us who are of the family of God."

He put his hand over hers. "I wish you were coming with me."

She lowered her hand to her lap. "I am where I must be." She rose slowly. "I must go to Lady Julia." She limped toward the antechamber. Prometheus went with her, measuring his steps to hers. She looked up at him as she limped toward the door. "Will you remain here until the villa is sold?"

"Yes. What about your things?" he said, seeking any way he could to delay her departure.

"They were packed and sent along with Julia's. I've nothing left to carry but this walking stick." She saw his deep concern and tried to reassure him. "It's not a far distance, Prometheus. I'll manage very well."

"When will I ever see you again?"

"I'll attend meetings whenever possible. We'll see one another there."

He was afraid of the separation. "It's not enough. You've kept me accountable," he said, and she knew to what he referred.

"Solomon said, 'Trust in the Lord with all your heart, and lean not on your own understanding; in all your ways acknowledge Him, and He shall direct your paths.'"

"I'll try to remember."

"Don't *try*. Say it over and over to yourself until it's engraved upon your heart. And remember this as well." She recited the song of the shepherd. "Say it to me." She repeated it with him until he had it memorized. "Say it over morning, noon, and night, and lay it upon your mind as a pattern for thinking."

She opened the door and went out. Prometheus gave her support as she went down the steps. When they reached the gate, he opened it for her. She paused and looked up at him. "Do you know what happened to make Lord Marcus hate his sister so much?"

"No," he said. "I was too caught up in my own misery to notice anyone else's. Besides that, it wasn't long after you were sent to the arena that I ran away."

Hadassah sighed. "I wish I knew what happened between them."

"Perhaps it was you."

She glanced back at him in surprise. "Why would you think that?"

"He was in love with you, wasn't he?"

She was deeply saddened by his words, for they roused poignant memories. Had Marcus ever truly loved her? "I think I was merely different from the women he had known. A challenge of sorts. But I don't think he ever loved me in a way that would have lasted." Had he loved her, wouldn't he have listened to her words about the Lord?

She remembered Marcus' declaration of love in Julia's bedchamber. She remembered his anger when she had refused to marry him. She had wounded his pride, not his heart. And because of it, he had cursed her and left. She had never seen him again until the day he bumped into her outside the public baths. She had never thought to see him again after that, and now she was to live under his roof. She was filled with trepidation—and a disturbing excitement. Marcus might never have truly loved her, but she was still in love with him.

"Primus thought Marcus Valerian loved you," Prometheus said. "He used to taunt Lady Julia about it. He'd say Lord Marcus came to see a slave rather than his own sister."

"That wasn't true. He was absolutely devoted to Julia. Marcus always loved his sister. He adored her."

"He doesn't love her anymore."

She was silent, wondering. "Perhaps he will again." She reached out and touched Prometheus' arm. "You'll be in my prayers each day. Stand firm in the Lord."

"I will."

"He will protect you." Stretching up, she embraced him. "You are my dear brother, Prometheus. I love you very much."

"I love you, too," he said hoarsely, unable to say more. His eyes were moist.

Hadassah released him and went out the gate. He closed it behind her and leaned his forehead against it. "God, protect her. Lord, be with her." Turning away, Prometheus went up the steps to the deserted villa, repeating what she had taught him.

"The Lord is my shepherd; I shall not want. . . ."

41

Marcus was coming out of the triclinium with Iulius when one of the servants admitted the veiled woman to the antechamber. "Rapha!" Iulius breathed in surprised pleasure and went forward, leaving Marcus standing alone.

The woman was leaning heavily on her walking stick but put her hand out in greeting. "Iulius, you are looking well. How is Lady Phoebe?"

"The same as when you left. We didn't expect you this evening. Lady Phoebe has retired."

"I tend Lady Julia."

"You're the one? Lady Julia said she was expecting a personal maid, but I never guessed . . ."

"Nor should you have."

"How did this come to be?"

"The Lord brought us together. Where is she?"

"She was overwrought when she arrived. Lord Marcus had wine sent up to her. I checked on her a short while ago, and she was asleep."

Marcus came forward, his smile sardonic. "As you've probably guessed, she's drunk herself into a stupor."

Hadassah's heart quickened at the sound of his voice and approach. She looked up at him as he stopped before her. "Good evening, my lord."

He studied her coolly. "I didn't expect you."

"I told you I would come."

"Yes. I remember." He frowned, feeling a pang of discomfort. "I thought tomorrow or the next day."

"With your permission, I'll go up to her now."

"As you please."

She limped toward the steps. It was clear she was tired and in pain.

"Rapha, wait," Iulius said and went to her. He spoke too softly for Marcus to hear. She put her hand on his arm. Iulius shook his head and caught her up in his arms. Marcus watched him carry the woman up the steps.

Aggravated by her arrival, Marcus entered the peristyle. He sat in the small alcove he had often shared with Hadassah and leaned back against the wall. Closing his eyes, he listened to the fountain. He was perplexed by the veiled woman. She made him uncomfortable.

He heard footsteps coming down the steps. Opening his eyes, he sat forward. "Iulius, I would like to speak with you."

Iulius strode across the peristyle. "She *walked* here," he said upon reaching him. His tone was faintly accusing.

Marcus' demeanor darkened. "I would have sent a litter for her tomorrow."

"I had heard she had left Alexander Democedes Amandinus, but I had no idea she was ministering to Lady Julia. It's amazing!"

"Why? Who is she that anyone would care where she is or what she's doing?"

"She is *Rapha*." Grim-lipped, Iulius beckoned one of the maids and told her to take a tray up to Lady Julia's chamber.

"Oh! Rapha is here?" the girl said in bright surprise.

Marcus glanced at her. Did the whole household know of this woman?

"Indeed," Iulius said, "and she'll be remaining with Lady Julia indefinitely. Have a sleeping couch moved to her chambers and see that there is plenty of warm bedding. Rapha didn't ask for warm compresses, but I think she's in great pain from her long walk from Lady Julia's villa."

Marcus grew annoyed at the second mention of her walking. "Tell her she is free to use our baths," he said coolly.

"Thank you, my lord. I'm sure she will be most grateful," Iulius said.

Marcus glowered at him.

"One more thing, Lavinnia," Iulius said to the serving girl. "She asked that no outsiders be informed that she is here. Tell the others. She wants nothing to interfere with her care of Lady Julia."

"I will tell everyone." The girl hurried off with an air of excitement Marcus couldn't miss.

"One would think the proconsul had just entered the house, rather than a crippled slave woman in veils," Marcus said dryly.

Iulius shot him a confounded look. "Is it possible you've never heard of her?"

"I've been away a long time, Iulius. Remember? And I'm filled with questions. For one: Who *is* she?"

"She is a healer. I heard of her at the marketplace not long after your mother was struck down by paralysis. It was said Rapha could heal with a mere touch of her hand. We sent an appeal that she come."

"Obviously, she isn't the miracle worker she's reputed to be or Mother would be up and about walking and talking."

"Rapha made no claims of any kind, my lord," Iulius said quickly, "but it was she who convinced us that your mother understood what was happening around her. The other physicians who came all said it would be best to end her misery with a dose of hemlock."

Marcus went cold. "Go on."

"The physician who brought Rapha with him also suggested euthanasia. Rapha objected. She insisted your mother was *aware*, that her mind still functioned though her body did not. We were faced then with a terrible dilemma, my lord. What was best for your mother? Can you imagine what agony to be trapped within a useless body? I'd seen such fear and despair in your mother's eyes, but didn't know if she even knew what was going on around her. Rapha insisted she did and that she should live. She asked to be left alone with her, and when she readmitted us to the bedchamber, your mother was as she is now. Whatever Rapha said or did gave your mother *hope*. Equally important, Rapha gave her life purpose."

"What purpose?" Marcus said, stunned by all he had been told.

"She prays. Unceasingly, my lord. From the moment she awakens and is carried out onto the balcony to evening when she is carried back to her bed, she prays. Of course, since you have returned home, she has spent more time with you."

"Are you suggesting I'm interfering with her *work?*"

"No, my lord. Forgive me if I express myself badly. You stand in answer to many of your mother's prayers. Your return home has served to reaffirm and strengthen her faith. You are solid assurance that God hears her prayers and answers."

Marcus rose from the marble bench, his expression pensive. "You will forgive me if I still have doubts about this veiled woman. Lady Julia called her Azar, not Rapha. Perhaps she isn't the same person of whom you speak. It's a common enough practice for some women to veil themselves, and among them, I'm sure, are several cripples."

"I'm sure you're right, my lord, but there is no mistaking her. It's less how Rapha appears than what you feel when she's near."

Marcus frowned. "What do you feel?"

"It's hard to explain."

"Try," Marcus drawled sardonically.

"Trust. Reassurance. Comfort." He spread his hands. "In a strange way, her faith in God gives one a confidence in him as well, even those who don't believe."

"You don't?"

"Because of your mother's faith, I have come to believe, but there are times when I doubt."

Marcus understood only too well. He now believed Jesus had come to earth, that he had allowed himself to be crucified as an atonement for man's sin, and that he had been raised up from the dead. Yet, Marcus had difficulty believing Christ was sovereign. The world was too filled with evil.

It was these very doubts that roused his caution.

"Despite what you say, Iulius, I'm not so inclined to allow a stranger in our midst, especially one so mysterious as this one."

"I am sure she has sound reasons for changing her name."

"What might they be?"

"If you but ask, I'm sure she will explain."

343

42

Opportunity to speak with Rapha-Azar eluded Marcus. Word had reached his representatives that he was back in Ephesus. They came to see him, bringing with them records of the business transacted in his absence. He spent morning until evening of the next few days closeted with them in the bibliotheca. They urged him strongly to take the helm once again.

"The opportunities to make money now are vast, my lord, and your instincts have always proven sound," said one. "What eludes us is crystal clear to you."

Marcus' own nature and inclination tempted him to grasp the opportunities he saw from the reports given him. It would be so easy to reenter the business arena and focus his attention on things other than the problems in his family. Just listening to his representative and looking over the reports made his mind hum with ideas on how to increase his wealth.

Yet some small voice in his head bade Marcus resist his inclination to pour himself back into the business of making money. What was his motivation? He had wealth enough to last a lifetime now. And his mother needed him.

And there was still the unfinished matter of Julia.

His conscience plagued him constantly regarding his sister, while reason held him distant. Each time he went up the steps, he felt the urge to see his sister, to talk to her about what had happened to him in Palestine. At the same time, another voice reminded him of what Julia had done to Hadassah.

"There. It's finished," she had said, her face distorted by glee and hatred, and he would remember again Hadassah's body upon the sand.

Tonight, he was weary. He had spent most of the afternoon with Mother. He was tired of the sound of his own voice, exhausted with trying to think of pleasant things to say to amuse her. She gazed at him in a way that made him wonder if she understood his deeper feelings, those he tried so desperately to hide.

As he passed by Julia's bedchamber to go downstairs to the triclinium for a simple evening meal, he felt the urging within him again. The door was open, and he heard a soft voice. He paused and glanced in.

His sister was sitting sideways on her sleeping couch while the veiled woman sat behind her, brushing Julia's hair with long, smooth strokes. She was speaking to his sister. He shut his eyes tightly, for the scene reminded him piercingly of Hadassah. He opened his eyes again and watched Azar minister to Julia. He had seen Hadassah brushing Julia's hair with those same unhurried strokes while singing some psalm of her people. His heart ached with longing.

God, will I never forget her? Is this your way of punishing me for my part in it?

He stood in the doorway, filled with dismay that something so commonplace should rouse such pain. How long would it take before the love faded and the memories became bearable? Did Julia feel any remorse at all?

The veiled woman turned her head slightly. Seeing him, she lowered the brush to her lap. "Good evening, my lord."

Julia turned sharply, and he saw how pale she was.

"Good evening," he said, keeping his voice cool and under control.

"Come in, Marcus," Julia said, eyes pleading.

He almost did as she asked and then stopped himself. "I've no time this evening."

"When will you have time?"

He raised his brow at her peevish tone and directed his attention to her servant. "Have you all you need?"

"Why don't you ask *me*, Marcus? *Yes*, most gracious lord, we have all the *physical* comforts we could possibly want."

Ignoring her, he spoke coolly to Azar. "When you've tucked your mistress in for the night, come to the bibliotheca. I've some questions that need answering."

"What questions?" Julia demanded.

Hadassah wondered as well, her heart beating even more rapidly. Marcus stood rigidly in the doorway, staring at her with hard, dark eyes.

Julia sensed Azar's tension. "You don't have to tell him anything, Azar. You've nothing to do with my brother."

"She'll answer or leave this house."

At his coldness, Julia's tenuous control snapped. "Why did you bring me back here, Marcus?" she cried out. "To make my life more unbearable than it already is?"

Angry at her accusation, Marcus left the doorway and headed down the corridor.

"Marcus, come back! I'm sorry. Marcus!"

He kept going. How many times before had she wept to get her own way? Not this time. Not ever again. Closing his heart off to her, he went down the steps.

The cook had prepared a succulent meal, but Marcus had no appetite. Annoyed, he went to the library and tried to lose himself in reviewing some of the documents his representatives had left with him. Finally, he brushed them aside impatiently and sat staring glumly ahead, his emotions in turmoil.

He wished he hadn't brought Julia back here. He could've paid her debts, seen she had the servants she needed, and left her in her own villa.

"My lord?"

Marcus saw the veiled woman standing in the doorway. He turned his mind from the dark memories to the problem at hand.

"Sit," he commanded and gestured to the seat facing him.

She did so. He found it surprising that a cripple could move with such grace. She sat straight-backed, her body turned slightly so that she could extend her bad leg.

"Iulius tells me your name is Rapha, not Azar," he said pointedly.

Hadassah bit her lip, wishing she could still the fluttering in her stomach whenever she was in Marcus' presence. She had tried to prepare herself for this interview, but sitting here in this small room with him so close filled her with trepidation.

"Rapha is what I was called, my lord. It means 'the healer' in Hebrew."

She spoke in a soft rasping voice that reminded him pleasantly of Deborah. Was it the accent?

"Then you are a Jew. It was my understanding from Julia that you were a Christian."

"I am both, my lord. By race, I am a Jew, by choice, a Christian."

Ever defensive, he took offense. His mouth curved in a cool smile. "Does that place you on a higher plane than my mother, who is a Gentile Christian?"

Stunned by his accusing question, she was filled with dismay.

"No, my lord," she said, explaining quickly. "In Christ, there is neither Jew nor Roman, slave nor free, male nor female. We are all one in Christ Jesus." She leaned forward slightly, her voice softening as though to reassure him. "Your mother's faith makes her as much a child of Abraham as I, my lord. *Anyone* who chooses becomes an heir to the promise. God is impartial."

Her words eased his misgivings. "By anyone, you mean me."

"Yes, my lord."

It was on the tip of his tongue to say he had accepted the Lord in Galilee, but pride held him from it. "I'm told that you saved my mother's life."

"I, my lord? No."

"Iulius said the physician who came with you suggested my mother's life be ended with a draught of hemlock. You interceded on her behalf. Is that not so?"

"Your mother lives because it is God's will she do so."

"That may be, but Iulius said after you were alone with my mother, she was changed."

"I spoke with her."

"Only spoke?"

Hadassah was grateful for the veils that hid the heat that rose into her face. Unlike what she had done with Phoebe, she knew she could never show her face to Marcus. She would rather be sent back to the arena than have him look upon her scars with the same revulsion she had seen in the faces of others.

"I cast no spells, nor did I utter incantations," she said, thinking it answered the question behind his words.

He held up his hand. He could sense her increased tension but could not fathom the reason for it. "I'm making no accusations, Azar. I'm merely curious. I like to know something about the people in my household."

She was quiet a moment. "I knew when I looked in your mother's eyes that she was aware. She heard what was being said and understood. She was afraid and in great distress over her condition. I think she would've drunk the hemlock Alexander offered gladly for no other reason than to spare others the responsibility of her care. I simply told her what she already knew."

"What she knew? What was that?"

"That God loves her, my lord, as she is. And she's alive for a reason."

Marcus ran his hand along the edge of the writing table, his thoughts in turmoil. He wanted to know more about this woman. "Iulius tells me you were very well known in Ephesus."

Hadassah said nothing.

"Why did you give up your position?"

The cold abruptness of his question surprised her. "I chose to be with your sister."

"Just like that. Why did you change your name?" The question came out harder than he intended.

"Because I am not Rapha. Jesus is the healer, not I," she said, telling him what she had told Alexander and hoping he would better understand it.

"And Azar is your real name?"

"Azar means 'helper.' That's the position I hold and all I hope to be."

He caught the careful way she answered. "Why did you choose Julia?"

"I can't answer that, my lord."

"Can't or won't?"

"I know I'm where the Lord wants me. I do not know why he wants me here."

He frowned darkly, for her words struck him on the raw, bringing back the conviction he had felt in Galilee. God wanted him here also. With Julia. He rebelled against what more he knew God wanted of him.

"I suppose, in your opinion, God loves my sister too and has a purpose for her life, such as it is." Before she could respond, he waved his hand. "You may go."

As soon as she did, he rose in frustration.

Perhaps he only needed to get out of the villa for a while. He went out into the corridor.

"Do you want the litter, my lord?" Iulius said, seeing the cloak a servant handed him.

Marcus swung the garment on. "I feel like walking," he said, fixing the gold brooch at his shoulder. "If Mother awakens and sends for me, tell her I've gone to the baths." He strode to the door and yanked it open. He went down the steps and slammed the gate behind him.

He headed for the men's club where he had spent much of his time before leaving Ephesus, thinking he might find distraction in renewing old acquaintances. The night air cooled his anger, and by the time he reached his destination, he was relaxed. He was

greeted with surprised welcome, his back pounded by half a
dozen men he knew.

"We heard you were back in Ephesus, but saw no sign of
you," one said.

"Where have you been keeping yourself, Marcus?"

"No doubt he's been at his emporium poring over his ledgers
to see how much money's been made during his absence." They
all laughed.

"I heard you went to Palestine."

"Palestine!" one exclaimed. "By the gods, why would anyone
in their right mind go to that wretched country?"

Their exuberant company grated rather than soothed Marcus'
nerves. He laughed with them, but his heart wasn't in it. He felt
as though he was back in Rome with Antigonus, wishing he was
anywhere else. Was he the only one who had changed? Was he
the only one who sensed the foul corruption eating away at the
world?

"You should come to the games tomorrow."

"I'm bringing Pilia with me."

"Ah, Pilia," another groaned, rolling his eyes as though in
ecstasy.

The others laughed and made ribald remarks of how Pilia
implanted herself upon the memory of any man with whom she
spent a night, especially after the games.

Marcus thought of Arria.

He thought of his sister.

He dove into the pool, thankful when the water closed over his
head and shut out the sound of his friends' voices. Friends? He
didn't know them anymore. He swam to the far end of the pool
and lifted himself out. Striding between the pillars, he entered the
calidarium, where he remained until the sweat was pouring from
his body. Skipping the tepidarium, he dove into the frigidarium,
thankful for the shock of cold water that drove all thought from
his head.

Only briefly.

He submitted to a vigorous massage before leaving the club.
He walked down the street, one more body among the imper-
sonal chaos of the crowds that milled around near the Artemision. He stopped to look up at the temple. It was garishly
beautiful, an immense monument to man's engineering.

With his acute mind, he saw it as the grandest money-making

venture in Ephesus. Idol makers surrounded the massive complex, taking in money for crude statues of the goddess who supposedly inhabited the temple. Others raked in gold coin for sacrificial animals. Still others sold amulets and secret spells enclosed in expensive lockets. Incense was sold by the pinch and at prices to test a worshiper's depth of faith. Prayers were bought.

Inside were the temple prostitutes, male and female, at prices on a sliding scale—depending on the wealth of the man or woman who had come to pay proper homage to the goddess.

Marcus shook his head sadly. How much did a priest charge these days for a blessing? How much for hope that would prove empty?

Marcus looked down a street lined with inns that catered to those who had come far distances to see the temple and worship Artemis. Most came, worshiped, and departed, while others remained for months, delving into the volumes written by the priests on the sacred Ephesian letters carved into Artemis' headpiece. Did anyone really know what they meant? Did they mean anything at all?

He stood looking up at the Artemision. How many came to this building to find hope and went away in despair, their questions unanswered, their needs unfulfilled? How many felt the same aching emptiness and driving need he had felt for so long and were destined to remain that way to death and beyond?

Suddenly, in the midst of his contemplation, he sensed someone staring at him. He turned. An Arab stood across the street. People milled around him, moving steadily toward the Artemision or entering the shop behind him. The man didn't move, nor did he avert his gaze. Marcus felt warning in his stare and wondered at it. He didn't recognize the man and so could not understand the intensity of his perusal. Then the Arab seemed to vanish among the throng of people.

Perplexed, Marcus started walking again, trying to spot the man among the crowds moving to and from the Artemision. Had he entered an idol maker's shop?

Someone bumped him hard from the side, almost knocking him down. He lost his breath and stumbled, catching himself before falling. He swore, knowing it had been a deliberate action, perhaps intended as a way to strip him of his purse. He turned to see who had bumped him and saw the Arab again, moving quickly away in the direction of the Artemision. He mingled with the crowd so fast, Marcus couldn't catch up.

Shaking his head, Marcus turned back and went up Kuretes Street toward home.

His side began to burn with pain. When he put his hand to it, he felt moisture. His eyes widened as he looked at his bloody hand, and he swore. Feeling the blood dripping down his side, he hurried his pace toward home. Wincing, he pushed the gate open and went up the steps. As soon as he entered the villa, he threw off his cape. Clenching his teeth against the pain, he went up the steps.

Iulius came out of the Lady Phoebe's bedchamber. "My lord!" he said in concern, seeing the blood staining Marcus' tunic.

"I was attacked," Marcus said grimly, shaking off his support. "It's nothing more than a cut."

At Iulius' call, Lavinnia came running. "Get water and bandages. Lord Marcus has been attacked," he said, following Marcus. "Move, girl. Quickly!"

Hadassah came out of Julia's bedchamber and watched Iulius help Marcus into his room. Alarmed, she followed, but when she appeared in his doorway, he waved her off angrily. "Tend to Julia. I'll tend to myself."

She ignored him. Iulius immediately stepped back so she could see the wound. Marcus heard her soft gasp.

"It's nothing," he said and gave a laugh as she swayed slightly. "Does the sight of blood bother you?"

Only the sight of your *blood,* she wanted to say. "Not usually, my lord." She came closer, trembling as she looked at the slash along his ribs. "How did this happen?"

"An Arab, I think. God knows why."

She drew back as though stunned. Lavinnia arrived with a pan of water and bandages. He sucked in his breath as Hadassah began to cleanse the wound. "Let Iulius see to it," he said, seeing how her hands shook. He laughed softly. "I think I know why you left that physician," he said, amused.

"A little lower and he might have struck a vital organ," Iulius said, taking over.

Feeling faint, Hadassah left the room.

43

Alexander knew something was wrong the moment Hadassah was ushered into his atrium. She was greatly agitated.

"Where is Rashid?"

"He's not here," he said, alarmed. "What's happened?"

"Where is he?"

"I don't know. Why do you ask?"

"Because an Arab attacked Marcus this evening, and I must know if it was him."

Alexander made no attempt to suggest it was someone other than Rashid. The Arab had made no secret that he thought Marcus Valerian was a threat to Hadassah's life and should be killed. Rashid was nothing if not single-minded in his loyalty to Hadassah, whether she wanted it so or not.

"He went to find out how Julia's illness was progressing. . . ."

"Progressing?" Hadassah said in dismay, knowing full well that Rashid wished for Julia's swift demise.

Alexander's mouth tightened. "He learned from Prometheus that she had been taken to her brother's villa. He also informed Rashid that you went with her."

"By my own choice. What is he thinking?"

"He wouldn't have done anything unless he saw Marcus Valerian as a threat to your life."

Alexander's evasiveness only served to convince her. "Marcus is no threat to me. None of the Valerians are a threat to me."

"Rashid thinks otherwise."

"Then correct his thinking!"

Alexander was surprised. "I've never heard you speak in that tone. Do you think I condone Rashid's behavior? Don't blame me for his bloodthirsty nature. You were the one who chose him from all those left on the temple steps. Remember?"

"God chose him."

"Then it's God who is directing his steps."

"God does not direct a man's path to murder!"

Rashid entered the chamber, effectively silencing them both. As he threw off his cloak, Hadassah saw the hilt of a knife tucked

352

expertly into his belt. Rashid's face darkened, his eyes blazing.
"Valerian?"

She shuddered, her fears confirmed. "Alive, thank God,"
Hadassah said.

"Next time he will not be so fortunate," Rashid said with dark
promise.

Hadassah came to him. "If you hold me in any esteem at all,
Rashid, you will make no further attempts on Marcus' life."

His face hardened.

She put her hand on his arm. "Please, Rashid. I beg of you. I
would rather God strike me dead now than that you take the life
of another."

"I told you I would protect you, and I will."

"At what cost to me, Rashid?"

"His blood be on *my* head, not yours."

"If you kill Marcus, it will cost my heart."

Rashid frowned, not understanding. "Your heart?"

Alexander stood, staring at her. "You love him," he said in
amazement.

"You *love* him?" Rashid said, astounded.

"Yes, I love him," she said softly. "Since before the arena. And
afterward. For as long as I live."

Alexander turned away, pain washing over him at her fervent
words.

Rashid shook her hand off his arm and stepped away. He
looked back at her, eyes dark with contempt. "Only a fool
woman could love a man who tried to have her killed!"

"I don't know that Marcus had anything to do with it. It was
Julia."

"The woman you now serve," Rashid said in disdain.

"Yes," she said.

"How can you?" he demanded, filled with wrath at what had
happened to her, and at her for not wanting retribution.

"Christ loved us in the same way. While we were yet sinners,
he died for us that we might be saved. How can I do less?"

"Ah, then you speak of another kind of love."

"I speak of a woman's love for a man as well, Rashid," she
said. "Please. Do nothing to harm Marcus Valerian."

Alexander stood on the far side of the room beneath the archway. "Do as Hadassah asks, Rashid," he said tonelessly, looking
out over the city. "Trust in God to take his own vengeance."

353

Rashid drew himself up, the blood of the warrior pounding in his veins. "Have you not said yourself that I was chosen to protect her?"

Alexander turned. "You know as well as I that God has set his hand upon the mother and daughter. Be assured, Rashid. The son is in God's hand as well."

Rashid stood silent, dark eyes enigmatic.

Hadassah limped near again. "Please, my friend," she whispered. "Give me your promise."

Rashid swept the veils up from her face and studied the terrible scars openly. "You plead mercy for those who did this to you?"

She blushed. "Yes."

He let go of the veils as though they burned him. "You are a fool!"

"That may be, but promise me anyway, Rashid. I know if you give me your word, you will never break it."

Her words of confidence and trust in him gave him pause. He glanced at Alexander and saw the rueful look on the physician's face. Alexander thought he knew him better. Rashid's face hardened as he looked down again at the diminutive woman who stood before him, crippled and scarred. Her eyes were clear, confident. Against his will, his heart softened. It didn't seem to matter that he would never understand her. She understood him.

"I promise to withhold my hand from him until he raises his against you."

Hadassah took his hand. "I wished for more, but will be content with that." She smiled, her eyes softening with affection. "God will have his way with you, my friend." She drew the veils down over her face again.

Alexander gave her the herbs she needed to treat Marcus Valerian's wound. He instructed her to cauterize the wound before applying a poultice and binding it. "Are you sure you don't want me to go with you?"

"I know what to do."

He walked with her to the litter and lifted her in. "Take care," he said, afraid for her. She took his hand in hers and pressed it to her veiled cheek. When she released him, he drew the curtains closed and stepped back. The servants lifted her and bore her away. Alexander had never felt more lonely in his life.

He found Rashid cleaning his knife. "Will you keep your word?"

Rashid's hand stilled. He lifted his head slowly and looked at him. Alexander felt chilled by the dark depths of those eyes. Without a word, Rashid returned to cleaning his knife.

44

"Where is she?" Julia said, distressed when Lavinnia came at her summons rather than Azar.

"She left the house, my lady. She didn't say where she was going."

"When will she return?"

"She didn't say, my lady."

"By the gods, do you know nothing at all? What's happened that she would leave me?"

"Your brother was attacked, my lady."

Julia's eyes went wide. "Attacked?" She started to rise from her couch, but her head swam and she sank down again, a trembling hand to her forehead.

"He will be all right, my lady. Do not distress yourself."

"How can I not be distressed? Who would dare attack my brother?"

"He said it was an Arab, my lady."

"Did Marcus know him by name?"

"I don't think so."

She wanted to go to Marcus to see for herself that he was all right, but she was too dizzy to do so. Even if she were able to go to him, he would not admit her to his chamber. "Azar said she wouldn't leave me," she said plaintively.

"I'm sure she will return, my lady." Lavinnia straightened the covers for her. "Perhaps she's gone to the physician."

"A cool cloth," Julia said. "My head aches."

Lavinnia dipped a clean cloth into the basin of water and wrung it before placing it gently over Julia's forehead and eyes.

"See what you can find out," Julia said and waved her away.

When Lavinnia didn't return within a few minutes, Julia became restless and worried. She brushed the cloth aside and sat up slowly, clutching the edge of the sleeping couch until her head stopped spinning. Once it did, she rose and walked unsteadily to the doorway. The house was very quiet. Had Marcus' wound been more serious than Lavinnia said? Had Marcus died?

Julia went out into the open corridor. She leaned heavily

against the wall. The marble was cold. She wished she had put on her wrap, but would not waste strength now to go back for it. She had to find out about Marcus.

Sliding her hand along the wall, Julia walked shakily down the corridor toward Marcus' chambers. She could hear voices. She reached the doorway and looked in. Iulius was leaning over the sleeping couch. She saw Marcus' leg, half-raised. On the floor was a discarded tunic stained with blood.

"How bad is it?" she said, her voice trembling. She gathered what strength she had and entered the room.

Marcus saw Julia just inside his bedchamber doorway. Clearly, she had come from her bed, for she was dressed in a rumpled gown that did little to conceal her gaunt body. Tangles of dark hair framed a white face. She was trembling, whether from fear or weakness he didn't know.

Nor did he care.

"Are you all right?" she said, staring at the blood-soaked bandage on his side.

"I won't die."

"I was afraid for you." She swayed slightly, her thin white hand against her breasts. "Would you like me to sit with you awhile?"

Marcus lay back on the couch. "See her to her room," he said, refusing to respond to her tremulous request. Iulius went to her. Marcus had spoken loudly enough for her to hear, and she made no protest when he supported her as he took her from the room.

Gritting his teeth, Marcus fought the rise of pity for her and remorse that he had turned her away so coldly. She was so wan and thin, as though she diminished each time he saw her. She had always prized her beauty. What must she feel now when she looked in a mirror and saw that gaunt, white face? Once, she would have taken pains to dress and have her hair braided and curled before leaving her room or receiving guests. Yet, tonight, she came straight from her sickbed to see what had happened to him.

Iulius returned. He didn't mention Lady Julia. Marcus started to ask, but sucked in his breath as the servant peeled the blood-soaked bandage from his ribs. "The wound is still seeping, my lord."

"Wash it again with wine and then bind it. If I die, I die," he said, annoyed.

"Drink some wine, my lord," Iulius said grimly, handing Marcus a full goblet. As Marcus propped himself up, the wound began to bleed again. He lay back once more, and Iulius soaked a cloth in the fine red vintage. Marcus' body stiffened as the slave washed the wound and then bound it again. He gave Marcus another goblet of wine, noting that his eyes were dark and clouding.

"Don't look so worried, Iulius," Marcus said drowsily. "Whatever liquid has seeped out, you've poured back in." His body relaxed as he passed out. Iulius bent over him, unsure whether it was loss of blood or too much wine that had so affected him.

Hadassah entered. Iulius hurried to her to take the small bundle she carried. "The wound still seeps, Lady Azar."

"Bring the brazier," she said, taking the bundle from him as she reached the bed. Leaning down, she touched Marcus' shoulder. He didn't rouse. She laid a trembling hand against his chest and felt the slow, firm beat of his heart.

Opening the bundle, she laid out the small packets of herbs and a cautery. She placed the end of it in the hot coals of the brazier. "We must seal the wound and pack it with herbs," she told Iulius. "You will need to hold him still."

She took the cautery from the fire and drew the hot metal along the wound, searing it closed. Marcus groaned, rousing slightly, only to faint again. The smell of burning flesh nauseated Hadassah, but she reheated the cautery and finished the task.

"I need a small bowl," she said, and Iulius brought one to her. She mixed the herbs with salt and made a poultice, which she bound to the wound. She sat down on the edge of Marcus' sleeping couch and drew her hand across his brow. "I will stay with him," she said.

"Lady Julia came to see him. Lord Marcus commanded me to take her back to her room."

"Did he speak with her?"

"No, my lady."

Hadassah sat thinking. She put her hand on Marcus' bare chest and felt the firm beat of his heart. "See if she's awake, Iulius. If so, bring her here so she can see that her brother is sleeping. It will set her mind at ease."

"Yes, my lady."

Julia came in, leaning upon Iulius' arm. Hadassah rose from the edge of Marcus' sleeping couch. She took Julia's hand and nodded for her to sit where she had been. Julia took her brother's hand. "He's so pale."

"He's lost blood."

"Will he be all right?"

"I think so, my lady," she said, then added to encourage her, "No vital organ was struck. We've cauterized the wound. The poultice should prevent infection."

"He didn't want me here," she said, putting her hand over his where it looked small and white against his large, strong, tanned hand. "He told Iulius to take me back to my room."

Hadassah came close and put her arms around her. She stroked the tangled hair back from Julia's face.

Julia leaned against her side and closed her eyes, feeling comforted. "I was afraid you'd left me, Azar."

"You need not fear, my lady."

"I know that in my head, but my heart . . ." She sighed, struggling against the invading weakness. This small effort was almost too much for her. "I'm so glad you're here with us."

Hadassah felt her trembling. "You must rest now, my lady. Your brother will be fine in a few days." She bent to help her rise.

"Iulius can help me back to my room. You stay with him. Please. I trust him in your care."

Hadassah touched her cheek. "You're thinking of others above yourself."

Julia's mouth curved wryly. "Am I? Or is it only that my last hope rests in him?" She leaned upon Iulius as she left the room.

Hadassah remained with Marcus through the night. He roused once and looked at her with dazed eyes. Frowning, he mumbled. She rose and leaned down. "What is it, my lord?" she said and put her hand on his forehead. It was cool.

He grasped the edge of her veils and tugged weakly. Her heart leapt. Straightening quickly, she gently loosened his fingers and sat again, trembling.

He moved again, relaxing into sleep, and her gaze moved over him. He filled her with wonder, for he was strongly built and beautifully made. She thought she could sit like this forever and just look at him. Tears pricked her eyes and she looked away. She prayed that the passion she felt for him might be transformed into agape. The memory of his kisses, given her so long ago, still sent her pulse racing. She prayed God would wipe it from her mind.

Still the longing persisted. He moved again, restless and in pain. She reached out and took his hand. At her touch, he calmed.

"Why, Lord? Why do you do this to me?" she whispered desolately. There was no answer.

As the dawn sent rays of sunlight over the wall of the balcony, Marcus awakened. Sluggish and disoriented, he turned his head and saw Azar sitting beside his sleeping couch. He rose slightly and sucked in his breath, immediately remembering the attack of the night before. Hadassah raised her head.

Wincing at the sharp pain in his side, he swore and lay back.

She put her hand lightly over his. "Lie still, my lord, or you will reopen the wound."

As she drew back slightly, Marcus captured her hand and pinned it down beneath his own. "You remained with me all night?"

"Lady Julia was concerned for you."

"She need not be. It's a superficial wound." He loosened his grasp on her, holding her hand lightly rather than captive.

"Perhaps, my lord, but a little lower and your attacker might have struck a vital organ."

"A little higher and he would have slit my throat." He frowned. "You tremble," he said, curious. She withdrew her hand, and he frowned.

Hadassah's heart raced as he studied her intently. What was he thinking? His gaze moved down and fixed upon her hands clenched in her lap. She tried to relax. Now that he was awake, she should call Iulius to tend him. She rose, but she had sat too long. Her bad leg cramped, drawing a gasp of pain from her lips before she could catch herself. Clenching her teeth, she took a step back, ashamed of her awkwardness.

Marcus noticed, but didn't care. "You're not going, are you?" he said. Frowning, he looked up at the veils again. He could see the shape of her face beneath, but made out no distinctive features. A thin line had been cut and the edges embroidered so that she could see out, but he couldn't see behind that wall of colored gauze. She lowered her head and turned slightly, and he knew, though the gesture seemed natural enough, she was avoiding his perusal and his touch.

"You should eat, my lord. I'll ask one of the servants to have food brought up to you."

Marcus wanted her to stay. He wanted to know more about her. He wondered why she roused his curiosity. As she turned toward the door, he grasped for any excuse. "The bandage seems to be slipping." Azar turned back, her head tilting slightly to study it critically. "Do you see?" he said and gave it a tug, gritting his teeth against the stab of pain.

"It will remain tight enough, my lord, if you stop pulling at it."

He grinned. "I will stop pulling at it if you sit and talk with me."

"You aren't a little boy anymore, my lord."

His grin softened into a wry smile. "No. I'm not, Lady Azar." He pointed toward the chair. "Sit and speak to me as a man and not a boy." He would use whatever means he had available to spend more time with her, even commanding her as master of his household. She roused his interest more than anyone had in a long, long time.

She sat where she had been, but he sensed the distance she put between them. "You speak with Julia by the hour but can't seem to abide my company for even a few minutes."

"I've just spent the night with you."

He laughed. "I was asleep."

"Your sister is very ill, my lord."

He had the feeling his interest embarrassed her. "I'm merely curious about you," he said frankly and sat up. Grimacing with pain, he set his feet on the floor.

"You must rest—"

"I'm sluggish with rest." And his head ached from far too much wine.

"You've lost a lot of blood."

"Not enough to keep me on my back like an invalid as you're intent upon treating me." He would leave the art of self-pity to his sister.

When Azar turned her head away, he wondered if his appearance bothered her. He wore a loincloth and nothing else. Considering her occupation, he thought the possibility remote but dragged the covering across his lap in case. "Should Lady Julia have need of you, I'm sure she will send Lavinnia running to fetch you."

She looked at him again. "What caused this breach between you and your sister, my lord?"

361

"A bold question," he said, annoyed by it. "We'll speak of other things."

"This plagues you most."

"What makes you think that?" he said, his mouth curving into a mocking smile. "Do you think you can see into me on such short acquaintance?"

She hesitated. "Are you at peace with the way things are?"

"At peace? My mother is paralyzed. Julia is beneath my roof again, dying of a foul disease brought on by her own promiscuity and foul living. You must admit these are hardly circumstances to make for peace, Lady Azar."

"Are you so pure you can condemn her, my lord?"

His eyes darkened. "Let's just say I limited my experiences to the opposite sex."

She said nothing.

"Do you doubt my word?"

"No, my lord, but sin is sin."

He felt heat flood his face. "How much has my sister told you about Calabah?"

"I know of Calabah."

"Sin is sin? Did Julia tell you they were lovers? That alone should tell you something about the depth of her depravity." He arched an imperious brow in condescension. "Did she bother to tell you her husband was a homosexual as well, with a proclivity for young boys? Prometheus was one of them. That's the reason I didn't want him in my house."

"Prometheus repented and gave his life to God," she said softly. "He returned of his own free will to serve Lady Julia. She said he ran away from Primus. He became a Christian and returned to your sister's household. If not for him, my lord, your sister would have had no one. Her servants had all deserted her."

"I concede you that," he said grimly, then regarded her ruefully. "This isn't the conversation I hoped to have with you."

"It's the truth."

"Nevertheless."

"You hold on to your anger against her like a shield. Why, I don't know. I wanted you to understand your sister was alone except for Prometheus. Whatever he was before—"

"Very well," he said impatiently, cutting her off. "I'll send for him if it pleases you."

"That wasn't my reason for telling you this. Prometheus is

well. Lady Julia gave him his freedom. It was a purely unselfish act on her part. He has work to do for the Lord. It's Julia who concerns me. And you. You mustn't abandon her."

Heat surged up in him. "I haven't abandoned her. She's here, isn't she?"

"Yes, she's here. You've given her shelter, food, servants to care for her. Yet you withhold from her what she needs most."

"And what's that?" he said derisively.

"Love."

A muscle jerked in his cheek. "Forgive me for keeping you from your duties, Lady Azar. You may go."

Hadassah rose slowly. She took up her walking stick. "Please, my lord. For her sake and yours, forgive her for whatever she's done."

"You don't know what she's done," he said, furious and wishing she would leave quickly.

"Nothing is so terrible it can't be set aside in the name of love, in the name of God."

"It's because of love I can't forgive her."

His passionate words left Hadassah more perplexed than before. Only one thing was certain in her mind. "Until you can forgive her, you'll never know the fullness of what it means to be forgiven yourself. Please, think on this. You haven't much time left."

Marcus did think on it long after Azar left. Despite his desire to put her words out of his mind, they kept repeating over and over. They cut him deeply. He remembered the relief and joy he had felt on the shores of the Sea of Galilee. He longed for those feelings to return, for somewhere along the road home he had lost sight of what he had found. It had taken the words of a veiled cripple to remind him again. And he didn't like it.

Raking his fingers through his hair, he stood and went out onto the balcony. He didn't know if he could set the past aside. He didn't know if he could forgive, let alone forget. He wasn't Jesus. He was a man, and the loneliness was sometimes so unbearable . . . God so distant. He had felt close to him in Galilee. Here he felt alone.

Azar was right. Peace would elude him until he obeyed the command he received in Galilee. He had felt briefly the tremendous relief of forgiveness on the shores of the Sea of Galilee. Forgiveness received could not be withheld. He must pour it out upon his sister, whether he wanted to or not.

Yet he still warred with his desire to punish her for what she had done, to make her suffer as she had made others suffer.

"I can't. . . ." Bowing his head, Marcus prayed for the first time since returning to Ephesus. Simple words, from his heart.

"Jesus, I can't forgive her. Only you can. Please . . . help me."

45

Julia lay on her sleeping couch, a cool cloth over her eyes. Hadassah had left to speak with the cook about preparing her a broth that might soothe her stomach. She hadn't been able to eat in three days, not since Marcus had ordered Iulius to remove her from his room. She couldn't stop thinking about Marcus and the way he had looked at her. She put a trembling hand over the cloth, pressing it against her throbbing head. She wished she could die now and have the pain and misery of her life over and done.

She heard someone enter her room and close the door. "I don't feel hungry, Azar," she said bleakly. "Please don't press me to eat. Just sit with me and tell me another story."

"It's not Lady Azar."

Julia froze at Marcus' voice. She lowered the cloth, thinking she might be imagining him here. "Marcus," she said in tentative greeting. Seeing he was real, she prepared herself for the inevitable attack.

He watched her sit up shakily and rearrange the coverings and cushions. Her hands were trembling as she pushed her hair back from her face. She was thin and white as death.

"Sit. Please," she said, gesturing gracefully toward the seat Azar usually occupied.

He remained standing.

Julia could tell nothing from his expression. His handsome face was like a stone facade. He seemed in good health despite the recent attack on his life. She, on the other hand, was growing worse daily. She wanted to weep as his dark eyes moved over her. She knew what she looked like with her scraggly, thinning hair, her emaciated body, her skin so pale it was almost translucent. The fever was upon her again, wilting her strength and making her tremble like an old woman.

She smiled up at him sadly. "You once took as much pride in my beauty as I did."

His mouth curved ruefully.

Her heart beat heavily with dread at his silence. "Have you

changed your mind, Marcus? Are you going to send me somewhere far away where you can forget you have a sister?"

"No. You'll remain here until you die."

He spoke of her death so matter-of-factly that she went cold.
"You're eager for that day, aren't you?" She lowered her gaze, for
his had become sardonic. "So am I."

"A ploy to make me pity you?"

She glanced up, hurt by his disdain. "Your pity is preferable to
your hatred."

Marcus let out his breath and walked across the room. He
stood at the foot of her couch. "I've come to tell you I've set my
mind against hating you."

"A difficult decision, no doubt. I'm ever so grateful."

Her tone roused his anger. "Did you expect more?"

She had no strength left for self-defense. "Why do you come to
me now, Marcus? To see what's befallen me?"

"No."

"I am cursed," she said, fighting the tears she knew he hated.
"You can see how accursed I am."

"The gods I called upon don't exist, Julia. If you're cursed, it's
by your own deeds."

She looked away. "So that's why you've come. To remind me
of what I did." She gave a bleak, humorless laugh of despair.
"You needn't. I look back upon my life with loathing. I see the
wretched things I did as though scenes are painted on these walls
I stare at every day." She balled one thin white hand against her
heart. "I remember, Marcus. I remember it all."

"I wish to God I didn't."

She looked up at him then, eyes dark with anguish. "Do you
know why I sent Hadassah to the arena? Because she made me
feel *unclean*."

Heat poured through his body, the sort that drove a man to
wrath and acts of violence. He gritted his teeth. "I want to forget
what you did to her."

"So do I." The dark circles beneath her eyes proclaimed the
ravages of illness. "But I don't think it's possible."

"I have to forget or go mad."

"Oh, Marcus, forgive me! I didn't know what I was doing."

His eyes flashed. "You knew," he said coldly, unable to abide
her lies.

Julia closed her eyes, her mouth trembling. For once she was honest with herself. "All right," she said in a choked voice. "I knew. I knew, but I was so consumed with misery myself that I didn't care what I did to anyone else. I thought if Hadassah was dead, everything would be the way it used to be." She looked up at him desperately. "Can you understand that?"

He stared at her coldly. "And was it?"

"You know it wasn't." She looked away from his cold face. "I loved her, too, Marcus, only I didn't realize it until it was too late."

"Loved her?" he said, eyes blazing. "You *loved* Calabah."

"I was deceived by Calabah."

"You walked into that relationship with your eyes wide open. I *warned* you myself, but you wouldn't listen. Don't tell me now you didn't know." Marcus turned and walked toward the archway to her private balcony, unable to stand being near her.

Julia looked at his rigid back and wanted to weep. "I don't expect you to understand. How can you? After Hadassah died, I felt this horrible void. Not just because you cursed me and left that day, but because . . . because Hadassah was the only one who ever really loved me."

Marcus turned on her. "Your self-pity sickens me, Julia. What of Father and Mother? Didn't they love you enough? What of me?"

"It wasn't the same kind of love," she said softly.

Marcus frowned.

"You know what she was like. Hadassah loved me for who I was, not for who she hoped I'd be. No expectations. No conditions. She saw me at my worst and still . . ." She shook her head, looking away.

Silence filled the room.

"Everything went bad," Julia said bleakly. "Life soured." She looked up at him, eyes pleading for his forgiveness.

"I don't want to hear this, Julia." He turned away. "I can't listen to it."

"I didn't know what was missing until Azar came. Oh, Marcus, she's like Hadassah. She's—"

Marcus turned, and she saw the pain in his eyes and the anger he tried so hard to deny. She knew it was her fault both were there. "I'm sorry. I'm so sorry, Marcus," she whispered brokenly. "What more can I say?"

"Nothing."

She swallowed. "I'd bring her back if I could."

He was silent for a long moment. "I can't be in this room with you unless we reach an understanding. We won't speak of Hadassah ever again. Do you understand me?"

She felt as though he had put upon her the sentence of death. "I understand," she said, her heart so heavy it was like a stone.

Neither spoke for a long moment.

"Have you seen Mother lately?" Marcus said with a faint lift of one brow.

"Azar took me in to her yesterday morning," Julia said in a dull voice. "It was nice to sit with her on the balcony and close my eyes and pretend things were the way they used to be."

"She's content."

"So it seems. Strange, isn't it?" Julia's mouth jerked as she fought the tumultuous feelings. Despite his neutral conversation, she knew: He hated her and would continue to hate her whatever he said. And why shouldn't he? She had to accept it. She almost wished her brother hadn't come. Not seeing him had been painful enough. Seeing him and feeling the wall between them was agony.

The door opened again, and Lavinnia entered with a tray. She was smiling and talking softly to someone behind her. She paused in the doorway as she saw Marcus, her cheeks blooming with color.

Julia recognized the look. How many other household servants had fallen in love with Marcus? Hadassah had only been one of many. "Put the tray on the table, Lavinnia, thank you." The girl quickly obeyed and departed, stepping past Azar as she entered the room.

"Lord Marcus," Azar said. "Good afternoon."

Her voice was warm and welcoming, drawing a smile from him. "Good afternoon, Lady Azar."

She limped across the room and set her walking stick aside. She touched Julia's shoulder. It was the merest brush of her fingers, but Julia relaxed as though reassured. She smiled up at the veiled woman, and Azar touched her forehead. "The fever has returned, my lady," she said and took the damp cloth from where Julia had dropped it. She set it aside and took up a fresh one, dipping it into the bowl of cool water. Wringing it out, she dabbed Julia's face lightly.

Julia lay back again, the tension Marcus hadn't noticed until then going out of her. She held her hand out and Azar took it, sitting on the edge of the sleeping couch. She lightly brushed the damp tendrils of hair back from Julia's temples and then turned her head toward him.

"I looked in on your mother a few minutes ago, my lord. Iulius put seed out for the birds. They come and sit on the wall where she can watch them."

"She always liked birds," he said, thankful for her presence. It eased the tension between him and his sister.

"A pair of turtledoves was looking over the stonework. Perhaps they'll nest there."

"Remember in Rome, Marcus, how Mother loved to work in the flower garden and watch the birds," Julia said wistfully. "Oh, Azar, I wish you could have seen it. It was so pretty there. You'd have loved it."

Marcus remembered Hadassah going out into the moonlit garden to prostrate herself before the Lord.

"There were trees that bloomed each spring," Julia went on, "and a stone walkway that wound around the flowerbeds. Mother even had a *fanum* built near the west wall." Julia looked at Marcus. "Was it the same when you returned?"

"It was the same, but empty. I was told when I returned from Palestine that Mother released her rights to the villa to one of Father's old friends in the Senate on the agreement that the proceeds would be used for the poor."

"Oh," Julia said, feeling a deep pang of loss. "I was so happy there as a child. I used to run along the pathways." To think of others living there was unsettling. Yet, she saw it was a good thing. Perhaps her mother had felt the same pleasant feeling she had when she had given Prometheus his freedom.

As he listened to Julia, Marcus was filled with memories as well. He remembered his sister, young and full of high spirits, racing to him and leaping into his arms. She had been innocent of the world then, eager to hear every detail of his adventures. She drank in the gossip of her friend Olympia and cajoled him into taking her to the games on the sly. He had agreed because he thought his father's restrictions unreasonable at the time. Now he wondered if Father hadn't seen Julia more clearly than he ever had. He had never considered what the effects might be of his own less-than-perfect example.

"Have you found the man who attacked you?" Julia asked, and he was grateful to have his thoughts diverted.

369

"I've had neither the time nor inclination to trace him."

"But you must, Marcus. He could try again."

"I'll know him the next time I see him. That'll be warning enough."

"What if you don't see him first?" she said, worried. "There's another possibility. What if this Arab is merely a hireling for someone else? There must be reason behind his mad attack. You must find him and learn what it is so you can destroy your enemies before they destroy you."

Marcus glanced at Azar. Though she said nothing and did nothing, he sensed she was disturbed by the course of this conversation. "He may have been a robber and nothing more," he said, wanting to dismiss the occurrence entirely.

"You aren't without resources, Marcus. You could find him if you chose to do so."

"*If* I chose to do so," he said pointedly.

Her expression fell at his brusqueness. "I didn't mean to argue, Marcus. I just don't want you hurt again."

He smiled down at her with an ironic twist of his mouth. No one had ever hurt him as much as she had done.

Comprehending that look, Julia went cold inside. She lowered her head.

Azar put her hand over Julia's and raised her head. Marcus could feel her looking at him through that veil. He couldn't see her face but felt her disappointment. A muscle jerked in his jaw. "I've work to do," he said tersely. Nodding to Azar, he walked across the room toward the door.

"Will you come visit me again, Marcus?" Julia said plaintively.

Marcus strode from the room without answering.

46

Julia finally slept, and Azar left Lavinnia to watch over her so that she could go down to the alcove in the peristyle and pray in solitude. Rashid was uppermost in her mind, but she was not so foolish she didn't recognize the danger to herself should Marcus trace the Arab. Rashid's rash act might also put Alexander at risk.

Hadassah considered revealing her identity to Julia and prayed for the Lord's guidance. What came to her was the conviction that Julia would assume some plot on the lives of her family members should she tell her who she was and her connection with the Arab. Even imagined wrongs had been enough for Julia to retaliate in the past. If her suspicions were aroused now, calamity could fall swiftly upon everyone. If that happened, what would become of Julia?

Be still and know that I am God, said the Spirit within Hadassah. And so she obeyed, waiting upon him while laying her hopes bare.

Hadassah heard a servant open the front door and greet Marcus. Her senses quickened. He had left the house after seeing Julia and been away all evening. As he walked through the antechamber, she saw him glance her way and stop. She sat back against the wall of the small alcove, her heart beating rapidly.

Unclasping the gold brooch at his shoulder, Marcus let the servant remove his cloak. As he entered the peristyle, Hadassah rose. "Please sit," he said and took the other side of the curved marble bench. He leaned back with a sigh, his hand over his side.

Hadassah studied his pale, weary face. "Your wound—"

"Is fine," he said curtly. "Iulius changed the dressing before I left."

"You must allow yourself time to heal, my lord."

"I am not a man accustomed to sitting around for long."

"So I see."

He heard the softening in her tone and smiled. He glanced around the small alcove remembering how often he had sat here with Hadassah. She had often come here in the late evening or early morning to pray.

371

"Thank you for seeing Julia," Hadassah said.

Drawing back to the present, he looked at Azar. "The visit didn't go very well," he said wryly. He found it strange that he felt so comfortable with a woman he scarcely knew. She intrigued him more each time he saw her.

"It's a beginning."

"Implying I should continue." His mouth curved sardonically. "I'm not sure I want to repeat the experience." His emotions had been raw all evening. He kept seeing Julia's face, white and strained, eyes pleading for something he didn't feel he could ever give. "It might be better if I left her alone."

"Better for whom?"

"You are direct, aren't you?" he said dryly. "Better for both of us. Some memories are best left buried."

Hadassah understood only too well. She had had to set her mind from the beginning to lay aside some of the things Julia had done to her and others. It hadn't been easy. Even while leaning on the Lord, there had been moments of great struggle. Yet sometimes, when she least expected it, Julia would surprise her with sweetness. Marcus needed to see that and be reminded.

"What was your sister like as a child?"

Marcus smiled bitterly. "Adorable."

"Tell me about her."

He did, drawing from their early life in Rome, of her spontaneity and hunger for life, her quick laughter and high spirits. As he talked, his sadness deepened, for he had loved his sister then, loved her with a fierce protectiveness and pride.

"And then she met Calabah," he said. "Olympia introduced them. I knew of Calabah long before Julia met her. She was well known in Rome. Rumors abounded that she murdered her husband, but nothing was ever substantiated. She had friends in high places. Julia wasn't the first to be corrupted by her influence, nor will she be the last."

"Do you think Julia's corruption was all Calabah's doing?" Hadassah said softly.

He looked at her, sensing a subtle challenge. Conceding, he let out his breath and put his head back again. "I had part in it," he confessed.

"What part, my lord?"

"I introduced Julia to the games, much to my father's displeasure. I think he would've been happy to keep Julia from the world. Looking back now, perhaps he was right after all. Some come to realize the depravity of what they see and turn away from it. Others become seared, numb to the suffering of others. They need more and more excitement to satisfy them, until nothing satisfies. Julia is like that."

"You no longer attend the games?"

"I haven't in a long, long time. I lost my taste for them rather suddenly." Just as he had lost the taste for other things he had once found desirable.

What might life have been had Hadassah lived? He shared her faith now. . . .

But if she had lived, you never would have gone on your quest to find God.

The sudden thought disturbed him.

"You look perplexed, my lord."

"Many things have changed within me since I went to Galilee."

"Galilee, my lord?"

He laughed. "You're surprised. It's understandable. Everyone thought I was mad. Why would a Roman go willingly to Palestine." His smile fell. "I had my reasons. I sailed to Caesarea Maritima, then rode to Jerusalem. What a city of death that place is. I didn't stay long. I spent some weeks in Jericho with a Jewish family and then traveled on to Nain." He smiled in fond amusement, remembering old Deborah.

"Nain?"

"You've heard of it? That's surprising. It's nothing but a speck of dust and little else. An old woman sent me on my way to the Sea of Galilee." He saw the way Azar wove her fingers together tightly and wondered what agitated her so about his story.

"Why did you go?" she said.

"There was once a young slave girl in this house," he said, looking around him. "She believed in Jesus Christ as the Son of the living God. I wanted to find out if he really existed."

"And did you?"

"Yes." He smiled. "The very moment I gave up hope of ever doing so," he said. "A man named Paracletos appeared to me and answered my questions. He told me to go to Capernaum where a man would be waiting for me at the gate. There was such a man, and his name was Cornelius. He baptized me in the Sea of Galilee and said God wanted me to return to Ephesus. So . . ." He gave her a rueful smile and spread his hands in self-deprecation. "Here I am."

"Oh, my lord," she murmured, and the warmth and joy of her voice reminded him of what he had felt when he had come up out of the sea, a new creation. "I didn't know."

He gave a dry laugh. "Why should you? I'm not much of a Christian."

"Oh, but the Lord is faithful, Marcus. He will mold you into his vessel."

His smile died. "If I don't shatter it to pieces first." He leaned forward, clasping his hands between his knees. "I know what God wants of me. I'm just not willing to do it. Not now. Maybe never."

Tears coursed down her cheeks. She leaned forward and took his hands, her own trembling. "Of ourselves, we can do nothing. It is God in us who works his purpose."

The love in her voice warmed his entire body. Her hands were strong and smooth. He didn't want to let go of her. His eyes burned, for Julia was right: Azar was very much like Hadassah. His heart raced. He wished he could see her face.

Hadassah withdrew her hands from his slowly and leaned back.

Marcus watched Azar clasp her hands in her lap. He could feel her tension and wished she could relax and talk to him as she did with his sister. "I'd like to know more about you," he said softly.

"You know me well enough already, my lord."

He smiled slightly, tilting his head. The same smile had won and broken the hearts of countless other women. "I know you practiced medicine with Alexander Democedes Amandinus, but little more."

"I'm here for Julia, my lord."

"Ah yes. Julia . . ." He sighed and leaned back against the wall, his face shuttered by shadows.

"Have you told her you've accepted Jesus as your Savior, my lord?"

"A neat turn of conversation." He gave a soft laugh. "No."

"Why not?"

"Because she'd never believe it. I'm not sure I do. Perhaps it was all a dream and never really happened. What I felt in Galilee I certainly don't feel now."

"What do you feel?"

"At odds with life."

"That's because you're no longer of the world."

His mouth curved wryly. "I felt at odds with life long before I went to Palestine, Azar. My discontent goes back as far as I can remember."

"God chooses his children from before the foundation of the earth. You were filled with thirst for the living water from birth, Marcus. Until you sought Christ, you failed to find a way to fill the emptiness within you. Only Jesus suffices. It's my prayer that Julia is one of his chosen as well."

"I doubt it."

"Then why is she so consumed with sorrow?"

"Because she's dying of a disease she brought on herself. Don't make the mistake of thinking it's regret over anything she ever did."

"Isn't it possible that the hunger that has driven you through life is the same hunger that's driving your sister?"

"Let's discuss something else."

"There's nothing else more important than that you forgive your sister."

"I don't want to talk about this!"

"She's flesh of your flesh. If her sorrow is according to the will of God, it will produce a repentance without regret leading to salvation."

"And if not?" he challenged coldly, incensed by her lack of obedience to his will.

"Then she will die without knowing Christ. She will stand before God Almighty and be judged for her sins. Is that what you want, Marcus? For God to judge her and cast her into the pit of fire for all eternity?"

Disturbed, he looked away, a muscle jerking in his cheek.

"My lord," Azar said gently, "God sent you home to bring Julia the Good News."

"Then *you* tell her."

"I have. I have told her over and over. And I will keep telling her for as long as God allows."

He heard tears in her voice. "If she hungers for God, she'll find God the same way I did."

"Not without your forgiveness, Marcus."

"Let God forgive her!"

"He will if she but asks, but sometimes people need to be

taken by the hand and guided to that moment because they're too afraid to take the step themselves. Take her by the hand."

He made a fist. "Curse you," he breathed. "Curse you for doing this to me."

Stunned and hurt, she fell silent.

He felt her withdrawal. "I'm sorry," he said, shutting his eyes. "It's not you I'm angry with. God asks too much."

"Does he? Jesus forgave the men who drove the nails into his hands and feet. He forgave the people who mocked him as he hung on the cross. He even forgave the disciples for deserting him. Aren't we all like that, Marcus? Fallible. Afraid. Weak in our faith. And still Jesus loves us and points the way to real freedom and what it means." She leaned forward slightly, and he felt her earnestness. "God forgave you in order that you forgive *her.*"

Marcus rose, angry to be so tormented. He had hoped for a few minutes of interesting conversation, not words to blister his conscience and renew his grief.

"You know in part, Lady Azar. I know the *whole.* If you knew everything Julia had ever done, you'd understand why I feel as I do."

"Then tell me."

"Leave well enough alone!"

"Is it well?"

"Julia can make her own confessions. And if it's forgiveness she needs, she can go to God for it!"

Hadassah watched him walk away. With a heavy heart, she bowed her head once more in prayer. She remained in the small alcove long after the servants were asleep. She finally rose to go to her own bed.

Marcus, alone and hurting, stood in the shadows of the corridor above, watching her.

47

Marcus sat with his mother on her balcony, talking to her of mundane things as the turtledoves fed upon the bread Iulius had put on the wall for them. He held his mother's hand, stroking it and wishing she could speak clearly enough for him to understand. When he had first come home, she had repeated "Ha . . . da . . ." over and over again. She would stare into his eyes with such intensity, he was sure she was trying to tell him something. But the constant reminder of Hadassah only served to bring him pain. She must have seen that, for, thankfully, she stopped mentioning Hadassah entirely.

"Ju . . . leee . . . ," she said today.

"I've seen Julia and spoken with her, Mother," he said, adding no more. "Azar is seeing to all her needs."

She made a soft sound. Marcus was aware how hard she tried to convey her thoughts to him and that she only relaxed when she had succeeded. He saw her relax now, resting her shoulders back against the cushioned chair. Her mouth sagged slightly, and he kissed her hand and sat in silence, head down, not knowing what to say.

He found less to talk about each time he came to sit with her. What could he say that would offer any consolation? That all was well in the household? That he was happy? No, none of this. Yet he felt his struggles were his own and best kept to himself. What could his mother, bound as she was by her illness, do to help him? He would only burden her further.

Phoebe watched her son and knew all was not well. She felt his unrest. She knew his silence was not a sign of contentment but a troubled heart. He didn't realize how much Iulius told her about what was going on in her family. She knew Marcus had seen Julia. She also knew he hadn't forgiven her. Iulius told her Marcus had informed Julia he had decided to set the past aside. Phoebe knew why. He didn't want to face it.

She often prayed when he was sitting beside her on the balcony. *What more can I do, Lord? Let the Spirit give me the words. I plead with you with all my heart for my children. I would pour out my life for them, but who better to know that kind of love than you. You poured out your life for them already. O God, if they could but see, if they could but know and fully realize. Oh, if I could only live to see that day. . . .*

"Azar intrigues me," Marcus said, breaking into her prayer. "I'd like to know more about her, but she always seems to turn the conversation to other matters."

"Ju . . . lee . . ."

"Yes. Julia. Azar doesn't leave the bedside until Julia's sleeping. I understand Azar visits with you daily, as well."

Phoebe closed her eyes and opened them in answer.

"I suppose she prays with you."

Again, Phoebe closed and opened her eyes.

"Prayer seems her only pastime," he said with a faint smile. "She sits in the alcove in the peristyle and prays. It's the one Hadassah used to like. She spent the entire night there a few days ago." He paused, then went on. "I upset her."

Restless, he kissed his mother's hand and placed it on her thigh as he rose. The turtledoves took flight. He stood at the wall and looked out at the city. "I may go talk to the physician. I don't seem to get the answers I want from her."

Phoebe made no sound. She had long since realized Hadassah must have good reason for not revealing her identity. Whatever those reasons were must be of God. If it was the Lord's will Marcus know Hadassah was alive, she trusted him to choose his own time for unveiling her.

Iulius came out onto the balcony. "I'm sorry to interrupt, my lord, but you have visitors. Ezra Barjachin and his daughter, Taphatha."

Surprised and delighted, Marcus bent to kiss his mother's cheek. "I'll return later. These are the people I mentioned who took me into their home in Jericho."

She closed her eyes and opened them. If not for them, Marcus would have perished along the road to Jericho. She longed to hear of what they spoke. As Marcus left the room, she looked at Iulius. He seemed able to read her thoughts. "I'll serve them myself," he said with a grin and gestured for Lavinnia to remain with her.

Marcus went down the stairs quickly. He laughed joyfully as he saw his friends. Ezra looked very little changed as he stood in his

robes in the center of the antechamber. The young woman beside
him was another matter.

"Ezra!" Marcus said, clasping the Jew's hand in warm welcome. "It's good to see you!"

"And you, Marcus," Ezra said, clasping his arm.

Marcus' gaze swept the girl standing just behind him. He
moved to her, hands held out. She took them, her own trembling
slightly. "Taphatha, you are even more beautiful than I remember," he said, smiling as he bent to kiss her cheek in greeting.

"You made it safely home, my lord," she said. "We wanted to
make certain."

"I made it without further mishap." He grinned. "Come into
the triclinium. Iulius, have refreshments brought in. No pork, and
bring the best wine."

Marcus watched as Taphatha's gaze swept the elegant room
with its Roman urns, Corinthian glass, and richly covered
couches and marble tables—then finally came back to rest shyly
on him. He had seen that look in other women's eyes and knew
she had not gotten over her infatuation. He felt his pulse quicken
and realized his own attraction to her was strong.

"My home is yours for as long as you remain in Ephesus,"
Marcus said, gesturing for Ezra to take the couch of honor. "Is
your wife with you?"

"Jehosheba died shortly after you left Jericho," Ezra said, making himself comfortable. He put his hand out to Taphatha, and
she took the place beside him.

Marcus gave his condolences, and they spoke briefly of Ezra's
wife. "What brings you to Ephesus?"

"Work of great importance," Ezra said, smiling once again.
"Before I tell you, there are things we must discuss."

"I've missed our debates, my friend. You must stay here with
us. There's plenty of room. You can come and go about your business as you please."

"Did you find God?" Ezra asked bluntly.

Marcus fell silent for a moment, sensing the urgency of the
question. Ezra and Taphatha both looked at him, waiting, and he
knew his answer would determine whether they stayed or went,
whether they trusted him or not.

"You will remember of whom we often spoke on your roof,"
Marcus said.

"Jesus," Ezra said, nodding.

Marcus told of his journey to Nain and of Deborah, who sent him on to the Sea of Galilee where he met Paracletos. He told of running to Capernaum where he found Cornelius waiting for him. "I believed then that Jesus was the Christ and was duly baptized in his name."

"That is good news!" Ezra laughed. "I was not baptized into Christ until I reached the church at Antioch. By then, Taphatha had accepted the Lord as well, and Bartholomew with her."

"Bartholomew?" Marcus said, glancing at her. She lowered her eyes.

"A young man from Jericho," Ezra said. "He often accompanied Taphatha home from the well. He has a heart for God. When I decided we must journey to Antioch and learn more of Jesus from the church there, Bartholomew chose to leave his father and mother and come with us."

"Will I meet this young man of yours?" Marcus said to Taphatha.

"We are not betrothed, my lord," she said too quickly. She blushed.

"My apologies," Marcus said, smiling slightly. "I thought. . . ." He glanced at Ezra.

"Bartholomew didn't want to interfere in any way with our reunion," he commented briefly, then he and Taphatha fell silent.

Marcus looked from father to daughter, his eyes coming to rest on Taphatha's face. She met his eyes shyly, and he saw hers were filled with deep emotion—and uncertainty. "You said you were here on a matter of great importance," Marcus said at last, looking away from Taphatha.

"I was told in Antioch that the apostle Paul wrote a letter to the church here. One of the brethren heard it and said it's a letter of great importance. I've come to hear it read for myself and ask permission to copy it and carry it to the church in Antioch."

"I wouldn't know about such a letter, nor of the church here."

Ezra looked surprised. "You haven't met with other Christians since your return?"

"I haven't had the time nor the inclination. My mother and sister are both in ill health, and I've the responsibilities of my ships and the emporium as well." Iulius poured the wine that had been set before them. He handed Ezra a golden goblet and another to Taphatha. When all were served, he withdrew and oversaw the food brought in.

"I find it strengthens my faith to receive the encouragement of fellow believers," Ezra said. "Our brothers and sisters in Antioch are praying for us during this journey."

They talked as easily as they had on the roof in Jericho. Marcus enjoyed the conversation. Taphatha said little, but her presence was pleasant, for her beauty graced the room. Watching her from time to time, Marcus remembered how he had thought about her a great deal during the first few weeks of leaving Jericho.

A movement caught his eye, and he glanced up to see Azar making her way laboriously down the steps. Quickly he rose from his couch. "There's a woman I would like you both to meet," he said to Ezra and went out into the antechamber. "Lady Azar, I've guests from Palestine. Please join us."

She limped slowly toward the archway into the triclinium where he waited for her. Marcus put his arm out. She hesitated and then put her hand on him for support, entering the room beside him. He made the introductions, hoping during the course of conversation she might reveal something of her past to those of her own country. Ezra Barjachin looked surprised and pleased when Azar greeted him in Aramaic. He spoke to her in the same language, and she answered.

Marcus seated her on the couch nearest him. "I would prefer you speak in Greek," he commanded her quietly before straightening.

"I apologize, my lord. Your friend asked my position in the household, and I told him I attend your sister Julia." She declined Iulius' offer of wine and turned her head toward Taphatha who was watching her with open curiosity.

"You can speak freely," Marcus told them. "Lady Azar is also a Christian." He gave them a lopsided grin. "A better one than I, my friend." He turned to Azar. "Ezra Barjachin and his daughter have come to Ephesus to meet with the church here."

Hadassah nodded wordlessly and sat listening with interest as Ezra told her why he had come to Ephesus.

"If not for Lord Marcus, we would still be in Jericho living under the weight of the Law."

"If not for these two, my bleached bones would be lying in a wadi alongside the road to Jericho." Marcus told how he had been attacked by robbers and left for dead. "Taphatha nursed me back to health."

"It was the Lord who led us to you," Taphatha said softly, "and the Lord who restored your health."

Feeling a dull ache in her heart, Hadassah saw the way the young and beautiful Taphatha looked at Marcus. It was clear that, during the weeks Marcus had been in their house, she had fallen in love with him. Did he love her as well?

Hadassah had never been more aware of her own scars and lameness than at that moment. She couldn't look at Marcus' face, sure she would see the feelings that shone on Taphatha's face mirrored on his own. How could he not have fallen in love with so sweet and beautiful a girl?

Lavinnia came to the archway. "Yes?" Marcus said, annoyed, fairly certain of why she had come.

"Lady Julia has awakened, my lord. She's asked for Lady Azar."

"You will excuse me, my lord?"

"Of course," he said, hiding his displeasure at the interruption. One would think Julia could do without the woman for an hour or two.

Hadassah rose, aware that Ezra, Taphatha, and Marcus all watched her. She felt awkward and embarrassed to draw so much attention. She spoke briefly to Ezra and Taphatha, telling them it was a pleasure meeting them and wishing them success in their venture. When she left the room, she spoke briefly with Lavinnia about bringing a meal up for Julia.

"Her accent is Galilean," Ezra said.

"She's told me very little about herself or her homeland," Marcus said, watching Azar limp toward the steps. "In fact, at times I think she's evasive."

Ezra grew thoughtful. "Perhaps she has cause."

Marcus frowned, wondering what cause she might have.

Taphatha turned from having watched Azar go up the steps. "Why does she veil herself like that?"

"She told me she's badly disfigured. She wasn't known by that name until she came to attend my sister. The people called her Rapha."

"'The healer,'" Ezra translated.

"She objected to the title."

Ezra's brows raised in interest, but the conversation soon returned to his mission.

"I was hungry to read accounts of Jesus when I first arrived in

Antioch," Ezra said. "However, I learned only one apostle wrote a full account of Jesus' life—Levi—and I haven't had the opportunity to read the account for myself because of the scarcity of copies. Luke, the physician who traveled with Paul, has chronicled a history. John Mark, who accompanied Paul on his first missionary journey, set down what he was told."

Ezra sat forward. "It came to me in Antioch that copies must be made of these documents for all the churches. The copies must be accurate, down to every jot and tittle, so that the gospel remains pure. We need the written accounts of eyewitnesses to instruct us."

"Many believers think the Lord will return any day, and there isn't the need to spend such time and money on this mission," Taphatha said.

Ezra appealed to Marcus. "Which is why I believe your gift to me was manna from heaven, Marcus. The gold you left in Jericho has funded this journey and is funding others. If the apostle John will permit me, I will copy Paul's letter in its entirety and take it back to Antioch, where it will be copied again by two other scribes whose work is meticulous. The documents will be carefully scrutinized and compared to assure that not one letter or word is changed. We *must* preserve these eyewitness accounts for future generations."

Taphatha didn't seem to share her father's conviction or zeal. "Jesus was said to promise that this generation would not pass away before he returned."

"Yes," Ezra said, "but the Lord God gave His only begotten Son, that whoever believes in Him should not perish but have everlasting life. By that promise alone, Daughter, we know this generation of believers will *never* pass away."

He turned to Marcus. "God has put in my heart a zeal for his Word, the Word he has given through his apostles to followers of the Way. We must not live for today as the Gentiles do. We must think of tomorrow and of our children and their children. The eyewitness accounts must be copied and preserved."

Marcus saw how Ezra's eyes burned with determination and excitement, and his own blood stirred within him. "Whatever more you need to further your purpose, my friend, I will gladly give."

Ezra nodded. "God prepared you for this day," he said, smiling broadly and relaxing. "If this journey accomplishes what I hope, I want to find other scribes with the same burden upon their hearts and send them to Corinth and Rome. The Corinthian church is said to have received four lengthy letters from Paul. Another scribe could be sent to Rome, where I've heard there's a letter to all the saints that's in the keeping of a husband and wife in whose home the church meets."

Marcus shook his head. "Rome is not a healthy place for a Christian."

"Nor is Ephesus," Ezra said.

"No, it isn't," he said, remembering Hadassah's death. "Ephesus is the center of worship for Artemis and second only to Rome in worshiping the emperor as a god."

"God did not give us a spirit of fear, Marcus. If this work is of the Lord, he will protect us."

Troubled, Marcus looked at Taphatha. If she traveled with her father, she would be in great danger. She seemed far less convinced about this mission than he, but remained obedient.

As Hadassah had been obedient.

Marcus looked back at Ezra and saw the older man considering him carefully. Something was on Ezra's mind, but he was apparently not ready to speak of it now in his daughter's hearing.

Marcus had a feeling he knew what it was.

48

Long hours later, after Ezra and Taphatha had departed for the evening, Marcus went upstairs. As he was walking down the corridor, he heard Azar speaking. He stood outside Julia's door, listening.

"Yes, my lady, but consider the mouse who lives in the wheat field. He has no thought for the future, either. The high stalks of wheat provide food and shelter, and he has no fear of tomorrow. But then the harvest comes and his world is stripped away, and his life with it. Not once did that poor mouse give thought to the owner of that field, nor even acknowledge his existence. Yet the day of harvest came anyway."

"And is coming," Julia said with a weary sigh. "I understand what you're saying, Azar. I am the mouse."

"My lady . . . ," Azar said, her voice full of hope.

"No. Please, listen. It's a good thing to know there will be justice someday. But don't you see? Justice is being served now. Whether I acknowledge God or not doesn't matter, Azar. My fate is fixed."

"No, Julia . . ."

"It's too late for me. Don't speak of the Lord anymore," Julia said bleakly. "It only hurts to hear of him."

"He can remove your pain."

"The pain will stop when I die."

"You needn't die."

"Oh yes. I *need* to die. You don't know the things I've done, Azar. Unforgivable things. Marcus used to tell me everything costs something. He was right."

Marcus shut his eyes, pierced by the utter hopelessness in Julia's voice. He had wanted to punish her—and so he had. Now he heard her anguish, and it echoed inside him. Did he want his sister to die? He had accepted Christ. He was saved. He had hope. What did she have?

What had he left her?

Oh God, forgive me! Even as he prayed, he knew God was there . . . and he knew what he needed to do. Marcus entered the room quietly, unnoticed, but as he came closer, Azar lifted her head. Julia's face was turned away. Azar let go of Julia's hand and took up her walking stick and stood, drawing back for him to take her place. "Please don't go," Julia said, turning her head. Then she saw Marcus.

He took the seat Azar left vacant for him. Julia's eyes were dull and lifeless, utterly resigned to whatever came. He took her hand. "Julia, I was wrong," he said huskily.

Her mouth curved sadly. "No you weren't."

"I said things in anger. . . ."

"You have every right to be angry with me," she said. "But let's not talk of it ever again. I can't talk about it."

He held her hand to his lips. "I'm sorry, little one," he said, full of regret. He felt Azar's hand on his shoulder, squeezing gently, and his eyes filled with tears.

Julia curled her fingers around his. "Do you remember when I had the abortion, the first one in Rome? Calabah said it would be so easy, that once the problem of my pregnancy was over everything would be fine again. It never was." She looked up bleakly at the ceiling. "Sometimes I find myself counting back and thinking how old that child would be today. I wonder if it was a boy or a girl." She blinked back the tears.

She swallowed convulsively and her fingers tightened in Marcus' hand, clinging to him. "I killed my baby. As I killed Caius."

"What?" Marcus said softly, stunned.

"I murdered him. Calabah gave me the poison, and I gave it to him in small doses so his death would seem natural." She looked at her brother with haunted eyes. "But he knew what I was doing at the end. I could tell by the way he looked at me. It didn't bother me until then, Marcus. And then I couldn't stop thinking about it."

She shook her head against her pillows, eyes tormented. "I kept telling myself it was justice. He was unfaithful to me with other women, not once but many times. He was cruel and evil. Do you remember when you came to me and asked if I'd slept with the Greek who owned the horses? I did. I did it to pay his debts. But mostly, I did it to pay Caius back for hurting me. He beat me for it. He would've beaten me to death if . . ." She closed her eyes, remembering how Hadassah had covered her and taken the blows.

Marcus could see the rapid pulse in her throat. Her skin was white and beaded with perspiration. "It's all right, Julia. Go on."

"She covered me." Her eyes welled with tears that spilled over. "She *covered* me," she whispered, amazed, as though she had just remembered the incident that had happened so long ago. Her face convulsed, and she looked away and said very quietly, "Did you know I told Hadassah to put Atretes' baby on the rocks here in Ephesus?"

She turned her head back again and searched his face. "You didn't, did you? I'm full of terrible secrets, aren't I? I loved him so much, and he hated me because I married Primus. I wished I hadn't, but there was nothing I could do. Calabah made such terrible sense, but Atretes wouldn't listen. When he turned from me, I wanted to hurt him, too, and I used my own child to do it. I used my own child. . . ."

Marcus put his hand on her hair. "Hadassah wouldn't have gone through with it."

"She told me my baby was a boy, a perfect baby boy, and I commanded her—"

"She obeyed God above everyone and everything, Julia. You know she did. Your child lives. You can be sure of that."

The tears ran down the sides of Julia's face, into her hair. "Oh, I hope so," she whispered brokenly. "O God, please, I hope so. . . ." She drew in her breath, curling slightly on her side as pain gripped her. She wept softly, inconsolable.

Azar mixed a mandragora into watered wine and held Julia so she could drink it. Julia relaxed slowly as Azar dabbed the perspiration from her forehead and murmured to her, touching her face tenderly. Sighing, Julia turned on her side and held Azar's hand against her cheek.

"She will sleep now," Azar said and began to clean the room.

Marcus could see Azar was exhausted, for as she gathered the clothes, her limp was more pronounced. He took her walking stick from her and set it aside. Before she could protest, he swept her up in his arms. "As you will also," he said and carried her to the sleeping couch against the wall.

As he held her, he caught the subtle scent of her, and his heart began to pound heavily. She was slender and light, and he remembered catching Hadassah up in his arms once in the same manner. As he laid Azar down, he sensed her tension. The veil had shifted slightly, and he saw her scarred throat. Unable to stop himself, he reached out to gently touch her skin, and she stiffened, her hands flying up to press the veils to her face.

Marcus drew back slowly, his heart racing. What was happening to him? "Azar . . . ," he said hoarsely.

"*Go,*" she said, her voice choked with tears. "Go away, please."

Marcus did as she asked, but rather than go to his own bedchambers for the night, he went downstairs again. Throwing a cloak over his shoulders, he went out of the villa.

He had to know about her.

Striding down the street, he headed toward the center of Ephesus. It was late, and crowds of people milled about, gathering on corners and in doorways to laugh and talk. He wove through them and kept going with purposeful strides. When he reached his destination, he pounded on the door with his fist. A servant opened it. "Office hours are—"

Marcus pushed the door open and entered the antechamber. "Tell the physician Marcus Lucianus Valerian is here to see him on a matter of importance."

He paced the antechamber while he waited.

Alexander entered, his expression cold. "Did Rapha send you?"

"I didn't come about my sister," Marcus said and noticed Alexander's eyes narrow. "I've some questions I'd like answered."

Alexander's mouth curved wryly. "Questions about your health?"

"Questions about the woman you sent to take care of my sister."

"I didn't send her, Valerian. In fact, if I could have my way, Rapha would still be here with me!" With that, the physician spun and walked away.

Undaunted, Marcus followed him toward the inner courtyard. Alexander turned to face him, eyes dark with anger. "Rapha is wasting her time on your sister. I told her that when we first saw her. There's nothing she can do unless she can call down another miracle from God."

"*Another* miracle?"

"You don't even know what you have in your house, do you, Valerian?"

"Then tell me."

"It began months ago when we were called to the house of an idol maker whose wife had been in labor two days. When I examined her, I knew the baby would have to be removed or she and the child would die. Rapha said no. She touched the woman's abdomen. The child turned and came out. Just like that." He snapped his fingers at Marcus. He gave a hard laugh. "Your sister called for us because she'd heard of Rapha's reputation. She wanted a miracle, too. She didn't get one."

Marcus' eyes narrowed. "You've a singularly nasty way of speaking about Julia. Surely you've taken care of other women who've lived as freely as she has."

"More than I care to recount."

"And you commend them all to oblivion?"

"Promiscuity has its own rewards."

Marcus' eyes narrowed, and he considered the other man for a moment, then shook his head. "Your dislike of my sister goes far deeper than some generalized distaste for her lifestyle. It's *personal.*"

"I'd never seen your sister before the night Rapha and I were called to her villa. But even on short acquaintance, I found her to be one of the most self-centered women I'd ever met. Frankly, I was more than willing to leave her to her fate."

"But Azar had other ideas."

Alexander was silent for a moment. He wanted to strike Marcus, to call Rashid in to finish what he had tried to do with his treasured knife. But he knew both options were impossible. He was allowing his feelings to get in the way of his better judgment. He forced himself to answer calmly. "She didn't like the fame she was receiving. People were beginning to look upon her as a goddess. She said God is Rapha, not her. That's why she left."

"She could have gone anywhere. She could have left Ephesus all together. Why did she choose to attend my sister?"

"Maybe she took pity on her, Valerian. Why question your good fortune? Your sister had no money. Rapha had more than she wanted."

"What?" Marcus said, stunned.

"Rapha provided for your sister until you returned and moved her into your villa." Alexander saw this information was new to Marcus and wished he had kept silent. "Money means nothing to Rapha. She gives it away as fast as she receives it."

"I don't understand. Why would she help Julia?"

"You're never going to understand, Valerian." He gave a self-deprecating laugh. "I don't know if I ever will." How many people were there in the world who would give up fame and fortune to care for someone who had tried to kill them?

After a moment, Marcus muttered in a troubled voice, "She reminds me of someone I used to know."

Alexander went cold, small prickles of apprehension licking up his spine. He studied Valerian's face.

"I know she comes from the district of Galilee," Marcus said.

Alexander's dread grew. "How do you know that?"

"I recognize the accent. And she's a Christian." He shook his head and glanced at Alexander, then frowned slightly at the look on the young physician's face. The man was afraid! "You know something about her, don't you?"

Someone entered the antechamber. As the sound of footsteps came near the courtyard, Marcus turned slightly and caught a glimpse of a man in long, flowing white robes. The man halted and looked at him with unblinking dark eyes under a red burnoose with a black band.

"*You!*" Marcus said, recognizing him as the man who had attacked him near the Artemision.

Rashid drew his blade.

"Put the knife away, you fool!" Alexander shouted.

"Who is this man, Amandinus?" Marcus demanded. "And what has he to do with you?"

"I am Amraphel Rashid Ched-or-laomer," the Arab said coldly.

Marcus assessed him disdainfully. "I suggest you inform me of the reason you tried to slit me open in front of the Artemision. Then you may *attempt* to do so again." His eyes glittered. "But I warn you, I am not so easily murdered when attacked face-to-face."

"Rashid, don't be a fool!" Alexander said.

A dark, pulsating silence ensued as Rashid measured Marcus. Many young Roman men enjoyed the sport of training for hand-to-hand combat. Valerian was strongly built, and Rashid saw no fear in his eyes.

"You do not respond?" Marcus mocked. He addressed his next words to Alexander who stepped between them. "Who is this man to you, Democedes?"

"A hot-headed fool," Alexander said, angry to be placed in this position. "Put the knife away, Rashid."

Rashid ignored the command. Valerian had recognized him. One word from Valerian and Rashid knew he would be dead. If not for his oath to Rapha, he would kill Valerian right now. "What does this Roman pig want?"

"Answers! Now!" Marcus demanded imperiously. "Who is this man?"

"He's already told you," Alexander said, angered by Valerian's innate arrogance. Perhaps it was bred into Romans to think they could command anyone they chose. He fixed Rashid with a furious glare. "Have you forgotten your oath?"

A muscle ticked by Rashid's right eye. He glared at Marcus a moment longer and then slipped the knife expertly into the scabbard attached to his cloth belt. His hand remained lightly on the hilt.

It was clear to Marcus that he wasn't going to get any answers from Alexander. The physician stood by, looking between the two of them with an air of annoyance. "What have I to do with you, Ched-or-laomer?" Marcus said, directing the question directly to the stony-faced Arab.

Black eyes burning like coals, Rashid stood contemptuous and silent.

Alexander knew one slight movement on either's part and one or both of them would die. "As Rashid is too stubborn to speak his mind, I'll tell you he's given his oath not to raise his hand against you again." Alexander didn't add the conditions upon which Rapha had gained that oath.

Marcus was derisive and unconvinced. His look made it clear he thought Alexander was behind it.

"Think whatever you will, Valerian, but I had nothing to do with his attack on you. Rashid has a mind of his own," he said, glaring at the hard-faced Arab who had placed him in the untenable situation. Valerian had friends in high places. One word to the right ear and he and Rashid and Hadassah would find themselves in the arena. And this time, no one would come out alive.

"As you found it necessary to extract an oath, you know more than you're telling me," Marcus said.

"I know he's blood minded and irrational! But that might be due to the fact that his Roman owner left him for dead on the steps of the Asklepion." Alexander gave a brittle laugh. "It was my ill fate that Rapha chose him from all the rest to take back to the booth where I started my medical practice. We treated him there." He gave Rashid a dark look. "Unfortunately, he lived."

"Not all Romans are contemptible," Marcus retorted.

"Have you ever owned an Arab?" Alexander asked to confuse the matter.

"I've never in my life left a slave to die on the temple steps, nor would I. And to answer your question, no, I have never owned an Arab slave." He gave Rashid a scornful look. "Nor do I ever intend to have one."

Rashid grinned coldly.

"I told you it was a case of mistaken identity," Alexander said to Rashid, hoping the fool would have the good sense to keep up the ruse. "Perhaps now, you'll believe me."

"Should I accept the word of a Roman?" Rashid said.

Marcus stepped closer. "What was the name of this owner of yours?"

"Rashid is a freeman now," Alexander said when it became all too clear Rashid had no intention of gracing Marcus with a response to anything he said.

"By whose authority?" Marcus demanded, not turning his back on Rashid. "Yours, Democedes?"

"By all that is decent and just! Should I save a man and give him back to the ones who very nearly caused his death?"

Marcus was surprised at Democedes' anger. It seemed far too intense, far too passionate. What reason had he for such depth of emotion regarding Romans and their slaves? He studied him, considering his words. "Do you make a habit of rescuing those who were discarded in such a despicable manner?"

Alexander was grateful the subject had moved away from Hadassah, while disturbed that he must now defend his medical practices.

"I needed patients on whom to practice my skills."

"Practice?" Marcus said with distaste.

"Like most physicians, I despise the practice of vivisection," Alexander said angrily. "This seemed my only other alternative for studying human anatomy. If one loses an abandoned slave, no one cares. When I did this, I chose carefully, treating only those I thought I could save. Either that, or challenging cases that gave me opportunity to try to affect a cure."

"How many of these experiments of yours died?"

A muscle jerked in Alexander's cheek. "Too many," he said, "but fewer than would have if I hadn't interceded. Perhaps you're like so many others who don't know what happens beyond your own private little kingdom. Anyone who's observed the practices of the temple can tell you the priests only take in those whose chances of survival are good. They nurse slaves back to health in order to sell them and pocket the money. The rest of the poor souls left on the steps are abandoned by everyone. I've seen a few who suffered with particularly repulsive diseases dispatched by the priests before dawn. That way their bodies can be removed before the crowds come with votive offerings." His mouth curved cynically. "After all, it wouldn't be good for business to have worshipers see so many dying on the steps of a temple honoring a god of good health and healing, would it?"

"Is this how you found Rapha?"

Alexander froze at the question. He thought quickly and saw a way to protect her identity while still telling the truth. "She was the first," he admitted. "I've never since treated anyone so grievously injured. It was by the grace of God she lived at all, Valerian, not by my skills."

"What made you choose her then?"

"She would say it was God. Perhaps it was. I just knew when I saw her that I had to do everything I could to keep her alive. It wasn't easy. She suffered months of pain, and she'll bear the scars of what happened to her for the rest of her life. That's why she's veiled, Valerian. Whenever someone saw her face, they turned away." His mouth curved sardonically. "It's an unfortunate trait of mankind, isn't it? Most people don't see past surface scars to the beauty within." He stared coldly into Marcus' eyes. "And some just want to satisfy their morbid curiosity."

Marcus' eyes flashed. "You think that's all there is to my being here, don't you? That I want my curiosity satisfied?"

"Isn't it? Whatever mystery you think there is, Valerian, it's in your own mind. Rapha's reasons for covering herself are obvious and well founded. Anyone with half an ounce of decency would respect her wishes. It might be good for you to think of her feelings, especially since it's Rapha alone who stands between your sister and the hottest fires of hell!"

Marcus looked between the two men and knew he would learn nothing more here. He strode across the antechamber to the door.

As it slammed, Rashid looked back at Alexander. "Do you think he believed you?"

"Why shouldn't he? I told him the truth."

"Not all of it."

"Enough." His voice was cold, filled with anger. "And far more than he deserved to hear."

49

Marcus looked in on Julia when he returned to the villa. When he saw Azar standing on the balcony in the moonlight, her hands raised to the heavens, a sharp stab of pain struck him. He watched her for a moment, trying to calm his emotions. Shaking his head, he turned his attention away from Azar and approached Julia's bed.

He frowned. Even in sleep, Julia seemed troubled. Perhaps it was because death was so close. He leaned down and lightly brushed some of the tendrils of dark hair from her pale face. Sadness filled him. How was it possible that the sister he had adored had come to this? How was it possible he had thought he didn't love her anymore?

She stirred at his touch but didn't awaken.

Straightening, he went out to Azar who now stood with her hand lightly resting on the wall. "She seems to be sleeping soundly," he said, standing beside her.

Hadassah's heart beat like the wings of a trapped bird. She had hoped Marcus would leave the room after checking on Julia, rather than come out to her. "It's the mandragora, my lord. She won't awaken until morning," she said, looking out over the city because she couldn't bear the heartbreak of looking at him. Whenever she did, she thought of the beautiful young girl who had come with her father to see him.

Her fingers whitened on the wall as she struggled against her turbulent emotions. She was still in love with Marcus. She had known it the first time she had seen Marcus again. She had tried to will herself against it, but her love only grew stronger each day. When she had seen Taphatha looking at him with the eyes of love, she had wanted to flee the pain that swelled within her.

Only later during her prayers had it come to her how cunning Satan could be. Her love for Marcus could become a tool against her, for when her heart and mind were on Marcus, Julia lay forgotten.

Nothing must distract her from her mission here. And no one. She mustn't waste time mourning what might have been with

Marcus or being overcome by sorrow that he might marry another. It was right and natural he marry. God had said it was not good for man to be alone. And Marcus was alone.

So are you, came the insidious thought tapping at the door of her mind. She refused to open herself to it.

O God, help me not to waste a single moment of Julia's time thinking of myself and the things that might have been.

And yet, pain had gripped her heart again as the man she loved came to stand beside her.

"She's close to the end, isn't she?" Marcus said grimly.

"Yes."

"She's set her mind against believing in a Savior, Azar, *any* savior." He knew what that was like. Hadn't he done likewise during all those months he had traveled through Palestine?

"I won't give up on her."

He looked out at the dark, sleeping city. Despite its affluence and grandeur, he sensed it was dying of its own corruption, just as Julia was dying of hers. Yet, he had seen the same hunger in her that he had felt. Why hadn't he recognized it earlier for what it was?

Marcus shut his eyes. How much of Julia's refusal to accept Christ now was due to his own unforgiveness? Sometime during the last weeks she had moved from rebellion and self-defense to self-loathing and acceptance of her fate. But salvation required more than remorse. It required repentance. It required Christ. Julia had to keep moving along the road, but she was so close to the end now, she seemed unable to comprehend any other avenue open to her but the one she had paved for herself. Death.

O God, how much of this is my doing because I wasn't willing to forgive her as you forgave me?

"Oh, my lord," Azar whispered softly. "If only I could make her see."

Her words stilled Marcus' thoughts of himself. He wasn't sure if she was praying or speaking to him. "You've tried, Azar," he said, wanting to comfort her. It was he who hadn't done what God sent him to do.

She bowed her head. "I want Julia to know that death is not a sunset but a sunrise. O God, how do I do that?"

Hearing the tears in her voice, Marcus put his hand over hers. Her head came up, and she withdrew her hand from beneath his. Though she didn't step away, Marcus felt the yawning distance between them. "Why must it be like this?" he said hoarsely, not even sure what he was asking or of whom.

"You must help with Julia," Azar said, her hand clenched against her heart. "You must help me."

"How?"

"Forgive her."

"I have," he said, growing angry in self-defense. "Do you think I want my sister to burn in hell?" And then he looked away, ashamed. Hadn't he? Up until a few hours ago, hadn't that been exactly what he wanted?

"Forgive her again, Marcus. Forgive her again and again, no matter what she's done to hurt you. Do it as many times as it takes for her to believe you mean it. I've said and done all I know, and I haven't reached her. Perhaps God waits upon you to show her the way. Please, Marcus, show her the way."

She started to turn away, but he clasped her wrist. "Why do you love her so much?"

"Does there have to be a reason?"

"Yes."

"Jesus asks us to love one another as he loved us."

"Don't give me a commandment for an answer, Azar. It should be easier for me to love her. She's my sister. Yet, it's been you who has loved her. All the time, it's been you more than anyone else." He felt her tension and wished he could tear away the veils, but Democedes' warning was still fresh in his mind. What of her feelings? What of Julia?

"I can't give you answers when I haven't any myself," she said in a voice softly broken with emotions he knew she wanted concealed. Why? "All I know is that the first time I saw your sister, I loved her as I did my own flesh and blood. There have been moments when I wished God would relent, but he burdened me with love for Julia. And love her I will until God leads me otherwise."

Marcus released her slowly. Turning away from him, she limped back into Julia's bedchamber and sat down on the chair beside the bed. He came and stood behind her. She had given him a glimpse of her own struggle. He put his hands on her shoulders and felt her stiffen.

Always she pulled away from him. Why? And why did he so desperately want it otherwise? Confused, disturbed, he backed away. "Send for me when she awakens," he said and left the room.

Julia wakened only briefly in the morning and then lapsed into a coma.

50

Ezra Barjachin came to speak with Marcus the same afternoon. While they were closeted in the bibliotheca, Alexander Democedes Amandinus arrived at Rapha's request.

"She's been like this all day," Hadassah said. "The mandragora wore off hours ago."

He lifted Julia's eyelids and drew back. "It's unlikely she will come out of it," he said frankly. "It's the final stage before death comes."

"She can't die, Alexander! Not yet. You must help me bring her out of this state."

"That's what I'm trying to tell you. There's nothing we *can* do to bring her out of it. It's *over*. Finished. Everything's been done that can be done. Let her go."

"So she just drifts away like this?"

"Peacefully."

Hadassah sank down on the chair and wept.

Alexander frowned heavily. For whatever crazy reason Hadassah had devoted herself to this selfish, cruel young woman, she had done it wholeheartedly. He found himself wishing that everything had gone as Hadassah had hoped.

Her tears disturbed him. For her sake, Alexander made another closer examination of Julia. She had wasted away to almost skin and bones since he had seen her last. The lesions were worse, spreading the infection throughout her body. For the first time since he had met Julia Valerian, he was moved to pity. Whatever she had been or done, she was a human being.

As he straightened, he saw the tray of untouched food. "If she awakens, don't give her anything solid to eat. Broth or thin gruel only," he said, unaware the tray had been brought up for Hadassah. "But I think it would be wiser not to hope."

He took a small drug box from his case and handed it to her. She turned it in her hand, recognizing the carvings. "I still have some mandragora left," she said, handing it back to him. He took it and clenched it in his hand. With a sigh he dropped it back into his case and set it aside.

"We must talk," he said, putting his hand beneath her arm and drawing her firmly to her feet. When they were out on the balcony, he turned her to face him. "You have done all you can, Hadassah. You have to let her go."

"I can't. Not yet."

"When?"

"When she accepts Christ—"

"If she hasn't to this point, she never will."

"Don't say that!"

Alexander drew her into his arms, cupping the back of her head. "You can't save the world, little one."

She clutched his tunic. "I can't save anyone," she said in defeat, her cheek against his chest. She was so physically tired. She felt overcome and heartsick.

"I've decided to sail to Rome and offer my services to the Roman army," Alexander said unexpectedly.

Stunned, Hadassah drew back.

Alexander wasn't prepared to tell her all his reasons, choosing only those she would easily accept.

"Military doctors have fewer restrictions than I do, and traveling with the legions will expand my knowledge and experience. I'll be able to learn about and collect new herbs. Think of the possibilities, Hadassah. You know the styptic *barbarum* was discovered on the frontier. So was *radix britannica*. It's been successful in countering the effects of scurvy. We need to learn more, and I can't do it here in the comfort of Ephesus."

He gripped her shoulders, and his eyes burned in their intensity. "Your work here is done, Hadassah. I want you to come with me."

Looking at him, seeing his love and concern, she was tempted. A few moments before Alexander's arrival she had overheard Lavinnia telling one of the other maids that Marcus was speaking with Ezra Barjachin. She was even more certain now that Ezra Barjachin had come to offer his daughter in marriage to Marcus. And it would be to Marcus' best interests in finding happiness to agree.

Now that Julia was no longer even conscious of her presence, Hadassah wondered what purpose she served by staying any longer. She wondered why God had brought her here at all.

"Come with me," Alexander said. She wanted to. She wanted to escape the hurt and sense of failure that washed over her now.

What more could she do for Julia? And loving Marcus as she did only brought anguish because nothing would ever come of it. God had plans for him—plans that included a beautiful young Jewish Christian from Jericho, not a woman who was scarred and lame.

"Think of all those you could help," Alexander went on persuasively, encouraged by the uncertainty he saw in Hadassah's eyes. "You've been here for months taking care of one dying woman when you could've helped a dozen or more live during that time. Why stay any longer when it's so clearly hopeless?"

She closed her eyes, trembling as though standing against a dark wind.

"Come with me." He lifted the veil and cupped her face. "Please, Hadassah. Come with me."

Oh God, why can't I say yes? Why do you hold me here? her heart cried. But she knew, no matter what she felt, no matter how much it hurt, she had made her choice long ago.

Her eyes traveled his face, willing him to understand. "I can't leave her, Alexander. Until she breathes her last breath, I must remain with Julia."

Pain flickered across his face. He took his hands from her. "Are you sure it isn't Marcus Valerian that holds you here now?"

She drew the veils down without answering.

Alexander wouldn't let her turn away from him. He took hold of her arms and held her fast. "What would you say if I told you *I* love you? Because I do! Hadassah, I love you! Doesn't that make a difference?"

"I love you, too, Alexander." At her quiet words his spirit soared, only to be crushed in the next second as she continued. "I'll always love you for your kindness to me, for your compassion to countless others, for your hunger to know truth. . . ."

"I wasn't speaking of brotherly love."

She reached up and touched his face tenderly. She said nothing for a long moment, then she smiled sadly. "Oh Alexander, I wish I could give you what you want. But I don't love you the way I love Marcus." The words pierced his heart, and he would have turned away, but she kept her hand on his cheek, urging him to look at her. He did so, meeting her warm eyes. "Nor do you love me the way you do your medicine."

He wanted to deny it, to argue. But he couldn't. He knew she was right. He let his breath out softly and looked away. "You do have a way of cutting to the heart of things."

"Not always," she said, thinking of Julia. Had she known the heart of things, couldn't she have found a way to reach Julia? *O God, except for you, Lord, I feel so alone.*

Alexander decided to tell her the rest. Letting her go, he said, "Marcus Valerian came to call on me last night."

Her heart began to drum. "What did he want?"

"He wanted to know more about you. He's putting the pieces together, Hadassah. Rashid arrived at the wrong moment."

"Marcus saw him?"

"Yes, and there were a few moments when I thought it necessary to remind Rashid of his oath. Marcus will satisfy his curiosity about you one way or another. What he'll do when he finds out who you are, I can't tell you. But don't ever forget these are the same people who threw you to the lions." He slipped his hand beneath the veils to brush her cheek. "You'd be safer with me."

"Even so, I must stay here."

He looked at her, wanting to accept her words and respect her decision. But he couldn't. He kept pressing, using whatever means he could to dissuade her from staying. Had he stopped to ask himself why he was so determined, he would simply have thought it was his concern for her that drove him. . . .

He would never have imagined or believed that there was a deeper, darker purpose at work.

"And if I leave Ephesus?" he said in gentle challenge. "Where will you go when she dies? If I'm no longer here, what will you do?"

She shook her head, unable to think beyond now.

"You need to think, Hadassah. We belong together. Think of what we could learn and what we could do for others. Once Julia's gone, you'll have to leave."

"When will you be leaving?"

"In a few days," he said, lying to her for the first time and having no compunction about it because he thought it was for her own good. "I'll be referring all my patients to Phlegon and Troas." He gave her a wry smile. "Needless to say, they'll both be surprised to hear from me. We don't agree on a lot of things, but they're still the most skilled and knowledgeable physicians in Ephesus. I'd rather entrust patients to them than have them seek help from the priests of the Asklepion."

Hadassah shook her head. "I've done everything I know to do here," she whispered.

Alexander wasn't sure if she spoke to him or to herself, but he sensed her weakening. A force he didn't recognize urged him to grasp the opportunity. "You've done everything known to man. What more can you do but that?"

"Trust in God."

He moved away in frustration. "I'll be leaving as soon as I settle the practice."

"What of Rashid?" she asked.

"He'll stay and watch."

"Take him with you."

He looked at her in surprise. "Even if I wanted him along, he wouldn't go. You know that. And now that Marcus knows Rashid attacked him, his life might be forfeit. You know what they do to a slave who raises his hand against a Roman."

"Then he must go with you."

"He won't go unless you do."

Hadassah was torn; Rashid's situation seemed to overshadow the concerns she had fixed upon Julia.

It was what Alexander had hoped, convinced he was putting her first. "Send word what you decide." He leaned down to kiss her cheek through the veils. "You can do no more here. Let the poor girl rest in peace, Hadassah. Let her go."

Hadassah watched him leave the room, disturbed by what he had said. *Let her go? Let her go to hell?* Out of habit, she went to the Lord. *What am I to do? Show me what is true.*

She knew Alexander had spoken out of sincere concern for her and Rashid. Yet as she prayed, she knew something was not quite right in all he said.

And then it came. She saw clearly what lay behind her sense of unrest, for the Spirit within her revealed it to her. All was not lost. Nothing was too hard for God. Even impending death could not keep him from those who were his own . . . and Julia might still be one of God's own. Were Hadassah to leave now, she would be abandoning Julia when she most needed her.

O Lord God, forgive my doubt, and renew your Spirit within me that I may fulfill your purpose here. Let me not lean upon my own understanding or Alexander's.

As she rose, she knew Alexander had not recognized the unseen forces at work in what he had just tried to do. He had not recognized the seed of the tare, nor the dark, malevolent enemy who had given him the words to sow and thus weaken her.

It might have worked. Might well have done so. But for the grace of God . . . awed, grateful, Hadassah once again took her place beside Julia's bed, praising God for his protection.

Lavinnia came in with a tray of food at dusk. She looked at the untouched food she had brought at midday and glanced at Azar. "Was the meal not to your liking, my lady?"

"I'm sure the food is wonderful, Lavinnia, but please take the trays away. I will send for something when I'm ready." The girl did as she asked, knowing from her words that Lady Azar would fast and pray until the end came. Lavinnia returned and took the second tray. "May I bring you wine, my lady?"

"A bowl of cool water from the fountain would be nice."

Lavinnia came back quickly with what Hadassah wanted. "Thank you, Lavinnia." She dipped a fresh cloth in the water and wrung it out. She washed Julia's face gently. Julia didn't awaken.

Marcus came during the next afternoon. Hadassah rose, making way for him as he sat down beside the bed. He seemed preoccupied, and Hadassah wondered if he was thinking over whatever it was that Ezra Barjachin had come to discuss with him. He took his sister's limp hand between his and watched her face. When he spoke, Hadassah knew he addressed her.

"Iulius says Mother refuses to eat. She sits on the balcony with her eyes closed. He says he doesn't know if she's fasting and praying or simply drifting away." He bowed his head. "My God," he said in a voice husky with pain, "am I going to lose both of them at the same time?"

Hadassah's eyes filled with tears, for his face was lined with weariness and grief. She ached for him. "We must not give up hope, my lord." She meant the words sincerely, but they sounded hollow in the quiet room with Julia's still form on the bed.

"Hope," Marcus said bleakly. "I thought I'd found hope, but I don't know anymore." He leaned forward and combed his fingers lightly through the dark hair that lay against the pillow. He stood slowly and leaned down, kissing Julia's forehead. "Send for me if there's any change."

Hadassah took his place at Julia's side.

THE
GOLDEN VESSEL

51

Marcus entered the room as morning light crept over the wall. Hadassah glanced at him and saw how pale and strained his face looked. She rose from the seat beside Julia's bed so that he could sit beside his sister.

"No change?" he said.

"No, my lord."

"It's been three days," he said grimly. "Please speak with my mother, Azar. She still won't eat anything, and she was awake most of the night. I'm worried about her. She's not strong enough to fast."

"I will pray with her, my lord." She would do no more than that, for if Phoebe felt God called her to fast and pray, so be it, whatever came. Marcus sat down wearily. She felt his distress and put her hand on his shoulder, pressing lightly. "Trust in the Lord, Marcus. We're all in his hands, and he's assured us all things will work to his good purpose."

"I haven't your faith, Azar."

"You've faith enough."

As he started to reach up and cover her hand, she withdrew. He watched her limp toward the door and go out. Depressed, he rested his elbows on the edge of the bed. Raking his fingers through his hair, he held his head.

"Jesus . . . ," he said, but no other words came. "Jesus . . ." He was too tired and despondent to pray or even think. In the three days since Julia had fallen asleep his mother seemed to be fading away as well. He was going to lose both of them, and he had to resign himself to it.

Jesus . . . , his heart cried yet again.

A gentle wind came in from the balcony and, like a whisper of kindness, brushed Julia's brow. She drew in a soft breath of it and exhaled, turning her head toward it. Opening her eyes, she saw Marcus sitting beside her bed with his head in his hands. His posture was so utterly dejected, she reached out weakly and brushed her fingertips against him, wanting to give comfort. Marcus started slightly and raised his head. "Julia," he said hoarsely, staring at her.

"I'm glad you came back," she said softly. He grasped her hand and held it tightly, kissing it. Tears filled her eyes so she could hardly see his face. He did love her after all. Oh, God, he did love her!

A breeze brushed her face, oddly comforting. She felt so weak and light, as though that soft wind could lift her and carry her away like an autumn leaf. But she wasn't ready. She was afraid where it would carry her. An oppressive darkness seemed to be closing in around her, and the heaviness within her heart had not eased, even for a moment.

"I'm so sorry for everything, Marcus," she whispered.

"I know. I forgive you, Julia. Everything is forgotten."

"Oh, if it were only that easy."

"It is, little one. Listen to me, Julia. I've been such a fool, and I've so much to tell you." And there was so little time left. "Do you remember how Hadassah used to tell you stories? I want to tell you a story, *my* story." And thus he began, starting with the days in Rome when three emperors had reigned in a year, and half of his friends had been killed. He spoke of his lust for women, of endless banquets, of drinking, of the games—all of which he had used to sate the hunger within him. He'd lived by the adage "Eat, drink, and be merry, for tomorrow we die." Yet nothing had satisfied, nothing had filled the empty aching place inside him.

Then Hadassah had come into their lives, roped among other survivors of the holocaust in Jerusalem. "Mother bought her and gave her to you. There was something different about her from the beginning. Despite everything she'd endured, there was a peace about her. I'd find her at night in the moonlit garden praying to God. For you. For me. For all of us." He sighed, pressing his sister's hand between his.

"You weren't the only one who mocked her."

Hadassah limped along the upper corridor from Phoebe's chambers. As she neared Julia's open door, she heard Marcus speaking indistinctly. She entered quietly, her heart leaping as she saw Julia's open eyes. She was listening intently to Marcus, who was telling her about the desolation of Jerusalem and an old man who stood crying beside the last remaining remnant of the temple wall.

Marcus glanced up as Azar came into the room. Then he went on, telling his sister of being attacked by robbers on the road to Jericho. He told how Ezra Barjachin and his daughter Taphatha had saved his life. "I told him what Hadassah had told me about the Lord and saw him change, Julia."

Hadassah heard the deepening emotion in his voice as he told his sister of following the road to the village of Nain. Her hand whitened on her walking stick.

"I found the house where Hadassah lived, and I moved in. I'd wander over the hillsides, then buy wine and drink myself into oblivion. The people must have thought I was mad. They left me alone. No one dared question a Roman. All except one old woman who pestered me constantly." He gave a hoarse laugh. "Deborah."

Hadassah sat down heavily on the other side of Julia's bed. Without looking away from Marcus, Julia's hand searched for and found hers. Hadassah looked at Marcus through her veil . . . and her tears.

Marcus went on, telling how Deborah had taken him out on the hillside and sent him down to the Sea of Galilee, where he met Paracletos, and then, in Capernaum, Cornelius.

"I have never known a feeling like I had that day, Julia," he said. *"Freedom.* Joy beyond all understanding. It was as though I'd been dead my whole life and was suddenly alive." He put his hand lightly on her forehead. "You can feel that way, too."

"You didn't do what I did," Julia said sadly. "You never sinned the way I sinned."

Hadassah pressed her hand gently. "We all sin, Julia, and no sin is greater than any other. God sees all sin the same. That's why he sent Jesus to atone for us. For each of us."

Julia blinked back tears and looked up at the ceiling. "Neither of you can understand. You're good. I'm bad."

"Julia," Hadassah said. *O God, open her ears so that she can hear with her heart!* "Do you remember the Samaritan woman at the well? Do you remember Mary of Magdala? The Samaritan woman was the first to know Jesus was the Messiah, Mary the first to know he had risen from the grave."

"Azar doesn't understand," Julia said to her brother. "She doesn't know. Oh, Marcus, I know you never wanted me to speak of her again, but I can't help it. I can't stop thinking of it. I can't. . . ."

"Then say what you must."

She looked up at the ceiling again, feeling wretched and lost. "She was my best friend," she whispered, mouth trembling as she confessed the sin that weighed heaviest on her heart. "She loved me and I sent her to the arena to die because I was jealous. I might as well have killed love itself when I killed Hadassah."

Azar drew back as though stunned. Marcus glanced at her, sensing her turmoil.

Julia blinked back tears as she looked at her brother. "Marcus, you loved her. I heard you ask her to marry you. I told you at the arena I had her killed because she refused you, but it was more than that. I killed Hadassah because she was everything I wasn't. She was faithful. She was kind. She was *pure*. No matter how I treated her, or how Calabah and Primus treated her, she never changed."

Julia fumbled for Marcus' hand and clutched it tightly. "It cost her to say no to you, Marcus. I know you didn't think so. You were so angry you didn't even see me when you left. But it did. I looked in my room, and she was on her knees crying. I didn't want to tell you."

Marcus bent his head.

Julia cried, too, remembering. "May her God forgive me. I sat cheering when she died, and when it was over and she was dead and you were gone, I just screamed and screamed. I kept hearing the roar of those lions and I could see her lying dead on the sand. I knew what I'd done. I knew. Oh, God, I *know*. And Calabah and Primus mocked me for it."

She shook with weeping. "I can't be forgiven! How do you ask forgiveness of someone you murdered? Hadassah's dead. Oh, she's gone and it's my fault. My fault."

Anguished, Marcus looked at Azar. "Give her a drink of mandragora," he said, not knowing any other way to comfort his sister or be spared more pain himself.

Hadassah was trembling violently. "Leave me alone with her, my lord."

"Curse you, give her *something!*"

"Please," she said, her gentle voice instilled with urgency and command. "Do as I ask."

"Don't leave me," Julia wept when he let go of her hand and rose. "I'm afraid."

"*Go!*"

Marcus left, as much to escape the grief as to do as Azar said. He went out and gripped the railing across from Julia's chamber trying to regain control of his emotions. How much of this was his own fault?

Dear God, how much death had to come from his blindness?

Hadassah sat on the edge of the bed. "You must be calm now, my lady," she said, stroking Julia's brow. "I'll call Marcus back in a moment, but I must talk to you alone."

Her heart beat fast as she laid Julia's hand down. "I forgive you, Julia." She saw the slight frown flicker across Julia's brow. "I forgive you," she said again as she lifted her veils.

At first Julia stared at her without recognition, seeing only the terrible, disfiguring scars. Then she looked into Azar's eyes, and her own widened until they dominated her white face. Drawing in her breath, she strained back.

Hadassah had lived with fear herself and knew the power it had over people. "Don't be afraid of me, Julia. I'm not a ghost," she said. "I am alive and I love you."

Julia's breathing was rapid. "You're dead. I saw the lion. I saw your blood."

"I was badly injured. God spoke to Alexander, and he claimed me at the Door of Death so that I might live." She put her hand lightly over Julia's. "I love you."

"Oh . . . ," Julia said and with trembling fingers, reached up and touched Hadassah's face. "I'm sorry. Oh, Hadassah, I'm so sorry." She wept again. "I'm sorry. I'm sorry."

"Oh, Julia, you needn't be sorry anymore," Hadassah's voice was clear, though it trembled with emotion. "I forgave you everything before I ever walked into the arena. I blessed your name because it was through you, through being sent to the arena, that God freed me from *my* fear." She told Julia of her fear of Jerusalem and persecution should anyone discover she was a Christian. She told her of her struggle to bring the Good News to Julia and her family while being afraid to let anyone know of her faith in Jesus.

"And then I beat you," Julia said, ashamed. "I called you names and reviled you." How could Hadassah still say she loved her? How could she?

Hadassah took Julia's hand and kissed her palm. "Think no more of it. We've other matters more important now. You must make your choice. I've always prayed for you. I have pleaded with God that he would open your eyes and heart. Do you believe in Jesus?"

"Oh, Hadassah," Julia said, feeling the weight of her burdens being lifted. "How can I deny he exists when only he could have saved you from death?" She touched her cheek and lips. "I'm so glad. I'm so glad your Jesus loved you so much he couldn't let you die."

Tears filled Hadassah's eyes. "Not *my* Jesus, Julia. *Our* Jesus. Don't you see? God didn't spare my life for *me*. He spared my life for *you*."

Julia blinked, amazed and, for the first time she could remember, hope swept over her.

Hadassah touched the ill woman's pale cheek. "Why else would God have done such a miracle? What other purpose could there be? Why else would he send me here for you?"

Julia's face was transfixed. "Despite it all?"

Hadassah laughed softly in joy. "Oh yes! That's the almighty God he is." She took Julia's hand firmly between hers. "Despite ourselves, he loves us! You've confessed your sins, Julia. Will you confess your faith in him? He's knocked at the door of your heart all your life. Let him in, beloved. Please, Julia. Let him in."

"How can I not?" Julia said, holding tightly to Hadassah's hand and seeing the love shining in her eyes. "O God, O Jesus, please." Even as she uttered the words, it was as though something rushed into her very being, filling her, lifting her, overwhelming her. She felt lighter. She felt free. And she felt weak, so very weak. Her hand loosened. "So easy," she said with a sigh.

Hadassah stroked her cheek and smiled. "Awake, you who sleep, and arise from the dead, and Christ will give you light."

Julia held Hadassah's hand against her heart. "It shouldn't be so easy."

"Jesus did all the work."

"She must be baptized," a voice said from behind her, and Hadassah stiffened slightly, her heart jumping. Marcus! She let go of Julia's hand and covered her face quickly with the veils.

"Yes," she said shakily and rose, pain shooting up her bad leg. Grasping her walking stick, she stepped back from the bed. Had he seen her face? She couldn't bear it if he had.

"Hadassah's *alive*," Julia said, smiling radiantly up at Marcus as he leaned down to her.

He had never seen her eyes shine as they did now. "I know, Julia. I heard." He couldn't look at Hadassah, for he knew if he did, he would forget everything and want to know why she had hidden herself from him. His heart pounded wildly and his throat was suddenly dry. Joy and rage churned within him, and one word screamed in his mind: *Why?*

Why hadn't she revealed herself to him? Why hadn't she told him she was alive? Why had she left him in his despair?

But now was not the time to get the answers he so desperately wanted. Now was the time to concentrate on Julia. One glance at Hadassah and Marcus knew he would forget Julia in her desperate need—and so he didn't glance at her or speak to her. He simply lifted his sister gently, cradling her against his heart. Julia was so light she was like a child in his arms.

Julia stretched out her hand toward Hadassah. "Come with me."

"I'll follow," Hadassah assured her, unable to look into Marcus' face. He hesitated at the door and glanced back at her. "Don't wait for me, my lord," she said. "Go. Go now."

Marcus carried Julia along the upper corridor and down the stairs. He crossed the peristyle, which was filled with sunlight, and went down another corridor that led through more archways to the family baths. Without removing his sandals, he went down the marble steps. The cool water rose around his legs and hips, dampening Julia's thin gown.

"God forgive me if I overstep myself in doing this," Marcus said aloud, "but there's none other here." He lifted Julia slightly as he bent his head and kissed her. Then he lowered his sister into the water, immersing her. "I baptize you in the name of the Father and the Son and the Holy Spirit," he said, raising her up. Water streamed from her face and hair and body. "You have been buried with Christ and raised again in the newness of life."

"Oh Marcus," Julia said softly in wonder. Her eyes seemed to look past him, their focus on something he could not see.

Marcus pushed back through the water until he reached the steps. He walked up them and sat down on the edge of the pool, his sister cradled in his lap.

He heard Hadassah's steps and glanced up as she entered the bath chamber. His heart beat heavily. She hesitated and then continued toward him, her walking stick tapping the marble tiles. "It is done," he said hoarsely, and his voice echoed softly off the muraled walls.

"Praise the Lord," she said with a soft sigh of relief.

Suddenly Julia's breathing changed. It became more rapid, as though she was excited by something. Her eyes opened wide. "Oh! Can you see them?"

"See what, little one?" Marcus said, holding her closer, his hand lightly cupping her damp face.

"They're so beautiful," she murmured, her face filled with awe. "So beautiful." She blinked sleepily. "Oh, Marcus, they're singing. . . ." Her face softened and became beautiful again. She gave a long, deep sigh and closed her eyes. Her body relaxed completely in Marcus' arms, her head resting against his shoulder.

"All is well," Hadassah said, bowing her head in thanksgiving. She pressed her hand against her heart and closed her eyes. "She is home."

"Thank God," said a familiar voice that trembled with emotion.

Marcus glanced up sharply and saw the woman standing in the archway, Iulius just behind her.

"*Mother!*"

52

Phoebe came forward without assistance. "I knew the moment she accepted Christ," she said, looking at her daughter's face—a sweet, beautiful child, sleeping. "Feeling and strength returned to my body."

Marcus lifted Julia and stepped out of the water, carrying her to his mother. Tears streamed down Phoebe's cheeks, but she was smiling, her eyes shining. "Oh, how I prayed I would see this day," she said and kissed Julia's brow. "And I have. I have. . . ." She began to weep. "Oh, my child . . . my child . . ."

Iulius drew close to comfort her. He put his arm around her waist, and she turned toward him. Hadassah watched them leave the room with Marcus, who still cradled Julia close to his heart. After a moment, Hadassah limped to a carved marble bench against the wall and sat down. She was tired after her long vigil. She leaned her head back against the cool stone. She wanted to dance and leap and sing praises, but for now she was content to rest.

Lavinnia entered the bath chamber. "My lady? Are you all right?"

"Just tired, Lavinnia. All is well. I'm fine."

"Will you eat now, my lady? It's been three days since you've touched food."

Hadassah would have preferred her bed to food, but she saw the girl's deep concern and rose, bracing herself with her walking stick. "The time for fasting is over."

Lavinnia smiled brightly. "I will tell the cook."

"Speak with Iulius first, Lavinnia. Lady Phoebe will be hungry as well."

"Yes, my lady," she said, bowing in respect and then leaving quickly.

Hadassah wished she could leave the villa and avoid seeing Marcus again, but she was a slave again, belonging to this household. She was no longer free to come and go as Azar or Rapha had been.

She rose and limped down the corridor and entered the peristyle. Her leg ached, and she sat in the small alcove to rest and try to think. The morning sun warmed the courtyard and she had always liked the soothing sound of the fountain. She saw Lavinnia and another servant carrying trays up the stairs. The house was quiet, a peaceful quiet unlike that of the past weeks. The shadows were gone, the darkness lifted.

She remembered something her father had said long ago: The last shall be first, and the first last. Julia was with the Lord while she had to wait. She closed her eyes in thanksgiving.

God is merciful. Julia's redemption was proof of that, and Hadassah felt that her purpose here was now fulfilled, her work finished.

If only she could die right now and be with the Lord as well. She was tired, her body hurt, and her heart ached.

What do I do now, Lord? Where do I go from here?

She heard firm footsteps on the upper corridor and wanted to rise and run away. Her heart beat wildly and then calmed again as she saw it was Iulius, not Marcus, who came down the steps and crossed the peristyle to her.

"Lady Phoebe wishes you to join her."

Hadassah rose and followed.

Iulius glanced back at her as he reached the steps. Every step she took bespoke her weariness. "I will carry you," he said. As he lifted her, he heard her soft catch of pain.

Phoebe was sitting in the thronelike chair on her balcony. The couch used by friends who had come to visit was near her, a table set between was laden with food and wine. Iulius lowered Hadassah to her feet and left.

Phoebe smiled up at her. "Please sit down, Hadassah. You look far beyond exhaustion."

Hadassah sat, back straight, head slightly bowed, hands folded loosely in her lap. She felt light-headed from her fast and clenched her teeth against the pain shooting up her thigh into her hip.

"You have been a good and faithful servant," Phoebe said. She smiled, her eyes glowing with warmth. "Long ago, in Rome, I entrusted my daughter to you. I asked you to watch over and care for her. I asked that you stand by her in all circumstances. You have done more than that, Hadassah. Despite everything Julia did to you and to herself, you remained her friend." Her eyes welled with tears. "I thank God for bringing you into our lives and shall continue to do so every day until I leave this earth."

Hadassah lowered her head, overwhelmed by such praise and promise. "It was the Lord, my lady, not I." *Ah yes. You, Lord.*

"I would ask one more thing of you, Hadassah, but know it is not my place to do so," she said tremulously. "It is just as you encouraged me months ago when you came here with the physician. I have learned to trust in the Lord in all things." Whatever God willed for Marcus would come to be. It wasn't for a mother to interfere with God's plan by attempting to arrange things in her own strength. She could only do what she knew should have been done long ago and then pray for that which her heart desired. She could hope.

"As you have given to us, so I give to you," Phoebe said and held out a small scroll. Hadassah took it with trembling fingers.

"A document of manumission, Hadassah. You are free. You may stay or you may go, as you wish."

Hadassah couldn't speak. Emotion filled her, but it was not elation. Rather, she was overwhelmed with sadness. Perhaps this, then, was God's answer. She was free to leave the Valerians, free to go back to Alexander and travel with him, free to study herbs and cures on the frontier.

Phoebe saw how Hadassah sat, head down, her small hand clutching the document in her lap. Her heart sank. "It is my hope you will stay," she said softly, "but I know whatever you do, you will do according to the will of God."

"Thank you, my lady."

"You must be as hungry as I," Phoebe said briskly, blinking back tears. She broke bread and handed half to her.

Hadassah dipped the bread in the wine Phoebe poured for her. She held the veils out slightly so she could eat without revealing her face.

They dined in companionable silence.

"Marcus would join us, but he's decided to make all the arrangements for Julia's burial himself," Phoebe said.

"I will prepare her body, my lady."

"No need, my dear. It's already being done. Iulius and Lavinnia are seeing to it," Phoebe said. "You must rest. Your work is done, Hadassah. Julia is with the Lord." She held her hand out slightly. "Please, be at ease here with me. Stretch out upon the couch as you would if you were visiting a friend. I consider you one." *And even more so,* Phoebe's heart said. *I consider you my daughter.* "It would please me if you stayed awhile." *O Lord, let her remain forever.*

Hadassah obeyed and reclined, releasing her breath in relief as the strain left her bad leg. Replete, she fought sleep and tried to listen to Phoebe speak of Julia as a child. Her eyes felt heavy.

"It has been a long, hard time," Phoebe said. She rose and pinched off pieces of bread to put on the wall for the turtledoves. A small bird lighted a few feet away and hopped closer. It had the plain plumage of a female sparrow. Charmed, Phoebe held out her hand, but the bird took flight, perching on the flowering vine some distance away.

Phoebe wondered if Hadassah would do the same thing—take flight. She glanced back at the young woman lying on the couch. She was so still and relaxed, Phoebe knew she was asleep. She smiled and came to her, bending down to kiss her brow through the veils. *I have given up one daughter to you, Father. I pray you will let this one remain.*

Hearing Marcus' footsteps, she straightened. As he entered the room, she saw his face and intent and raised her hand quickly to her lips for silence, then joined him beneath the arch. She took his arm, turning him back into the bedchamber.

"I want to speak with her."

"Let her sleep for now, Marcus."

"I can't wait!"

"She is past endurance. Lavinnia said she's fasted since Julia fell into a coma, and you know very well how many hours she has sat at Julia's side."

"I will speak to her."

"Later. Not now when you're tired and angry."

He let out his breath, seeing sense in what she said. "Why didn't she tell me, Mother?" he said, deeply hurt. "She's been here for months. I've sat with her in the alcove. She had every opportunity to tell me who she was. Why did she keep silent?"

"She must've felt the need to hide herself from you or she wouldn't have done so."

"Did she think I was a threat?"

"How could she?"

"That Arab servant of hers thought I was. She must think I had some part in sending her to the lions. The plain truth is she didn't trust me."

"Had she reason?"

"I asked her to marry me!"

"And left her in anger when she refused," Phoebe reminded him gently.

"I'm not the shallow boy I once was."

"Then cease acting like one, Marcus," Phoebe said more firmly. "Put her needs before your own."

Marcus raked his hand back through his hair and turned away in frustration. He thought of the look of cold contempt on Rashid's face. He remembered Alexander's every word about the months she had suffered because of wounds caused by her master. Both had been convinced that he was part of what had happened to her. Where else would they have gotten such an impression but from Hadassah? "She must think I wanted her dead as much as Julia did."

"Perhaps it's something less complicated than that. Something far too human."

"What?"

"I don't know, Marcus. It was just a thought." She saw the strain of emotion he was under. "Do you remember when Hadassah first came to us? She was a pathetic, skinny little thing with eyes too big for her face and her hair growing back in tatters. You said she was ugly, and your father and Julia shared the same opinion. I didn't know what it was about her then that made me so sure she was right for Julia. I just knew. Now I know God works in our lives even before we believe. He sets his plan in motion and fulfills it in his time."

She approached her son and put a comforting hand on his arm. "I believed her about Jesus, Marcus. Your father believed at the end. You went to curse God for taking her life and returned praising him. And Julia, our rebellious, beloved Julia, stubborn to the last moment, is now with the Lord. Each one of us has come to know Christ because we saw him at work in Hadassah's life. She was God's gift to us."

"I know that, Mother." Even when he had thought she was dead, Hadassah had been the very air he breathed. "I love her," he said hoarsely.

"So do I." Her hand tightened on his arm. "Because we love her, we will treat her with the same care and sensitivity she has always shown us." She hesitated, knowing what she had to tell him would come as a surprise. "I've granted her freedom."

Marcus turned abruptly. "In writing?" he said in alarm.

"Of course."

He glanced at Hadassah and saw the small scroll that had fallen onto the marble tiles. "You had no right, Mother!" he said, angry again, afraid.

"You don't want her to be free?"

"Not yet."

Phoebe saw clearly. "Ah, I see. She's not to be free until she's answered your questions and agreed to whatever demands you might make of her."

"You think me so callous?"

"At times, you are very callous," she said sadly. "I'm sorry if this upsets you. I simply did what I felt led to do, Marcus."

"That document isn't worth the parchment on which it's written," he said in a tone he had often used in business dealings. "Not unless *my* signature is on it. Legally, Hadassah is my property, not yours."

Phoebe had nursed him at her breast and was not daunted. "Your father gave Hadassah to me, and I gave her to Julia. Upon Julia's passing on to the Lord, I felt justified in believing Hadassah mine again. And I have given her the freedom she deserves. Would you rescind that now? What of her feelings?"

"What if she leaves?"

Phoebe smiled in complete understanding and touched his cheek lightly. "You have two legs, Marcus. There's nothing to stop you from going after her."

53

Hadassah awakened in the moonlight, still lying comfortably on Phoebe Valerian's couch. The air was coolly refreshing, the sky a dark indigo blue with sparkling starlight. "The heavens declare your glory and the skies proclaim the work of your hands . . . ," she whispered as she looked up. She lifted her veils and smiled, gazing up at the beauty of it in wonder, watching the blue lighten. Dawn was coming.

She rose and held her hands up to the Lord in thanksgiving for Julia and Phoebe, both restored. Then she drew the veils down over her face again. Quietly entering the bedchamber, she saw a small brass oil lamp burning on a table. Phoebe was asleep.

Hadassah left the room. She limped along the upper corridor and entered Julia's chamber. Julia's bed had been removed and the room scrubbed clean. Except for her own bed, which remained by the wall, the few possessions she had brought with her, and a table on which was a basin and pitcher of water, the room was empty.

Feeling rumpled, Hadassah removed her veils and dark palus. She poured water into a basin and washed, then chose a blue palus to wear, covering her face with the matching veils. She went out onto the balcony to watch the sunrise.

"Your work is done," Phoebe had said, and Hadassah knew she had no reason to stay. Yet her heart broke at the very thought of leaving. And staying would be worse, infinitely worse.

"She's ugly," Marcus had said so long ago in the garden of the Rome villa. It was the first time she had seen him, the first words she had heard him utter. *"She's ugly."* If he had thought her ugly then, what would he think now, scarred as she was, mauled and torn by a lion of Rome?

What would others think if they were to see someone like her standing beside Marcus Lucianus Valerian?

Bowing her head, she struggled with her feelings. If she didn't do what she knew she must, she would waver, and worse heartache would happen. Turning away, Hadassah went through the archway into Julia's room. Without stopping, she passed through to the corridor above the peristyle. She went down the steps and out the front door.

It was a long distance to Alexander, but she needed time to settle her mind and put all those things that might have been with Marcus behind her. Her father had often said to commit her work to the Lord. She was trying hard to do just that.

A man she didn't know answered her knock. "May I speak with Alexander Democedes Amandinus, please?"

The door was drawn back abruptly, and she saw Rashid. "My lady!" he said and shouted for Alexander. "Rapha has returned, my lord!" He caught her up in his arms.

Alexander came running. "You walked all the way?" he said, taking her from Rashid's arms and striding into the courtyard, where he placed her on a comfortable couch. "Why didn't you send word to me or come by litter?"

"I didn't think of it," she said dully, her head against his shoulder. "I just wanted to get away as quickly as possible."

"You see that I was right," Rashid said darkly, glaring at Alexander.

"Bring her some wine," Alexander said. "We'll talk of what is to be done later."

"Who was the man who answered the door?" Hadassah said.

"Someone I picked up on the temple steps a few weeks ago," Alexander smiled, sweeping the veils from her face so he could see if she was all right. His smile dimmed. "You've been crying."

She put her hand on his arm. "It's all right now. It's finished, Alexander," she said, eyes alight. "Julia has passed on. She accepted Christ at the end."

He smiled wryly. "I will be glad if you are glad."

"I am. She is with the Lord."

Rashid handed her a goblet. "She has received justice. She is dead, and there it ends."

Hadassah glanced up at him.

"A woman who ate and drank her fill of blood and lived a life of depravity will not receive reward," he said with certainty.

"She repented."

"A convenient repentance at the end does not alter her fate."

"Not convenient, Rashid, heartfelt."

"And you think that makes a difference to God who takes vengeance?" he said coldly, eyes black and glittering. "Has he not done it before? As long as they obeyed, God blessed them. Sons of Abraham." His mouth twisted. "Look to Zion. Jerusalem was crushed for its iniquity. It is no more. Just as the Valerian is no more."

Hadassah looked at him and saw what he was: a child of wrath. "She repented, Rashid. She proclaimed her faith in Christ. She is saved."

"And so, despite everything she did to you and others, she receives eternal reward? A few words uttered with her dying breath and she inherits heaven with such as you?"

"Yes," she said simply.

"I think not. God is a God of *justice.*"

"Oh, Rashid, if God were only just, we would all perish, down to the last human being on the face of the earth. Don't you see? Have you not murdered in your heart? I have denied him when he gave me opportunities to proclaim him to others, and I let fear reign. Thanks be to God, he is *merciful.*"

Rejecting the Good News, the Arab turned away.

"You are back," Alexander said into the silence and put his hand over hers. "That's all that's important."

Just then, Andronicus entered. "Marcus Lucianus Valerian is here, my lord. He's asking to see Lady Hadassah."

Uttering a soft gasp, Hadassah covered her face with the veils.

Alexander rose and stood in front of her. "Tell him to go to Hades."

"Tell me yourself," Marcus said, striding into the courtyard. He saw Hadassah rising from the couch. He paused, then spoke quietly. "You left without word."

Rashid's hand went to the hilt of his knife, drawing it with a smooth ease of long practice as he moved to stand in Marcus' path. "And you think to take her back?"

"By rights, she still belongs to my family." Marcus' words were more harsh than he had intended.

"My lord, your mother granted me freedom."

"Where is the document to prove it?"

Alexander and Rashid both looked at her. She shook her head. "I don't know," she stammered. "I guess I lost it."

"Lost it?" Alexander said, astounded. "How could you lose something so important?"

Marcus produced the small scroll from his belt. "She left it lying on the balcony." He held it out to Hadassah.

Surprised, Rashid stared at the Roman for a beat, as though

debating with himself, then, slowly, he stood aside and allowed Marcus to face Hadassah. Alexander was struck by the tender look in Valerian's eyes.

He is in love with her! he thought, stunned by the realization. *And he doesn't care who sees it.*

"You left without saying good-bye," Marcus said, his voice soft again. "To Lavinnia or Iulius. Or even to Mother."

"I'm sorry." She could hardly breathe past the racing of her heart.

"Were you running from me?"

She lowered her head, unable to look at him.

"Mother tried to tell me you were alive, but I didn't understand."

"I thought it best you didn't know."

"Why, Hadassah?" His voice broke. "Did you think I had anything to do with what happened? Did you think I knew Julia sent you to the arena?"

Too filled with confusing emotions, Hadassah shook her head, silent. Love for him washed over her at the desperate sadness in his voice—but loving him made staying so much more difficult.

"I swear to you I didn't know you'd been sent to the arena. As God is my witness, I didn't know until I was sitting in the stands with Julia and—" He broke off, his face convulsing at the memory.

Alexander glanced at Rashid.

"When I saw you, there was nothing I could do," Marcus rasped. "I'd been sitting with Julia for hours, drinking wine, laughing at Primus' crude jokes, pretending to enjoy myself because I wanted to forget you." He gave a harsh, self-deprecating laugh. "Then the Christians were being brought out to face the lions." He drew a ragged breath, seeing himself as he had been, ashamed.

"I'd watched people die all day long without feeling anything, but I couldn't watch Christians die. I knew any one of them could have been you." He gave a bleak sigh. "I excused myself to buy more wine. I wanted to get drunk and forget. Julia stopped me. She said she had a surprise for me. She said she'd done something that would set everything right again. When I saw the look in her eyes, I knew." Hadassah could see the pain of that realization still reflected on his face, in his tormented eyes. "Oh, God, I knew in my soul what she had done, but I didn't want to believe it! Then I saw you. You walked away from the rest into the center of the arena. Do you remember? You stood alone." His face contorted again with remembered anguish.

He came closer, wishing he could see through the veils, wishing he could see her eyes and know what she was thinking. "Do you believe me, or do you still think I was part of it?"

"I believe you."

"But you've been afraid, unsure what I might do if I found out you lived."

She shook her head.

"Others feared for you," he said, his gaze sweeping Alexander and Rashid. "They were right to fear for you. Julia might have sent you back in the beginning."

"I knew that."

"But you didn't know what *I* would do," he said sadly. "Did you?" When she said nothing, he thought he had assumed correctly. "Do you remember telling me once that you prayed God would open my eyes? He did, Hadassah. With holy vengeance. I *saw* that day. Everything. I saw Julia and her friends and myself as though a lamp had been lit in a dark room and everything was suddenly illuminated." He clenched his fist.

"When the lion took you down, I felt my own life go out of me. Everything that meant anything—everything that mattered— was stripped away, like dust before a wind. I blamed Julia. I blamed myself. I blamed Jesus."

Alexander did not move from Hadassah's side. Marcus looked at him and knew he loved her, too. It had been this man who had taken care of her when she had needed help most. For a moment, Marcus' pride told him he should leave now and let Hadassah stay with Alexander. Why bare his soul only to be rejected? But he couldn't leave. Whatever feelings were between Hadassah and the physician, Marcus had to tell her everything, his pride be cursed.

He drew a calming breath and went on. "I went to Palestine to curse God because I thought he had abandoned you as I had. I went because I loved you. I still love you."

Alexander frowned. Glancing down, he saw how Hadassah trembled. Yet when Marcus reached out to touch her, she withdrew. What held her distant from the man? Was it fear? Or was it something else?

Rashid was frowning as well, troubled and embarrassed by

Valerian's passionate appeal. The Roman had no shame in laying his heart before a woman. Yet that very fact made one thing glaringly clear: This man could have had no part in sending Hadassah to the arena. He would sooner have faced the lions himself.

Silence fell in the courtyard, a hush that trembled.

Alexander let his breath out slowly, his mouth curving ruefully. He met Marcus' eyes, then stepped back. "We'll leave you alone with her."

Reluctantly, Rashid slipped his knife back into his belt.

Hadassah clutched Alexander's arm. "Please, don't go," she whispered.

He put his hand over hers. "You know I love you," he said softly, "but you'd better hear him out and decide what it is you really want."

"It won't change anything," she said tearfully. "It can't."

"Can't? Have you forgotten your own claim, Hadassah? God can accomplish the impossible." He touched her veils tenderly. "Is it God's will at work that holds you back, or your own?" When she didn't answer, he took her hand. "You'd better find out." Kissing her palm, he released her and motioned to Rashid.

Her heart thumped madly as Alexander and Rashid left the room. Marcus stood looking down at her with an intensity that made her senses swim.

"I love you," he said again. "I loved you then and I love you now. Don't you realize that I began falling in love with you all over again, even when I thought you were someone else, someone called Azar."

She felt weak. "You honor me, Marcus," she said tremulously, tears burning her eyes.

"Honor," he said. "A hollow word when it's love I want."

Her stomach tightened.

"I didn't know what forgiveness was until you unveiled yourself to Julia," he said heavily. "When I accepted Christ in Galilee, I felt forgiven, but it took you to teach me what it means to forgive." Would she forgive him for not protecting her?

"I didn't teach you, Marcus. God taught you."

"You were his instrument. You have always been the light in my household, even when you were so afraid of me you shook. I should have taken you from Julia's villa that day, no matter what you said."

"And then what would have become of *us*? What would have become of *her*?" God's timing had been perfect.

He heard the tears in her voice and came the last few steps separating them. Heart pounding, he handed her the small scroll. Her hand trembled as she took it. She kept her head down. "I asked you to marry me once and you refused. You said it was because I didn't believe in God. I believe now, Hadassah."

"That was long ago, Marcus."

"It was yesterday for me."

She stepped away from him. "I'm not the same girl." She was trembling all over, her knees weak. She wanted him to leave . . . but if he did, she thought she would die.

"Tell me you don't love me, Hadassah. Tell me straight out that you don't feel anything for me, and I'll leave you alone."

She blinked back tears. "I love you as a Christian brother."

He brushed his fingers lightly against the veil, and she jerked away. "Swear to me, it's only that."

"Christians don't swear to anything."

"Then say it plainly. Tell me you don't love me as I love you."

She shook her head, unable to speak.

"I want to marry you, Hadassah. I want to have children with you. I want to grow old with you."

She closed her eyes. "Don't say any more, please. I can't marry you."

"Why not?"

"You will marry, but you won't marry someone like me, Marcus. You'll marry a beautiful young girl from Jericho."

He put his hands on her shoulders and felt her tense. "There's only one woman I've ever wanted to marry. *You.* There's only one woman I ever will marry. *You.*"

"Taphatha is in love with you."

"She thinks she is," he said without arrogance. "She'll get over it."

She turned and looked up at him. "You must reconsider. She's beautiful and kind and she loves the Lord."

"I already told Ezra no. Bartholomew is far better suited to be Taphatha's husband."

"Bartholomew?"

"A young man who followed them from Jericho. Ezra wouldn't consider him before because Bartholomew's father is a Greek." He laughed softly. "I reminded him I'm a Roman."

"It doesn't matter now that you're in Christ. We are all one. . . ."

"Bartholomew is a Christian. He's Ezra's second convert. Ezra just needs to put aside old prejudices. The boy loves Taphatha the way I love *you*." He touched her veils, and she stepped back, turning away from him. He frowned slightly.

"Hadassah, do you remember when I asked you to marry me the first time? You said you couldn't be yoked to an unbeliever. You said I was stronger than you. You were afraid I'd pull you away from God. Do you remember?"

"I remember." She had told him her desire to please him would eventually become more important than pleasing God.

"We'll pull together now, Hadassah. I believe that Jesus is the Christ, the Son of the living God."

She had yearned to hear him speak those words. She had prayed unceasingly for it over the past years. She had set her heart upon them long ago in the garden of the Roman villa. And now she couldn't speak past the tears choking her.

"You were in love with me then," Marcus said. "I felt it every time I touched you. And I felt it again the other day when we were sitting in the alcove and I took your hand." He saw the soft fluttering of the veil with each breath she took, and his heart began to beat faster. "Let me see you."

"*No!*" she said in anguish and pressed the veils to her face, turning away from him. "No!"

He knew then what held her back.

"Is that what keeps you from me? Your scars?" He turned her around firmly and took her wrists, forcing her hands down.

"Marcus, *no!*"

"Do you think it matters to me?"

"Please, don't!"

Ignoring her protest, he removed the veils and let them drop carelessly to the floor. Weeping, Hadassah turned her face away. He caught her chin and forced her head up so he could look at her. She closed her eyes tightly.

"Oh, beloved." The wounds had been deep, the scars running from her forehead to her chin and throat. Releasing her wrists, he touched her face tenderly, tracing the mark of the lion. "You are beautiful." He cupped her head in his hands and kissed her forehead, her cheek, her chin, her mouth. "You are beautiful."

She opened her eyes as he drew back slightly, and he looked into them. What she saw melted all resistance, removed all shame.

"You are more beautiful to me than any woman in the world," he said huskily, "and more precious than all the gold of a thousand ships." He kissed away the tears on her cheeks and lowered his mouth to cover hers. When she relaxed in his arms, he drew her closer. When her arms slid around him, he thought he had entered heaven.

"Oh, Hadassah," he said, breathing in the intoxicating scent of her. He drew back trembling and combed his fingers into her hair. "Marry me," he said. "Marry me *now.*"

She smiled up at him, eyes shining through her tears. Once again God had brought her face-to-face with her greatest fear: Marcus had seen her face. He had seen her scars. And the love in his eyes had only grown more tender.

Oh, God, what a wonder you are! her heart cried out in gladness as she spoke the words she had longed to speak to Marcus for years.

"I will marry you, my lord."

He laughed, drinking in the love in her eyes. "Oh, beloved," he said, caressing her face. "I feel the way I did when I rose from the Sea of Galilee." The joy he had felt then poured over him in wave upon wave. Tears wet his cheeks, and he didn't even know he was crying. "I missed you. I have missed you as if half of myself had been torn away."

She reached up and touched his face in wonder. "As I have missed you."

He kissed her again, his desire for her as intense as it had ever been, even stronger, growing. He loved the smooth, silky texture of her skin. He loved the look in her eyes when he touched her, a reflection of the wonder and pleasure he felt. Love filled him so full that the spirit within him sang in celebration. And he knew it was a gift—a gift from a loving Father who had been waiting for him to come home.

The echo in the darkness had not been Hadassah's voice at all but God's, calling out to him, never letting him go.

O Lord, Lord, what a wondrous thing you've done. You've given me the desire of my heart. Me, the least deserving of men. O Lord God, my God, your love amazes me. O Abba, I love you. I thank you. Christ Jesus, Father, I will praise and worship you

429

for as long as I draw breath upon this earth, and beyond that, on my knees before your throne in heaven.

He pressed Hadassah to his chest, his heart overflowing. At last . . . at long last, he was home.

EPILOGUE

Yet I hold this against you: You have forsaken your first love. Remember the height from which you have fallen! Repent and do the things you did at first. If you do not repent, I will come to you and remove your lampstand from its place. (Revelation 2:4-5, NIV)

The marriage of Marcus Lucianus Valerian and Hadassah, freewoman, conducted and blessed by the apostle John, had the people of Ephesus talking for months. After all, when was the last time the heir of one of Rome's greatest merchant families married a former Jewish slave? And when had present and retired generals and proconsuls socialized openly with dockworkers, former slaves, and exprostitutes? For that is what Marcus had commanded at the end of the ceremony: that his slaves be freed and that they be invited to join in the wedding celebration with all the other guests.

Hadassah, radiant with joy, stood beside Marcus and pledged him her life and her love. Those standing near enough to see her face could not help but be stirred by the love shining there. Two such people were Alexander and Rashid. And though Alexander's heart felt strangely empty as he watched Hadassah and Marcus joined together, he was content to know Hadassah was happy. Soon after the wedding, Alexander closed his practice and volunteered his services to a Roman legion that was to sail for Britannia. He sent a brief note of farewell to Hadassah . . . and never returned to Ephesus.

As for Rashid, immediately after the wedding, he disappeared. There were those who reported, much later, that Rashid had returned to Syria, married, and raised a family. Others, however, were certain that, from time to time, they saw an Arab in the shadows of Ephesus, near Marcus and Hadassah's home, watching those who came and went, surreptitiously guarding Hadassah and her family. And family there was, for Hadassah and Marcus were blessed with seven sons and three daughters! All of whom brought unending joy to Phoebe during the last few years of her life. But Phoebe could not deny her special love for one granddaughter in particular: a beautiful, laughing, dark-eyed little girl whom her parents named Julia.

431

As persecution of Christians intensified, John was exiled to the island of Patmos. Marcus began using all of his political and financial connections to protect his family. When he laid his mother to rest, he breathed a prayer of thanks that she was free from the coming strife. Before long, he added a new cargo to his ships: fugitive Christians who needed transport to safety.

With each passing day, the church in Ephesus backslid more and more into worldly doctrine and practices. Finally the Lord came to John and revealed the future to him. John warned Ephesus in his written Revelation what would happen if they did not repent and return to their initial love of and devotion to the Lord.

Marcus, who had been spending increasing time in prayer with Hadassah, awoke one morning with a clear message in his heart and mind: Leave. Without hesitation, he liquidated all the family assets in Ionia, loaded Hadassah and the children on board his finest ship, and, with a handpicked crew, set sail. No one ashore knew their destination.

Within two centuries, in A.D. 262, Ephesus fell. What had been the second most powerful city in the Roman Empire was destroyed by Goths, and even the Artemision, one of mankind's Seven Wonders of the World, was burned and razed. To this day, only scattered ruins remain of a once glorious cosmopolitan city.

The Lord had removed the lampstand.

You met him in *A Voice in the Wind.*

Atretes.

German warrior. Revered gladiator. A man who won his freedom through his strength and fierceness . . . a man whose life was changed forever by an encounter with a dark-haired woman, a young Christian Jewess named Hadassah.

Now his story continues.

In *As Sure As the Dawn,* Atretes vows to move heaven and earth to find his son—the baby whose life Hadassah saved—and take him back to Germania. Only one thing stands in his way: Rizpah, a young widow who adopted his baby. But Atretes is undaunted. After all, he has faced fierce warriors and pitiless gladiators. One woman should be no trouble at all.

It doesn't take him long to find out just how wrong he is.

As Sure As the Dawn, the third book in Francine Rivers' acclaimed Mark of the Lion series. Don't miss it! Available in a bookstore near you.

As Sure As the Dawn

Rizpah turned and saw Atretes striding toward her. She knew he was angry. Everything about him exuded his foul mood. Shifting the baby in her arms, she sighed. What had she done to displease him now?

Lord, will I ever do what is right in this man's eyes?

When he reached her, she saw his blue eyes glittering dangerously. "You're not to leave the villa unless I order you to do so!"

"You wish to make your son a prisoner, my lord?" she said, striving for calm.

"I wish to protect him!"

"As do I, Atretes. I'm within the walls."

"You will stay in the *villa!*"

"What possible harm can come to Caleb out here? You have guards—"

"Woman, you will do as I say!"

Her hackles rose at his imperious tone. The man was impossible. She was not his servant, and she did not intend to be treated as such. She had never taken well to being commanded to obedience. Stephen had always dealt with her in a more gentle fashion than this thick-headed German. Would that her husband were still alive.

"If you are reasonable," she told him in icy tones, "I will obey. In this case, you aren't!"

His eyes narrowed dangerously. "Press me and I'll throw you right out that gate."

She looked straight back at him. "No, you will not."

Hot color flooded his face. "What makes you so sure?"

"Because you're as concerned for Caleb's good health as I. I am the only mother he has known, and he needs me. Besides, I don't know why you're so incensed, Atretes. You watched me walk Caleb around the yard yesterday and the day before and had no objections. Today you look like a melon ready to burst."

Atretes struggled to hold his temper. She was right, which only maddened him further. He *had* watched her yesterday and the day before, and he'd found himself enjoying the activity, possibly

434

for the same reasons Sertes had just enjoyed watching her. She was beautiful. And she knew, for the sake of his son, he couldn't throw her out the gate. His hands sorely itched to throttle her. He had seen the look of speculation in Sertes' eyes before he'd left.

Rizpah saw the conflicting emotions in the German's face, anger overriding everything else—and felt remorse. God still had much work to do with her and her sharp tongue. She should have handled things differently. She should have sealed her lips and gone into the villa and chosen a better time to state her opinions. With a resigned sigh, she sat Caleb on her hip. "What's happened that you think it necessary to keep Caleb in the confines of the villa?"

Atretes watched his son grasp the front of her tunic, pulling it slightly. "It's enough that I command you."

"Must we go through this again?" she said with strained patience. "Has it something to do with the friend that was visiting with you?"

"He is no friend! His name is Sertes, and he's editor of the Ephesian games."

"Oh," she said. "He came to talk you into fighting again, didn't he?"

"Yes."

She frowned. "Did he succeed?"

"No."

She sensed there was something very serious behind his anger. She tried again. "You must tell me where the danger lies, Atretes. I seem to have blundered, but I don't know how."

He saw no other way to convince the stubborn woman but to tell her the truth. "If Sertes could find a way to force me to fight again, he would do it. He asked who you were. I said you were a servant. He asked about *him.*" He nodded curtly at his son.

Her heart began to race as she sensed the danger. "And?"

"I said the child was yours."

She let out her breath, her mouth curving ruefully. "That must have choked you."

"You think the situation amusing?" he said through his teeth.

Rizpah sighed. In another moment he wouldn't be able to think clearly through the red haze of his rising temper. "No," she said calmly. "I don't think it's amusing. I think it's very serious, and I'll do as you say."

Her capitulation took him off guard. It was the one thing he had not expected. She always fought him, always had something to say in response to his demands. He'd known that coming to her would involve a fight—at least, so he'd thought. And he'd been ready for that. But he hadn't been ready for this calm agreement! *Cursed woman!* he thought irrationally. *What is she up to now?*

Speechless with frustration, Atretes watched her walk away. She went around the side of the villa. Still hungry for a good fight, he went after her. She was entering the back door of the villa when he caught up with her. She glanced back at him. "Would you like to play with your son for a while?"

He stopped inside the doorway. "Play?" he said, taken aback.

"Yes, *play.*"

"I haven't time."

"All you have is time," she said and entered the bath chamber.

"What did you say to me?"

She turned to face him, smiling sweetly. Too sweetly. "I said, all you have is time." He opened his mouth for a scathing reply, but she cut him off. "You'd enjoy playing with Caleb more than running around in the hills and jumping over rocks or spending hours in your gymnasium lifting weights and terrorizing your guards."

A hot flush came over his face.

"Here," she said, and before he could think of a retort burning enough, she handed the baby to him.

His rage evaporated in a wave of alarm. "Where are you going?"

"I need to find some clean linen. Caleb's soaking through those wraps." Smiling faintly, she walked away.

Atretes grimaced. He could feel the dampness seeping through his fresh tunic where he clutched the infant to his chest. When his son began nuzzling his chest hairs, Atretes held him away. "He's hungry!" he called out, unaware of the slightly frantic note in his voice.

Rizpah stopped beneath the archway. "Be at ease, Atretes. He's not *that* hungry." She laughed, and the musical sound floated around him in the marble-tiled chamber. Her eyes sparkled with amusement. "Besides, I doubt he'll draw much blood. Not until he has teeth." And with that, she walked from the room.

Alone with his son, Atretes paced nervously. He held the babe at arm's length, but Caleb squirmed and looked ready to cry, so

Atretes held him close again, cold sweat breaking out on the back of his neck. He found it ironic that he had faced death hundreds of times and never been reduced to the vulnerability he felt now, holding a baby—*his* baby.

Caleb's tiny, pudgy fingers grasped the ivory chip hanging from a gold chain around his father's neck and stuffed a corner of it into his mouth.

Scowling, Atretes tugged the medallion declaring its freedom from his son's mouth. He tucked it quickly out of reach inside his tunic, muttering under his breath about women who deserted their babies. His son's lip quivered.

"Don't start crying," he said gruffly.

Caleb's mouth opened wide.

"By the gods, not again," Atretes groaned. He winced at the howling wail that came forth. How was it possible for such a small creature to make so much noise? "Very well. Eat it!" he said, pulling the chain out from beneath his tunic and dangling it temptingly before his son. Still whimpering, Caleb grasped the chip and gummed it.

Atretes carried his son over to a massage table and placed him on it. The child positively reeked.

"*Rizpah!*" Her name echoed off the marble muraled walls around him. Caleb lost hold of the chip again and screamed. Gritting his teeth and holding his breath, Atretes unwound the soiled wraps and tossed them in a heap near the wall. "You need a bath, boy. You stink!" He picked the baby up and carried him into the pool. Caleb stopped screaming as he felt the warm water of the tepidarium swirl up around him. Gurgling happily, he grabbed the chip again and pounded it against his father's chest, splashing water into Atretes' face.

Supporting his son under the arms, Atretes held him away and dipped him up and down in the water. Caleb squealed with delight, fists hitting the water. Atretes' mouth softened and tipped up on one side. He studied Caleb as he splashed. The babe had Julia's dark eyes and hair. Frowning, he wondered how much else of her was in him.

Suddenly he knew he was no longer alone. He looked up to see Rizpah standing in the archway, linens draped over her arm. "You called, my lord?" she said dryly, eyes dancing with laughter. She came to the edge of the pool and watched him wash Caleb. Laughing, she said, "He's a baby, Atretes, not a garment."

"He needed a bath," Atretes said as he walked up the steps out of the pool. Caleb didn't like the cool air as much as the warm water and began fussing again. "Take him," Atretes said, holding him out to her.

Tossing the linens onto her shoulder, she did as he asked. She kissed Caleb's wet cheek. "Did you have a nice bath?" she said, laughing at his happy chuckle. She bounced him gently as she headed for the massage table.

Atretes stood watching the woman. Her voice was soft and sweet, and she laughed and leaned down, letting Caleb grab her thumbs. Kissing the baby's chest, she blew air into his belly button. Caleb gave out that funny chuckle again. Mouth tipping, Atretes walked over to watch his son kicking and waving his arms happily. Rizpah ignored his presence and talked to the baby the whole time she swaddled him in linen, but as she lifted Caleb, she glanced up at Atretes. Her expression held awareness.

His pulse jumped, and with it, his wariness. He'd seen beautiful dark eyes like hers before.

Rizpah was disturbed by the intensity of his look, for it touched her in some instinctive elemental realm. When his gaze moved downward, she felt a flush of warmth spread through her entire body. *Lord, no!* She drew back a step, holding Caleb against her like a shield. "You will please excuse me, my lord," she said, eager to take Caleb and escape those predatory eyes.

"No, I will not."

She blinked. "My lord?"

"Take him into the triclinium."

"Why?"

"Do I need a reason?"

She hesitated, uncertain as to his motives, distressed by the emotions stirring within her.

"Do I?" he said, eyes narrowing.

"No, my lord."

"Then do what you're told."

Why must he use that tone with her? She was not his servant! True, she was there, in his home, by his permission to care for his son—for the babe she loved as her own. But she was *not* a servant. "Caleb is ready to be fed and put down to rest," she said, trying to keep calm.

"He can do both in the triclinium."

Seeing he had no intention of relenting, she carried Caleb out

438

of the baths with Atretes following. The inner corridor was thankfully cool. She entered the lavishly furnished dining room and sat down on a couch. Within minutes, Caleb fell asleep, and she wrapped her shawl around him, laid him on the couch, and placed cushions around him. Her hands shook as she folded them tightly in her lap and waited.

Atretes looked at her. "Are you hungry?" he said dryly.

"Not very," she said frankly. Feeling his gaze, Rizpah took up Caleb and held him, comforted by the warmth of his small body.

Atretes looked at the way she held his son cradled tenderly on her thighs. "It's occurred to me I know very little about you," he said, reclining on the couch opposite her and studying her face. She was beautiful.

Even relaxed, Rizpah sensed the alertness about him.

"What happened to your husband?" Atretes asked in a low voice.

Surprised and dismayed by the question, she said, "He died."

"I know he died," Atretes said with a cold laugh. "You wouldn't be a widow had he not. What I want to know is *how* he died."

She looked down at Caleb's precious face, stilling the pain rising inside her. Why must he ask about such things? "My husband was struck down by a chariot," she said softly.

"Did you ever find out who was driving the chariot?"

"I knew on the day it happened. The man was a Roman official."

"I wager he didn't even stop."

"No, he didn't."

Atretes' mouth curved slightly. "It seems we share a common hatred of Romans."

His observation caused swift concern. "I don't hate anyone."

"Don't you?"

She paled, wondering. Hadn't she overcome her feelings about what had happened? Was she still harboring anger against the man whose carelessness had cost the life of a man for whom she had cared deeply.

Lord, if it be so, cleanse me of it. Search me and change my heart, Father. "It's not the Lord's will that I hate anyone."

"The Lord?"

"Jesus, the Christ, the Son of the living God."

"Hadassah's God."

"Yes."

"We will not talk of him," he said dismissively as he rose from the couch. He poured wine into a silver goblet. A second goblet was on the tray, but he offered her nothing.

"It's the one thing I would wish to talk about with you," she said quietly.

He slammed the pitcher down so hard she jumped. Caleb awakened and started to cry.

"Pacify him!"

She lifted Caleb to her shoulder and rubbed his back. He cried harder.

"Make him stop crying!"

She rose, distressed. "May I have your permission to leave the room?"

"No!"

"He'll go back to sleep if I nurse him."

"Then do so!"

"I can't! Not with you staring at me!"

Atretes paced on the other side of the room, his face rigid as he glared at her. "By the gods, woman. Sit down and give him what he wants!"

"Stop shouting!" she responded with equal heat, then was immediately ashamed of her outburst. This wretched man brought out the worst in her!

Shaking with frustration, Rizpah plunked down. Presenting her back to Atretes, she set about tending the baby. Her shawl was wrapped around Caleb, and she needed it to drape over herself for modesty. Her hands shook as she removed it.

She let out her breath as Caleb began nursing and the room fell silent. She heard the scrape of metal against metal and knew Atretes was pouring himself more wine. Did he intend to get drunk? He was intimidating enough when sober. She didn't even want to think what he would be like reeling from too much wine.

An image of her own father rose like a demon, gripping her mind with anger and fear. Remembered violence. She shuddered and pressed it away. *Judge not lest ye be judged. Forgive and be forgiven. Ask and it shall be given.* She grasped hold of the promises, clinging.

Lord, walk with me through this valley. Talk with me. Open my ears and heart that I may hear.

"What are you muttering?" Atretes growled.

"I'm praying for help," she snapped, heart still pounding fast and hard. She was surprised Caleb didn't notice her tension.

"Is he asleep yet?" Atretes said quietly from behind her.

"Almost." Caleb's eyelids looked weighted. His mouth relaxed and then began to work again. Finally, he relaxed completely.

"Thank the gods," Atretes said with a sigh and reclined. He watched Rizpah's back as she readjusted her clothing. Sitting sideways on the couch, she began wrapping his son in her shawl again. "What happened to your own child?" Her hands went still, and he saw the soft color ebb from her cheeks.

"She took fever and died in her third month," she said tremulously. She lightly brushed Caleb's cheek. Turning on the couch, she looked at Atretes, her eyes awash with tears. "Why do you ask me these questions?"

"I'd like to know a little more about the woman who nurses my son."

Her dark eyes flashed. "How much did you know about the woman you bought to nurse him, other than that she was German?"

"Perhaps my interest in you has changed."

His cold, cynical smile had a dismaying effect upon her. Color swept into her face, but when she spoke, it was in cool, level tones. "You may play with Caleb any time you wish, my lord. But do not think you can play with me."

His brow lifted. "Why not?"

"Because it would strain an already tenuous relationship when I said *no* to you."

Atretes laughed at her.

"I am sincere, my lord."

"It would *seem* so," he said dryly. "But then, sincerity is a trait rarely found among women. I've only known three who possessed it: my mother, my first wife, Ania, and Hadassah." He gave a bleak laugh. "And all three of them are dead."

Rizpah felt a wave of compassion for him.

Atretes saw her dark brown eyes soften and fill with warmth, and his heart responded even as his mind rebelled. "You may go," he said, jerking his head in rude dismissal.

With relief, Rizpah scooped Caleb into her arms and rose. She felt Atretes' gaze follow her as she went to the archway. She paused there and looked back at him. For all his fierceness and hardness of heart, she knew now she was looking upon a man in

441

terrible pain. Praying for his release from the torment she saw in his face, she offered him what she could.

"I give you a solemn vow, Atretes: I never lie."

"Never?" he said mockingly.

She looked straight into his beautiful, empty blue eyes. "Even if it costs my life," she said softly, then left him alone.

GLOSSARY OF TERMS

abaton: a sacred dormitory adjacent to the Asklepion; people who were seeking a healing were "incubated" there for the night

alimenta: a portion of money set aside to aid the poor

Aphrodite: Greek goddess of love and beauty. Identified with the Roman goddess Venus.

Apollo: Greek and Roman god of sunlight, prophecy, music, and poetry. The most handsome of the gods.

Artemis: Greek moon goddess. Her main temple was in Ephesus, where a meteor fell (the meteor was then kept in the temple), supposedly designating Ephesus as the goddess' dwelling place. Although Romans equated Artemis with Diana, Ephesians believed she was the sister of Apollo and daughter of Leto and Zeus, viewing her as a mother-goddess of the earth who blesses man, beast, and the land with fertility. Unlike Diana, who was the goddess of the forest and of childbirth, Artemis was sensuous and orgiastic.

Asklepios, Asclepius: Greco-Roman god of healing. In mythology, Asklepios was the son of Apollo and a nymph (Coronis) and was taught healing by a centaur (Chiron).

Asklepion: the temple of Asklepios

atrium: the central courtyard of a Roman dwelling. Most Roman houses consisted of a series of rooms surrounding an inner courtyard.

aureus (pl. aurei): a Roman gold coin equivalent to twenty-five denarii and weighing between five and eleven grams

bibliotheca: library room of a Roman dwelling

calidarium: the room in the baths that was nearest to the boilers and thus was the hottest. Probably similar to a Jacuzzi or steam room of today.

catamite: a boy used by a man for homosexual purposes

Charon: in the Roman arena, Charon was one of the *libitinarii* ("guides of the dead") and was portrayed by a person wearing a beaked mask and wielding a mallet. This portrayal was a combination of Greek and Etruscan beliefs. To the Greeks, Charon was a figure of death and the boatman who ferried the dead across the Rivers Styx and Acheron in Hades (but only for a fee and if they had had a proper burial). To the Etruscans, Charun (Charon) was a figure who struck the deathblow.

civitas (pl. civitates): a small city or village

corbita: a slow-sailing merchant vessel

Cybele: Phrygian goddess of nature worshiped in Rome. In mythology, Cybele was the consort of Attis (the god of fertility), and she represented universal motherhood. Part of her following involved a strong hope for an afterlife.

denarius (pl. denarii): a Roman unit of money equivalent to one day's pay for a common laborer. (See also *aureus, sesterce, quadrans.*)

fanum (pl. fana): a temple that was larger than a shrine but smaller than the regular temples

frigidarium: the room in the baths where the water was cold

Hades: Greek god of the underworld

haruspex (pl. haruspices): a person at a temple who supposedly could interpret supernatural signs by examining the vital organs of animals sacrificed by the priests

Hera: Greek queen of the gods. In mythology, Hera was the sister and wife of Zeus and was identified with the Roman Juno.

Juno: Roman goddess, comparable to the Greek goddess Hera. Juno was the goddess of light, birth, women, and marriage. As wife of Jupiter, Juno was the queen of heaven.

Jupiter: the Roman supreme god and husband of Juno. Jupiter was also the god of light, sky/weather, and the state (its welfare and laws). Jupiter was comparable to the Greek god Zeus.

lararium: part of a Roman dwelling. The *lararium* was a special room reserved for idols.

lying-in: Roman term for labor (during childbirth)

mandragora: mandrake. A Mediterranean herb of the nightshade family used especially to promote conception, as a cathartic, or as a narcotic and soporific.

Mars: Roman god of war

mensor (pl. mensores): a shipyard worker who weighed cargo, then recorded the weight in a ledger

mezuzah: (pl. mezuzoth): originally the Hebrew word for doorframe, *mezuzah* also came to refer to a box mounted on the doorframe or, more importantly, to the parchment inside the box. On the parchments were written certain key Scriptures (two passages from Deuteronomy) and also Shaddai, the name of the Almighty. God had commanded the Jewish people to (perhaps metaphorically) "write them on the doorposts *[mezuzoth]* of your house and on your gates." The parchments were replaced after time and a priest would come to bless the *mezuzah* and household. (See also *phylactery.*)

Neptune: Roman god of the sea (or water). Seven sacred dolphins often accompanied his representation. Comparable to the Greek god Poseidon.

palus: a cloaklike garment worn by Roman women over a *stola*

peculium: an allotment of money given to slaves by their owner. Slaves could treat *peculium* as their own personal property, but under certain circumstances their owner could take it back.

peristyle: a section of a Roman dwelling (often a secondary section) that enclosed a courtyard and was surrounded by columns on the inside. Often located in the *peristyle* were the bedrooms of the family, the domestic shrine (*lararium*), the hearth and kitchen, the dining room (*triclinium*), and the library (*bibliotheca*). In wealthier homes, the courtyard in the *peristyle* became a garden.

phylactery: a small, square, black calfskin case that held strips of parchment on which were written four select passages, two from the book of Exodus and two from Deuteronomy. The *phylactery* was fastened by long leather straps on the inside of a devout Jew's arm between the elbow and shoulder nearest the heart. Another *phylactery* was tied to the forehead during prayers. This was in response to God's words in Deuteronomy 6:6: "These words which I command you today shall be in your heart. . . . You shall bind them as a sign on your hand, and they shall be as frontlets between your eyes."

posca: a drink made from *acetum* (a vinegarlike alcohol) and water

proconsul: a governor or military commander of a Roman province; answered to the Senate

propylon: (also called *propylaeum*) an architechtural term for an outer monumental gateway, arch, or vestibule

quadrans (pl. quadrantes): a bronze Roman coin. It took four of them to equal a copper coin, sixteen to equal a sesterce, and sixty-four to equal a denarius.

rennet: lining membrane of a stomach or one of its compartments

sacrarii: shipyard workers who carried cargo from wagons and dropped it on a scale

scimitar: a saber (sword) made of a curved blade with the cutting edge on the convex side

sesterce: a Roman coin, worth one-fourth of a denarius

sicarii (sing. sicarius): zealots who had turned to attacking travelers on the roads in Judea

sopherim: Jewish term for a scribe, a man who copied the Holy Scriptures for *phylacteries* and *mezuzoth*

statio (pl. stationes): a stopping place along the road where horses could be changed for hire and where garrisons of soldiers who patrolled the roads were stationed. Generally there were *stationes* every ten miles along the roads.

stola: a long, skirtlike garment worn by Roman women

stuppator: a shipyard worker who balanced on scaffolding to caulk ships when they docked

tabernacle: a small tent commonly found on the roof of a Jewish home

tallis: a shawl worn over the head or around the shoulders by orthodox and conservative Jewish men during morning prayers. The shawl is made from wool or silk and is rectangular with fringes at the corners.

tepidarium: the room in the baths where the water was warm and soothing

toga: the characteristic outer garment worn by Romans (although its use was slowly abandoned). It was a loose, oval-shaped piece of cloth worn draped about the shoulders and arms. The color and pattern of a toga were rigidly prescribed—politicians, persons in mourning, men, and boys each had a different toga that was to be worn. Boys wore a purple-rimmed toga, but when they came of age, they were allowed to wear the *toga virilis,* or man's toga, which was plain.

triclinium: the dining room of a Roman dwelling. The *triclinium* was often very ornate, having many columns and a collection of statues.

usus: the least binding form of marriage for Romans. It was probably similar to what we might today call "living together."

Way, the: a term used in the Bible (the book of Acts) to refer to Christianity. Christians probably would have called themselves "Followers of the Way."

Yeshua: Hebrew name for Jesus

Zeus: Greek king of the gods and husband of Hera; identified with the Roman god Jupiter

DISCUSSION GUIDE

Dear reader,

We hope you enjoyed this story and its many characters by Francine Rivers. It is the author's desire to whet your appetite for God's Word and His ways—to apply His principles to your life. The following character study is designed for just that! There are four sections of discussion questions for each of the four main characters:

- Character Review—gets the discussion going
- Digging Deeper—gets into the character
- Personal Insights/Challenges—gets you thinking
- Searching the Scriptures—gets you into God's Word

When writing this story, Francine had a key Bible verse in mind: "Trust in the Lord with all your heart; do not depend on your own understanding. Seek his will in all you do, and he will direct your paths" (Proverbs 3:5-6). We can choose to be self-sufficient or to rely on God. We can act on our own understanding regarding life's circumstances, or we can seek God's will in every situation. But only one choice assures us that God will direct our paths. Making wise choices is an ongoing process. With this in mind, let me encourage you to get together with some friends and discuss your favorite scenes, characters, and personal insights from this novel. May your insights never end, and may your discussion "runneth over"!

Peggy Lynch

HADASSAH

CHARACTER REVIEW
1. What is your favorite encounter with Hadassah and why?
2. What changes are evident in Hadassah since the arena (other than physical)?

DIGGING DEEPER
1. Discuss how Hadassah perceived herself.
2. Describe how Hadassah moved from fear and timidity to power and love.
3. What fears keep you from experiencing God's love and power?

PERSONAL INSIGHTS/CHALLENGES
1. In what ways do you identify with Hadassah? How are you different?
2. What do you think motivated Hadassah? What motivates you?
3. "Trust in the Lord with all your heart; do not depend on your own understanding. Seek his will in all you do, and he will direct your paths" (Proverbs 3:5-6). How did Hadassah demonstrate her trust in God?

SEARCHING THE SCRIPTURES
As you discuss Hadassah and how she grew in her faith, read the following Bible verses. They may shed light on her journey and yours as well.

> *O Lord my God, I cried out to you for help, and you restored my health. You brought me up from the grave, O Lord. You kept me from falling into the pit of death.* PSALM 30:2-3

> *Don't be concerned about the outward beauty that depends on fancy hairstyles, expensive jewelry, or beautiful clothes. You should be known for the beauty that comes from within, the unfading beauty of a gentle and quiet spirit, which is so precious to God.* 1 PETER 3:3-4

> *For God has not given us a spirit of fear and timidity, but of power, love, and self-discipline.* 2 TIMOTHY 1:7

MARCUS

CHARACTER REVIEW
1. Discuss Marcus' journey. What do you think he was looking for?
2. Did Marcus understand the real meaning of truth? Describe his attitude toward truth and how it affected his actions and decisions.

DIGGING DEEPER
1. Describe some of the changes you have observed in Marcus.
2. Contrast Marcus' understanding and response to "truth" with Julia's.
3. Recount Marcus' conversion to Christianity. What were the steps that led him to this point?

PERSONAL INSIGHTS/CHALLENGES
1. In what ways do you identify with Marcus? How are you different?
2. Why do you think Marcus began his journey for truth? In what ways do you seek truth?
3. "Trust in the Lord with all your heart; do not depend on your own understanding. Seek his will in all you do, and he will direct your paths" (Proverbs 3:5-6). In what ways did Marcus experience God's direction in his life?

SEARCHING THE SCRIPTURES
As you think about Marcus' journey in faith, look up the following Bible verses. They may reveal his motives and expose your own as well.

> *A wise person is hungry for truth, while the fool feeds on trash. Sensible children bring joy to their father; foolish children despise their mother.* PROVERBS 15:14, 20

> *We can gather our thoughts, but the Lord gives the right answer.* PROVERBS 16:1

> *And we know that God causes everything to work together for the good of those who love God and are called according to his purpose for them.* ROMANS 8:28

PHOEBE

CHARACTER REVIEW
1. Describe your favorite scene with Phoebe and what stands out about her.
2. Elaborate on Phoebe's relationship with her children.

DIGGING DEEPER
1. Discuss Phoebe's lifestyle and priorities. How did her lifestyle and/or priorities change in the course of the book?
2. In what ways did Phoebe demonstrate her faith in God?
3. What would your own list of priorities look like?

PERSONAL INSIGHTS/CHALLENGES
1. In what ways are you like Phoebe? How are your different?
2. Do you think Phoebe's prayer life was realistic? How does your prayer life compare?
3. "Trust in the Lord with all your heart; do not depend on your own understanding. Seek his will in all you do, and he will direct your paths" (Proverbs 3:5-6). In what ways did Phoebe learn to trust God?

SEARCHING THE SCRIPTURES
As you think about Phoebe's journey in faith, read the following Bible verses and see if they provide the reasons and hope that motivated her and hopefully you too.

Pure and lasting religion in the sight of God our Father means that we must care for orphans and widows in their troubles, and refuse to let the world corrupt us. JAMES 1:27

And the Holy Spirit helps us in our distress. For we don't even know what we should pray for, nor how we should pray. But the Holy Spirit prays for us with groanings that cannot be expressed in words. ROMANS 8:26

Confess your sins to each other and pray for each other so that you may be healed. The earnest prayer of a righteous person has great power and wonderful results. JAMES 5:16

JULIA

CHARACTER REVIEW
1. Choose a memorable or moving scene with Julia and discuss what caught your attention.
2. Describe Julia's lifestyle.

DIGGING DEEPER
1. Elaborate on some of Julia's choices and the consequences of those choices.
2. In what ways did Julia attempt to justify her choices?
3. In what ways do you justify your own attitudes or actions?

PERSONAL INSIGHTS/CHALLENGES
1. How do you identify with Julia? In what ways are you different?
2. When do you think Julia began to soften toward God and why?
3. "Trust in the Lord with all your heart; do not depend on your own understanding. Seek his will in all you do, and he will direct your paths" (Proverbs 3:5-6). In what ways did Julia struggle with her "own understanding"? In what ways do you?

SEARCHING THE SCRIPTURES
As you ponder Julia's journey to find the Savior, look up the following Bible verses. They may shed light on her struggles and your own as well.

> *Who can find a virtuous and capable wife? She is worth more than precious rubies. She will not hinder him but help him all her life.* PROVERBS 31:10,12

> *Another reason for right living is that you know how late it is; time is running out. Wake up, for the coming of our salvation is nearer now than when we first believed.* ROMANS 13:11

> *For if you confess with your mouth that Jesus is Lord and believe in your heart that God raised him from the dead, you will be saved. For it is by believing in your heart that you are made right with God, and it is by confessing with your mouth that you are saved.* ROMANS 10:9-10

BOOKS BY BELOVED AUTHOR
FRANCINE RIVERS

Visit www.francinerivers.com